D0994235

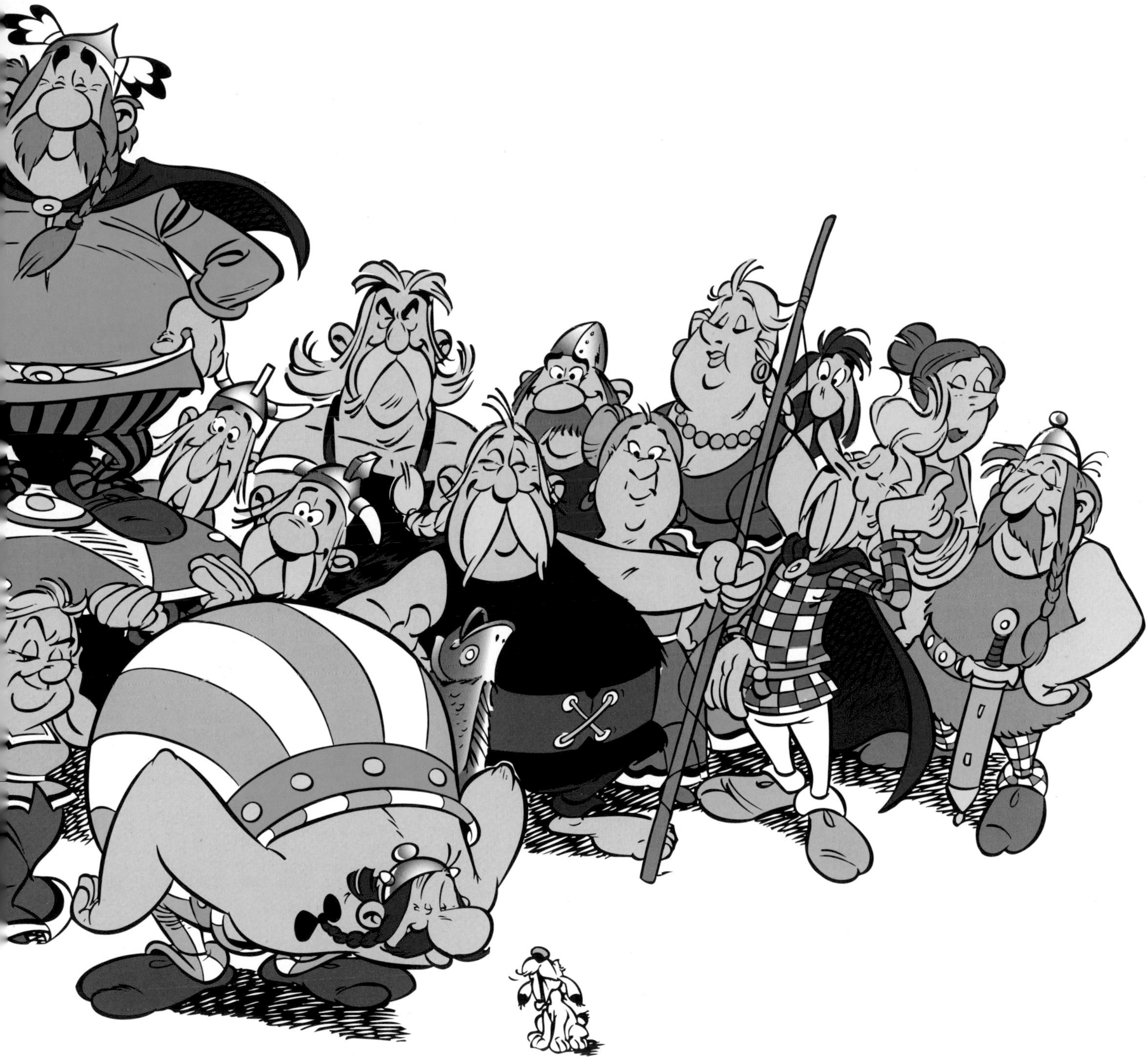

Asterix Omnibus 1

# ASTERIX THE GAUL, ASTERIX AND THE GOLDEN SICKLE, ASTERIX AND THE GOTHS

*Written by* RENÉ GOSCINNY

*Illustrated by* ALBERT UDERZO

Orion
Children's Books

ORION CHILDREN'S BOOKS

This omnibus first published in Great Britain in 2007 by Orion Books Ltd
This edition first published in Great Britain in 2011 by Orion Children's Books Ltd
Published in 2016 by Hodder and Stoughton

ASTERIX®-OBELIX®
This omnibus © 2007 Hachette Livre/Goscinny-Uderzo
Exclusive licensee: Hachette Children's Group
Translators: Anthea Bell and Derek Hockridge
Typography: Bryony Newhouse

All rights reserved

*Asterix the Gaul*
Original title: *Astérix le Gaulois*
© 1961 GOSCINNY/UDERZO
Revised edition and English translation © 2004 Hachette Livre

*Asterix and the Golden Sickle*
Original title: *La Serpe d'or*
© 1962 GOSCINNY/UDERZO
Revised edition and English translation © 2004 Hachette Livre

*Asterix and the Goths*
Original title: *Astérix et les Goths*
© 1963 GOSCINNY/UDERZO
Revised edition and English translation © 2004 Hachette Livre

The right of René Goscinny and Albert Uderzo to be identified as the authors of this work
has been asserted by them in accordance with the Copyright, Designs and Patents Act 1988.

5  7  9  10  8  6  4  2

A CIP catalogue record for this book is available from the British Library

ISBN 978 1 4440 0423 6

Printed in China

Orion Children's Books
An imprint of Hachette Children's Group, part of Hodder and Stoughton
Carmelite House, 50 Victoria Embankment
London EC4Y 0DZ
An Hachette UK Company

www.hachette.co.uk
www.asterix.com
www.hachettechildrens.co.uk

Every effort has been made to fulfil requirements with regard to reproducing copyright material.
The author and publisher will be glad to rectify any omissions at the earliest opportunity.

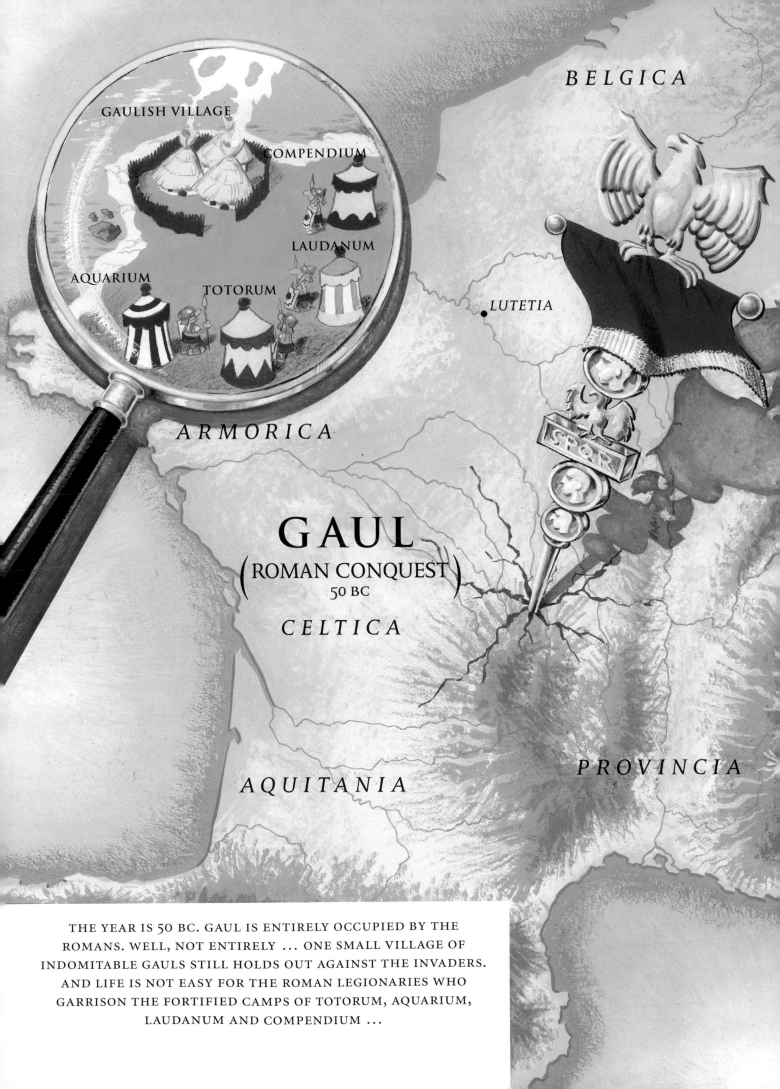

GAULISH VILLAGE

COMPENDIUM

LAUDANUM

AQUARIUM

TOTORUM

ARMORICA

BELGICA

LUTETIA

GAUL
(ROMAN CONQUEST)
50 BC

CELTICA

AQUITANIA

PROVINCIA

THE YEAR IS 50 BC. GAUL IS ENTIRELY OCCUPIED BY THE
ROMANS. WELL, NOT ENTIRELY ... ONE SMALL VILLAGE OF
INDOMITABLE GAULS STILL HOLDS OUT AGAINST THE INVADERS.
AND LIFE IS NOT EASY FOR THE ROMAN LEGIONARIES WHO
GARRISON THE FORTIFIED CAMPS OF TOTORUM, AQUARIUM,
LAUDANUM AND COMPENDIUM ...

ASTERIX, THE HERO OF THESE ADVENTURES. A SHREWD, CUNNING LITTLE WARRIOR, ALL PERILOUS MISSIONS ARE IMMEDIATELY ENTRUSTED TO HIM. ASTERIX GETS HIS SUPERHUMAN STRENGTH FROM THE MAGIC POTION BREWED BY THE DRUID GETAFIX . . .

OBELIX, ASTERIX'S INSEPARABLE FRIEND. A MENHIR DELIVERY MAN BY TRADE, ADDICTED TO WILD BOAR. OBELIX IS ALWAYS READY TO DROP EVERYTHING AND GO OFF ON A NEW ADVENTURE WITH ASTERIX – SO LONG AS THERE'S WILD BOAR TO EAT, AND PLENTY OF FIGHTING. HIS CONSTANT COMPANION IS DOGMATIX, THE ONLY KNOWN CANINE ECOLOGIST, WHO HOWLS WITH DESPAIR WHEN A TREE IS CUT DOWN.

GETAFIX, THE VENERABLE VILLAGE DRUID, GATHERS MISTLETOE AND BREWS MAGIC POTIONS. HIS SPECIALITY IS THE POTION WHICH GIVES THE DRINKER SUPERHUMAN STRENGTH. BUT GETAFIX ALSO HAS OTHER RECIPES UP HIS SLEEVE . . .

CACOFONIX, THE BARD. OPINION IS DIVIDED AS TO HIS MUSICAL GIFTS. CACOFONIX THINKS HE'S A GENIUS. EVERYONE ELSE THINKS HE'S UNSPEAKABLE. BUT SO LONG AS HE DOESN'T SPEAK, LET ALONE SING, EVERYBODY LIKES HIM . . .

FINALLY, VITALSTATISTIX, THE CHIEF OF THE TRIBE. MAJESTIC, BRAVE AND HOT-TEMPERED, THE OLD WARRIOR IS RESPECTED BY HIS MEN AND FEARED BY HIS ENEMIES. VITALSTATISTIX HIMSELF HAS ONLY ONE FEAR, HE IS AFRAID THE SKY MAY FALL ON HIS HEAD TOMORROW. BUT AS HE ALWAYS SAYS, TOMORROW NEVER COMES.

R. GOSCINNY **Asterix** A. UDERZO

# Asterix THE GAUL

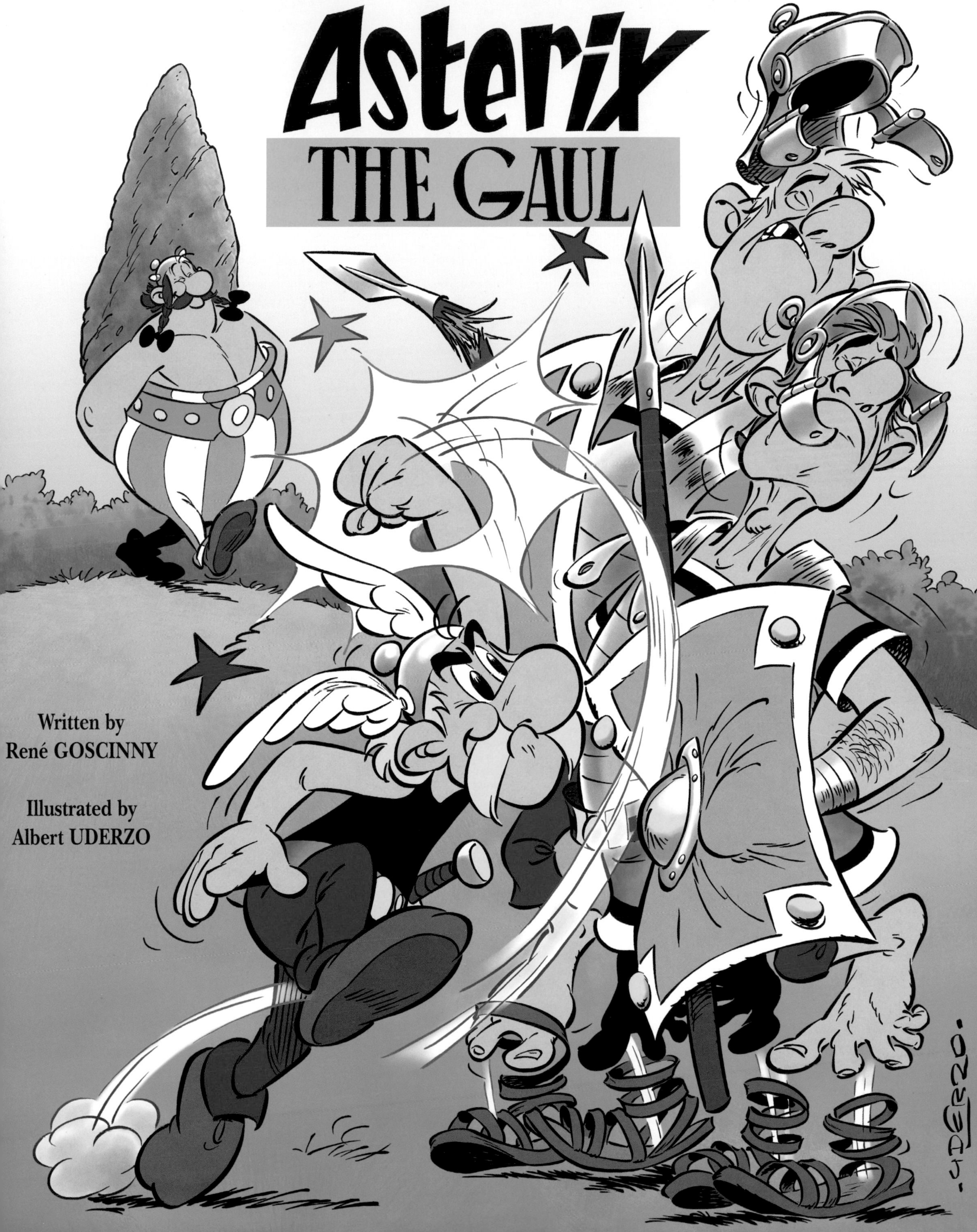

UDERZO


Written by
René GOSCINNY

Illustrated by
Albert UDERZO

GOSCINNY AND UDERZO
PRESENT
*An Asterix Adventure*

# ASTERIX
# THE
# GAUL

*Written by* RENÉ GOSCINNY *and Illustrated by* ALBERT UDERZO

*Translated by* Anthea Bell *and* Derek Hockridge

Orion
Children's Books

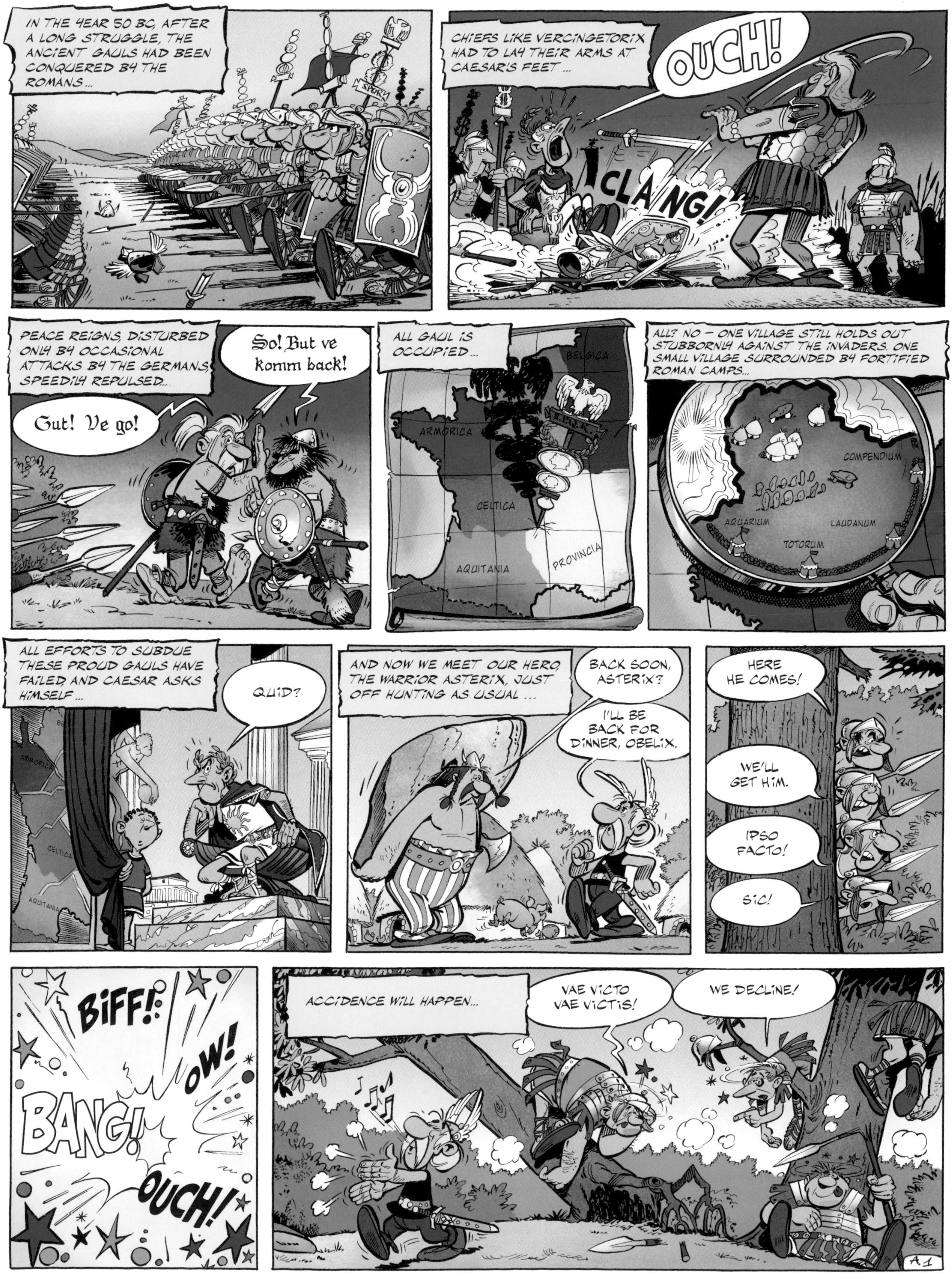
IN THE YEAR 50 BC, AFTER A LONG STRUGGLE, THE ANCIENT GAULS HAD BEEN CONQUERED BY THE ROMANS...
SPQR
CHIEFS LIKE VERCINGETORIX HAD TO LAY THEIR ARMS AT CAESAR'S FEET ...
OUCH!
CLANG!
PEACE REIGNS, DISTURBED ONLY BY OCCASIONAL ATTACKS BY THE GERMANS SPEEDILY REPULSED...
So! But ve komm back!
Gut! Ve go!
ALL GAUL IS OCCUPIED ...
BELGICA
ARMORICA
CELTICA
AQUITANIA
PROVINCIA
ALL? NO – ONE VILLAGE STILL HOLDS OUT STUBBORNLY AGAINST THE INVADERS. ONE SMALL VILLAGE SURROUNDED BY FORTIFIED ROMAN CAMPS...
COMPENDIUM
AQUARIUM
LAUDANUM
TOTORUM
ALL EFFORTS TO SUBDUE THESE PROUD GAULS HAVE FAILED AND CAESAR ASKS HIMSELF ...
QUID?
ARMORICA
CELTICA
AQUITANIA
AND NOW WE MEET OUR HERO, THE WARRIOR ASTERIX, JUST OFF HUNTING AS USUAL ...
BACK SOON, ASTERIX?
I'LL BE BACK FOR DINNER, OBELIX.
HERE HE COMES!
WE'LL GET HIM.
IPSO FACTO!
SIC!
BIFF!
OW!
BANG!
OUCH!
ACCIDENCE WILL HAPPEN...
VAE VICTO VAE VICTIS!
WE DECLINE!
A.1

AND AT THE ROMAN CAMP OF COMPENDIUM, IN THE TENT OF CENTURION CRISMUS BONUS...

AVE CRISMUS BONUS! THE PATROLS BACK!

AVE JULIUS POMPUS! I'LL GO AND INSPECT THEM.

AVE...

?!???

WHAT HAPPENED, BY ALL THE GODS? WERE YOU ATTACKED BY SUPERIOR NUMBERS?

SUPERIOR NUMBERS...

CAN'T QUITE SAY...

THERE WAS ONE OF THEM...

NOT A VERY LARGE ONE EITHER!

BY JUPITER! THERE MUST BE SOME SECRET BEHIND THE SUPERHUMAN STRENGTH OF THESE GAULS!

MEANWHILE ...

SO YOU'RE BACK, ASTERIX. ANYTHING INTERESTING HAPPEN?

NO...

OH YES! I KNOCKED FOUR ROMANS OUT.

OH, GOOD!

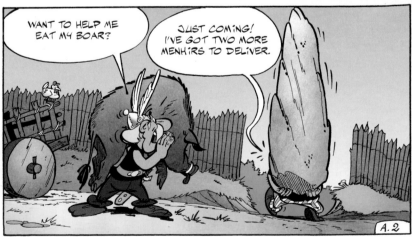

WANT TO HELP ME EAT MY BOAR?

JUST COMING! I'VE GOT TWO MORE MENHIRS TO DELIVER.

A.2

14

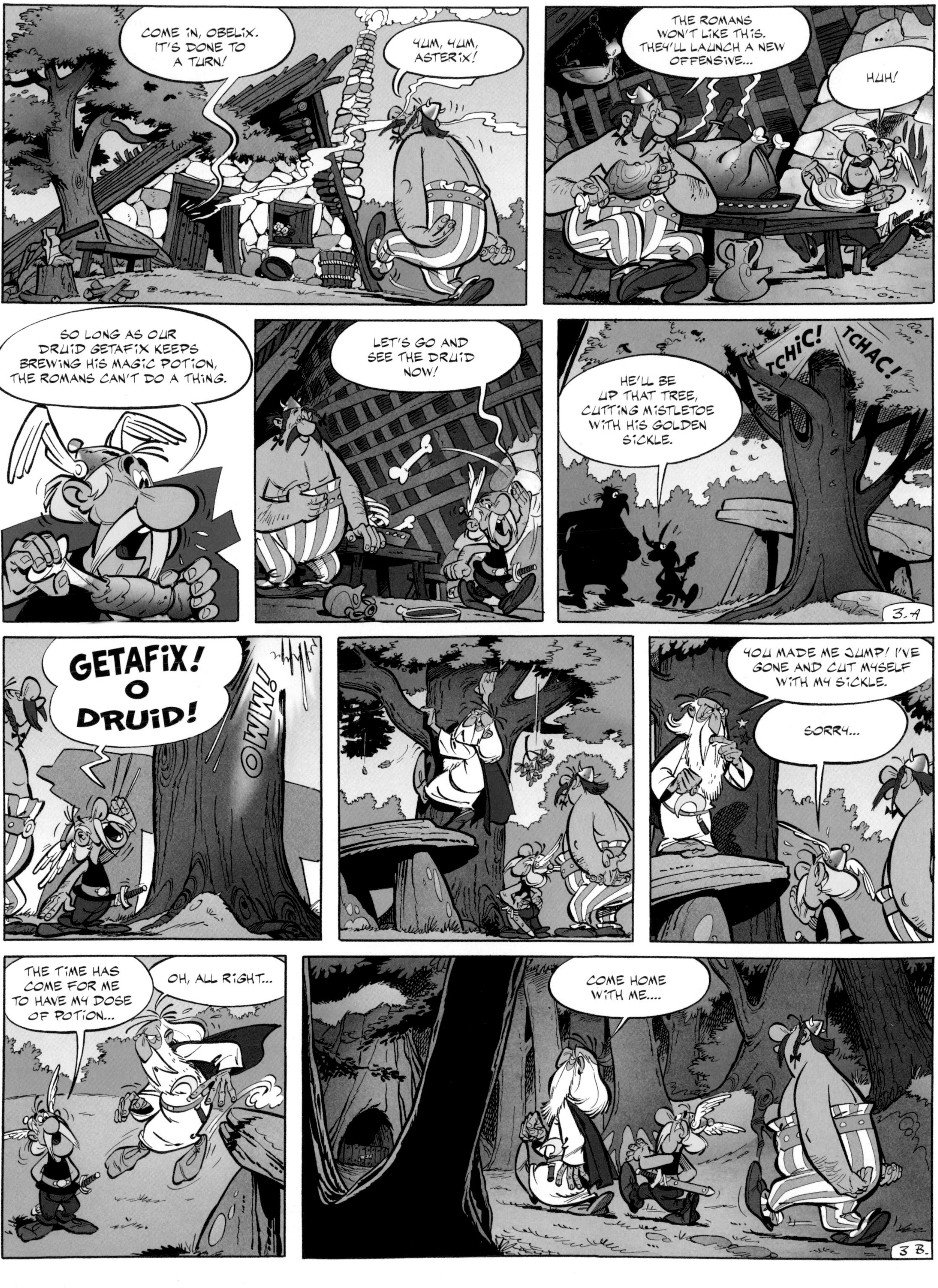
COME IN, OBELIX. IT'S DONE TO A TURN!
YUM, YUM, ASTERIX!
THE ROMANS WON'T LIKE THIS. THEY'LL LAUNCH A NEW OFFENSIVE...
HUH!
SO LONG AS OUR DRUID GETAFIX KEEPS BREWING HIS MAGIC POTION, THE ROMANS CAN'T DO A THING.
LET'S GO AND SEE THE DRUID NOW!
TCHIC! TCHAC!
HE'LL BE UP THAT TREE, CUTTING MISTLETOE WITH HIS GOLDEN SICKLE.
3.A
GETAFIX! O DRUID!
OWW!
YOU MADE ME JUMP! I'VE GONE AND CUT MYSELF WITH MY SICKLE.
SORRY...
THE TIME HAS COME FOR ME TO HAVE MY DOSE OF POTION...
OH, ALL RIGHT...
COME HOME WITH ME....
3 B.

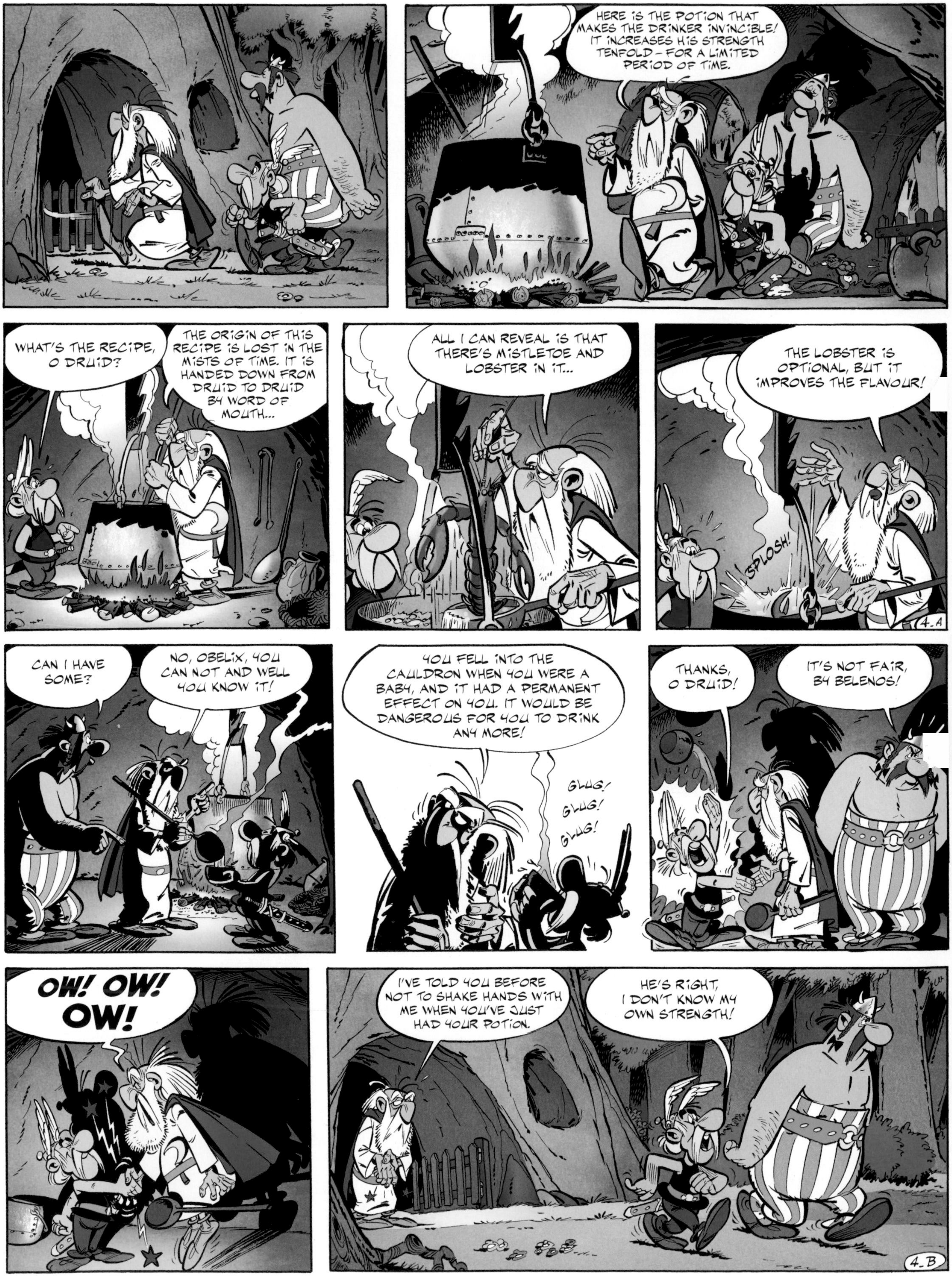
HERE IS THE POTION THAT MAKES THE DRINKER INVINCIBLE! IT INCREASES HIS STRENGTH TENFOLD – FOR A LIMITED PERIOD OF TIME.
WHAT'S THE RECIPE, O DRUID?
THE ORIGIN OF THIS RECIPE IS LOST IN THE MISTS OF TIME. IT IS HANDED DOWN FROM DRUID TO DRUID BY WORD OF MOUTH...
ALL I CAN REVEAL IS THAT THERE'S MISTLETOE AND LOBSTER IN IT...
THE LOBSTER IS OPTIONAL, BUT IT IMPROVES THE FLAVOUR!
SPLOSH!
4.A
CAN I HAVE SOME?
NO, OBELIX, YOU CAN NOT AND WELL YOU KNOW IT!
YOU FELL INTO THE CAULDRON WHEN YOU WERE A BABY, AND IT HAD A PERMANENT EFFECT ON YOU. IT WOULD BE DANGEROUS FOR YOU TO DRINK ANY MORE!
GLUG!
GLUG!
GLUG!
THANKS, O DRUID!
IT'S NOT FAIR, BY BELENOS!
OW! OW! OW!
I'VE TOLD YOU BEFORE NOT TO SHAKE HANDS WITH ME WHEN YOU'VE JUST HAD YOUR POTION.
HE'S RIGHT, I DON'T KNOW MY OWN STRENGTH!
4.B

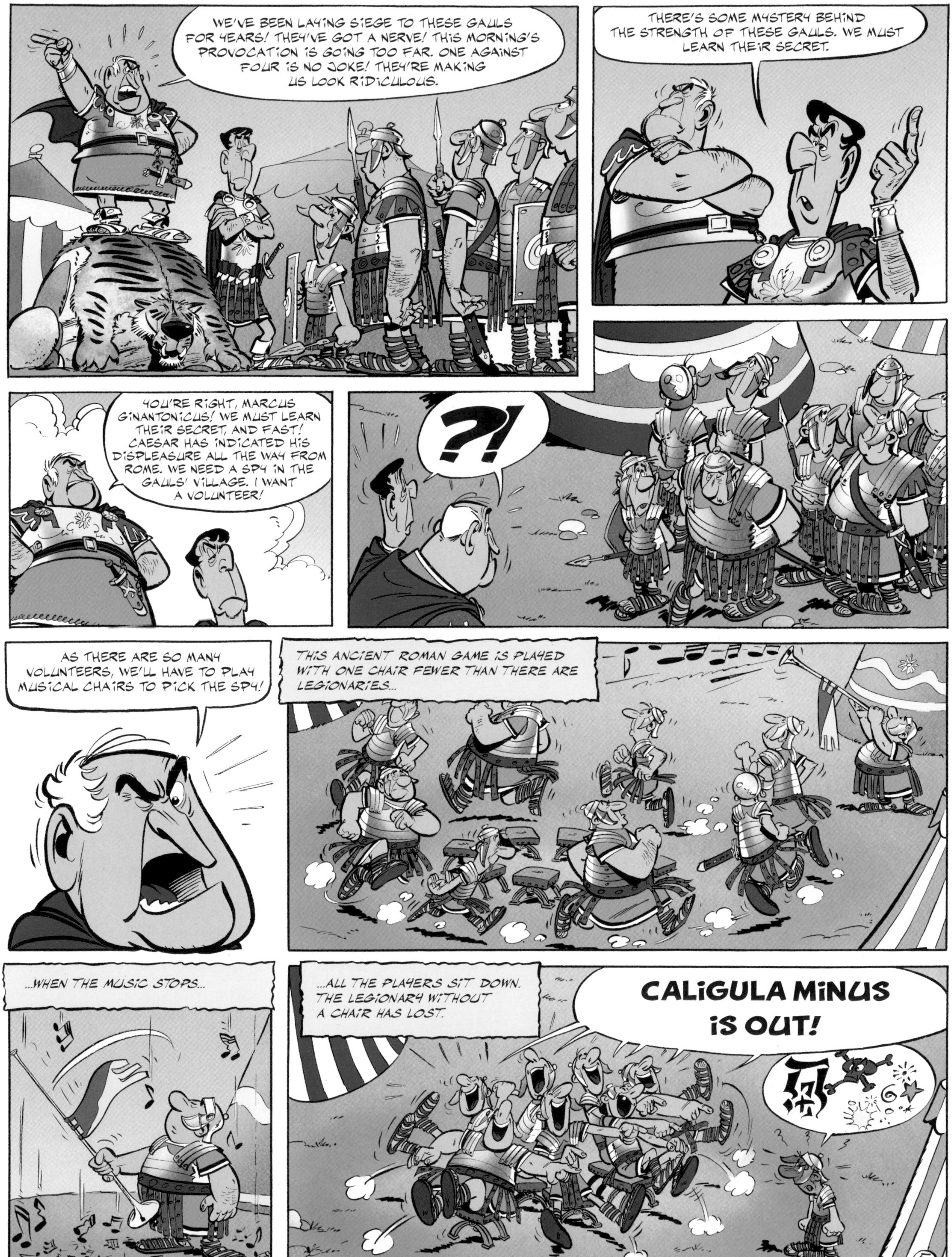
WE'VE BEEN LAYING SIEGE TO THESE GAULS FOR YEARS! THEY'VE GOT A NERVE! THIS MORNING'S PROVOCATION IS GOING TOO FAR. ONE AGAINST FOUR IS NO JOKE! THEY'RE MAKING US LOOK RIDICULOUS.
THERE'S SOME MYSTERY BEHIND THE STRENGTH OF THESE GAULS. WE MUST LEARN THEIR SECRET.
YOU'RE RIGHT, MARCUS GINANTONICUS! WE MUST LEARN THEIR SECRET, AND FAST! CAESAR HAS INDICATED HIS DISPLEASURE ALL THE WAY FROM ROME. WE NEED A SPY IN THE GAULS' VILLAGE. I WANT A VOLUNTEER!
?!
AS THERE ARE SO MANY VOLUNTEERS, WE'LL HAVE TO PLAY MUSICAL CHAIRS TO PICK THE SPY!
THIS ANCIENT ROMAN GAME IS PLAYED WITH ONE CHAIR FEWER THAN THERE ARE LEGIONARIES...
...WHEN THE MUSIC STOPS...
...ALL THE PLAYERS SIT DOWN. THE LEGIONARY WITHOUT A CHAIR HAS LOST.
CALIGULA MINUS IS OUT!

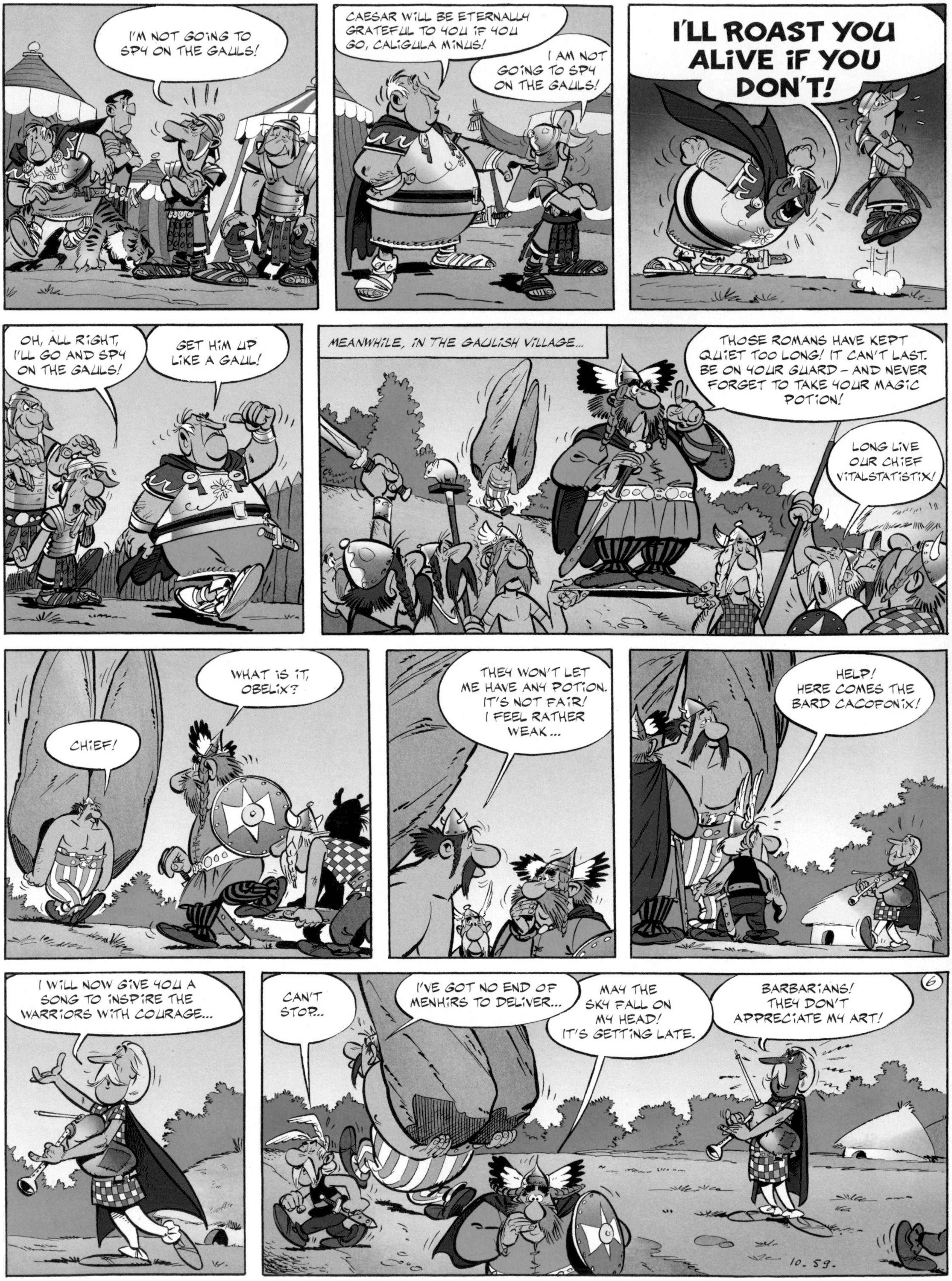
I'M NOT GOING TO SPY ON THE GAULS!
CAESAR WILL BE ETERNALLY GRATEFUL TO YOU IF YOU GO, CALIGULA MINUS!
I AM NOT GOING TO SPY ON THE GAULS!
I'LL ROAST YOU ALIVE IF YOU DON'T!
OH, ALL RIGHT, I'LL GO AND SPY ON THE GAULS!
GET HIM UP LIKE A GAUL!
MEANWHILE, IN THE GAULISH VILLAGE...
THOSE ROMANS HAVE KEPT QUIET TOO LONG! IT CAN'T LAST. BE ON YOUR GUARD – AND NEVER FORGET TO TAKE YOUR MAGIC POTION!
LONG LIVE OUR CHIEF VITALSTATISTIX!
CHIEF!
WHAT IS IT, OBELIX?
THEY WON'T LET ME HAVE ANY POTION. IT'S NOT FAIR! I FEEL RATHER WEAK...
HELP! HERE COMES THE BARD CACOFONIX!
I WILL NOW GIVE YOU A SONG TO INSPIRE THE WARRIORS WITH COURAGE...
CAN'T STOP...
I'VE GOT NO END OF MENHIRS TO DELIVER...
MAY THE SKY FALL ON MY HEAD! IT'S GETTING LATE.
BARBARIANS! THEY DON'T APPRECIATE MY ART!

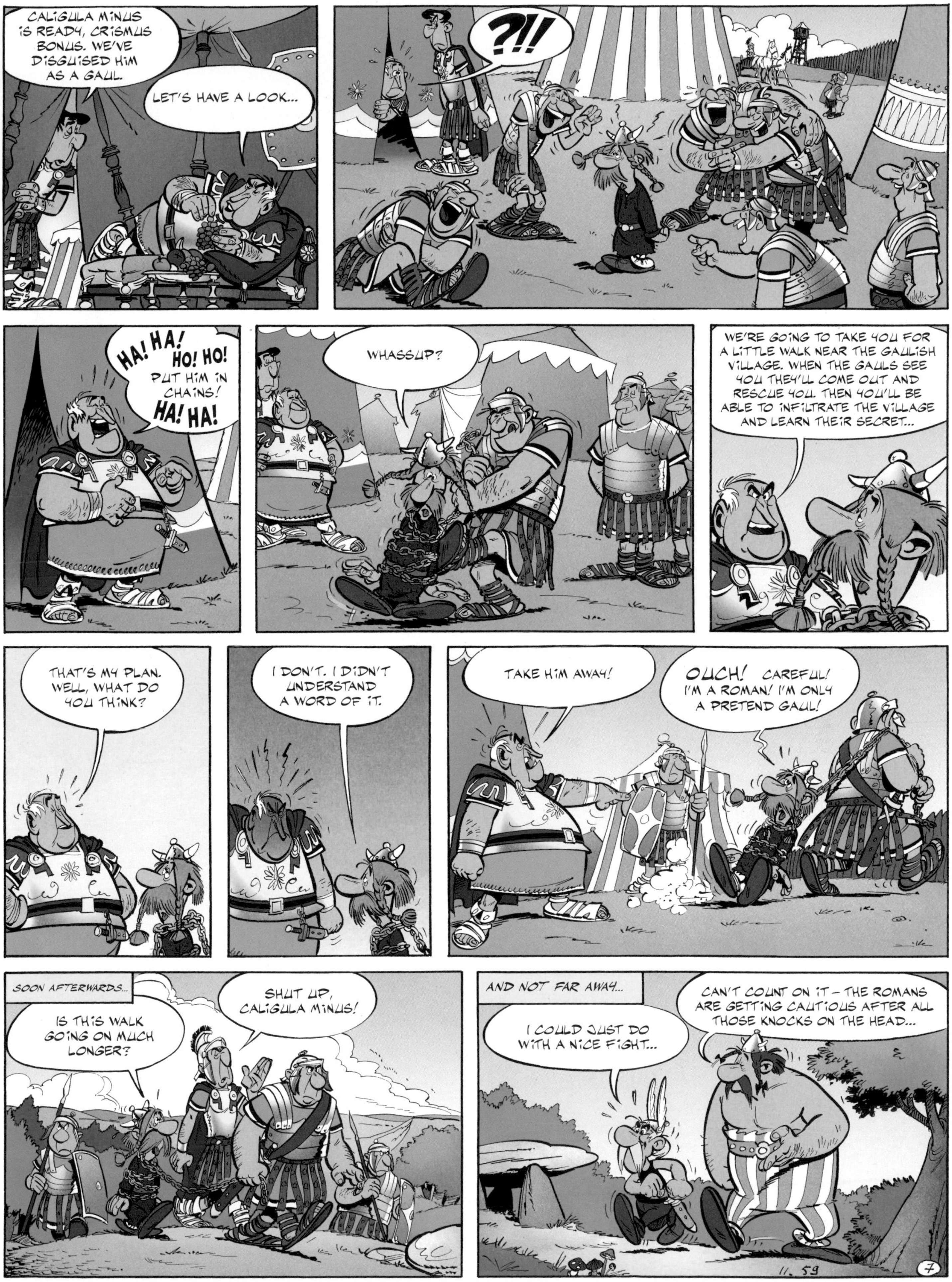

CALIGULA MINUS IS READY, CRISMUS BONUS. WE'VE DISGUISED HIM AS A GAUL.
LET'S HAVE A LOOK...
?!!
HA! HA! HO! HO! PUT HIM IN CHAINS! HA! HA!
WHASSUP?
WE'RE GOING TO TAKE YOU FOR A LITTLE WALK NEAR THE GAULISH VILLAGE. WHEN THE GAULS SEE YOU THEY'LL COME OUT AND RESCUE YOU. THEN YOU'LL BE ABLE TO INFILTRATE THE VILLAGE AND LEARN THEIR SECRET...
THAT'S MY PLAN. WELL, WHAT DO YOU THINK?
I DON'T. I DIDN'T UNDERSTAND A WORD OF IT.
TAKE HIM AWAY!
OUCH! CAREFUL! I'M A ROMAN! I'M ONLY A PRETEND GAUL!
SOON AFTERWARDS...
IS THIS WALK GOING ON MUCH LONGER?
SHUT UP, CALIGULA MINUS!
AND NOT FAR AWAY...
I COULD JUST DO WITH A NICE FIGHT...
CAN'T COUNT ON IT – THE ROMANS ARE GETTING CAUTIOUS AFTER ALL THOSE KNOCKS ON THE HEAD...

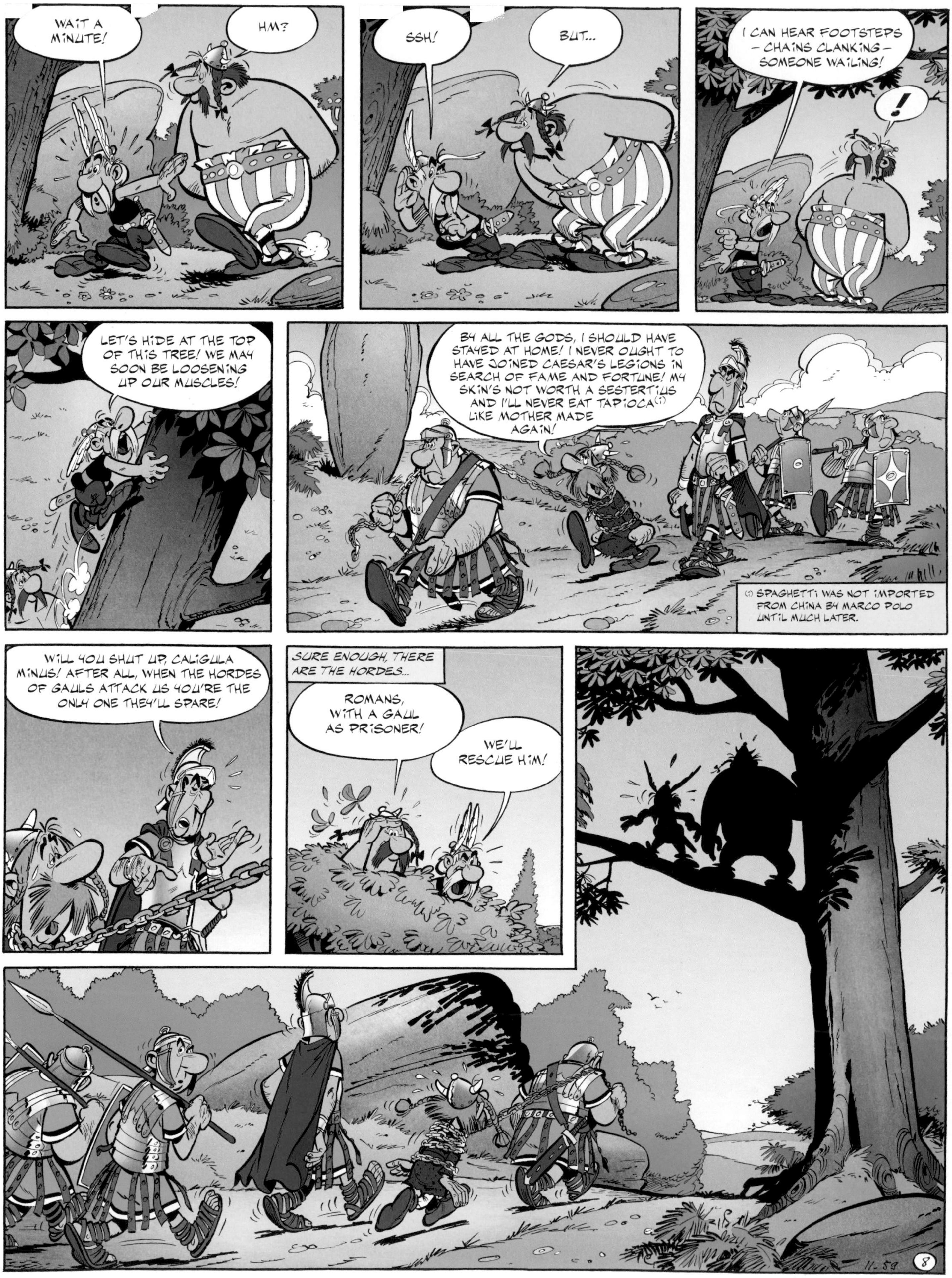
WAIT A MINUTE!
HM?
SSH!
BUT...
I CAN HEAR FOOTSTEPS – CHAINS CLANKING – SOMEONE WAILING!
!
LET'S HIDE AT THE TOP OF THIS TREE! WE MAY SOON BE LOOSENING UP OUR MUSCLES!
BY ALL THE GODS, I SHOULD HAVE STAYED AT HOME! I NEVER OUGHT TO HAVE JOINED CAESAR'S LEGIONS IN SEARCH OF FAME AND FORTUNE! MY SKIN'S NOT WORTH A SESTERTIUS AND I'LL NEVER EAT TAPIOCA(1) LIKE MOTHER MADE AGAIN!
(1) SPAGHETTI WAS NOT IMPORTED FROM CHINA BY MARCO POLO UNTIL MUCH LATER.
WILL YOU SHUT UP, CALIGULA MINUS! AFTER ALL, WHEN THE HORDES OF GAULS ATTACK US YOU'RE THE ONLY ONE THEY'LL SPARE!
SURE ENOUGH, THERE ARE THE HORDES...
ROMANS, WITH A GAUL AS PRISONER!
WE'LL RESCUE HIM!
11-59
8

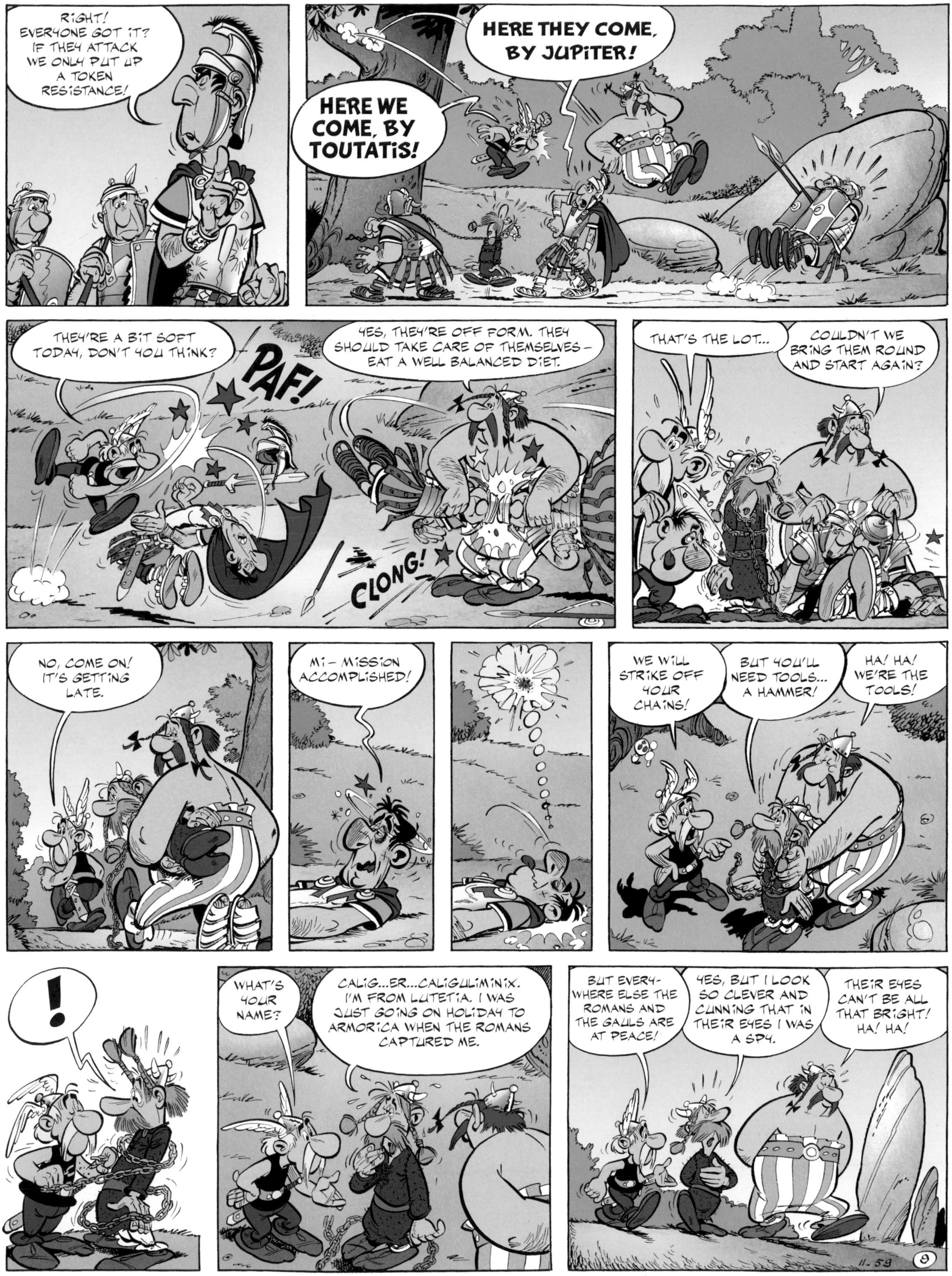
RIGHT! EVERYONE GOT IT? IF THEY ATTACK WE ONLY PUT UP A TOKEN RESISTANCE!
HERE THEY COME, BY JUPITER!
HERE WE COME, BY TOUTATIS!
THEY'RE A BIT SOFT TODAY, DON'T YOU THINK?
PAF!
YES, THEY'RE OFF FORM. THEY SHOULD TAKE CARE OF THEMSELVES – EAT A WELL BALANCED DIET.
CLONG!
THAT'S THE LOT...
COULDN'T WE BRING THEM ROUND AND START AGAIN?
NO, COME ON! IT'S GETTING LATE.
MI– MISSION ACCOMPLISHED!
WE WILL STRIKE OFF YOUR CHAINS!
BUT YOU'LL NEED TOOLS... A HAMMER!
HA! HA! WE'RE THE TOOLS!
!
WHAT'S YOUR NAME?
CALIG...ER...CALIGULIMINIX. I'M FROM LUTETIA. I WAS JUST GOING ON HOLIDAY TO ARMORICA WHEN THE ROMANS CAPTURED ME.
BUT EVERYWHERE ELSE THE ROMANS AND THE GAULS ARE AT PEACE!
YES, BUT I LOOK SO CLEVER AND CUNNING THAT IN THEIR EYES I WAS A SPY.
THEIR EYES CAN'T BE ALL THAT BRIGHT! HA! HA!

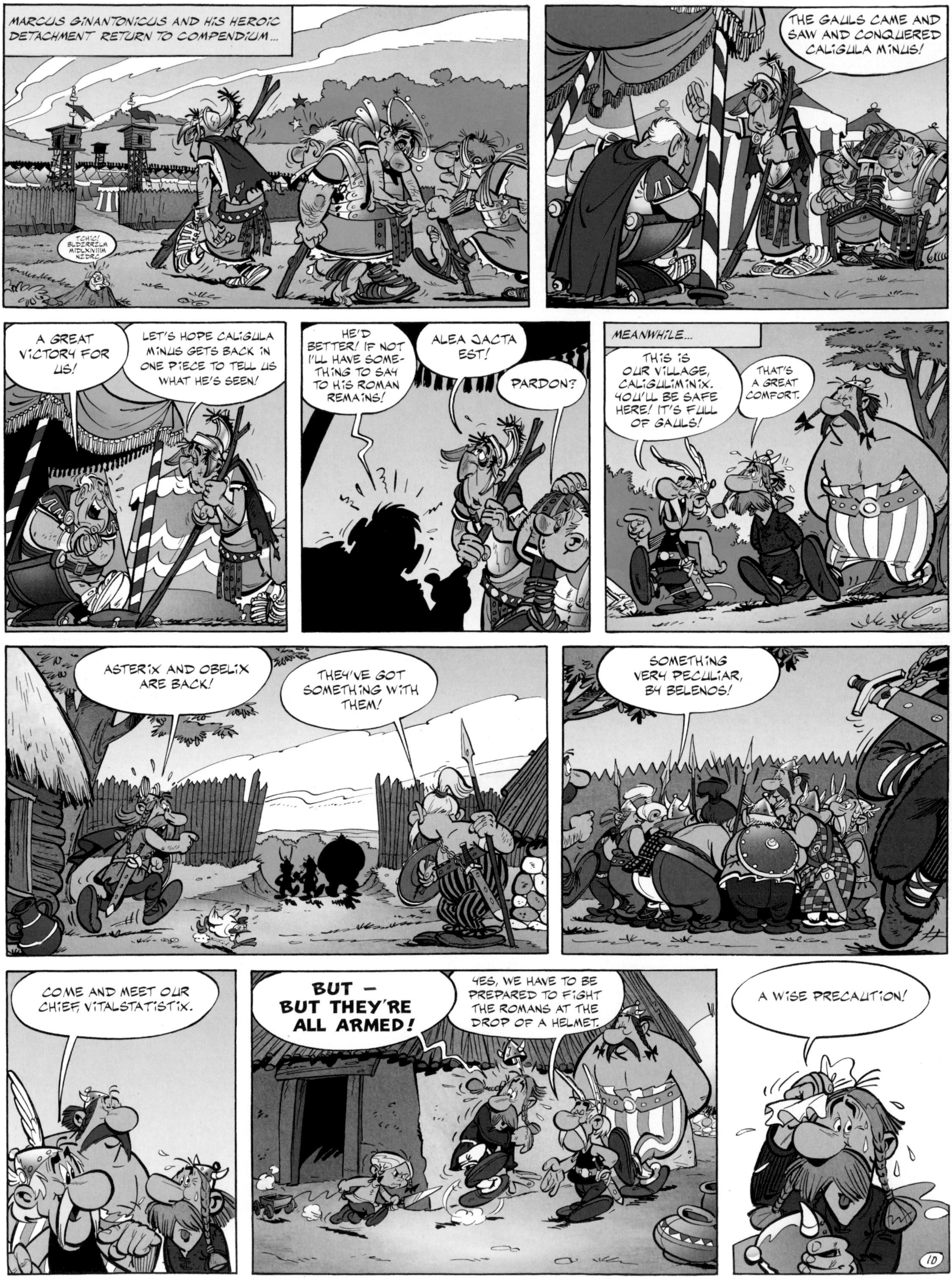
MARCUS GINANTONICUS AND HIS HEROIC DETACHMENT RETURN TO COMPENDIUM...
TCHIC! BLDZRRZLM MIDLXIVIIIM NZDRC
THE GAULS CAME AND SAW AND CONQUERED CALIGULA MINUS!
A GREAT VICTORY FOR US!
LET'S HOPE CALIGULA MINUS GETS BACK IN ONE PIECE TO TELL US WHAT HE'S SEEN!
HE'D BETTER! IF NOT I'LL HAVE SOMETHING TO SAY TO HIS ROMAN REMAINS!
ALEA JACTA EST!
PARDON?
MEANWHILE...
THIS IS OUR VILLAGE, CALIGULIMINIX. YOU'LL BE SAFE HERE! IT'S FULL OF GAULS!
THAT'S A GREAT COMFORT.
ASTERIX AND OBELIX ARE BACK!
THEY'VE GOT SOMETHING WITH THEM!
SOMETHING VERY PECULIAR, BY BELENOS!
COME AND MEET OUR CHIEF, VITALSTATISTIX.
BUT – BUT THEY'RE ALL ARMED!
YES, WE HAVE TO BE PREPARED TO FIGHT THE ROMANS AT THE DROP OF A HELMET.
A WISE PRECAUTION!
10

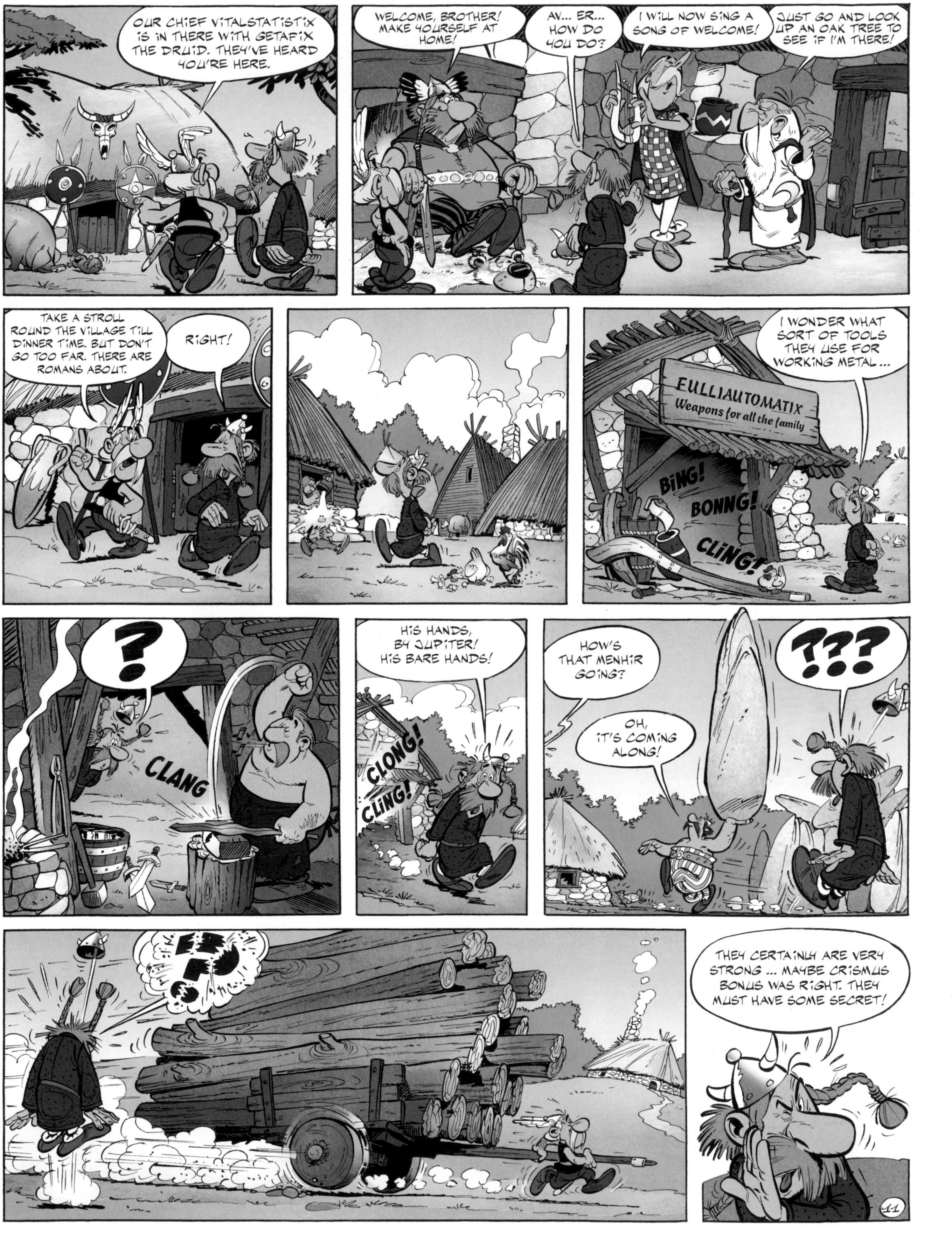

OUR CHIEF VITALSTATISTIX IS IN THERE WITH GETAFIX THE DRUID. THEY'VE HEARD YOU'RE HERE.
WELCOME, BROTHER! MAKE YOURSELF AT HOME!
AV... ER... HOW DO YOU DO?
I WILL NOW SING A SONG OF WELCOME!
JUST GO AND LOOK UP AN OAK TREE TO SEE IF I'M THERE!
TAKE A STROLL ROUND THE VILLAGE TILL DINNER TIME. BUT DON'T GO TOO FAR. THERE ARE ROMANS ABOUT.
RIGHT!
I WONDER WHAT SORT OF TOOLS THEY USE FOR WORKING METAL...
FULLIAUTOMATIX
Weapons for all the family
BING!
BONNG!
CLING!
?
CLANG
HIS HANDS, BY JUPITER! HIS BARE HANDS!
CLONG!
CLING!
HOW'S THAT MENHIR GOING?
OH, IT'S COMING ALONG!
???
THEY CERTAINLY ARE VERY STRONG ... MAYBE CRISMUS BONUS WAS RIGHT. THEY MUST HAVE SOME SECRET!
11

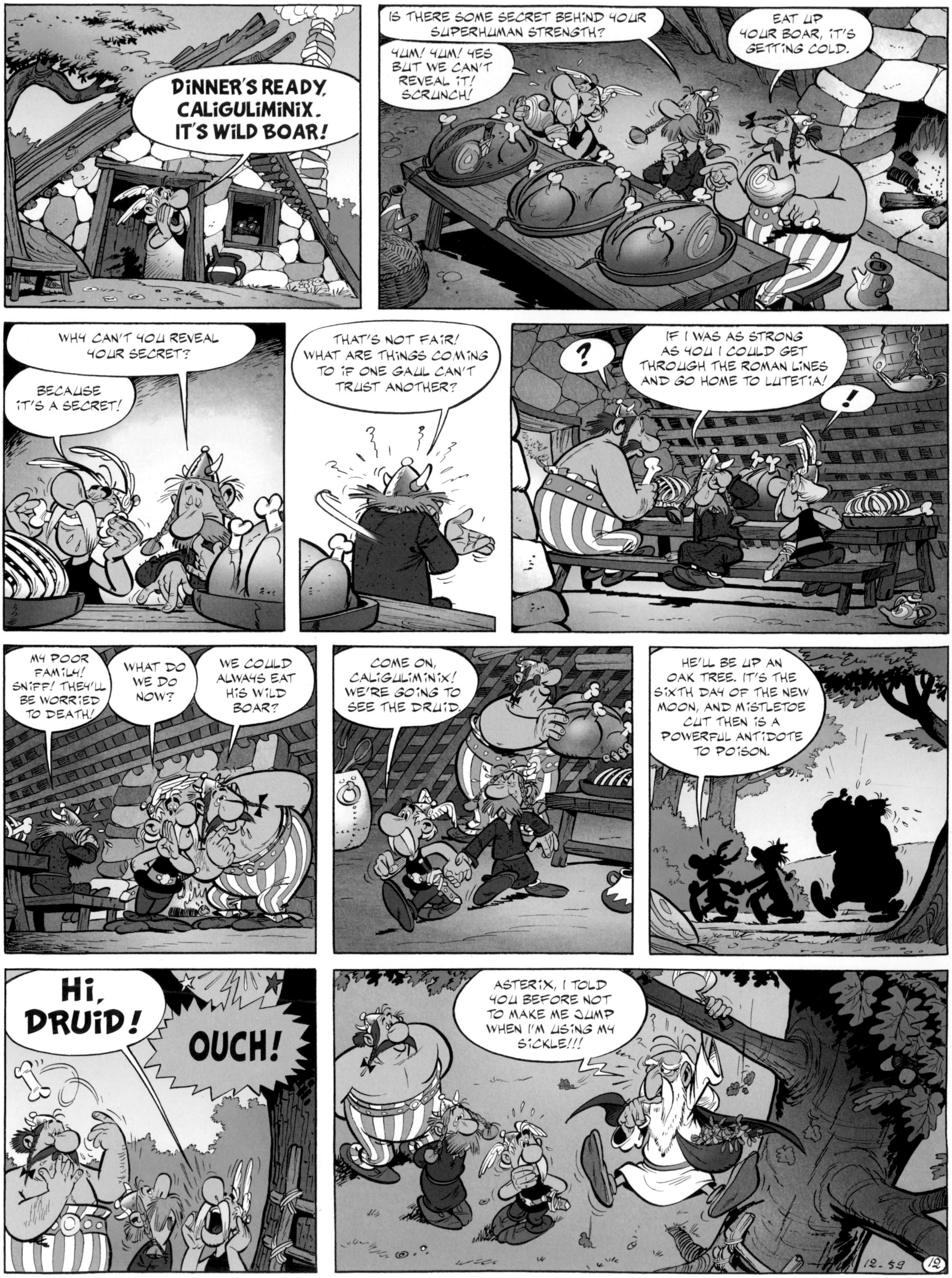
DINNER'S READY, CALIGULIMINIX. IT'S WILD BOAR!
IS THERE SOME SECRET BEHIND YOUR SUPERHUMAN STRENGTH?
YUM! YUM! YES BUT WE CAN'T REVEAL IT! SCRUNCH!
EAT UP YOUR BOAR, IT'S GETTING COLD.
WHY CAN'T YOU REVEAL YOUR SECRET?
BECAUSE IT'S A SECRET!
THAT'S NOT FAIR! WHAT ARE THINGS COMING TO IF ONE GAUL CAN'T TRUST ANOTHER?
?
IF I WAS AS STRONG AS YOU I COULD GET THROUGH THE ROMAN LINES AND GO HOME TO LUTETIA!
!
MY POOR FAMILY! SNIFF! THEY'LL BE WORRIED TO DEATH!
WHAT DO WE DO NOW?
WE COULD ALWAYS EAT HIS WILD BOAR?
COME ON, CALIGULIMINIX! WE'RE GOING TO SEE THE DRUID.
HE'LL BE UP AN OAK TREE. IT'S THE SIXTH DAY OF THE NEW MOON, AND MISTLETOE CUT THEN IS A POWERFUL ANTIDOTE TO POISON.
HI, DRUID!
OUCH!
ASTERIX, I TOLD YOU BEFORE NOT TO MAKE ME JUMP WHEN I'M USING MY SICKLE!!!
12-59
12

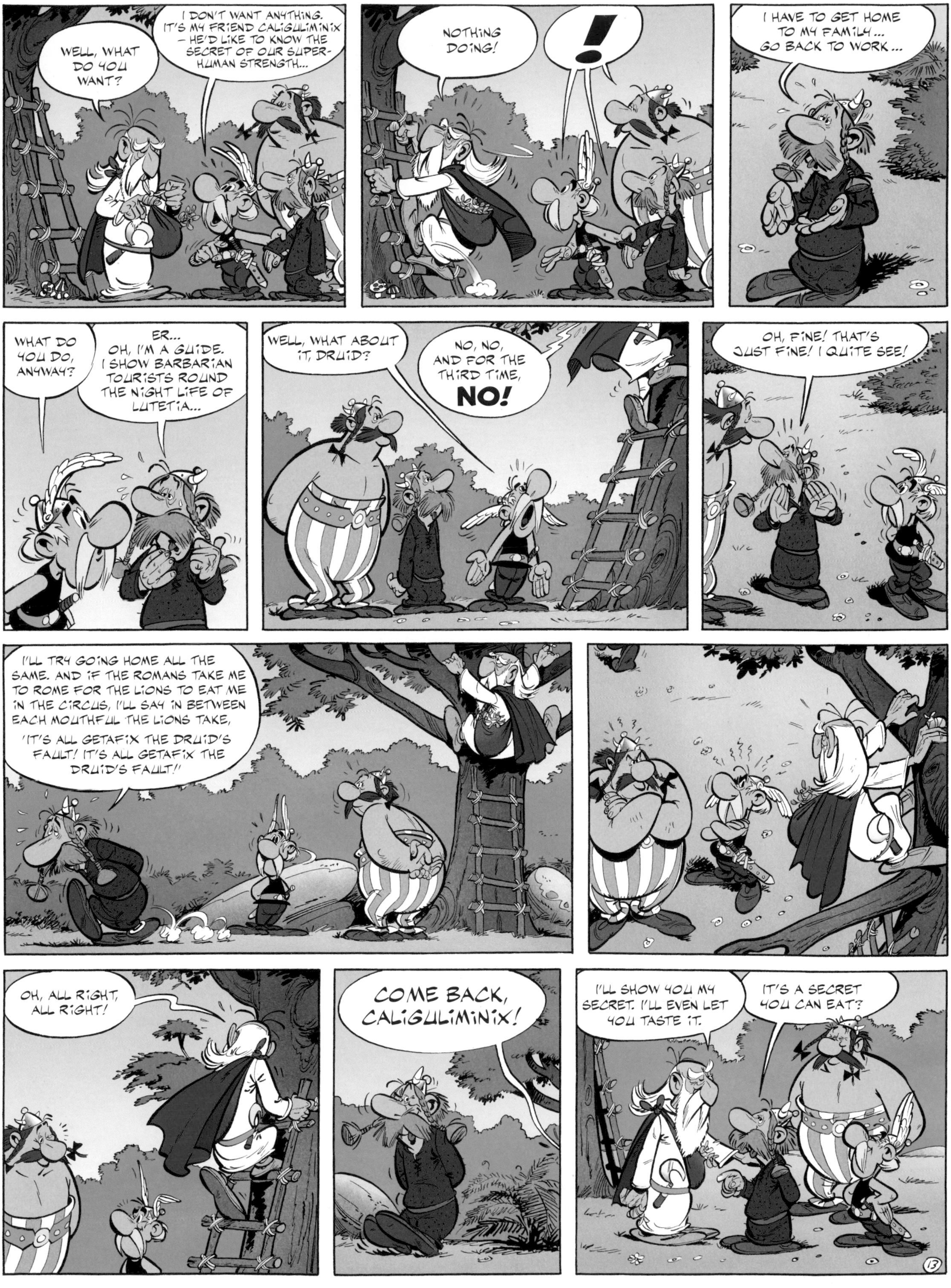
WELL, WHAT DO YOU WANT?
I DON'T WANT ANYTHING. IT'S MY FRIEND CALIGULIMINIX – HE'D LIKE TO KNOW THE SECRET OF OUR SUPER-HUMAN STRENGTH...
NOTHING DOING!
!
I HAVE TO GET HOME TO MY FAMILY... GO BACK TO WORK...
WHAT DO YOU DO, ANYWAY?
ER... OH, I'M A GUIDE. I SHOW BARBARIAN TOURISTS ROUND THE NIGHT LIFE OF LUTETIA...
WELL, WHAT ABOUT IT, DRUID?
NO, NO, AND FOR THE THIRD TIME, NO!
OH, FINE! THAT'S JUST FINE! I QUITE SEE!
I'LL TRY GOING HOME ALL THE SAME. AND IF THE ROMANS TAKE ME TO ROME FOR THE LIONS TO EAT ME IN THE CIRCUS, I'LL SAY IN BETWEEN EACH MOUTHFUL THE LIONS TAKE, 'IT'S ALL GETAFIX THE DRUID'S FAULT! IT'S ALL GETAFIX THE DRUID'S FAULT!'
OH, ALL RIGHT, ALL RIGHT!
COME BACK, CALIGULIMINIX!
I'LL SHOW YOU MY SECRET. I'LL EVEN LET YOU TASTE IT.
IT'S A SECRET YOU CAN EAT?
13

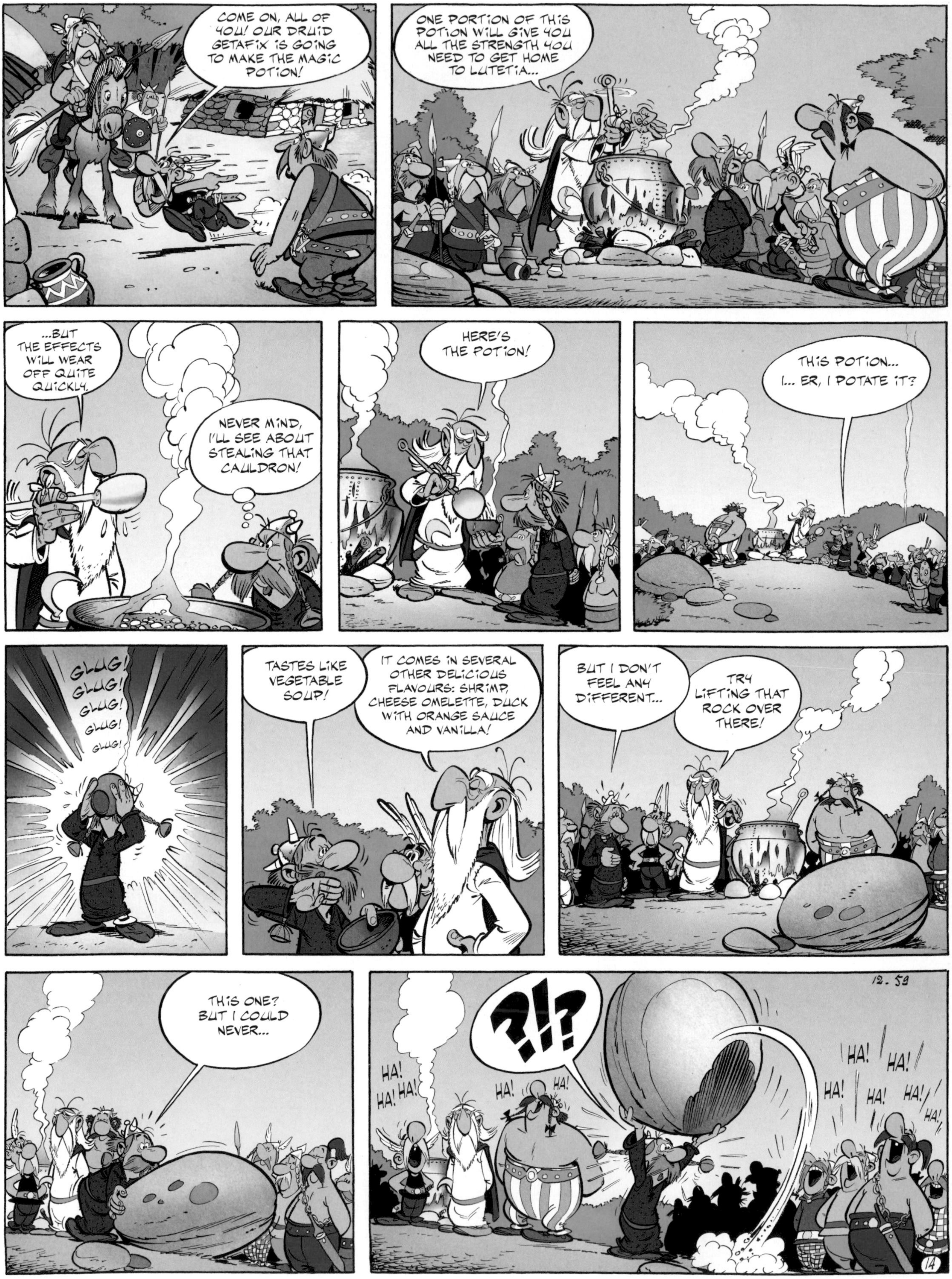
COME ON, ALL OF YOU! OUR DRUID GETAFIX IS GOING TO MAKE THE MAGIC POTION!
ONE PORTION OF THIS POTION WILL GIVE YOU ALL THE STRENGTH YOU NEED TO GET HOME TO LUTETIA...
...BUT THE EFFECTS WILL WEAR OFF QUITE QUICKLY.
NEVER MIND, I'LL SEE ABOUT STEALING THAT CAULDRON!
HERE'S THE POTION!
THIS POTION... I... ER, I POTATE IT?
GLUG! GLUG! GLUG! GLUG! GLUG!
TASTES LIKE VEGETABLE SOUP!
IT COMES IN SEVERAL OTHER DELICIOUS FLAVOURS: SHRIMP, CHEESE OMELETTE, DUCK WITH ORANGE SAUCE AND VANILLA!
BUT I DON'T FEEL ANY DIFFERENT...
TRY LIFTING THAT ROCK OVER THERE!
THIS ONE? BUT I COULD NEVER...
?!?
HA! HA! HA!
HA! HA!
HA! HA! HA! HA! HA! HA!
12 - 59
14

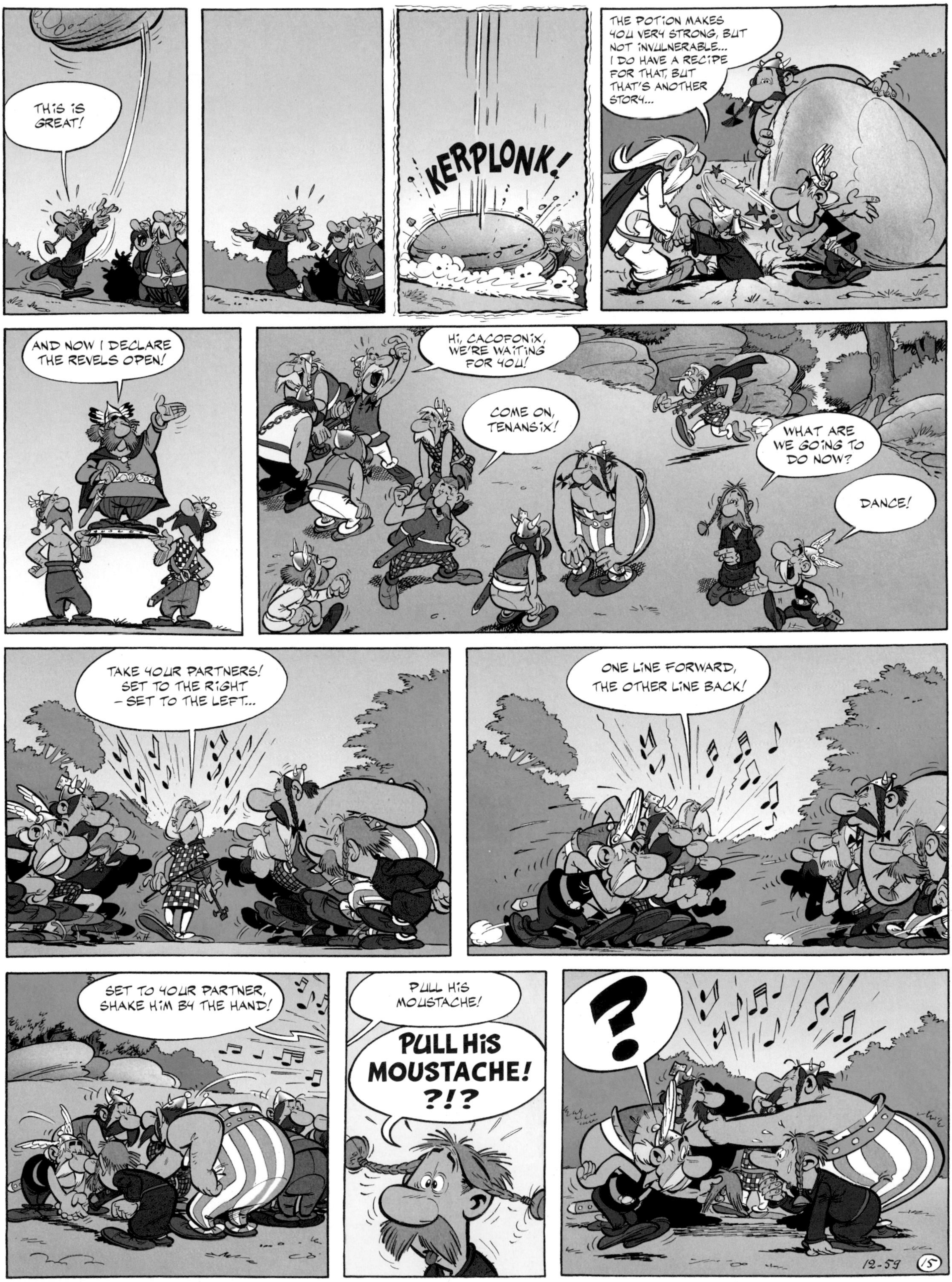
THIS IS GREAT!
KERPLONK!
THE POTION MAKES YOU VERY STRONG, BUT NOT INVULNERABLE... I DO HAVE A RECIPE FOR THAT, BUT THAT'S ANOTHER STORY...
AND NOW I DECLARE THE REVELS OPEN!
HI, CACOFONIX, WE'RE WAITING FOR YOU!
COME ON, TENANSIX!
WHAT ARE WE GOING TO DO NOW?
DANCE!
TAKE YOUR PARTNERS! SET TO THE RIGHT – SET TO THE LEFT...
ONE LINE FORWARD, THE OTHER LINE BACK!
SET TO YOUR PARTNER, SHAKE HIM BY THE HAND!
PULL HIS MOUSTACHE!
PULL HIS MOUSTACHE!
?!?
?
12-59 15

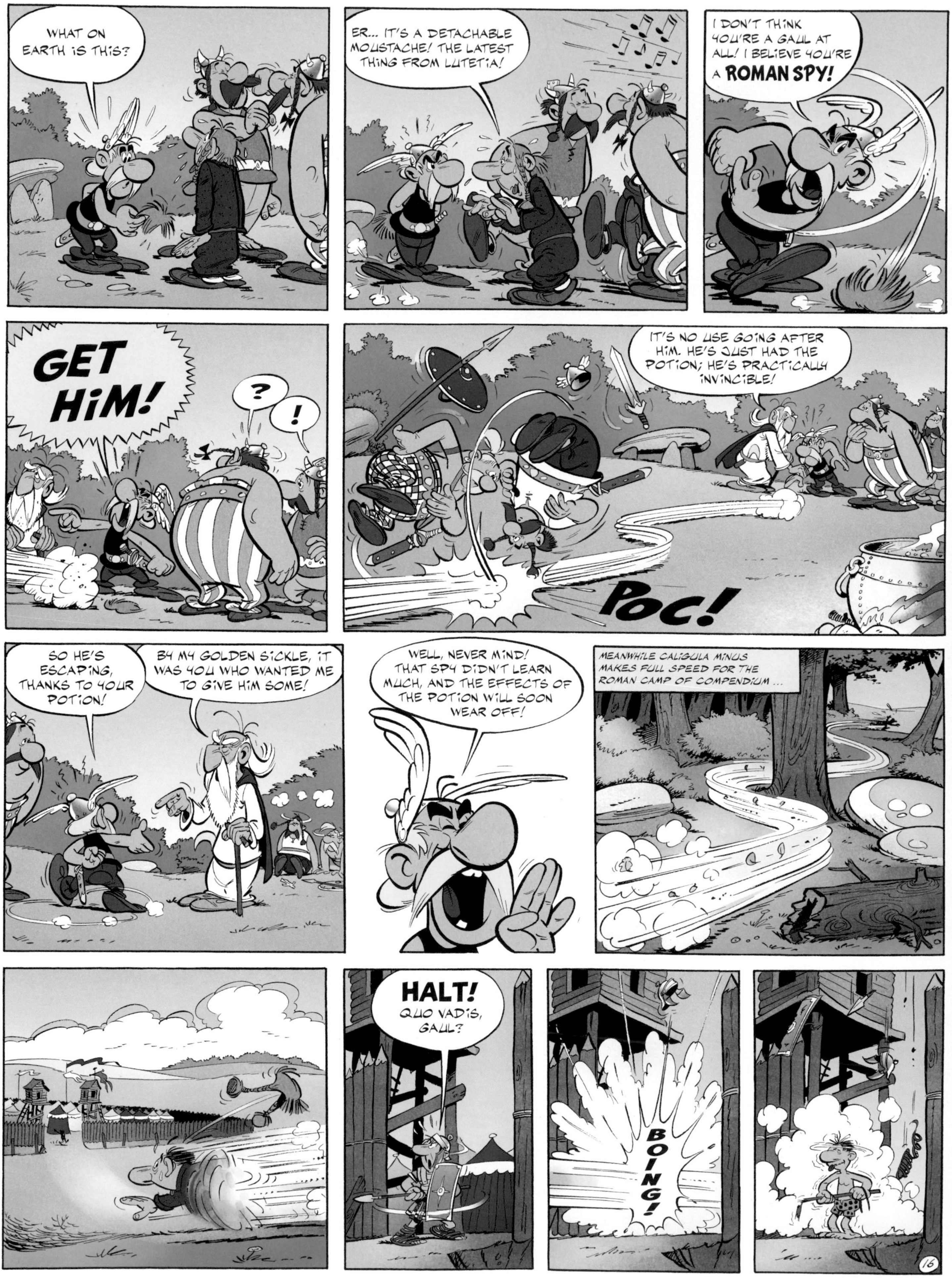
WHAT ON EARTH IS THIS?
ER... IT'S A DETACHABLE MOUSTACHE! THE LATEST THING FROM LUTETIA!
I DON'T THINK YOU'RE A GAUL AT ALL! I BELIEVE YOU'RE A ROMAN SPY!
GET HIM!
?
!
IT'S NO USE GOING AFTER HIM. HE'S JUST HAD THE POTION; HE'S PRACTICALLY INVINCIBLE!
POC!
SO HE'S ESCAPING, THANKS TO YOUR POTION!
BY MY GOLDEN SICKLE, IT WAS YOU WHO WANTED ME TO GIVE HIM SOME!
WELL, NEVER MIND! THAT SPY DIDN'T LEARN MUCH, AND THE EFFECTS OF THE POTION WILL SOON WEAR OFF!
MEANWHILE CALIGULA MINUS MAKES FULL SPEED FOR THE ROMAN CAMP OF COMPENDIUM ...
HALT! QUO VADIS, GAUL?
BOING!
16

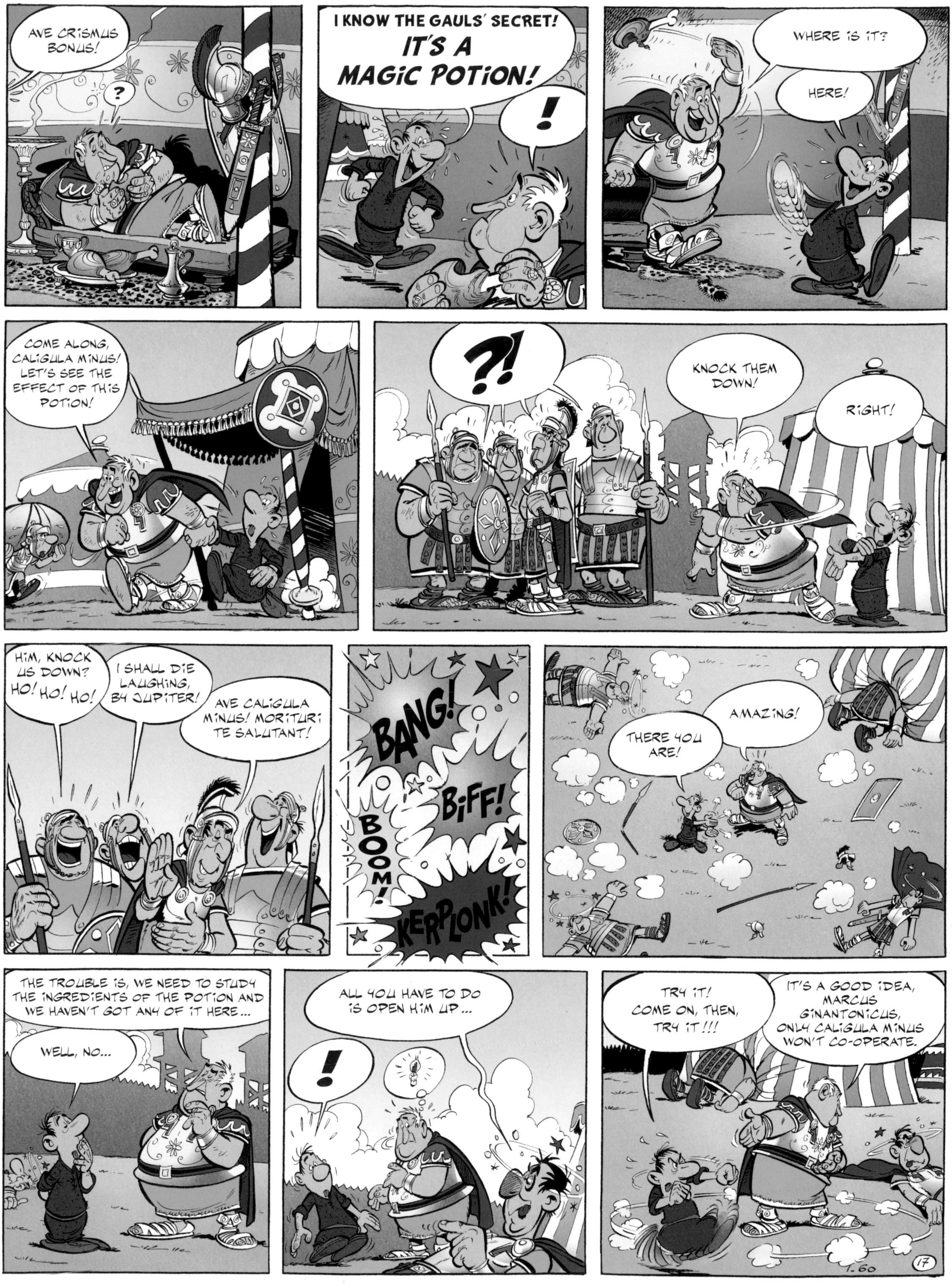

AVE CRISMUS BONUS!
?
I KNOW THE GAULS' SECRET! IT'S A MAGIC POTION!
!
WHERE IS IT?
HERE!
COME ALONG, CALIGULA MINUS! LET'S SEE THE EFFECT OF THIS POTION!
?!
KNOCK THEM DOWN!
RIGHT!
HIM, KNOCK US DOWN? HO! HO! HO!
I SHALL DIE LAUGHING, BY JUPITER!
AVE CALIGULA MINUS! MORITURI TE SALUTANT!
BANG!
BIFF!
BOOM!
KERPLONK!
AMAZING!
THERE YOU ARE!
THE TROUBLE IS, WE NEED TO STUDY THE INGREDIENTS OF THE POTION AND WE HAVEN'T GOT ANY OF IT HERE...
WELL, NO...
ALL YOU HAVE TO DO IS OPEN HIM UP...
!
TRY IT! COME ON, THEN, TRY IT!!!
IT'S A GOOD IDEA, MARCUS GINANTONICUS, ONLY CALIGULA MINUS WON'T CO-OPERATE.
17

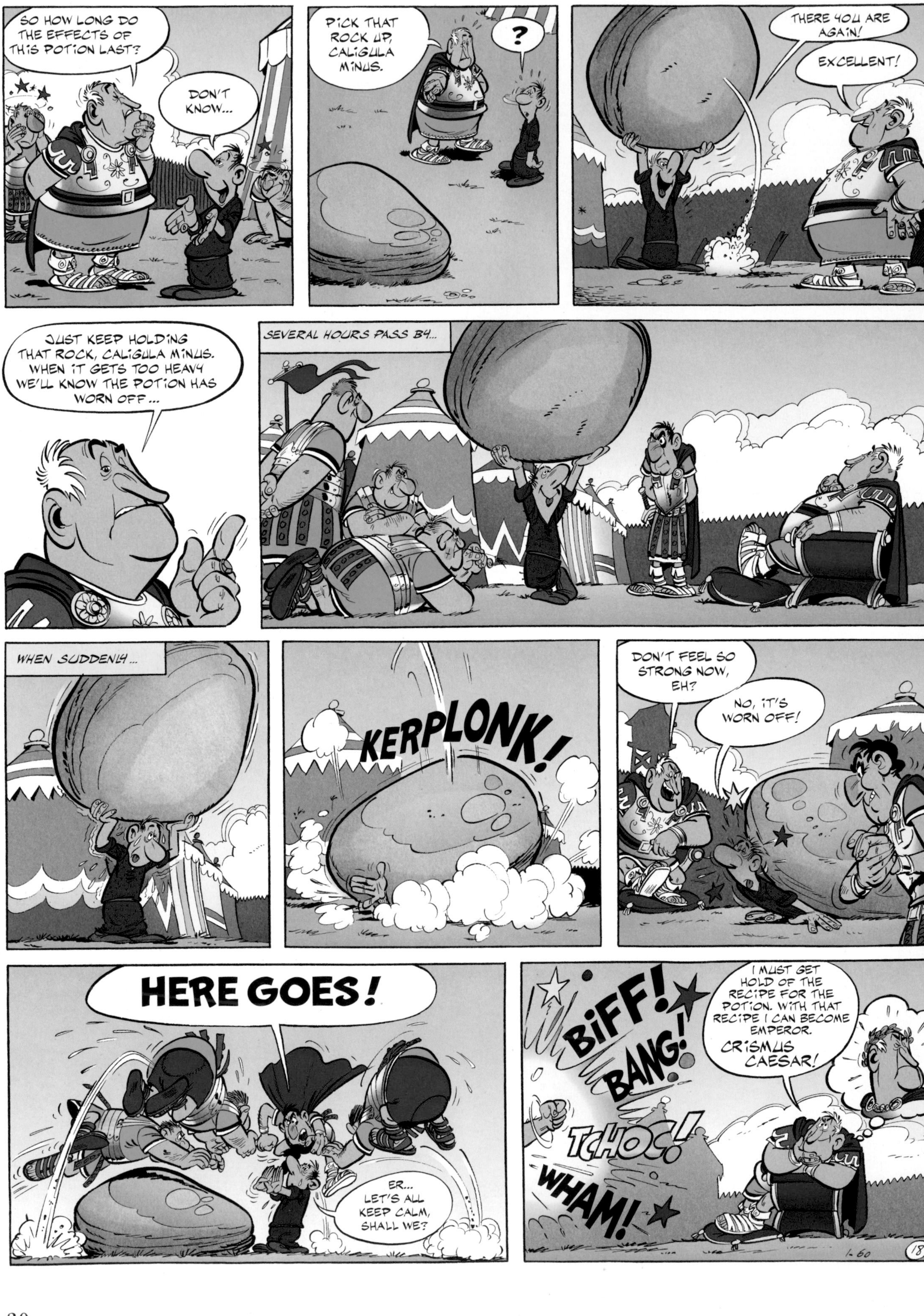
SO HOW LONG DO THE EFFECTS OF THIS POTION LAST?
DON'T KNOW...
PICK THAT ROCK UP, CALIGULA MINUS.
?
THERE YOU ARE AGAIN!
EXCELLENT!
JUST KEEP HOLDING THAT ROCK, CALIGULA MINUS. WHEN IT GETS TOO HEAVY WE'LL KNOW THE POTION HAS WORN OFF...
SEVERAL HOURS PASS BY...
WHEN SUDDENLY...
KERPLONK!
DON'T FEEL SO STRONG NOW, EH?
NO, IT'S WORN OFF!
HERE GOES!
ER... LET'S ALL KEEP CALM, SHALL WE?
BIFF!
BANG!
TCHOC!
WHAM!
I MUST GET HOLD OF THE RECIPE FOR THE POTION. WITH THAT RECIPE I CAN BECOME EMPEROR.
CRISMUS CAESAR!
18

SOON AFTERWARDS IN THE GAULISH VILLAGE...

I'M JUST GOING TO PICK SOME MISTLETOE IN THE FOREST.

WANT ME TO COME WITH YOU, DRUID?

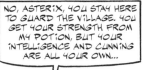

NO, ASTERIX, YOU STAY HERE TO GUARD THE VILLAGE. YOU GET YOUR STRENGTH FROM MY POTION, BUT YOUR INTELLIGENCE AND CUNNING ARE ALL YOUR OWN...

IT WOULD BE A DISASTER FOR US TO LOSE YOU! BESIDES, I'LL BE BACK SOON.

GOOD...

♪ (1)

(1) ANCIENT GAULISH AIR

OOPS!

GOT HIM!

⚡✶👊👀 (2)

(2) ANCIENT GAULISH SWEAR-WORDS

SOON AFTERWARDS...

WE GOT THE DRUID, O CRISMUS BONUS!

GOOD WORK, TULLIUS OCTOPUS!

AS A REWARD YOU SHALL HAVE 100 SESTERTII, AND YOU CAN GO TO ROME ON LEAVE TO SEE THE CIRCUS!

GOODY GOODY GUMDROPS! I'M GOING TO THE CIRCUS!

NOW, DRUID, YOU WILL TELL ME YOUR SECRET!

THAT'S WHAT YOU THINK!

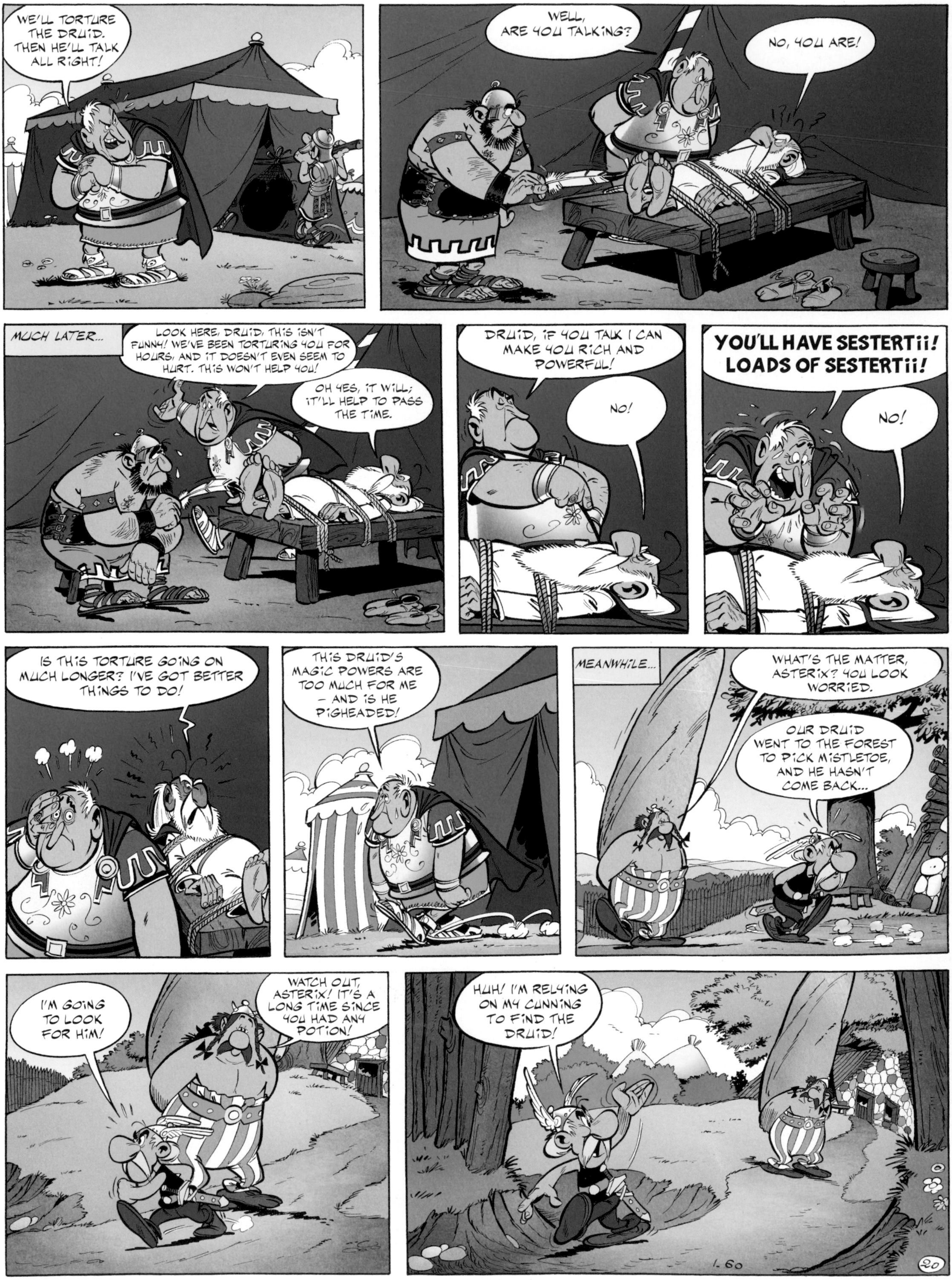

WE'LL TORTURE THE DRUID. THEN HE'LL TALK ALL RIGHT!
WELL, ARE YOU TALKING?
NO, YOU ARE!
MUCH LATER...
LOOK HERE, DRUID, THIS ISN'T FUNNY! WE'VE BEEN TORTURING YOU FOR HOURS, AND IT DOESN'T EVEN SEEM TO HURT. THIS WON'T HELP YOU!
OH YES, IT WILL; IT'LL HELP TO PASS THE TIME.
DRUID, IF YOU TALK I CAN MAKE YOU RICH AND POWERFUL!
NO!
YOU'LL HAVE SESTERTii! LOADS OF SESTERTii!
NO!
IS THIS TORTURE GOING ON MUCH LONGER? I'VE GOT BETTER THINGS TO DO!
THIS DRUID'S MAGIC POWERS ARE TOO MUCH FOR ME – AND IS HE PIGHEADED!
MEANWHILE...
WHAT'S THE MATTER, ASTERIX? YOU LOOK WORRIED.
OUR DRUID WENT TO THE FOREST TO PICK MISTLETOE, AND HE HASN'T COME BACK...
I'M GOING TO LOOK FOR HIM!
WATCH OUT, ASTERIX! IT'S A LONG TIME SINCE YOU HAD ANY POTION!
HUH! I'M RELYING ON MY CUNNING TO FIND THE DRUID!

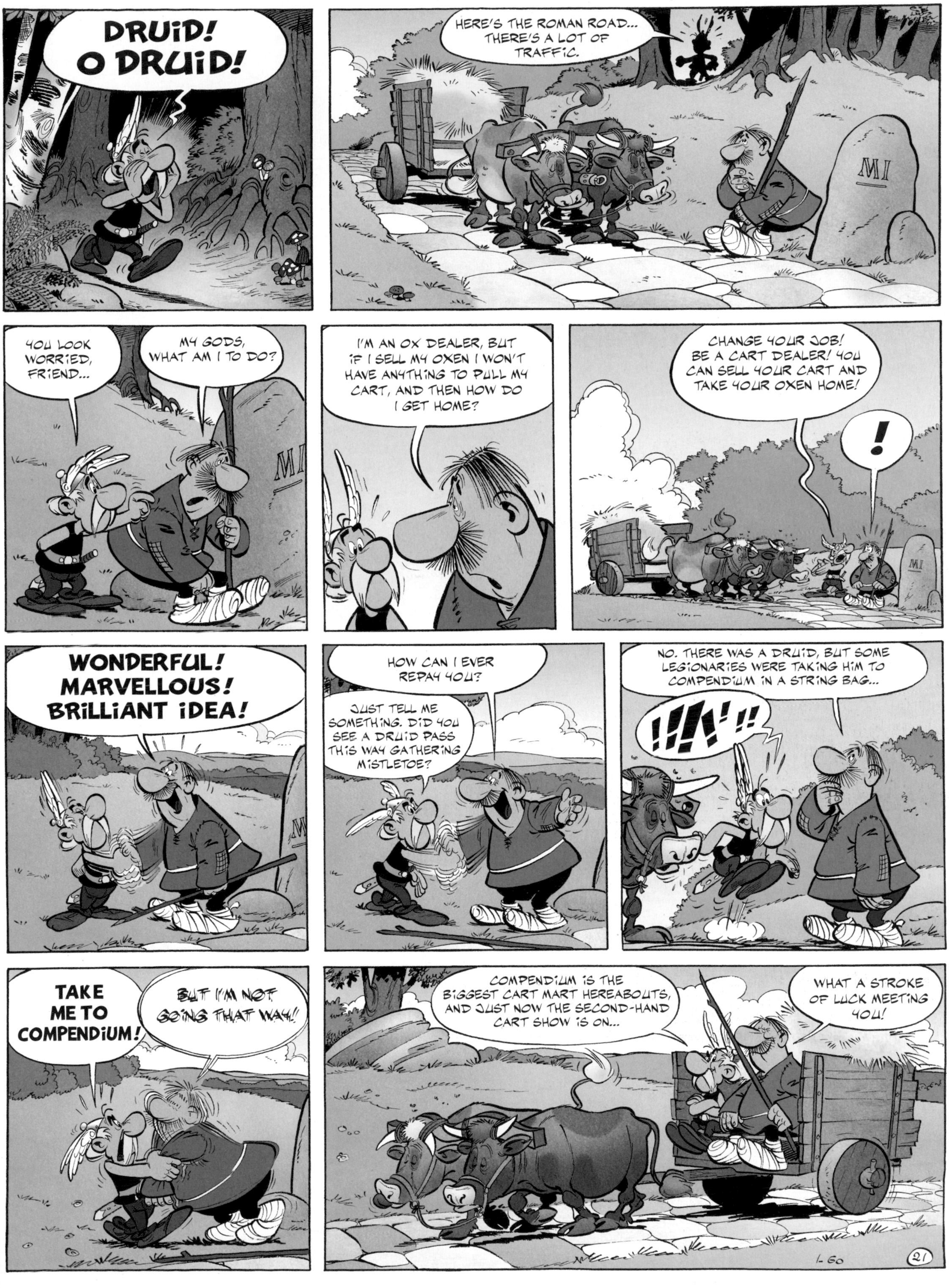
DRUID! O DRUID!
HERE'S THE ROMAN ROAD... THERE'S A LOT OF TRAFFIC.
MI
YOU LOOK WORRIED, FRIEND...
MY GODS, WHAT AM I TO DO?
I'M AN OX DEALER, BUT IF I SELL MY OXEN I WON'T HAVE ANYTHING TO PULL MY CART, AND THEN HOW DO I GET HOME?
CHANGE YOUR JOB! BE A CART DEALER! YOU CAN SELL YOUR CART AND TAKE YOUR OXEN HOME!
!
WONDERFUL! MARVELLOUS! BRILLIANT IDEA!
HOW CAN I EVER REPAY YOU?
JUST TELL ME SOMETHING. DID YOU SEE A DRUID PASS THIS WAY GATHERING MISTLETOE?
NO. THERE WAS A DRUID, BUT SOME LEGIONARIES WERE TAKING HIM TO COMPENDIUM IN A STRING BAG...
TAKE ME TO COMPENDIUM!
BUT I'M NOT GOING THAT WAY!
COMPENDIUM IS THE BIGGEST CART MART HEREABOUTS, AND JUST NOW THE SECOND-HAND CART SHOW IS ON...
WHAT A STROKE OF LUCK MEETING YOU!
21

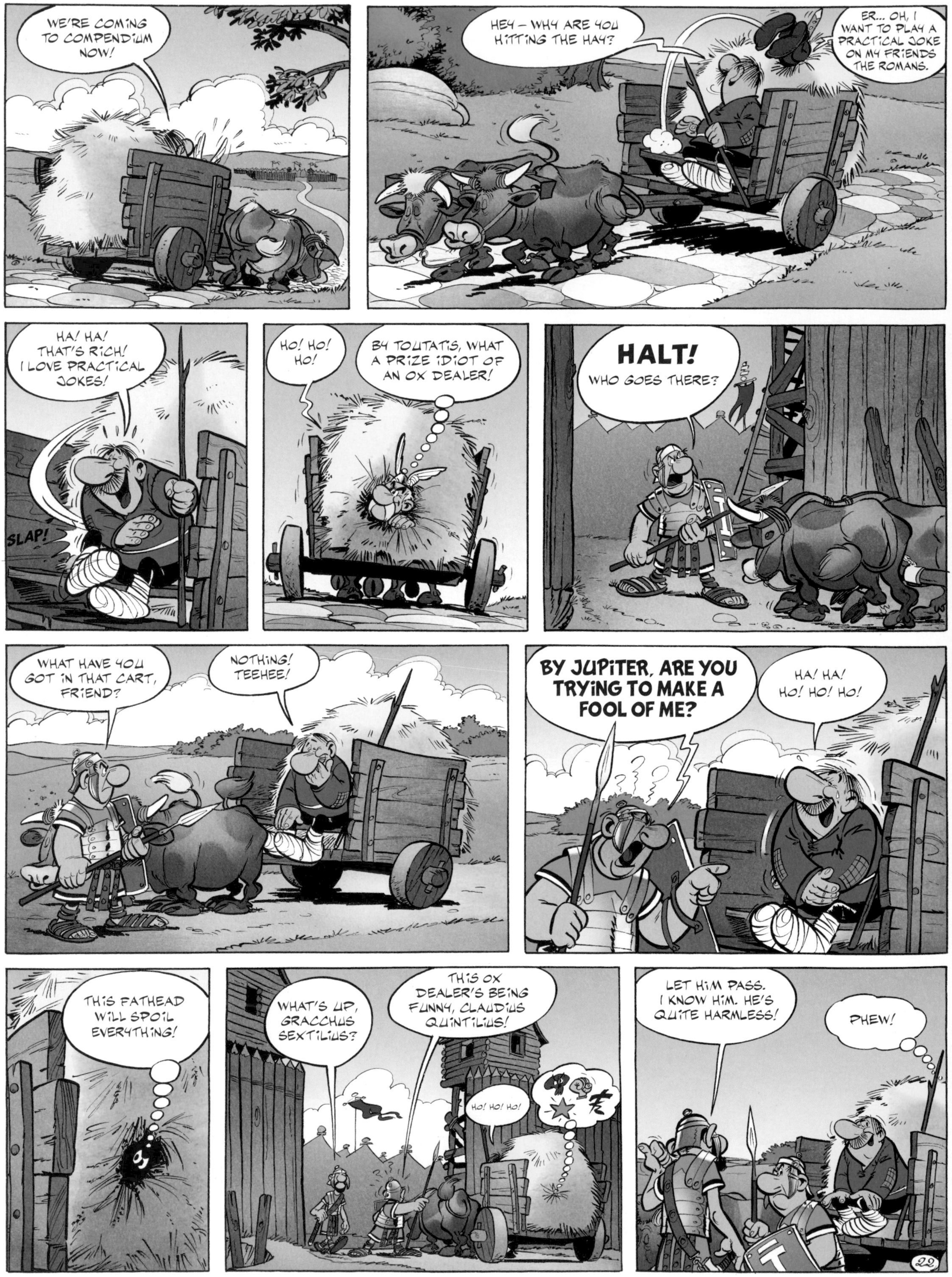
WE'RE COMING TO COMPENDIUM NOW!
HEY – WHY ARE YOU HITTING THE HAY?
ER... OH, I WANT TO PLAY A PRACTICAL JOKE ON MY FRIENDS THE ROMANS.
HA! HA! THAT'S RICH! I LOVE PRACTICAL JOKES!
SLAP!
HO! HO! HO!
BY TOUTATIS, WHAT A PRIZE IDIOT OF AN OX DEALER!
HALT! WHO GOES THERE?
WHAT HAVE YOU GOT IN THAT CART, FRIEND?
NOTHING! TEEHEE!
BY JUPITER, ARE YOU TRYING TO MAKE A FOOL OF ME?
HA! HA! HO! HO! HO!
THIS FATHEAD WILL SPOIL EVERYTHING!
WHAT'S UP, GRACCHUS SEXTILIUS?
THIS OX DEALER'S BEING FUNNY, CLAUDIUS QUINTILIUS!
HO! HO! HO!
LET HIM PASS. I KNOW HIM. HE'S QUITE HARMLESS!
PHEW!
22

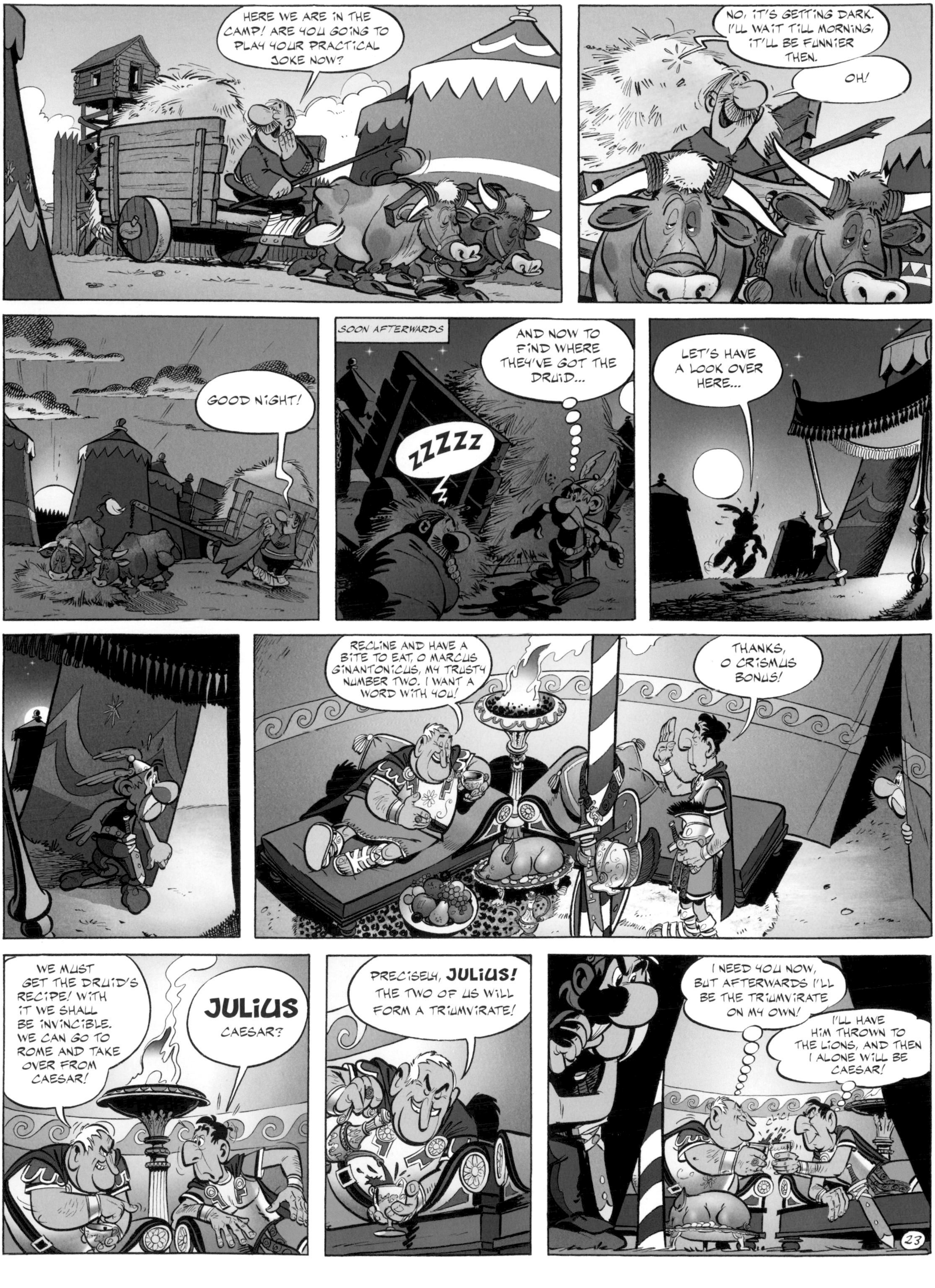
HERE WE ARE IN THE CAMP! ARE YOU GOING TO PLAY YOUR PRACTICAL JOKE NOW?
NO, IT'S GETTING DARK. I'LL WAIT TILL MORNING, IT'LL BE FUNNIER THEN.
OH!
GOOD NIGHT!
SOON AFTERWARDS
ZZZZZ
AND NOW TO FIND WHERE THEY'VE GOT THE DRUID...
LET'S HAVE A LOOK OVER HERE...
RECLINE AND HAVE A BITE TO EAT, O MARCUS GINANTONICUS, MY TRUSTY NUMBER TWO. I WANT A WORD WITH YOU!
THANKS, O CRISMUS BONUS!
WE MUST GET THE DRUID'S RECIPE! WITH IT WE SHALL BE INVINCIBLE. WE CAN GO TO ROME AND TAKE OVER FROM CAESAR!
JULIUS CAESAR?
PRECISELY, JULIUS! THE TWO OF US WILL FORM A TRIUMVIRATE!
I NEED YOU NOW, BUT AFTERWARDS I'LL BE THE TRIUMVIRATE ON MY OWN!
I'LL HAVE HIM THROWN TO THE LIONS, AND THEN I ALONE WILL BE CAESAR!
23

MOST INTERESTING, BUT IT TELLS ME NOTHING OF GETAFIX'S WHEREABOUTS!

HE MUST BE IN THAT HEAVILY GUARDED TENT...

THE BOLD APPROACH!

DO YOU MIND? I'VE JUST COME TO RESCUE GETAFIX THE DRUID. HE'S A FRIEND OF MINE.

?!?!

THANKS!

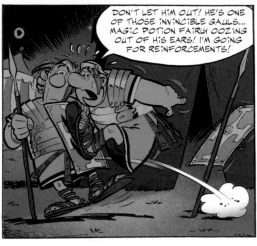

DON'T LET HIM OUT! HE'S ONE OF THOSE INVINCIBLE GAULS... MAGIC POTION FAIRLY OOZING OUT OF HIS EARS! I'M GOING FOR REINFORCEMENTS!

V...VERY WELL! BUT DON'T BE LONG, O CAIUS FLEBITUS!

AND INSIDE THE TENT...

ASTERIX!

ALL WELL?

BY BELISAMA, ASTERIX! WHAT MADNESS TO VENTURE RIGHT INTO THE JAWS OF THE ROMAN WOLF!

THE ROMANS CAN'T DO A THING AGAINST MY MAGIC POWERS!

EXACTLY! WE'LL HAVE SOME FUN WITH THEM! I'VE GOT A FEW IDEAS!

SIR! SIR!

24

36

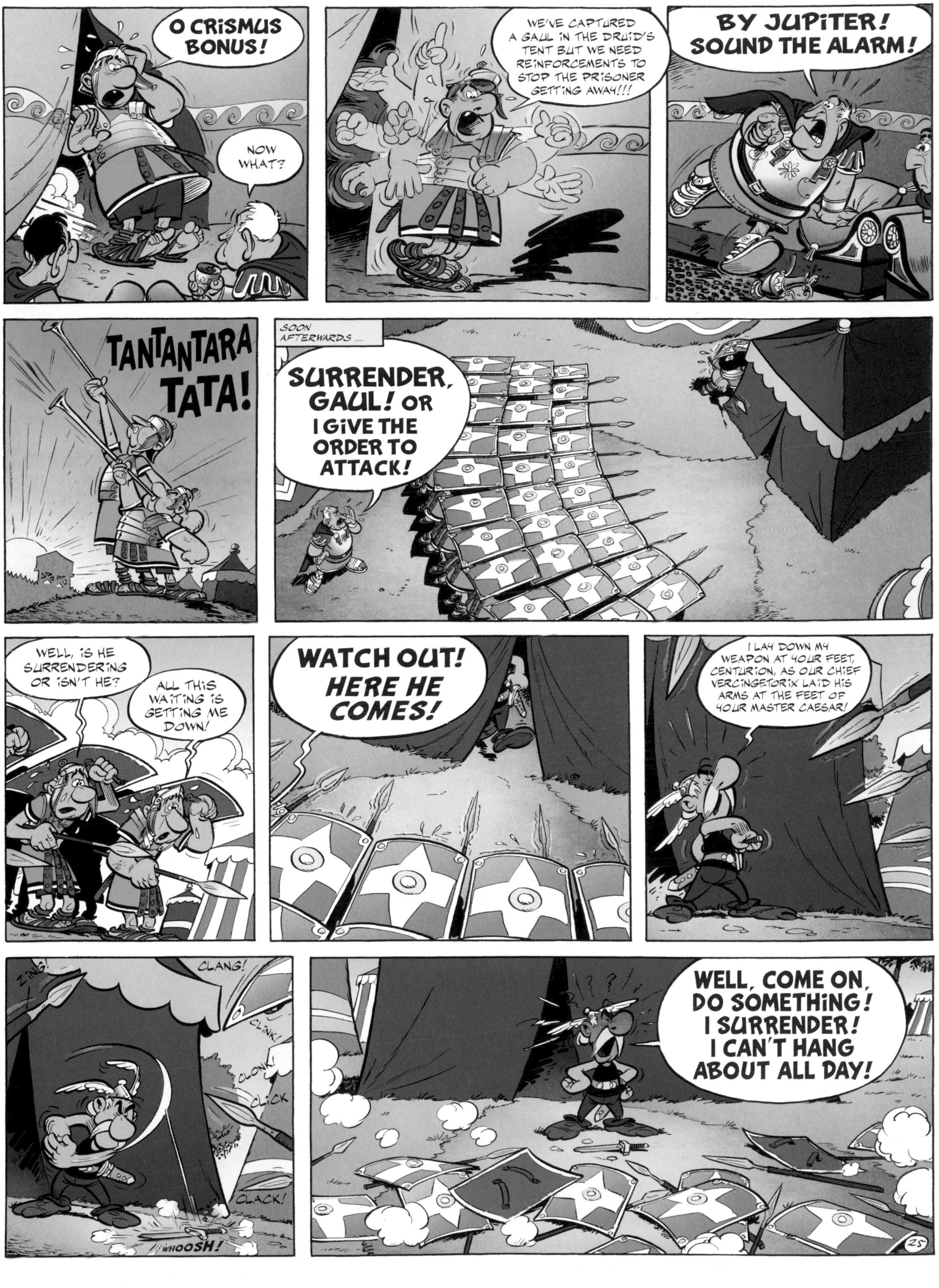
O CRISMUS BONUS!
NOW WHAT?
WE'VE CAPTURED A GAUL IN THE DRUID'S TENT BUT WE NEED REINFORCEMENTS TO STOP THE PRISONER GETTING AWAY!!!
BY JUPITER! SOUND THE ALARM!
TANTANTARA TATA!
SOON AFTERWARDS ...
SURRENDER, GAUL! OR I GIVE THE ORDER TO ATTACK!
WELL, IS HE SURRENDERING OR ISN'T HE?
ALL THIS WAITING IS GETTING ME DOWN!
WATCH OUT! HERE HE COMES!
I LAY DOWN MY WEAPON AT YOUR FEET, CENTURION, AS OUR CHIEF VERCINGETORIX LAID HIS ARMS AT THE FEET OF YOUR MASTER CAESAR!
ZING!
CLANG!
CLINK!
CLONK!
CLICK
CLACK!
WHOOSH!
WELL, COME ON, DO SOMETHING! I SURRENDER! I CAN'T HANG ABOUT ALL DAY!
25

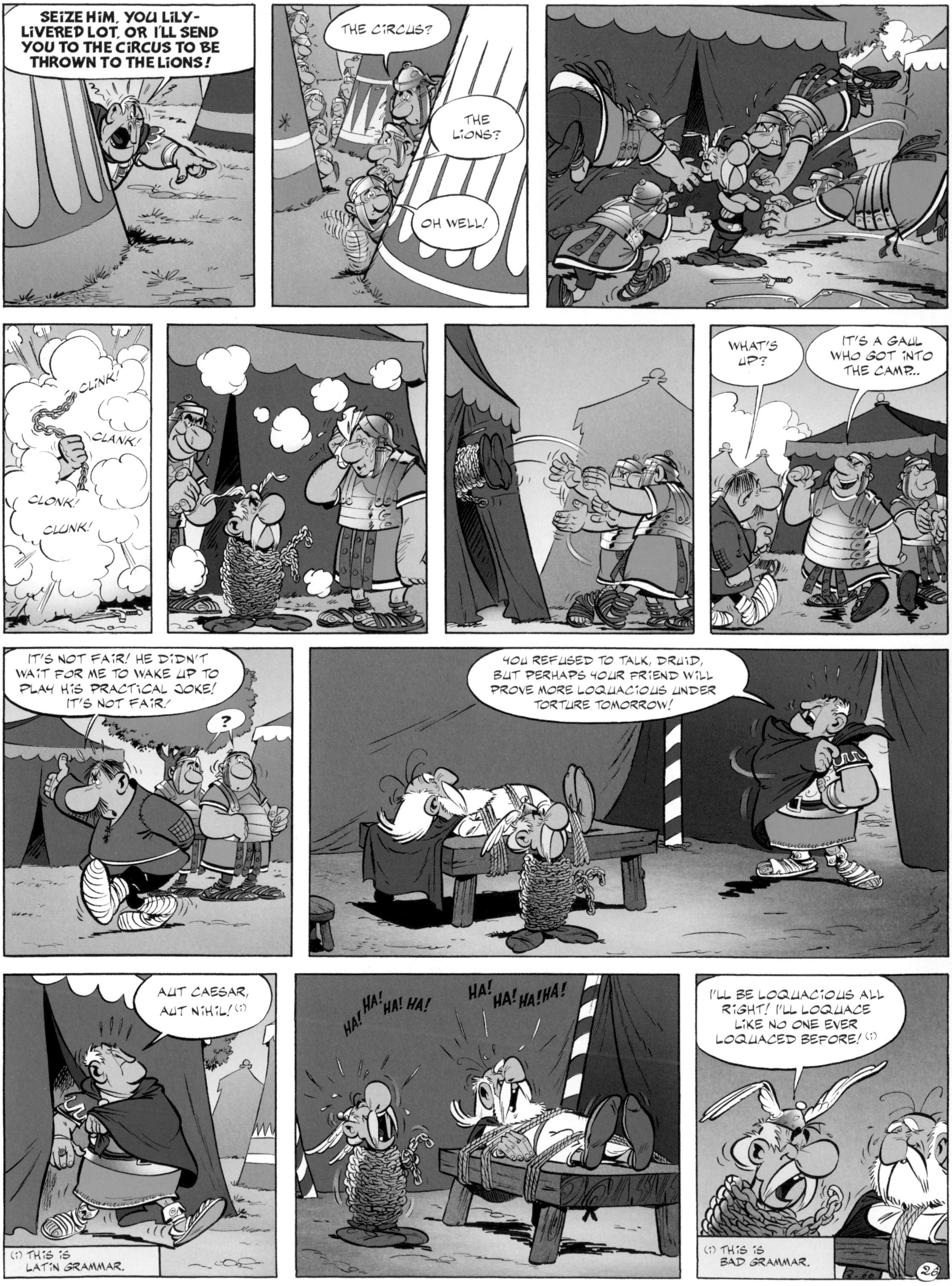
SEIZE HIM, YOU LILY-LIVERED LOT, OR I'LL SEND YOU TO THE CIRCUS TO BE THROWN TO THE LIONS!
THE CIRCUS?
THE LIONS?
OH WELL!
CLINK!
CLANK!
CLONK!
CLUNK!
WHAT'S UP?
IT'S A GAUL WHO GOT INTO THE CAMP...
IT'S NOT FAIR! HE DIDN'T WAIT FOR ME TO WAKE UP TO PLAY HIS PRACTICAL JOKE! IT'S NOT FAIR!
?
YOU REFUSED TO TALK, DRUID, BUT PERHAPS YOUR FRIEND WILL PROVE MORE LOQUACIOUS UNDER TORTURE TOMORROW!
AUT CAESAR, AUT NIHIL! (1)
(1) THIS IS LATIN GRAMMAR.
HA! HA! HA! HA!
HA! HA! HA! HA!
I'LL BE LOQUACIOUS ALL RIGHT! I'LL LOQUACE LIKE NO ONE EVER LOQUACED BEFORE! (1)
(1) THIS IS BAD GRAMMAR.
26

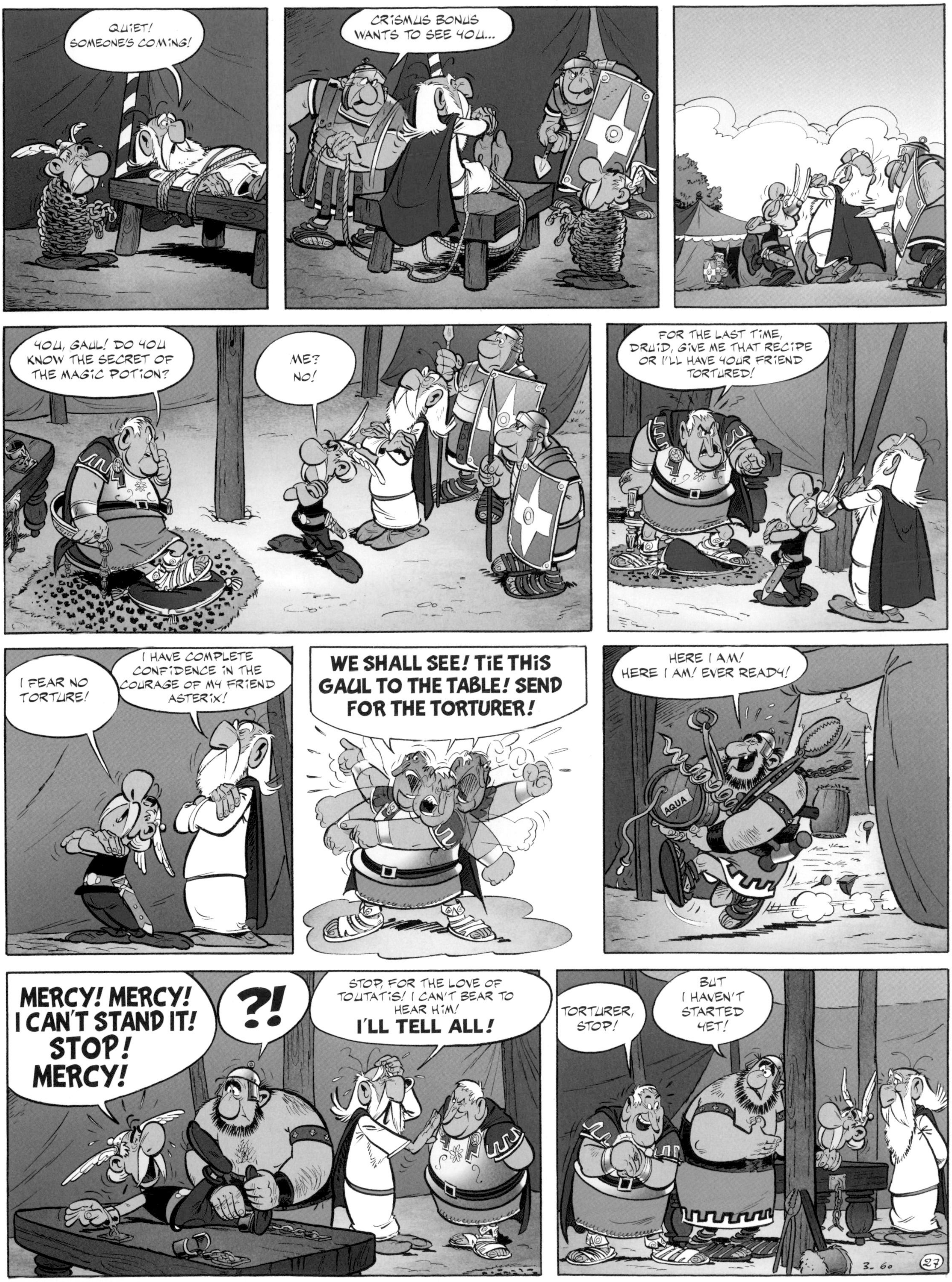
QUIET! SOMEONE'S COMING!
CRISMUS BONUS WANTS TO SEE YOU...
YOU, GAUL! DO YOU KNOW THE SECRET OF THE MAGIC POTION?
ME? NO!
FOR THE LAST TIME, DRUID, GIVE ME THAT RECIPE OR I'LL HAVE YOUR FRIEND TORTURED!
I FEAR NO TORTURE!
I HAVE COMPLETE CONFIDENCE IN THE COURAGE OF MY FRIEND ASTERIX!
WE SHALL SEE! TIE THIS GAUL TO THE TABLE! SEND FOR THE TORTURER!
HERE I AM! HERE I AM! EVER READY!
AQUA
MERCY! MERCY! I CAN'T STAND IT! STOP! MERCY!
?!
STOP, FOR THE LOVE OF TOUTATIS! I CAN'T BEAR TO HEAR HIM! I'LL TELL ALL!
TORTURER, STOP!
BUT I HAVEN'T STARTED YET!
3-60
27

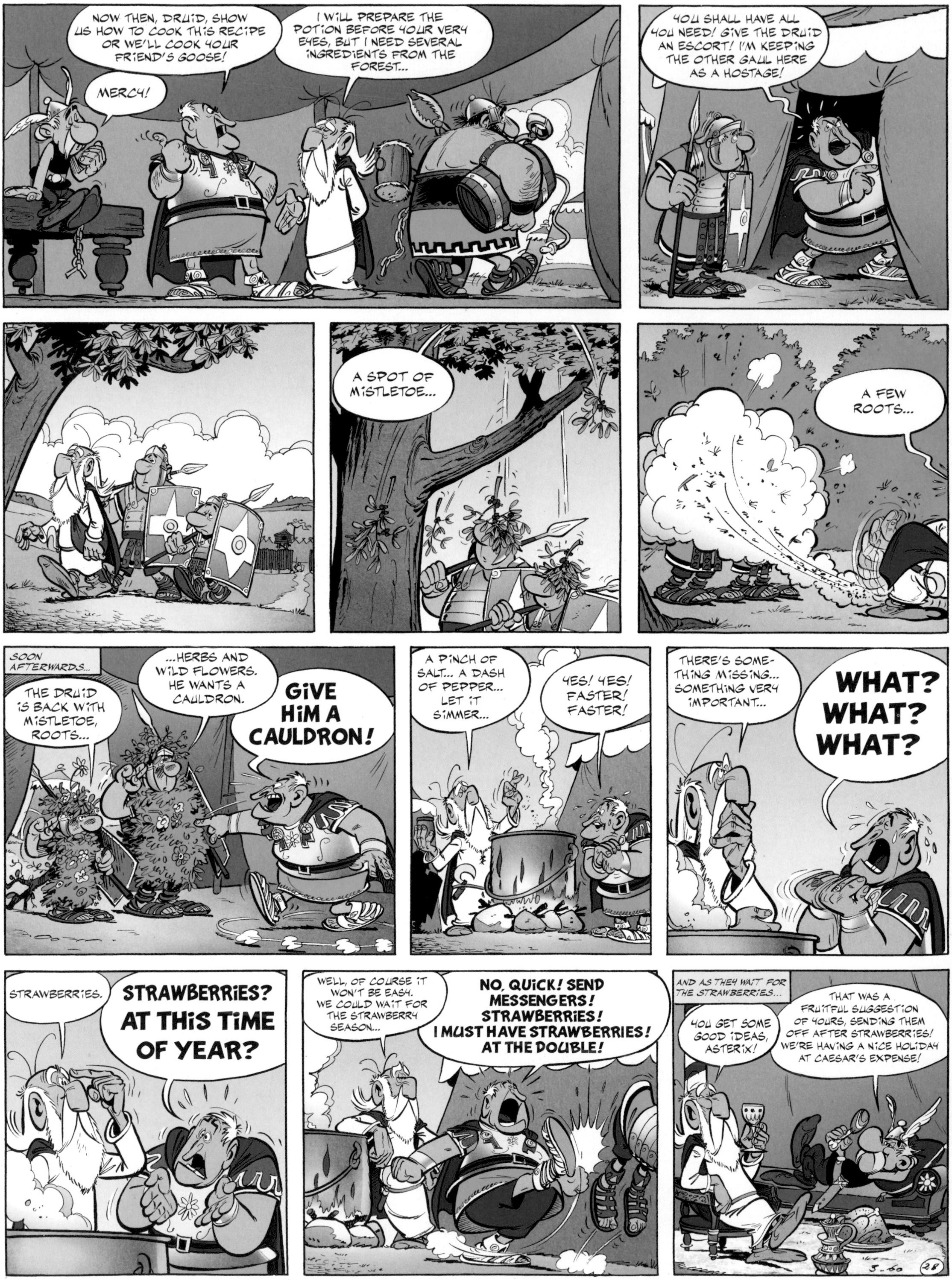
NOW THEN, DRUID, SHOW US HOW TO COOK THIS RECIPE OR WE'LL COOK YOUR FRIEND'S GOOSE!
MERCY!
I WILL PREPARE THE POTION BEFORE YOUR VERY EYES, BUT I NEED SEVERAL INGREDIENTS FROM THE FOREST...
YOU SHALL HAVE ALL YOU NEED! GIVE THE DRUID AN ESCORT! I'M KEEPING THE OTHER GAUL HERE AS A HOSTAGE!
A SPOT OF MISTLETOE...
A FEW ROOTS...
SOON AFTERWARDS...
THE DRUID IS BACK WITH MISTLETOE, ROOTS...
...HERBS AND WILD FLOWERS. HE WANTS A CAULDRON.
GIVE HIM A CAULDRON!
A PINCH OF SALT... A DASH OF PEPPER... LET IT SIMMER...
YES! YES! FASTER! FASTER!
THERE'S SOMETHING MISSING... SOMETHING VERY IMPORTANT...
WHAT? WHAT? WHAT?
STRAWBERRIES.
STRAWBERRIES? AT THIS TIME OF YEAR?
WELL, OF COURSE IT WON'T BE EASY. WE COULD WAIT FOR THE STRAWBERRY SEASON...
NO, QUICK! SEND MESSENGERS! STRAWBERRIES! I MUST HAVE STRAWBERRIES! AT THE DOUBLE!
AND AS THEY WAIT FOR THE STRAWBERRIES...
YOU GET SOME GOOD IDEAS, ASTERIX!
THAT WAS A FRUITFUL SUGGESTION OF YOURS, SENDING THEM OFF AFTER STRAWBERRIES! WE'RE HAVING A NICE HOLIDAY AT CAESAR'S EXPENSE!
5-60
28

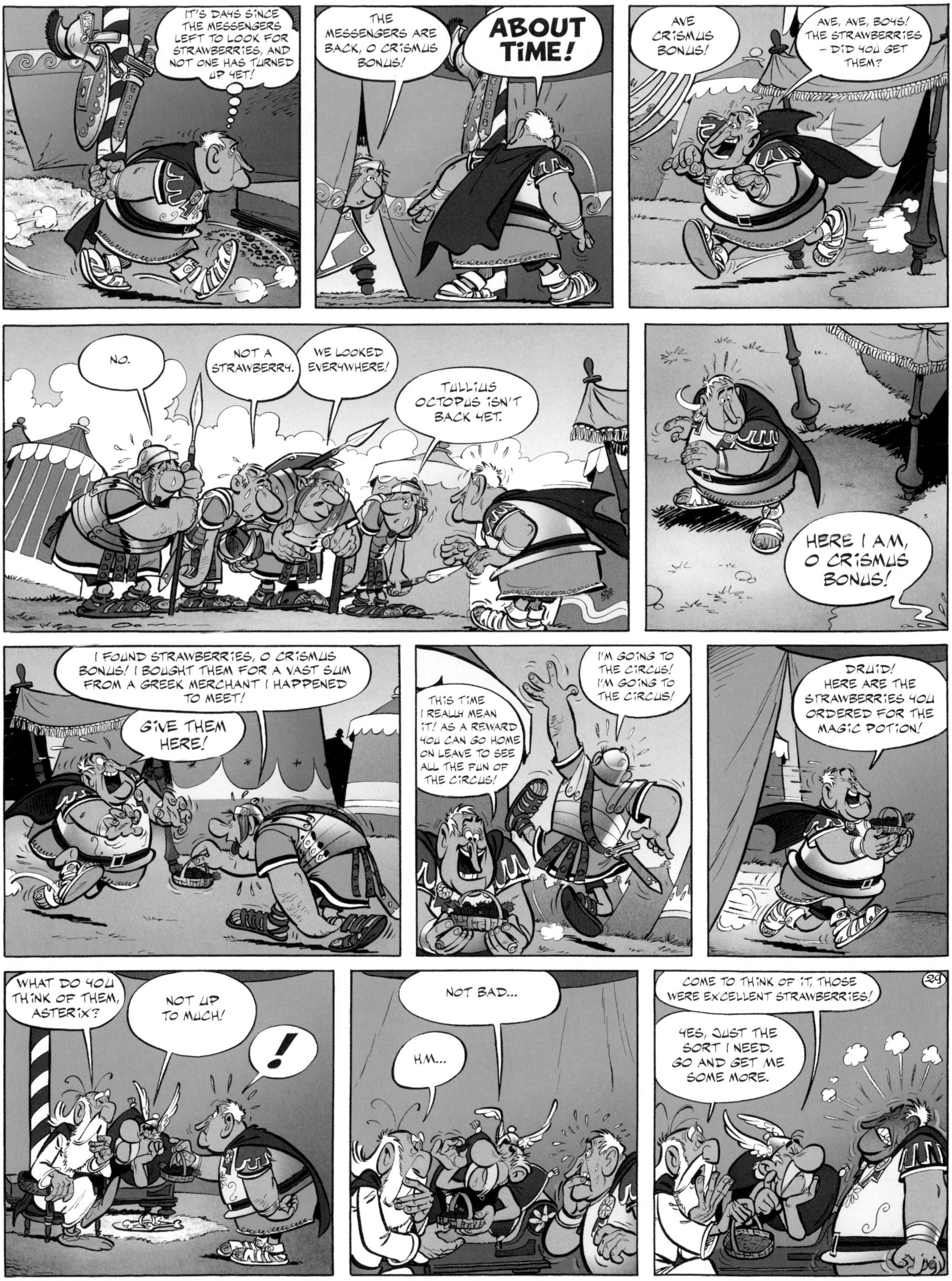

IT'S DAYS SINCE THE MESSENGERS LEFT TO LOOK FOR STRAWBERRIES, AND NOT ONE HAS TURNED UP YET!
THE MESSENGERS ARE BACK, O CRISMUS BONUS!
ABOUT TIME!
AVE CRISMUS BONUS!
AVE, AVE, BOYS! THE STRAWBERRIES – DID YOU GET THEM?
NO.
NOT A STRAWBERRY.
WE LOOKED EVERYWHERE!
TULLIUS OCTOPUS ISN'T BACK YET.
HERE I AM, O CRISMUS BONUS!
I FOUND STRAWBERRIES, O CRISMUS BONUS! I BOUGHT THEM FOR A VAST SUM FROM A GREEK MERCHANT I HAPPENED TO MEET!
GIVE THEM HERE!
THIS TIME I REALLY MEAN IT! AS A REWARD YOU CAN GO HOME ON LEAVE TO SEE ALL THE FUN OF THE CIRCUS!
I'M GOING TO THE CIRCUS! I'M GOING TO THE CIRCUS!
DRUID! HERE ARE THE STRAWBERRIES YOU ORDERED FOR THE MAGIC POTION!
WHAT DO YOU THINK OF THEM, ASTERIX?
NOT UP TO MUCH!
!
NOT BAD...
HM...
COME TO THINK OF IT, THOSE WERE EXCELLENT STRAWBERRIES!
YES, JUST THE SORT I NEED. GO AND GET ME SOME MORE.
29

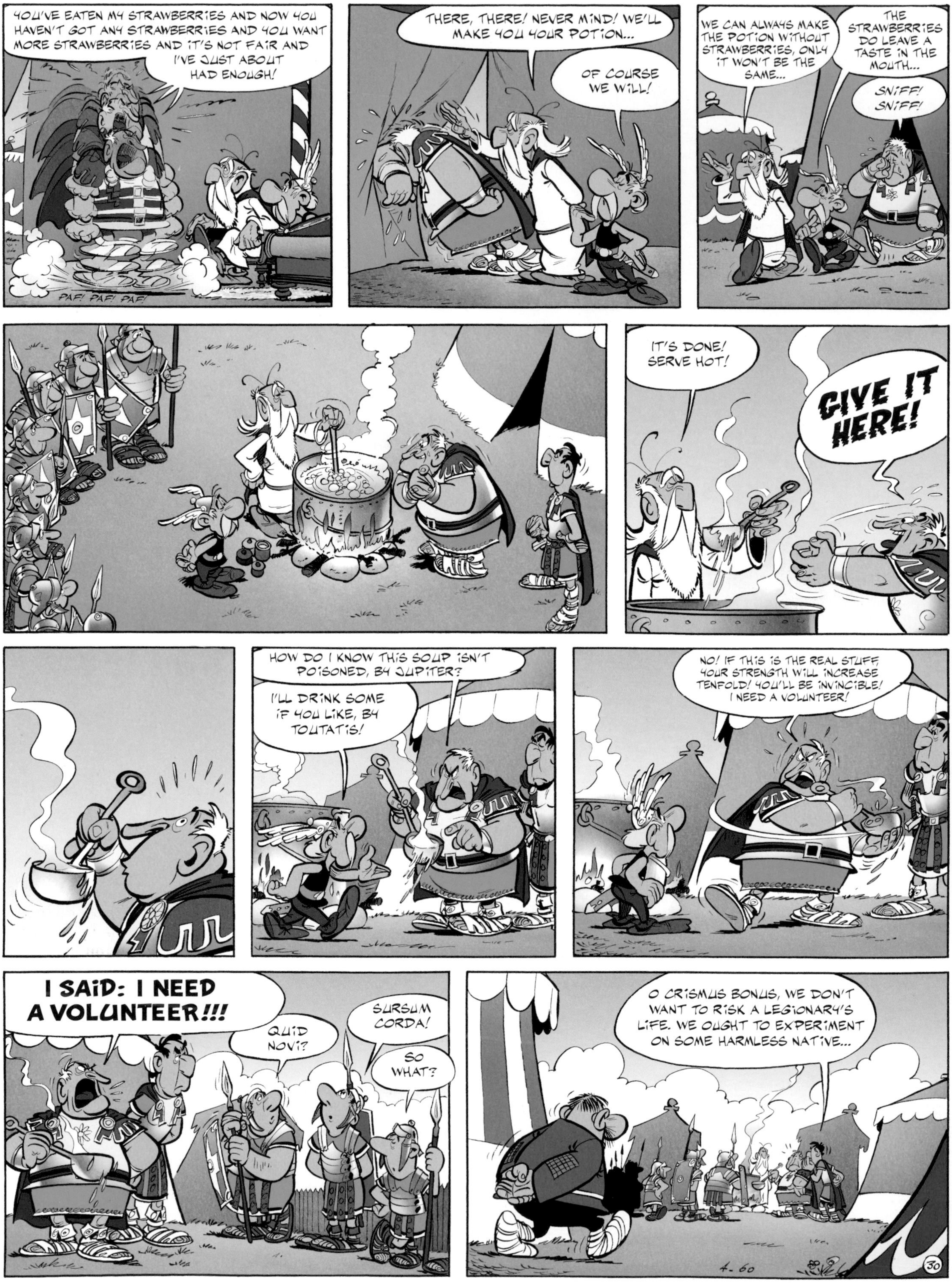
YOU'VE EATEN MY STRAWBERRIES AND NOW YOU HAVEN'T GOT ANY STRAWBERRIES AND YOU WANT MORE STRAWBERRIES AND IT'S NOT FAIR AND I'VE JUST ABOUT HAD ENOUGH!
PAF! PAF! PAF!
THERE, THERE! NEVER MIND! WE'LL MAKE YOU YOUR POTION...
OF COURSE WE WILL!
WE CAN ALWAYS MAKE THE POTION WITHOUT STRAWBERRIES, ONLY IT WON'T BE THE SAME...
THE STRAWBERRIES DO LEAVE A TASTE IN THE MOUTH...
SNIFF! SNIFF!
IT'S DONE! SERVE HOT!
GIVE IT HERE!
HOW DO I KNOW THIS SOUP ISN'T POISONED, BY JUPITER?
I'LL DRINK SOME IF YOU LIKE, BY TOUTATIS!
NO! IF THIS IS THE REAL STUFF, YOUR STRENGTH WILL INCREASE TENFOLD! YOU'LL BE INVINCIBLE! I NEED A VOLUNTEER!
I SAID: I NEED A VOLUNTEER!!!
QUID NOVI?
SURSUM CORDA!
SO WHAT?
O CRISMUS BONUS, WE DON'T WANT TO RISK A LEGIONARY'S LIFE. WE OUGHT TO EXPERIMENT ON SOME HARMLESS NATIVE...
30

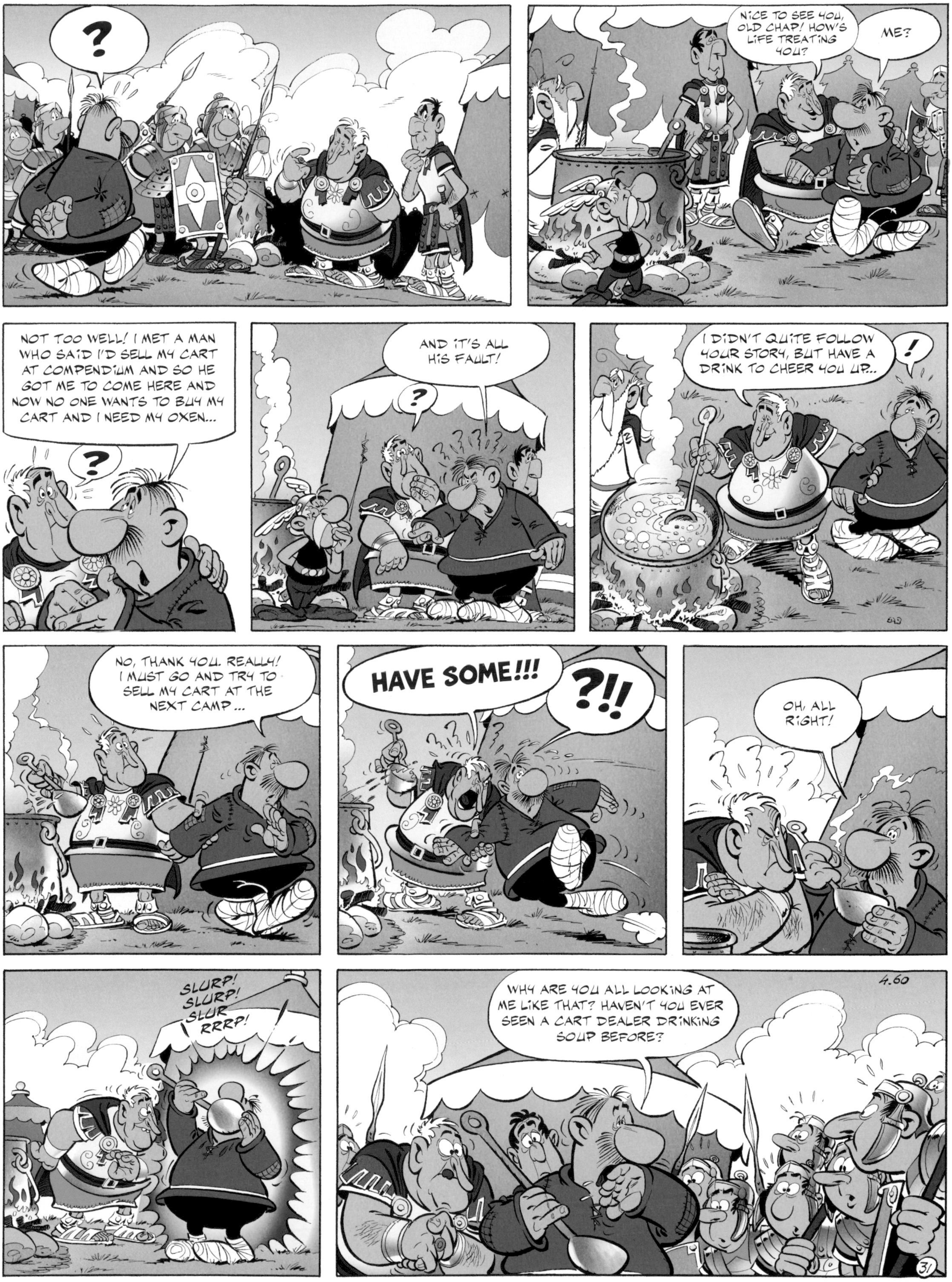
?
NICE TO SEE YOU, OLD CHAP! HOW'S LIFE TREATING YOU?
ME?
NOT TOO WELL! I MET A MAN WHO SAID I'D SELL MY CART AT COMPENDIUM AND SO HE GOT ME TO COME HERE AND NOW NO ONE WANTS TO BUY MY CART AND I NEED MY OXEN...
?
AND IT'S ALL HIS FAULT!
?
I DIDN'T QUITE FOLLOW YOUR STORY, BUT HAVE A DRINK TO CHEER YOU UP...
!
NO, THANK YOU. REALLY! I MUST GO AND TRY TO SELL MY CART AT THE NEXT CAMP...
HAVE SOME!!!
?!!
OH, ALL RIGHT!
SLURP! SLURP! SLUR RRRP!
WHY ARE YOU ALL LOOKING AT ME LIKE THAT? HAVEN'T YOU EVER SEEN A CART DEALER DRINKING SOUP BEFORE?

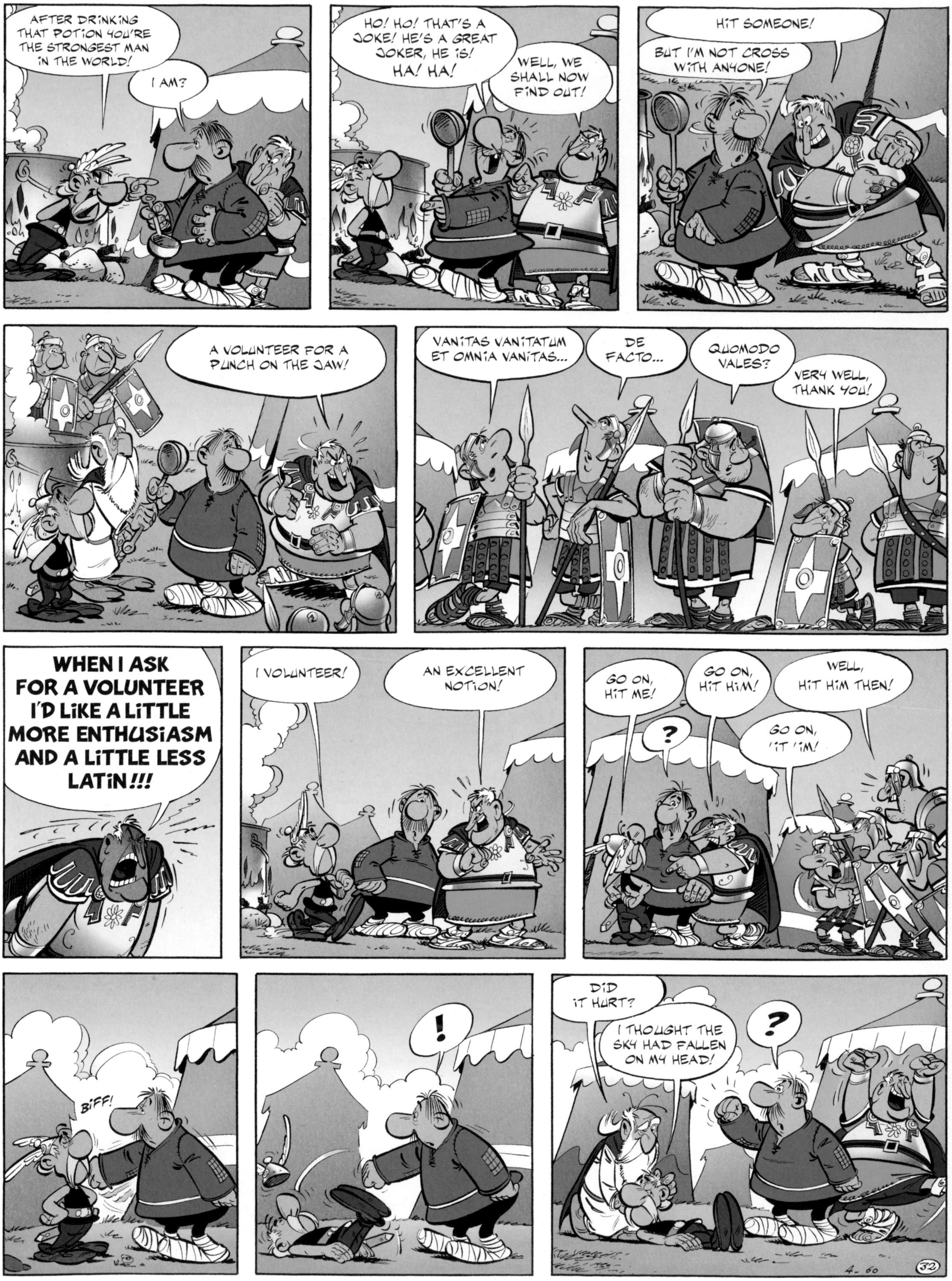
AFTER DRINKING THAT POTION YOU'RE THE STRONGEST MAN IN THE WORLD!
I AM?
HO! HO! THAT'S A JOKE! HE'S A GREAT JOKER, HE IS! HA! HA!
WELL, WE SHALL NOW FIND OUT!
HIT SOMEONE!
BUT I'M NOT CROSS WITH ANYONE!
A VOLUNTEER FOR A PUNCH ON THE JAW!
VANITAS VANITATUM ET OMNIA VANITAS...
DE FACTO...
QUOMODO VALES?
VERY WELL, THANK YOU!
WHEN I ASK FOR A VOLUNTEER I'D LIKE A LITTLE MORE ENTHUSIASM AND A LITTLE LESS LATIN!!!
I VOLUNTEER!
AN EXCELLENT NOTION!
GO ON, HIT ME!
GO ON, HIT HIM!
WELL, HIT HIM THEN!
?
GO ON, 'IT 'IM!
BIFF!
!
DID IT HURT?
I THOUGHT THE SKY HAD FALLEN ON MY HEAD!
?

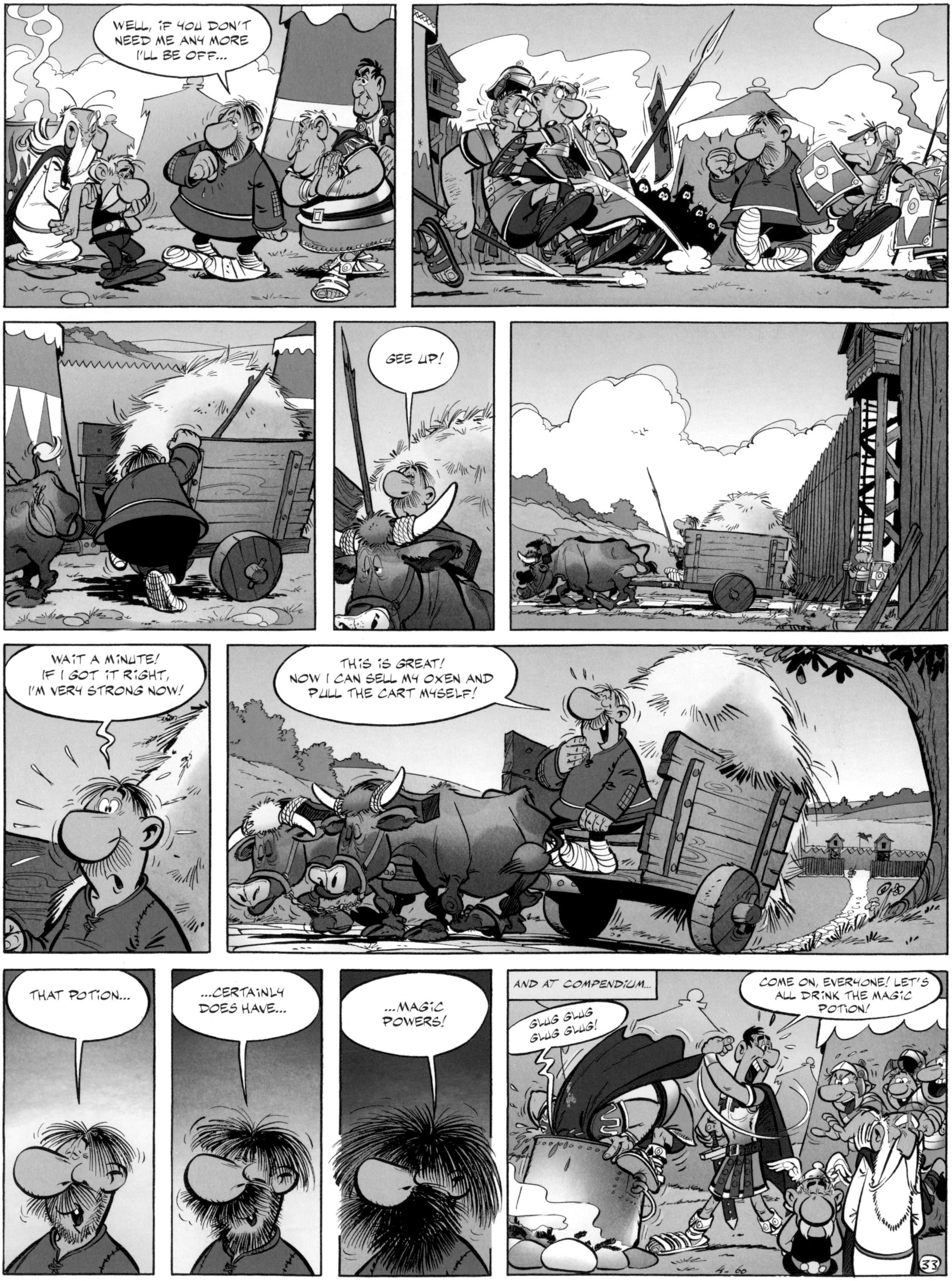
WELL, IF YOU DON'T NEED ME ANY MORE I'LL BE OFF...
GEE UP!
WAIT A MINUTE! IF I GOT IT RIGHT, I'M VERY STRONG NOW!
THIS IS GREAT! NOW I CAN SELL MY OXEN AND PULL THE CART MYSELF!
THAT POTION...
...CERTAINLY DOES HAVE...
...MAGIC POWERS!
AND AT COMPENDIUM...
COME ON, EVERYONE! LET'S ALL DRINK THE MAGIC POTION!
GLUG GLUG GLUG GLUG!
33

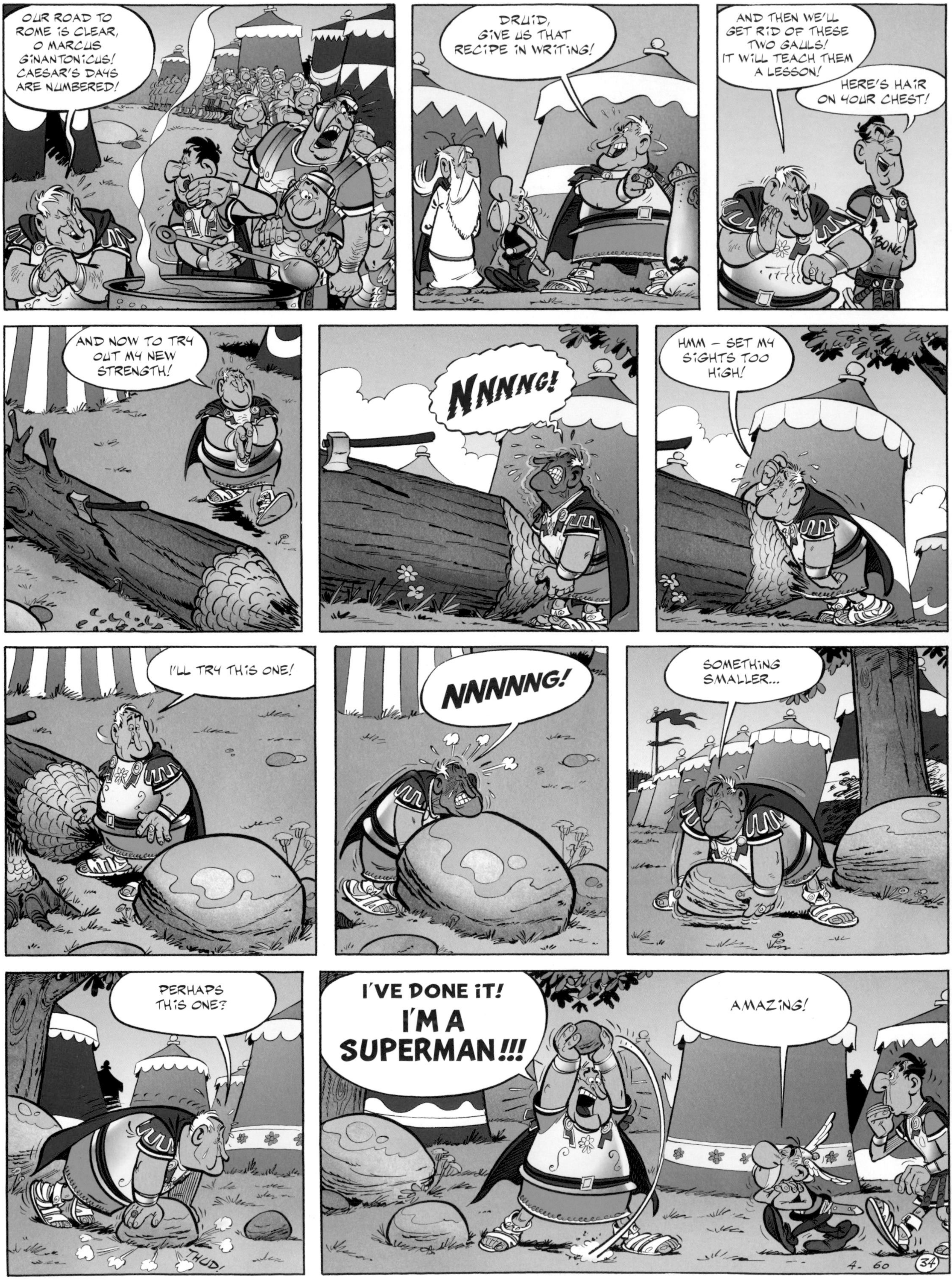

OUR ROAD TO ROME IS CLEAR, O MARCUS GINANTONICUS! CAESAR'S DAYS ARE NUMBERED!
DRUID, GIVE US THAT RECIPE IN WRITING!
AND THEN WE'LL GET RID OF THESE TWO GAULS! IT WILL TEACH THEM A LESSON!
HERE'S HAIR ON YOUR CHEST!
BONG
AND NOW TO TRY OUT MY NEW STRENGTH!
NNNNG!
HMM – SET MY SIGHTS TOO HIGH!
I'LL TRY THIS ONE!
NNNNNG!
SOMETHING SMALLER...
PERHAPS THIS ONE?
THUD!
I'VE DONE IT! I'M A SUPERMAN!!!
AMAZING!
4. 60
34

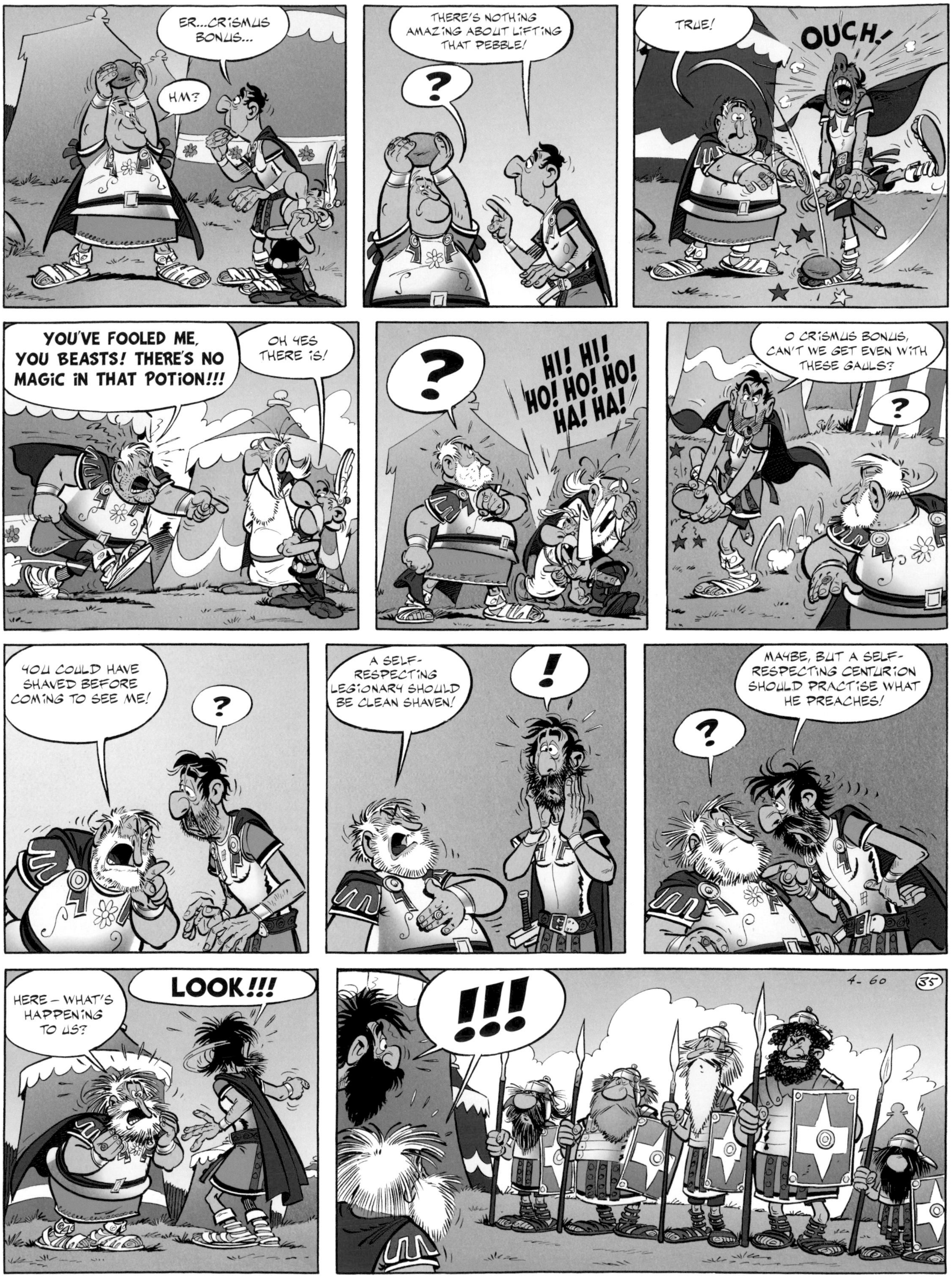

ER...CRISMUS BONUS...
HM?
THERE'S NOTHING AMAZING ABOUT LIFTING THAT PEBBLE!
?
TRUE!
OUCH!
YOU'VE FOOLED ME, YOU BEASTS! THERE'S NO MAGIC IN THAT POTION!!!
OH YES THERE IS!
?
HI! HI! HO! HO! HO! HA! HA!
O CRISMUS BONUS, CAN'T WE GET EVEN WITH THESE GAULS?
?
YOU COULD HAVE SHAVED BEFORE COMING TO SEE ME!
?
A SELF-RESPECTING LEGIONARY SHOULD BE CLEAN SHAVEN!
!
MAYBE, BUT A SELF-RESPECTING CENTURION SHOULD PRACTISE WHAT HE PREACHES!
?
HERE – WHAT'S HAPPENING TO US?
LOOK!!!
!!!
4-60
35

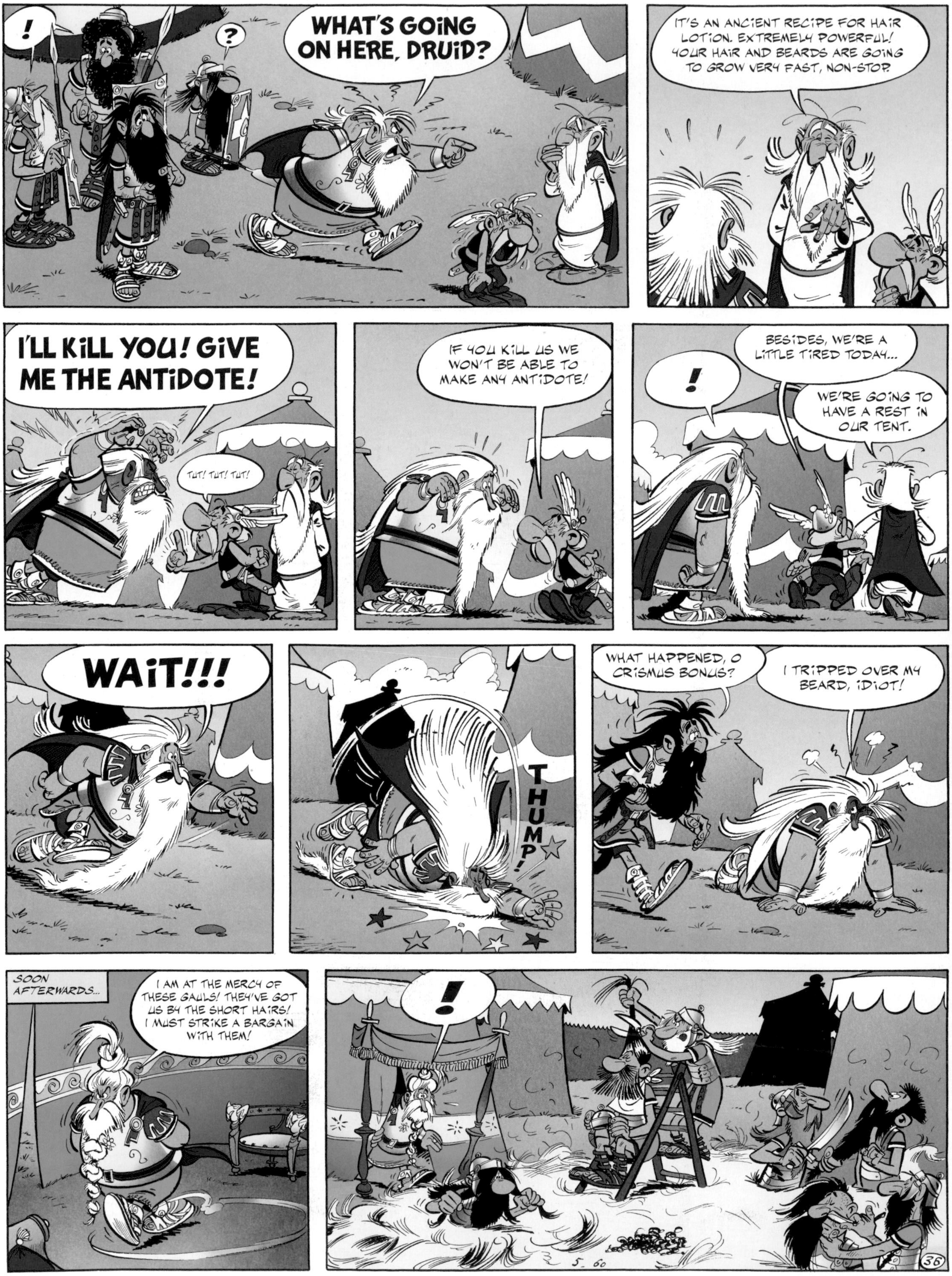
!
?
WHAT'S GOING ON HERE, DRUID?
IT'S AN ANCIENT RECIPE FOR HAIR LOTION. EXTREMELY POWERFUL! YOUR HAIR AND BEARDS ARE GOING TO GROW VERY FAST, NON-STOP!
I'LL KILL YOU! GIVE ME THE ANTIDOTE!
TUT! TUT! TUT!
IF YOU KILL US WE WON'T BE ABLE TO MAKE ANY ANTIDOTE!
!
BESIDES, WE'RE A LITTLE TIRED TODAY...
WE'RE GOING TO HAVE A REST IN OUR TENT.
WAIT!!!
THUMP!
WHAT HAPPENED, O CRISMUS BONUS?
I TRIPPED OVER MY BEARD, IDIOT!
SOON AFTERWARDS...
I AM AT THE MERCY OF THESE GAULS! THEY'VE GOT US BY THE SHORT HAIRS! I MUST STRIKE A BARGAIN WITH THEM!
!
36

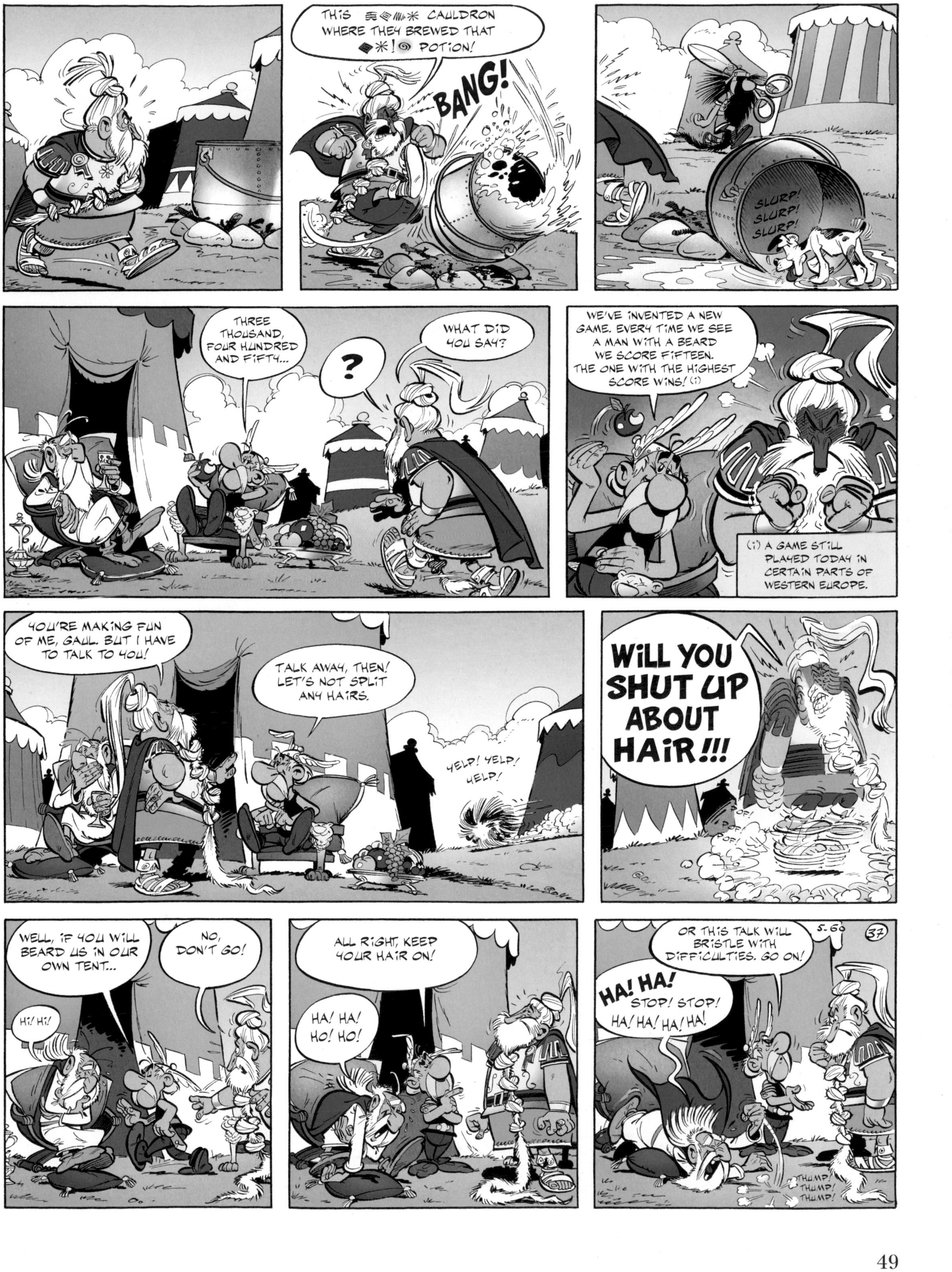
THIS CAULDRON WHERE THEY BREWED THAT POTION!
BANG!
SLURP! SLURP! SLURP!
THREE THOUSAND, FOUR HUNDRED AND FIFTY...
?
WHAT DID YOU SAY?
WE'VE INVENTED A NEW GAME. EVERY TIME WE SEE A MAN WITH A BEARD WE SCORE FIFTEEN. THE ONE WITH THE HIGHEST SCORE WINS! (1)
(1) A GAME STILL PLAYED TODAY IN CERTAIN PARTS OF WESTERN EUROPE.
YOU'RE MAKING FUN OF ME, GAUL. BUT I HAVE TO TALK TO YOU!
TALK AWAY, THEN! LET'S NOT SPLIT ANY HAIRS.
YELP! YELP! YELP!
WILL YOU SHUT UP ABOUT HAIR!!!
POF! POF! POF!
WELL, IF YOU WILL BEARD US IN OUR OWN TENT...
NO, DON'T GO!
HI! HI!
ALL RIGHT, KEEP YOUR HAIR ON!
HA! HA! HO! HO!
OR THIS TALK WILL BRISTLE WITH DIFFICULTIES. GO ON!
HA! HA!
STOP! STOP! HA! HA! HA! HA!
THUMP! THUMP! THUMP!

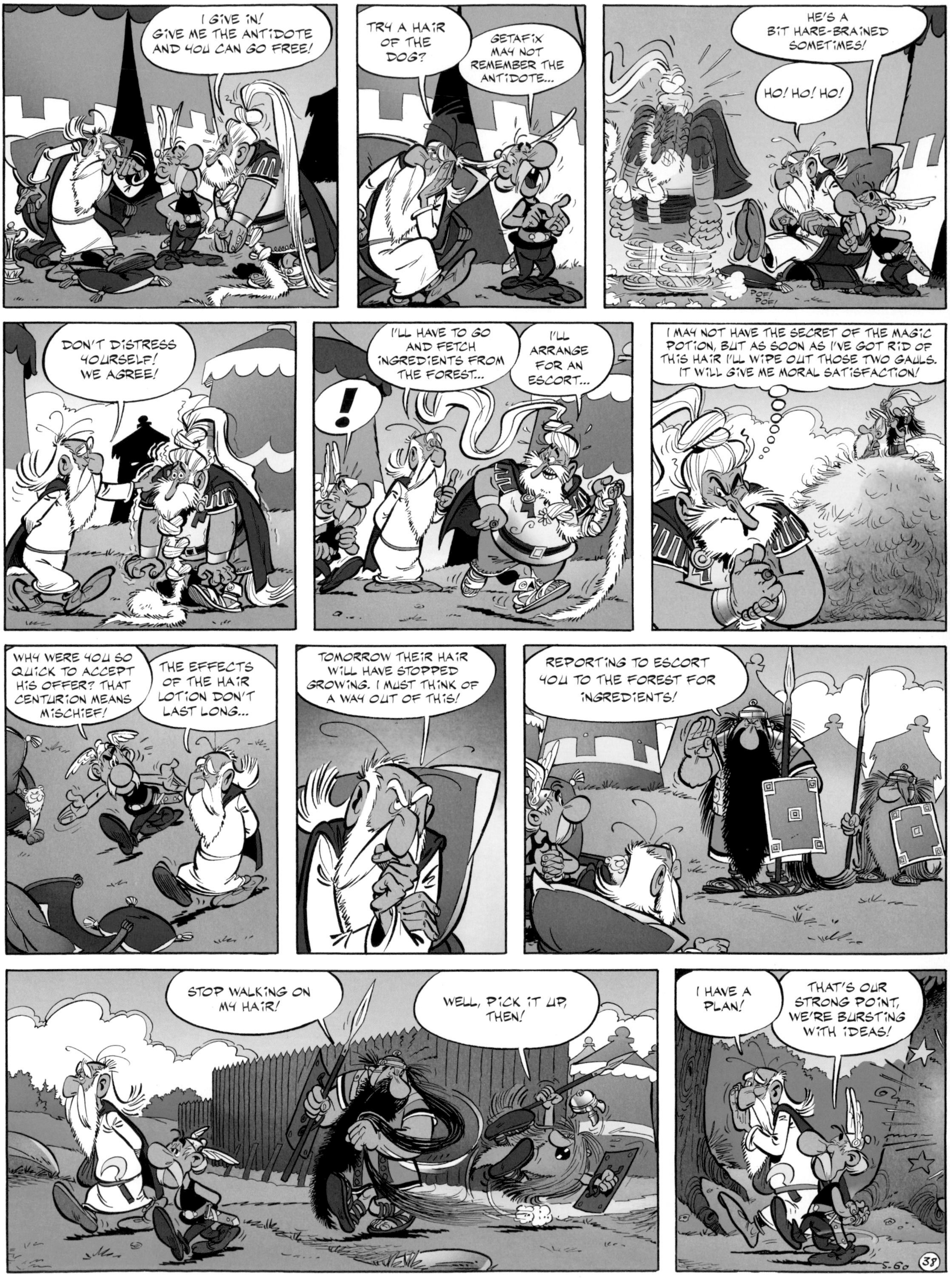
I GIVE IN! GIVE ME THE ANTIDOTE AND YOU CAN GO FREE!
TRY A HAIR OF THE DOG?
GETAFIX MAY NOT REMEMBER THE ANTIDOTE...
HE'S A BIT HARE-BRAINED SOMETIMES!
HO! HO! HO!
POF! POF!
DON'T DISTRESS YOURSELF! WE AGREE!
I'LL HAVE TO GO AND FETCH INGREDIENTS FROM THE FOREST...
I'LL ARRANGE FOR AN ESCORT...
!
I MAY NOT HAVE THE SECRET OF THE MAGIC POTION, BUT AS SOON AS I'VE GOT RID OF THIS HAIR I'LL WIPE OUT THOSE TWO GAULS. IT WILL GIVE ME MORAL SATISFACTION!
WHY WERE YOU SO QUICK TO ACCEPT HIS OFFER? THAT CENTURION MEANS MISCHIEF!
THE EFFECTS OF THE HAIR LOTION DON'T LAST LONG...
TOMORROW THEIR HAIR WILL HAVE STOPPED GROWING. I MUST THINK OF A WAY OUT OF THIS!
REPORTING TO ESCORT YOU TO THE FOREST FOR INGREDIENTS!
STOP WALKING ON MY HAIR!
WELL, PICK IT UP, THEN!
I HAVE A PLAN!
THAT'S OUR STRONG POINT, WE'RE BURSTING WITH IDEAS!
S.60
38

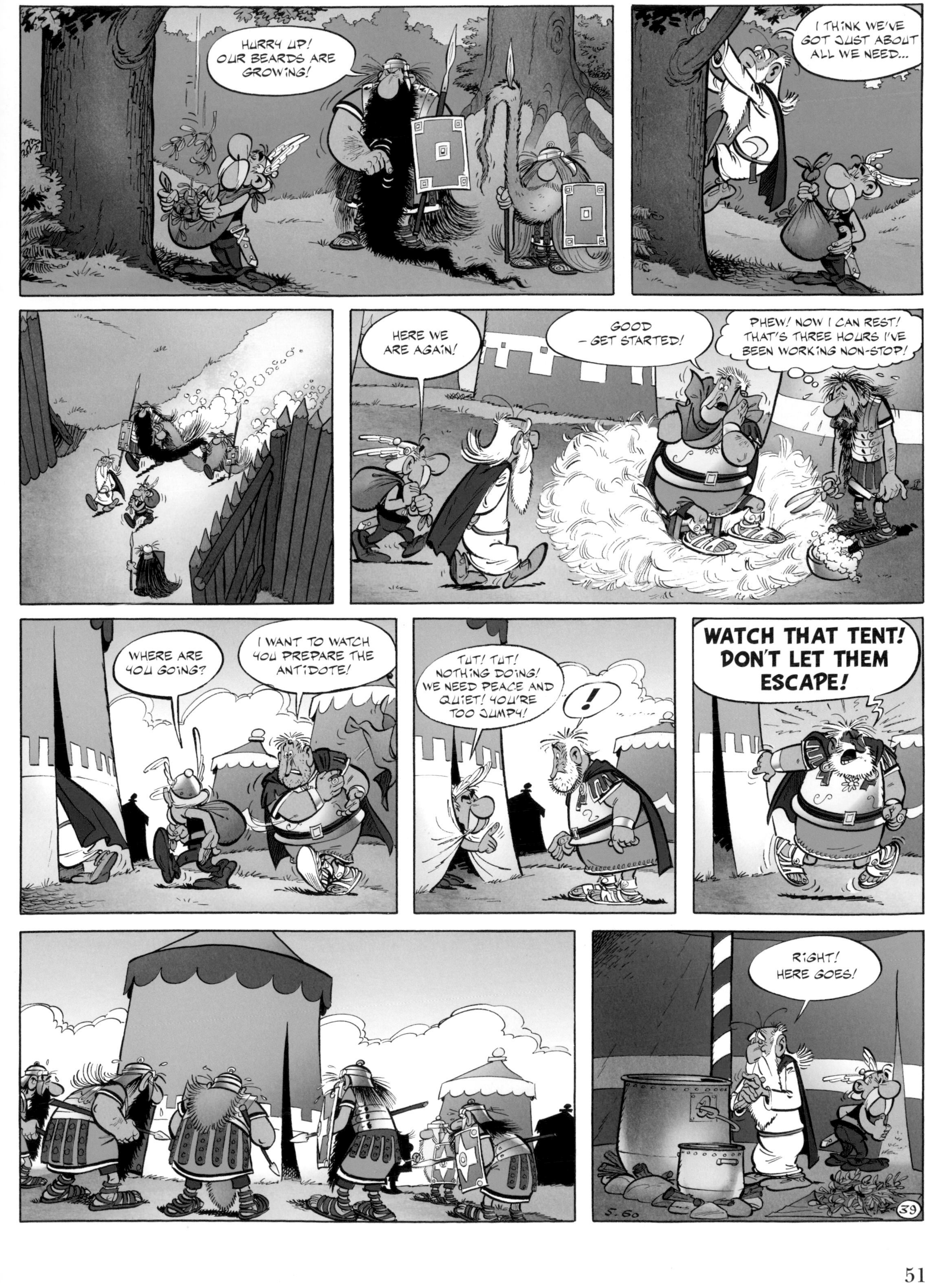
HURRY UP! OUR BEARDS ARE GROWING!
I THINK WE'VE GOT JUST ABOUT ALL WE NEED...
HERE WE ARE AGAIN!
GOOD – GET STARTED!
PHEW! NOW I CAN REST! THAT'S THREE HOURS I'VE BEEN WORKING NON-STOP!
WHERE ARE YOU GOING?
I WANT TO WATCH YOU PREPARE THE ANTIDOTE!
TUT! TUT! NOTHING DOING! WE NEED PEACE AND QUIET! YOU'RE TOO JUMPY!
!
WATCH THAT TENT! DON'T LET THEM ESCAPE!
RIGHT! HERE GOES!
39

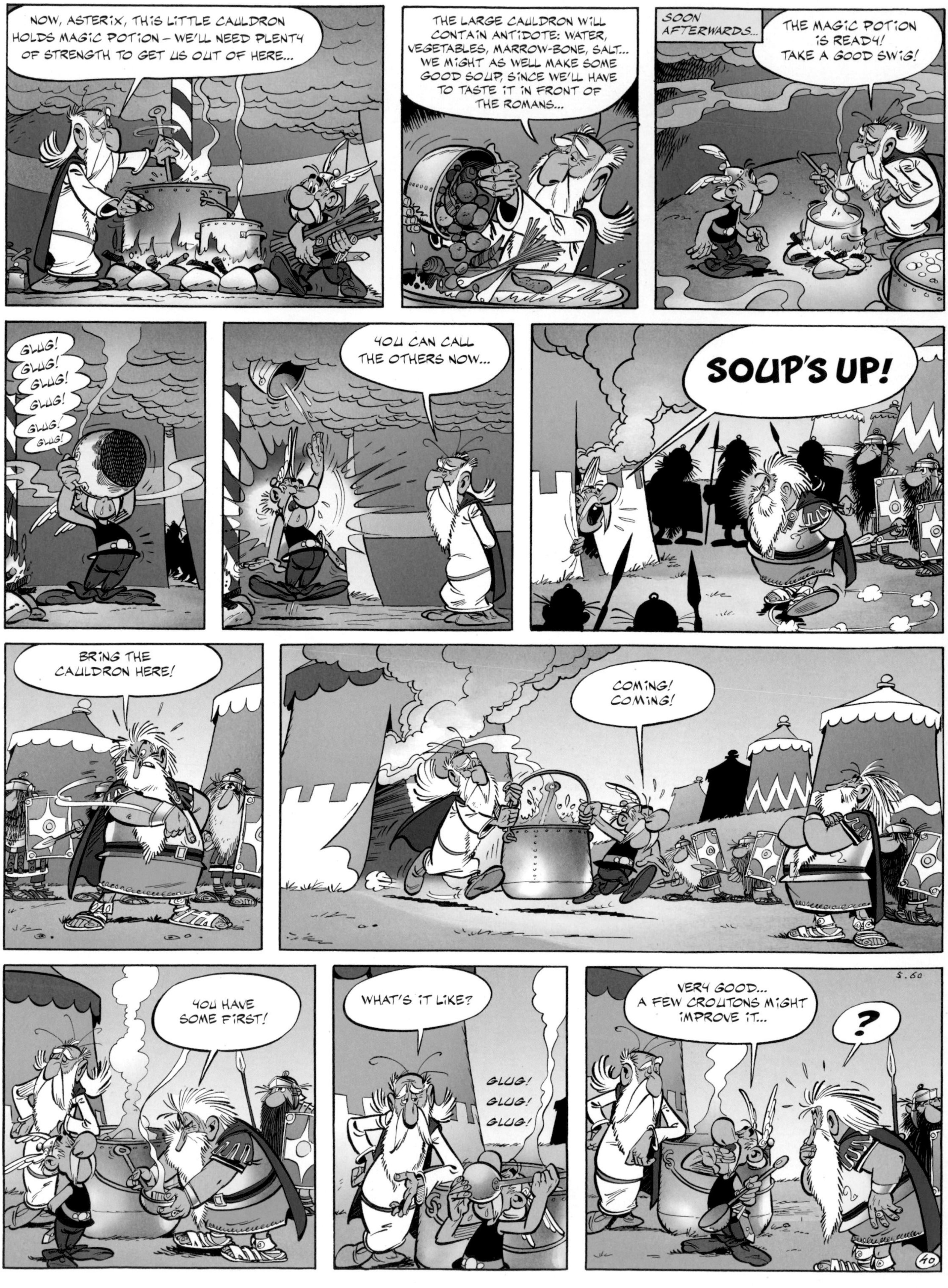
NOW, ASTERIX, THIS LITTLE CAULDRON HOLDS MAGIC POTION – WE'LL NEED PLENTY OF STRENGTH TO GET US OUT OF HERE...
THE LARGE CAULDRON WILL CONTAIN ANTIDOTE: WATER, VEGETABLES, MARROW-BONE, SALT... WE MIGHT AS WELL MAKE SOME GOOD SOUP, SINCE WE'LL HAVE TO TASTE IT IN FRONT OF THE ROMANS...
SOON AFTERWARDS...
THE MAGIC POTION IS READY! TAKE A GOOD SWIG!
GLUG! GLUG! GLUG! GLUG! GLUG! GLUG!
YOU CAN CALL THE OTHERS NOW...
SOUP'S UP!
BRING THE CAULDRON HERE!
COMING! COMING!
YOU HAVE SOME FIRST!
WHAT'S IT LIKE?
GLUG! GLUG! GLUG!
VERY GOOD... A FEW CROUTONS MIGHT IMPROVE IT...
?
5.60
40

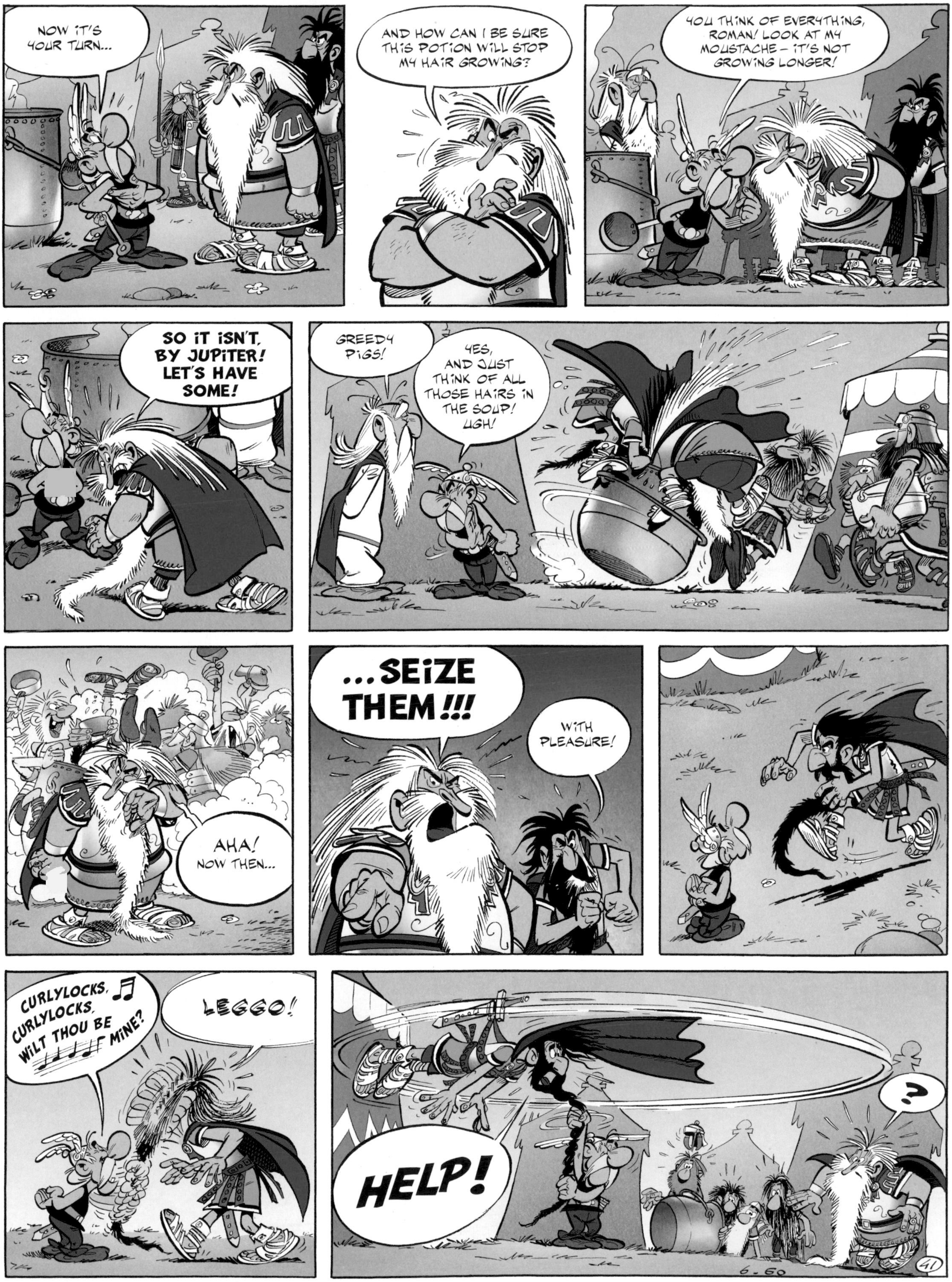
NOW IT'S YOUR TURN...
AND HOW CAN I BE SURE THIS POTION WILL STOP MY HAIR GROWING?
YOU THINK OF EVERYTHING, ROMAN! LOOK AT MY MOUSTACHE – IT'S NOT GROWING LONGER!
SO IT ISN'T, BY JUPITER! LET'S HAVE SOME!
GREEDY PIGS!
YES, AND JUST THINK OF ALL THOSE HAIRS IN THE SOUP! UGH!
AHA! NOW THEN...
...SEIZE THEM!!!
WITH PLEASURE!
CURLYLOCKS, CURLYLOCKS, WILT THOU BE MINE?
LEGGO!
HELP!
?
6.60
41

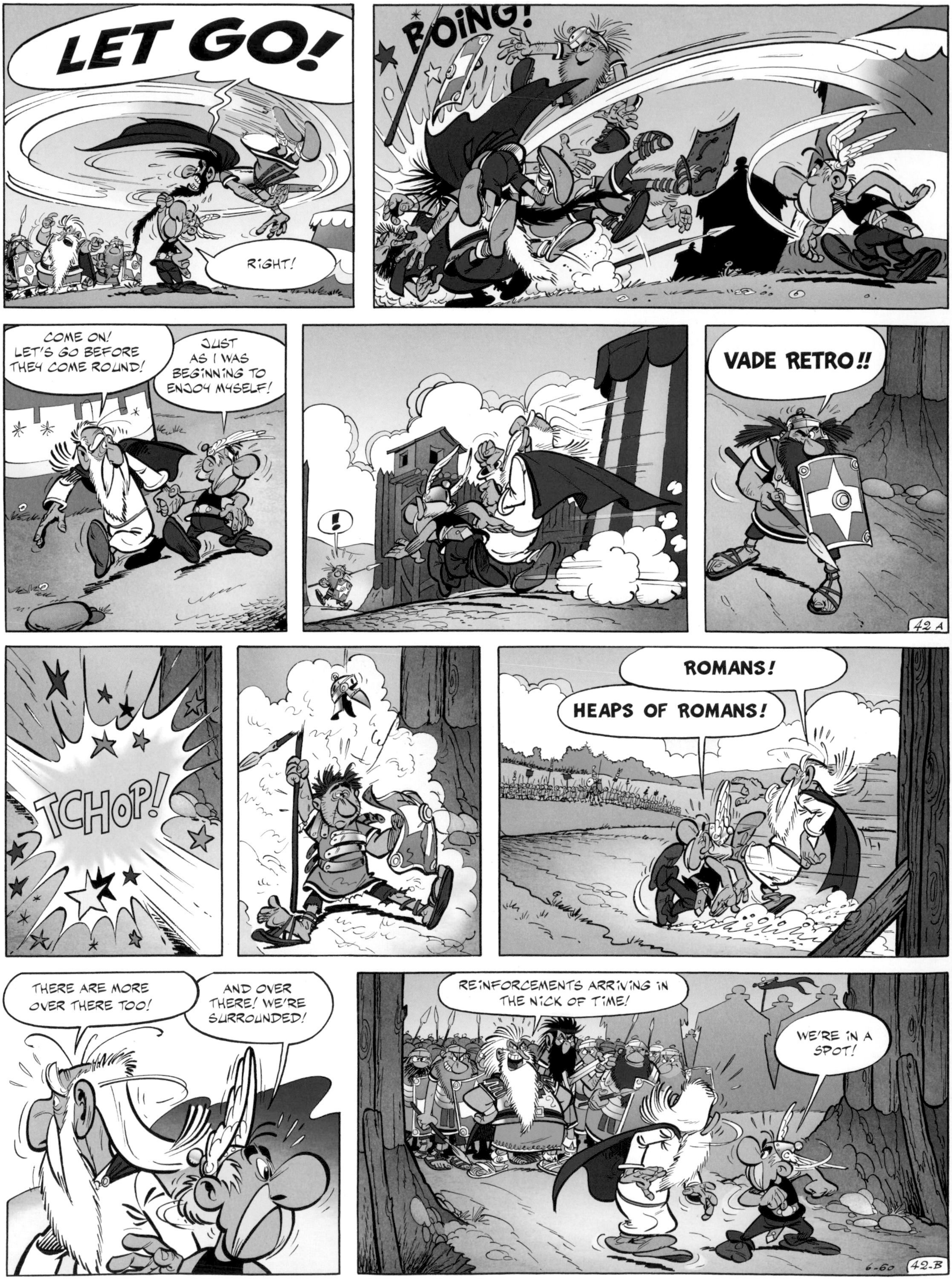
LET GO!
RIGHT!
BOING!
COME ON! LET'S GO BEFORE THEY COME ROUND!
JUST AS I WAS BEGINNING TO ENJOY MYSELF!
!
VADE RETRO!!
42 A
TCHOP!
ROMANS!
HEAPS OF ROMANS!
THERE ARE MORE OVER THERE TOO!
AND OVER THERE! WE'RE SURROUNDED!
REINFORCEMENTS ARRIVING IN THE NICK OF TIME!
WE'RE IN A SPOT!
6-60
42-B

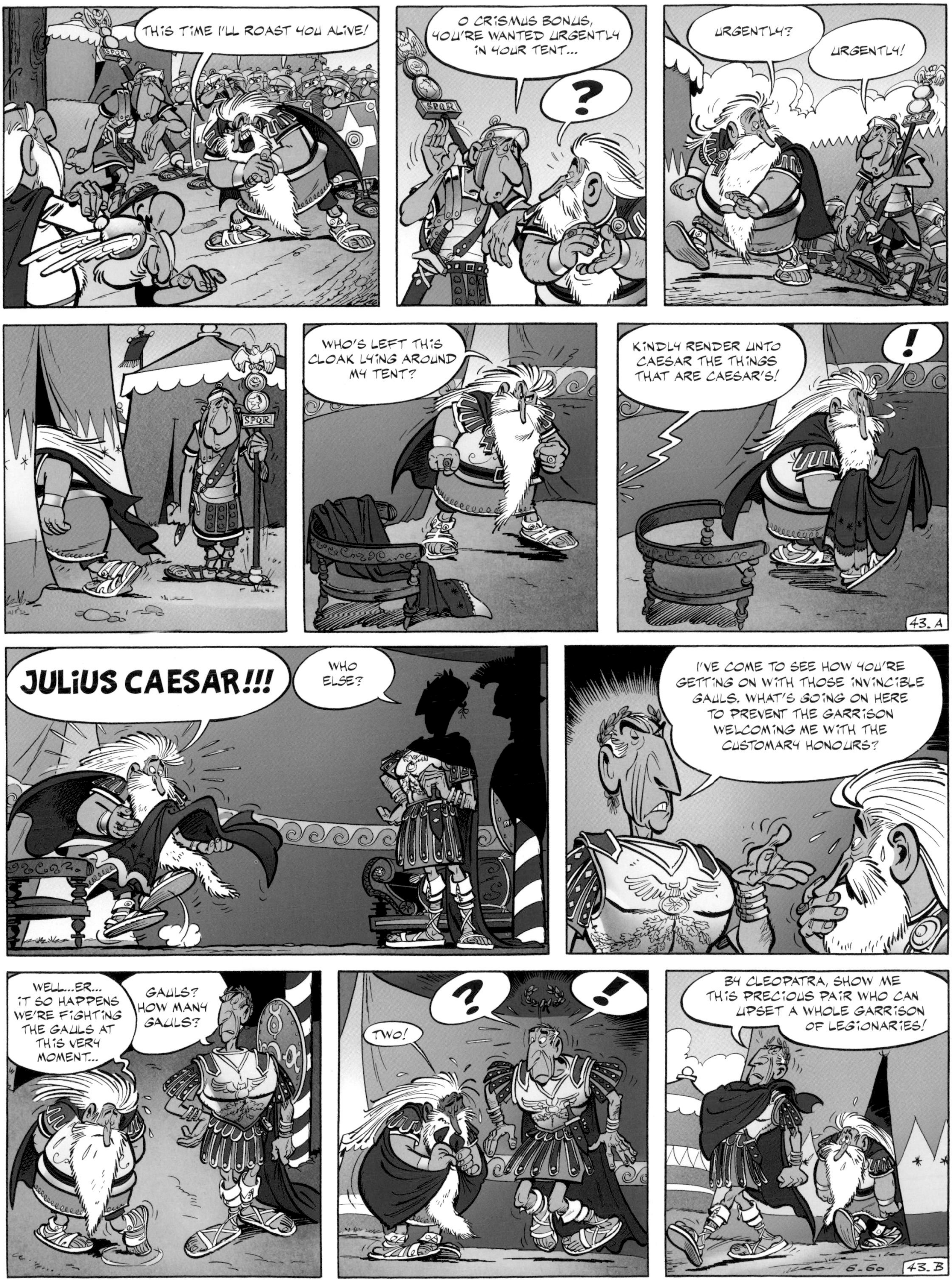

THIS TIME I'LL ROAST YOU ALIVE!
SPQR
O CRISMUS BONUS, YOU'RE WANTED URGENTLY IN YOUR TENT...
?
URGENTLY?
URGENTLY!
WHO'S LEFT THIS CLOAK LYING AROUND MY TENT?
KINDLY RENDER UNTO CAESAR THE THINGS THAT ARE CAESAR'S!
!
43. A
JULIUS CAESAR!!!
WHO ELSE?
I'VE COME TO SEE HOW YOU'RE GETTING ON WITH THOSE INVINCIBLE GAULS. WHAT'S GOING ON HERE TO PREVENT THE GARRISON WELCOMING ME WITH THE CUSTOMARY HONOURS?
WELL...ER... IT SO HAPPENS WE'RE FIGHTING THE GAULS AT THIS VERY MOMENT...
GAULS? HOW MANY GAULS?
?
!
TWO!
BY CLEOPATRA, SHOW ME THIS PRECIOUS PAIR WHO CAN UPSET A WHOLE GARRISON OF LEGIONARIES!
43. B

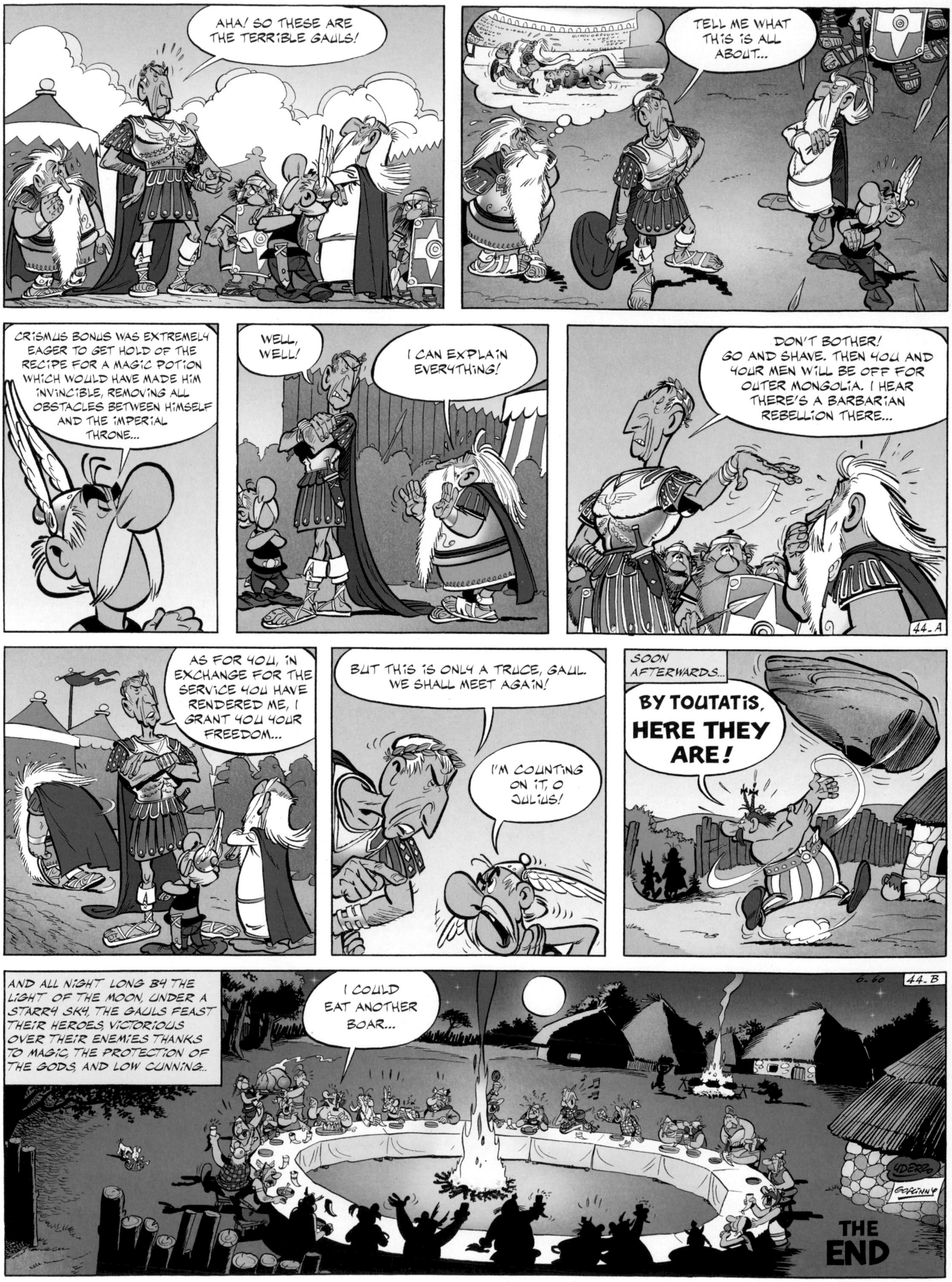
AHA! SO THESE ARE THE TERRIBLE GAULS!
TELL ME WHAT THIS IS ALL ABOUT...
CRISMUS BONUS WAS EXTREMELY EAGER TO GET HOLD OF THE RECIPE FOR A MAGIC POTION WHICH WOULD HAVE MADE HIM INVINCIBLE, REMOVING ALL OBSTACLES BETWEEN HIMSELF AND THE IMPERIAL THRONE...
WELL, WELL!
I CAN EXPLAIN EVERYTHING!
DON'T BOTHER! GO AND SHAVE. THEN YOU AND YOUR MEN WILL BE OFF FOR OUTER MONGOLIA. I HEAR THERE'S A BARBARIAN REBELLION THERE...
44-A
AS FOR YOU, IN EXCHANGE FOR THE SERVICE YOU HAVE RENDERED ME, I GRANT YOU YOUR FREEDOM...
BUT THIS IS ONLY A TRUCE, GAUL. WE SHALL MEET AGAIN!
I'M COUNTING ON IT, O JULIUS!
SOON AFTERWARDS...
BY TOUTATIS, HERE THEY ARE!
AND ALL NIGHT LONG BY THE LIGHT OF THE MOON, UNDER A STARRY SKY, THE GAULS FEAST THEIR HEROES, VICTORIOUS OVER THEIR ENEMIES THANKS TO MAGIC, THE PROTECTION OF THE GODS, AND LOW CUNNING...
I COULD EAT ANOTHER BOAR...
6-60
44-B
UDERZO
GOSCINNY
THE END

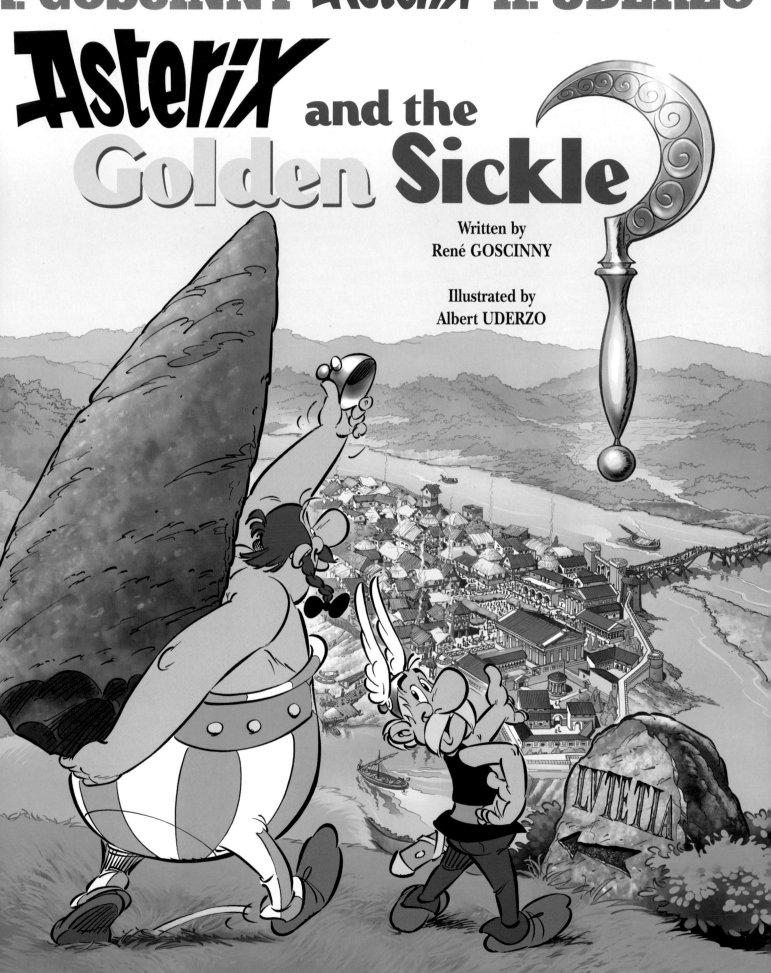

# R. GOSCINNY · Asterix · A. UDERZO

# Asterix and the Golden Sickle

Written by
René GOSCINNY

Illustrated by
Albert UDERZO

GOSCINNY AND UDERZO
PRESENT
*An Asterix Adventure*

# ASTERIX
# AND THE
# GOLDEN SICKLE

*Written by* RENÉ GOSCINNY *and Illustrated by* ALBERT UDERZO

*Translated by* Anthea Bell *and* Derek Hockridge

Orion
Children's Books

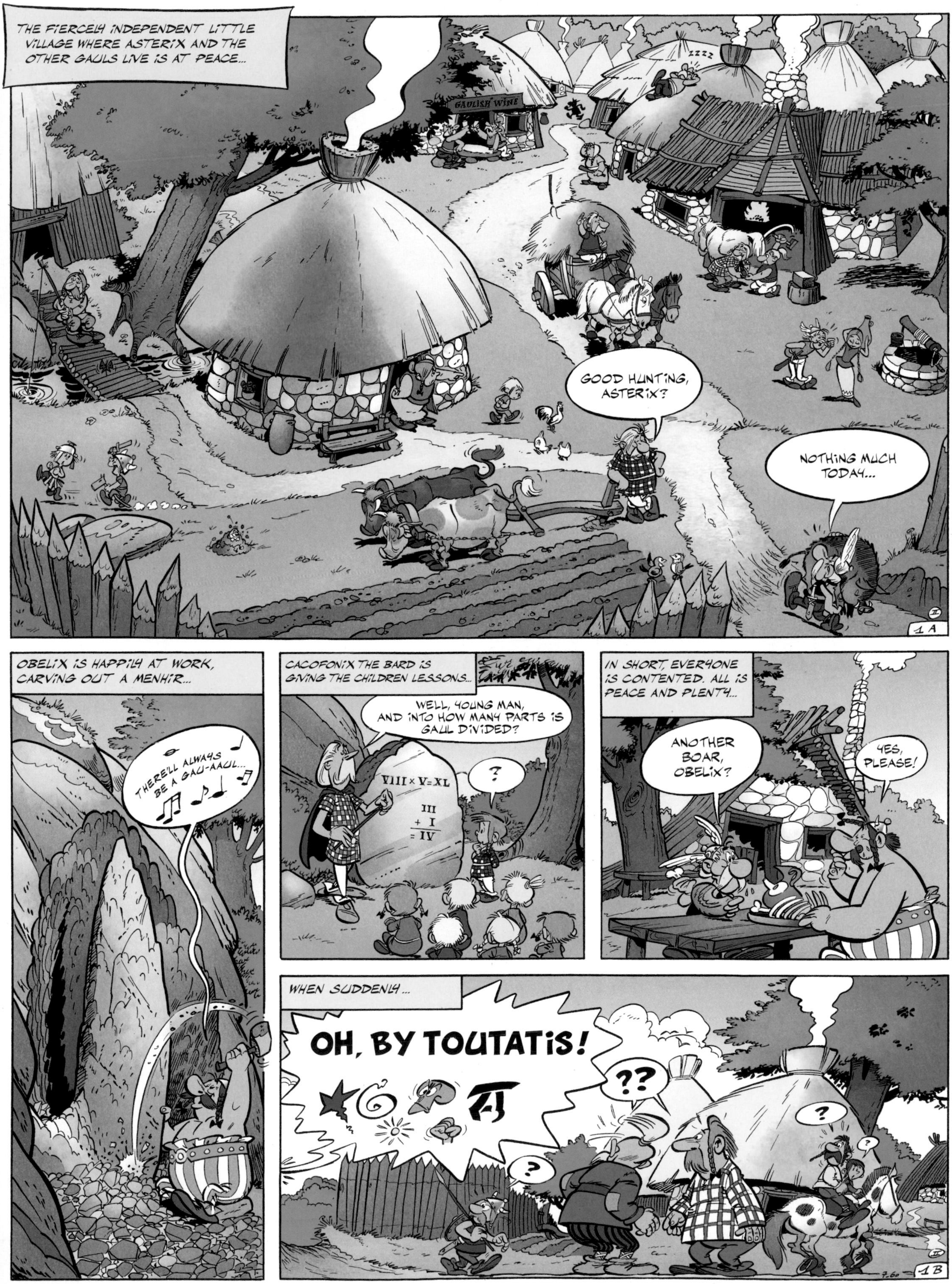
THE FIERCELY INDEPENDENT LITTLE VILLAGE WHERE ASTERIX AND THE OTHER GAULS LIVE IS AT PEACE...
GAULISH WINE
ZZZZ
GOOD HUNTING, ASTERIX?
NOTHING MUCH TODAY...
OBELIX IS HAPPILY AT WORK, CARVING OUT A MENHIR...
THERE'LL ALWAYS BE A GAU-AAUL...
CACOFONIX THE BARD IS GIVING THE CHILDREN LESSONS...
WELL, YOUNG MAN, AND INTO HOW MANY PARTS IS GAUL DIVIDED?
VIII × V = XL
III + I = IV
?
IN SHORT, EVERYONE IS CONTENTED. ALL IS PEACE AND PLENTY...
ANOTHER BOAR, OBELIX?
YES, PLEASE!
WHEN SUDDENLY...
OH, BY TOUTATIS!
??
?
?
?

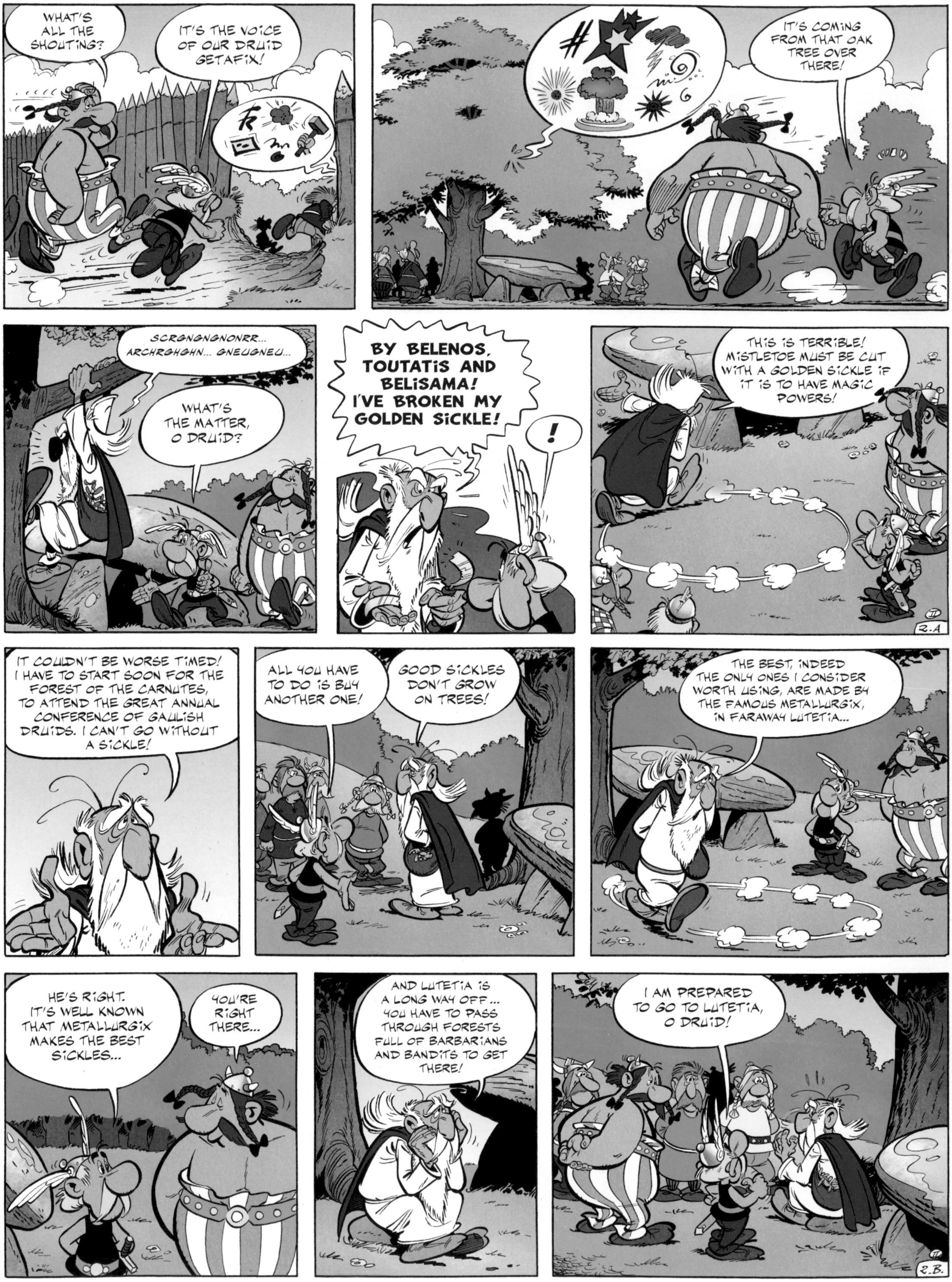
WHAT'S ALL THE SHOUTING?
IT'S THE VOICE OF OUR DRUID GETAFIX!
IT'S COMING FROM THAT OAK TREE OVER THERE!
SCRGNGNGNONRR... ARCHRGHGHN... GNEUGNEU...
WHAT'S THE MATTER, O DRUID?
BY BELENOS, TOUTATIS AND BELISAMA! I'VE BROKEN MY GOLDEN SICKLE!
!
THIS IS TERRIBLE! MISTLETOE MUST BE CUT WITH A GOLDEN SICKLE IF IT IS TO HAVE MAGIC POWERS!
IT COULDN'T BE WORSE TIMED! I HAVE TO START SOON FOR THE FOREST OF THE CARNUTES, TO ATTEND THE GREAT ANNUAL CONFERENCE OF GAULISH DRUIDS. I CAN'T GO WITHOUT A SICKLE!
ALL YOU HAVE TO DO IS BUY ANOTHER ONE!
GOOD SICKLES DON'T GROW ON TREES!
THE BEST, INDEED THE ONLY ONES I CONSIDER WORTH USING, ARE MADE BY THE FAMOUS METALLURGIX, IN FARAWAY LUTETIA...
HE'S RIGHT. IT'S WELL KNOWN THAT METALLURGIX MAKES THE BEST SICKLES...
YOU'RE RIGHT THERE...
AND LUTETIA IS A LONG WAY OFF... YOU HAVE TO PASS THROUGH FORESTS FULL OF BARBARIANS AND BANDITS TO GET THERE!
I AM PREPARED TO GO TO LUTETIA, O DRUID!
2.A
2.B.

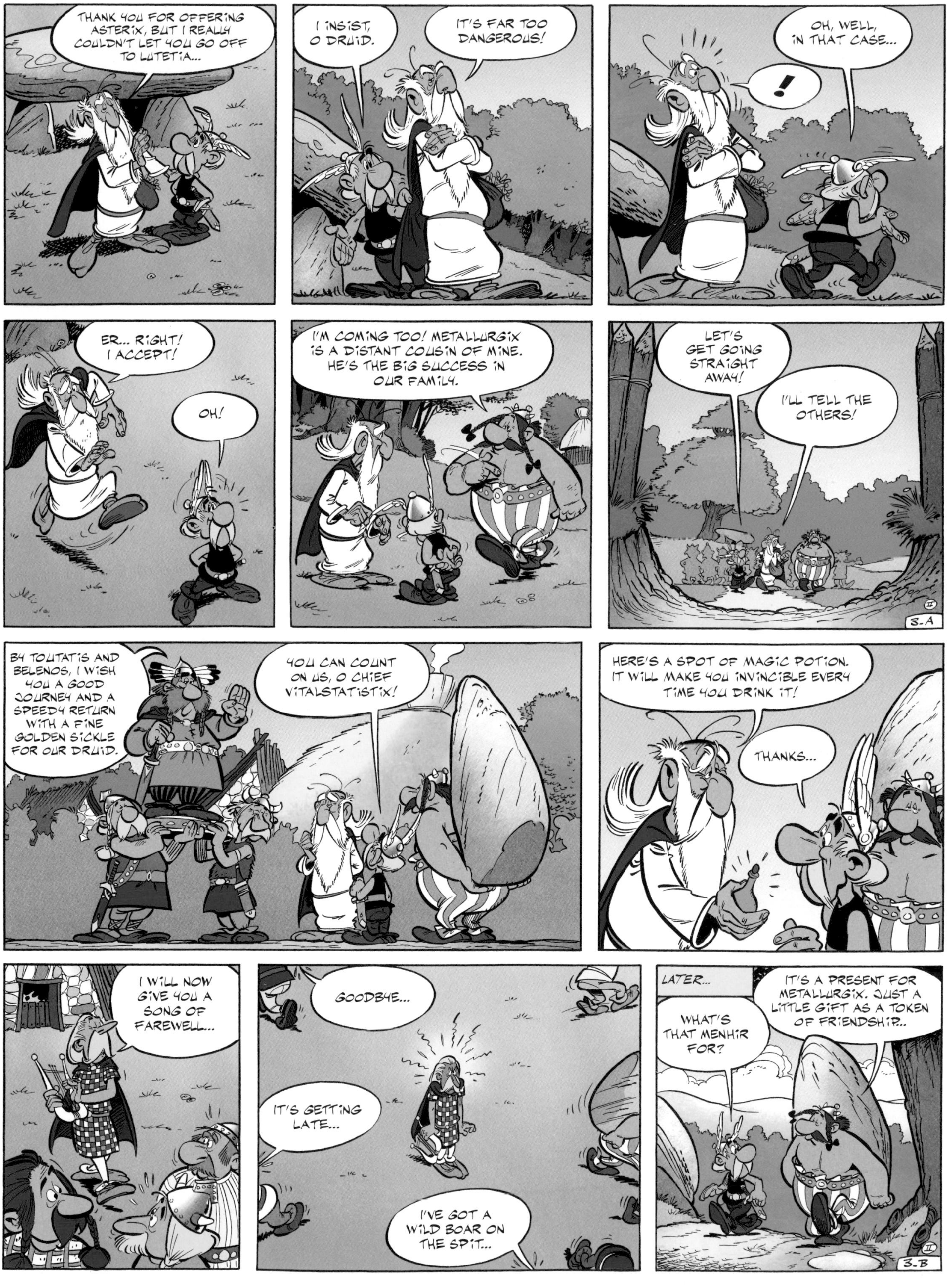
THANK YOU FOR OFFERING ASTERIX, BUT I REALLY COULDN'T LET YOU GO OFF TO LUTETIA...
I INSIST, O DRUID.
IT'S FAR TOO DANGEROUS!
!
OH, WELL, IN THAT CASE...
ER... RIGHT! I ACCEPT!
OH!
I'M COMING TOO! METALLURGIX IS A DISTANT COUSIN OF MINE. HE'S THE BIG SUCCESS IN OUR FAMILY.
LET'S GET GOING STRAIGHT AWAY!
I'LL TELL THE OTHERS!
3-A
BY TOUTATIS AND BELENOS, I WISH YOU A GOOD JOURNEY AND A SPEEDY RETURN WITH A FINE GOLDEN SICKLE FOR OUR DRUID.
YOU CAN COUNT ON US, O CHIEF VITALSTATISTIX!
HERE'S A SPOT OF MAGIC POTION. IT WILL MAKE YOU INVINCIBLE EVERY TIME YOU DRINK IT!
THANKS...
I WILL NOW GIVE YOU A SONG OF FAREWELL...
GOODBYE...
IT'S GETTING LATE...
I'VE GOT A WILD BOAR ON THE SPIT...
LATER...
WHAT'S THAT MENHIR FOR?
IT'S A PRESENT FOR METALLURGIX. JUST A LITTLE GIFT AS A TOKEN OF FRIENDSHIP..
3-B

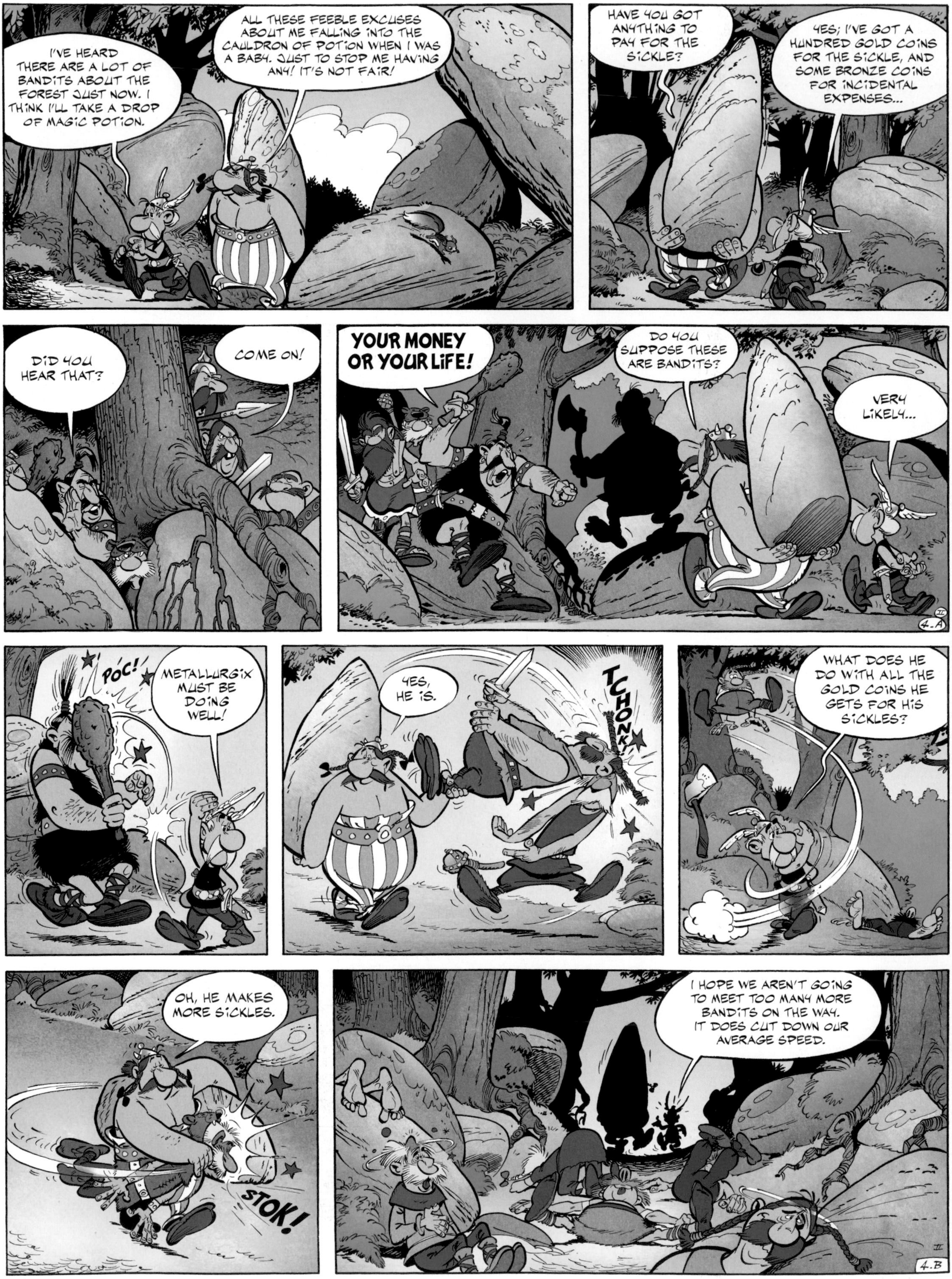
I'VE HEARD THERE ARE A LOT OF BANDITS ABOUT THE FOREST JUST NOW. I THINK I'LL TAKE A DROP OF MAGIC POTION.
ALL THESE FEEBLE EXCUSES ABOUT ME FALLING INTO THE CAULDRON OF POTION WHEN I WAS A BABY. JUST TO STOP ME HAVING ANY! IT'S NOT FAIR!
HAVE YOU GOT ANYTHING TO PAY FOR THE SICKLE?
YES; I'VE GOT A HUNDRED GOLD COINS FOR THE SICKLE, AND SOME BRONZE COINS FOR INCIDENTAL EXPENSES...
DID YOU HEAR THAT?
COME ON!
YOUR MONEY OR YOUR LIFE!
DO YOU SUPPOSE THESE ARE BANDITS?
VERY LIKELY...
4.A
POC!
METALLURGIX MUST BE DOING WELL!
YES, HE IS.
TCHONK!
WHAT DOES HE DO WITH ALL THE GOLD COINS HE GETS FOR HIS SICKLES?
OH, HE MAKES MORE SICKLES.
STOK!
I HOPE WE AREN'T GOING TO MEET TOO MANY MORE BANDITS ON THE WAY. IT DOES CUT DOWN OUR AVERAGE SPEED.
4.B

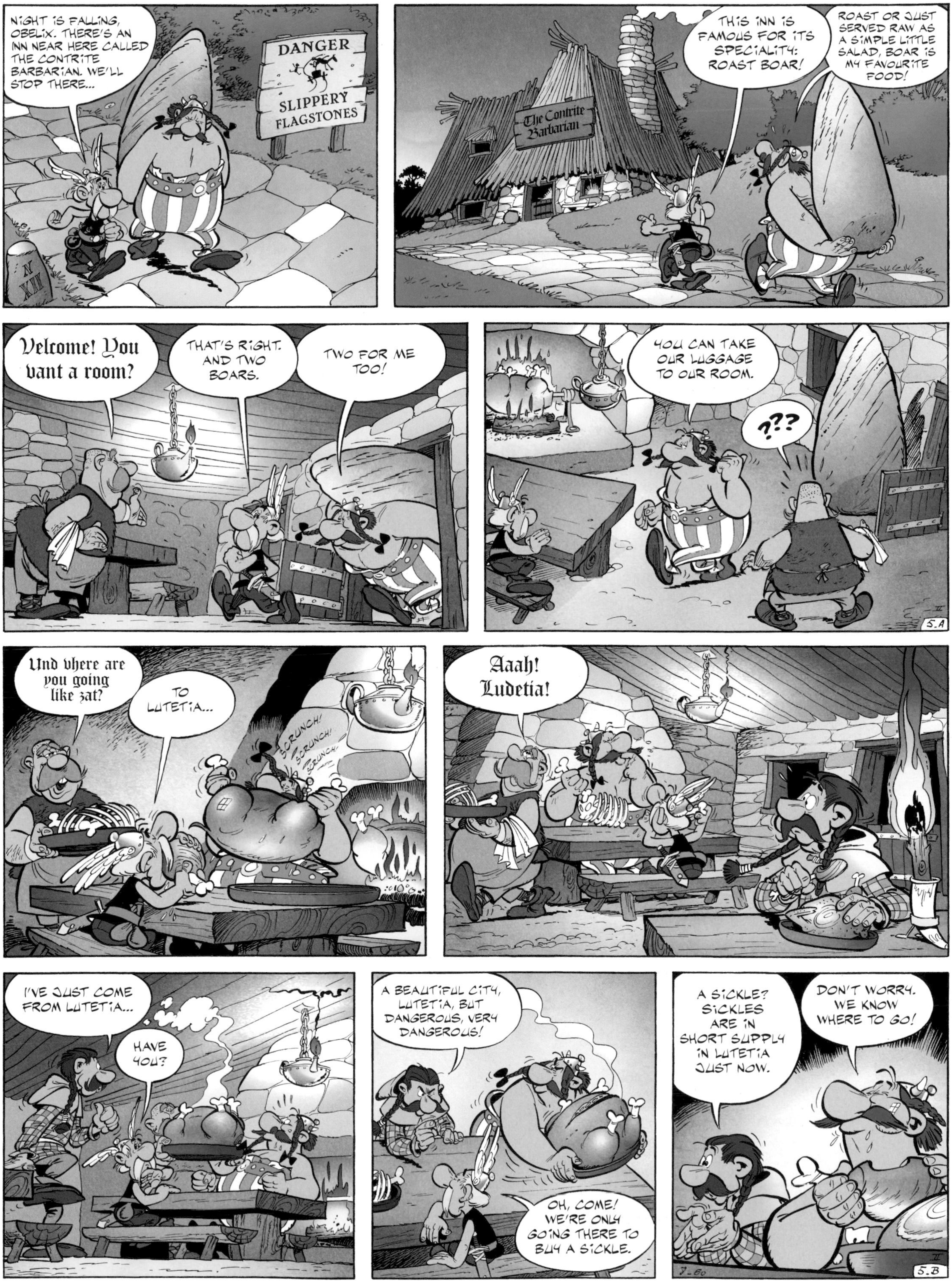
NIGHT IS FALLING, OBELIX. THERE'S AN INN NEAR HERE CALLED THE CONTRITE BARBARIAN. WE'LL STOP THERE...
DANGER
SLIPPERY FLAGSTONES
N XIII
THIS INN IS FAMOUS FOR ITS SPECIALITY: ROAST BOAR!
ROAST OR JUST SERVED RAW AS A SIMPLE LITTLE SALAD, BOAR IS MY FAVOURITE FOOD!
The Contrite Barbarian
Velcome! You vant a room?
THAT'S RIGHT. AND TWO BOARS.
TWO FOR ME TOO!
YOU CAN TAKE OUR LUGGAGE TO OUR ROOM.
???
Und vhere are you going like zat?
TO LUTETIA...
SCRUNCH! SCRUNCH! SCRUNCH!
Aaah! Ludetia!
I'VE JUST COME FROM LUTETIA...
HAVE YOU?
A BEAUTIFUL CITY, LUTETIA, BUT DANGEROUS, VERY DANGEROUS!
OH, COME! WE'RE ONLY GOING THERE TO BUY A SICKLE.
A SICKLE? SICKLES ARE IN SHORT SUPPLY IN LUTETIA JUST NOW.
DON'T WORRY. WE KNOW WHERE TO GO!

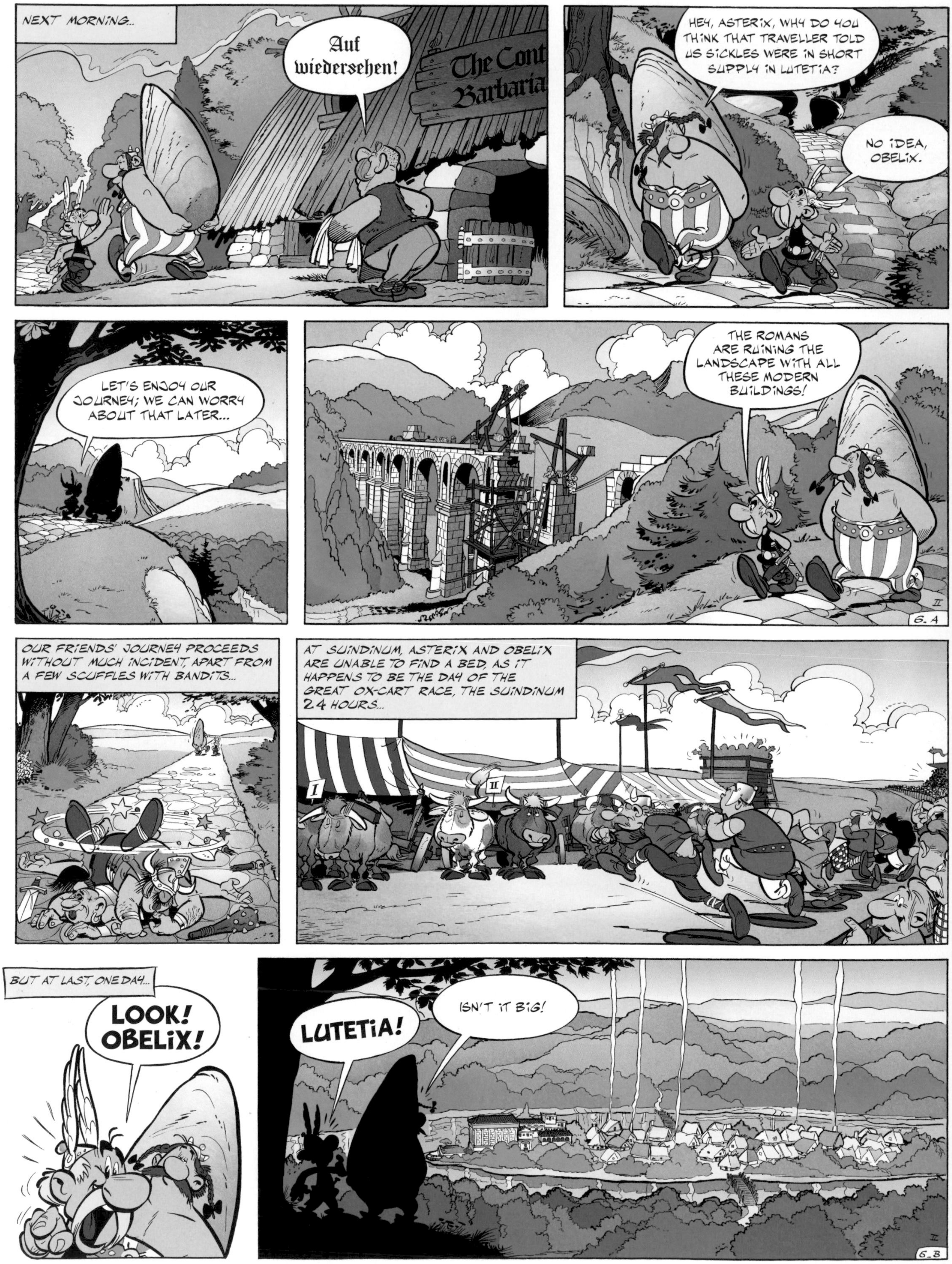
NEXT MORNING...
Auf wiedersehen!
The Cont
Barbaria
HEY, ASTERIX, WHY DO YOU THINK THAT TRAVELLER TOLD US SICKLES WERE IN SHORT SUPPLY IN LUTETIA?
NO IDEA, OBELIX.
LET'S ENJOY OUR JOURNEY; WE CAN WORRY ABOUT THAT LATER...
THE ROMANS ARE RUINING THE LANDSCAPE WITH ALL THESE MODERN BUILDINGS!
OUR FRIENDS' JOURNEY PROCEEDS WITHOUT MUCH INCIDENT, APART FROM A FEW SCUFFLES WITH BANDITS...
AT SUINDINUM, ASTERIX AND OBELIX ARE UNABLE TO FIND A BED, AS IT HAPPENS TO BE THE DAY OF THE GREAT OX-CART RACE, THE SUINDINUM 24 HOURS...
BUT AT LAST, ONE DAY...
LOOK! OBELIX!
LUTETIA!
ISN'T IT BIG!

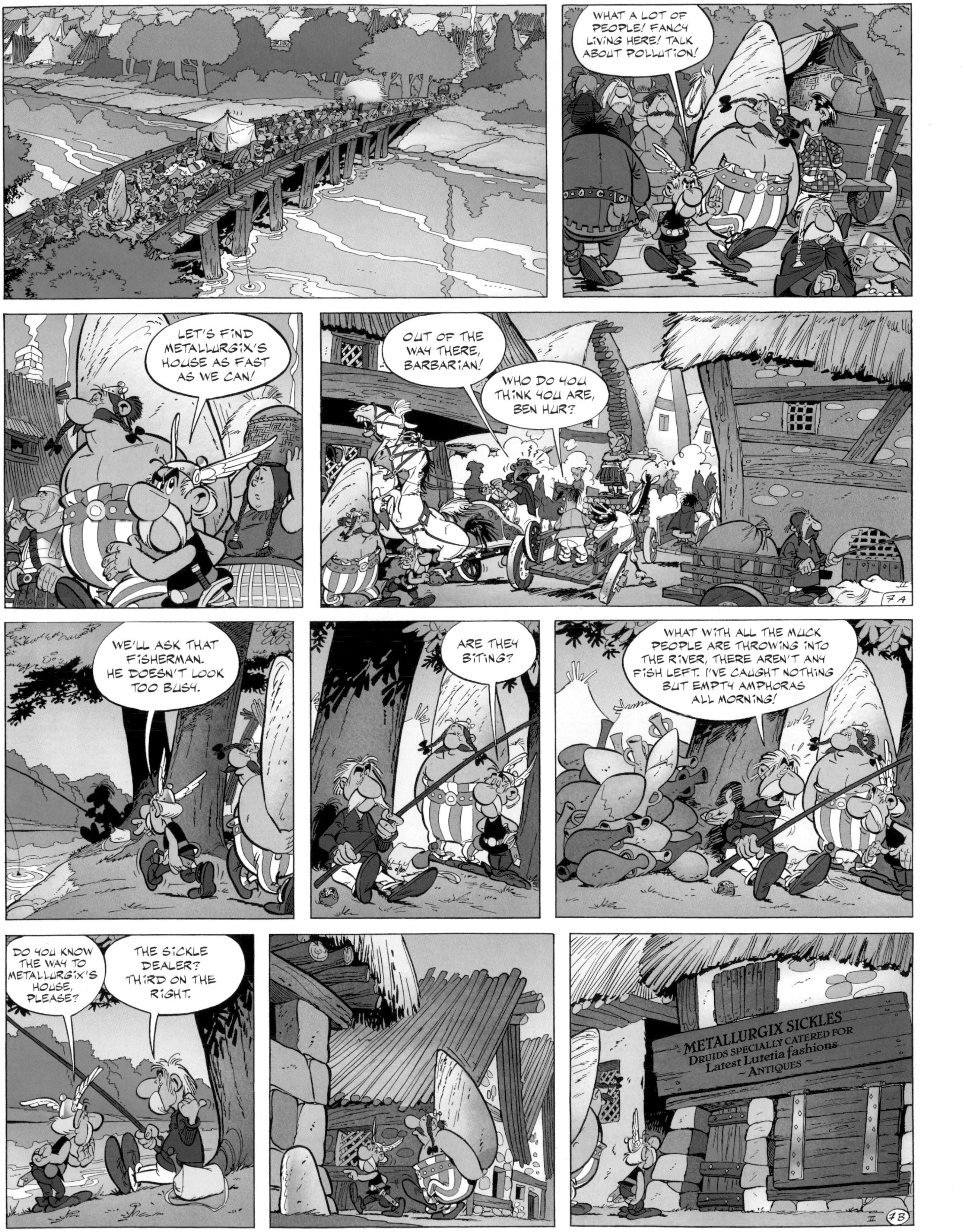

WHAT A LOT OF PEOPLE! FANCY LIVING HERE! TALK ABOUT POLLUTION!
LET'S FIND METALLURGIX'S HOUSE AS FAST AS WE CAN!
OUT OF THE WAY THERE, BARBARIAN!
WHO DO YOU THINK YOU ARE, BEN HUR?
WE'LL ASK THAT FISHERMAN. HE DOESN'T LOOK TOO BUSY.
ARE THEY BITING?
WHAT WITH ALL THE MUCK PEOPLE ARE THROWING INTO THE RIVER, THERE AREN'T ANY FISH LEFT. I'VE CAUGHT NOTHING BUT EMPTY AMPHORAS ALL MORNING!
DO YOU KNOW THE WAY TO METALLURGIX'S HOUSE, PLEASE?
THE SICKLE DEALER? THIRD ON THE RIGHT.
METALLURGIX SICKLES
DRUIDS SPECIALLY CATERED FOR
Latest Lutetia fashions
~ ANTIQUES ~

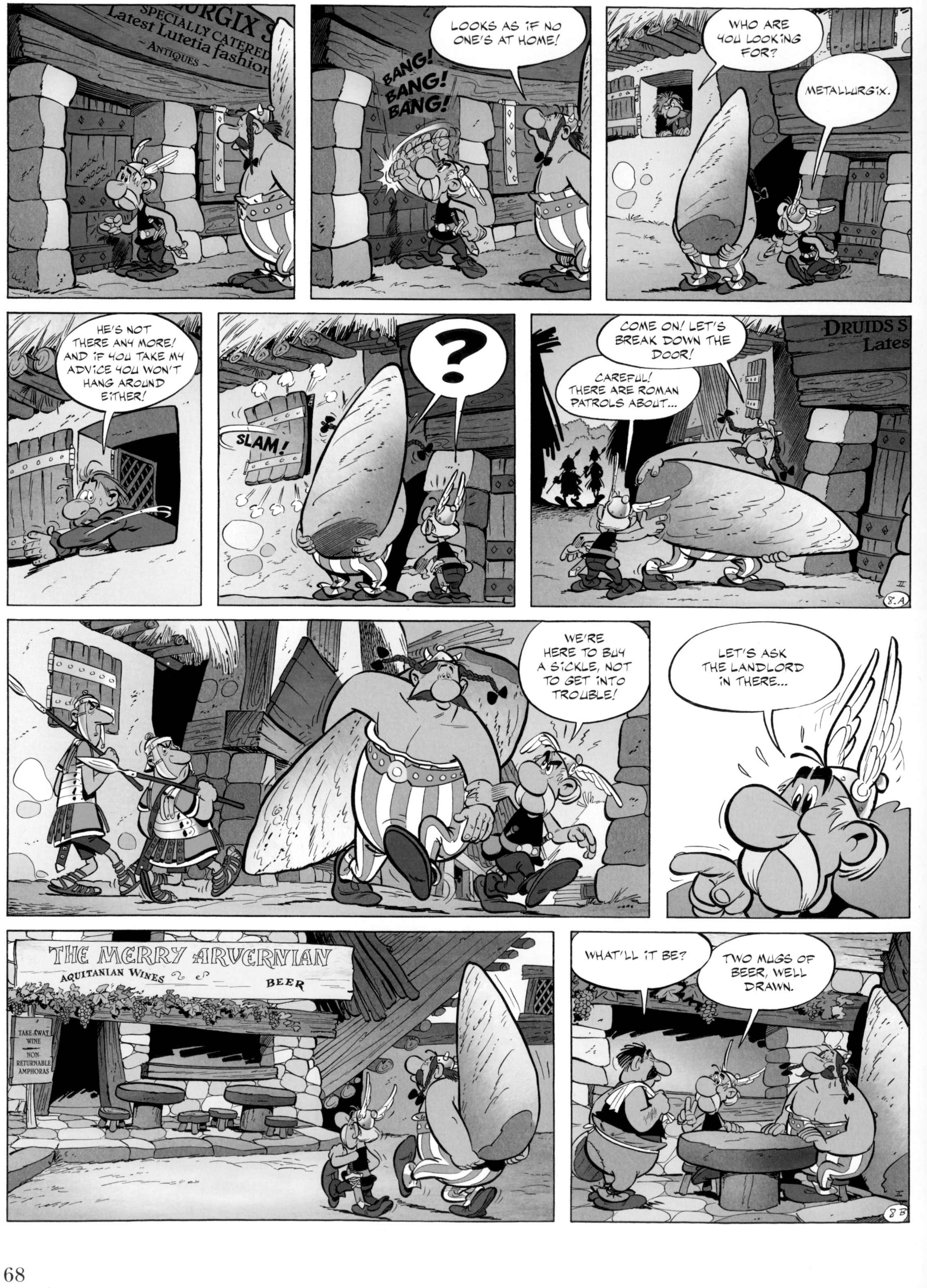
SPECIALLY CATERED
Latest Lutetia
~ ANTIQUES ~
KNOCK! KNOCK! KNOCK!
BANG! BANG! BANG!
LOOKS AS IF NO ONE'S AT HOME!
WHO ARE YOU LOOKING FOR?
METALLURGIX.
HE'S NOT THERE ANY MORE! AND IF YOU TAKE MY ADVICE YOU WON'T HANG AROUND EITHER!
SLAM!
?
COME ON! LET'S BREAK DOWN THE DOOR!
CAREFUL! THERE ARE ROMAN PATROLS ABOUT...
DRUIDS
WE'RE HERE TO BUY A SICKLE, NOT TO GET INTO TROUBLE!
LET'S ASK THE LANDLORD IN THERE...
THE MERRY ARVERNIAN
AQUITANIAN WINES
BEER
TAKE-AWAY WINE
NON-RETURNABLE AMPHORAS
WHAT'LL IT BE?
TWO MUGS OF BEER, WELL DRAWN.

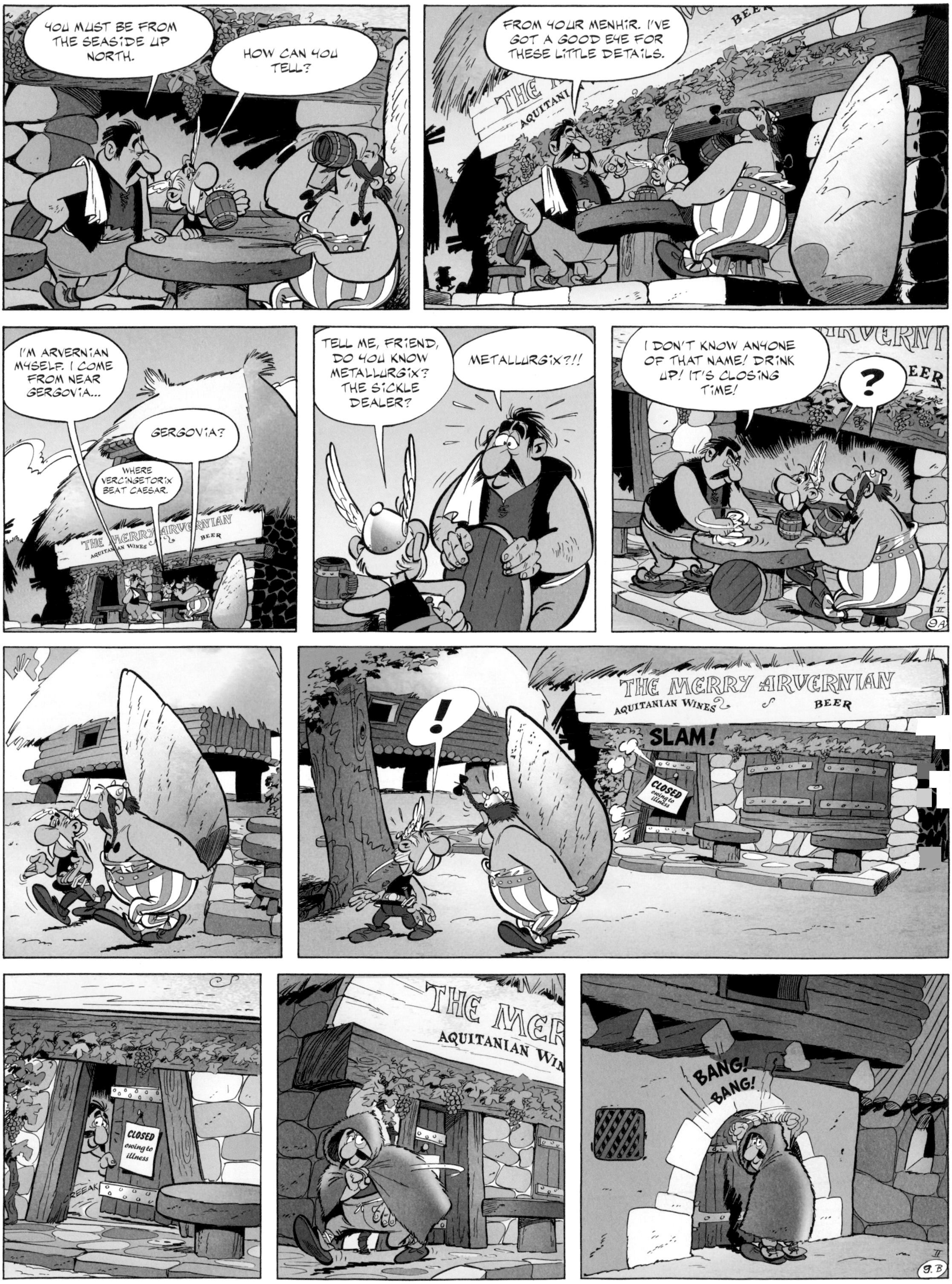

YOU MUST BE FROM THE SEASIDE UP NORTH.
HOW CAN YOU TELL?
FROM YOUR MENHIR. I'VE GOT A GOOD EYE FOR THESE LITTLE DETAILS.
I'M ARVERNIAN MYSELF. I COME FROM NEAR GERGOVIA...
GERGOVIA?
WHERE VERCINGETORIX BEAT CAESAR.
THE MERRY ARVERNIAN
AQUITANIAN WINES
BEER
TELL ME, FRIEND, DO YOU KNOW METALLURGIX? THE SICKLE DEALER?
METALLURGIX?!!
I DON'T KNOW ANYONE OF THAT NAME! DRINK UP! IT'S CLOSING TIME!
?
!
THE MERRY ARVERNIAN
AQUITANIAN WINES
BEER
SLAM!
CLOSED owing to illness
CLOSED owing to illness
THE MER
AQUITANIAN WI
BANG!
BANG!

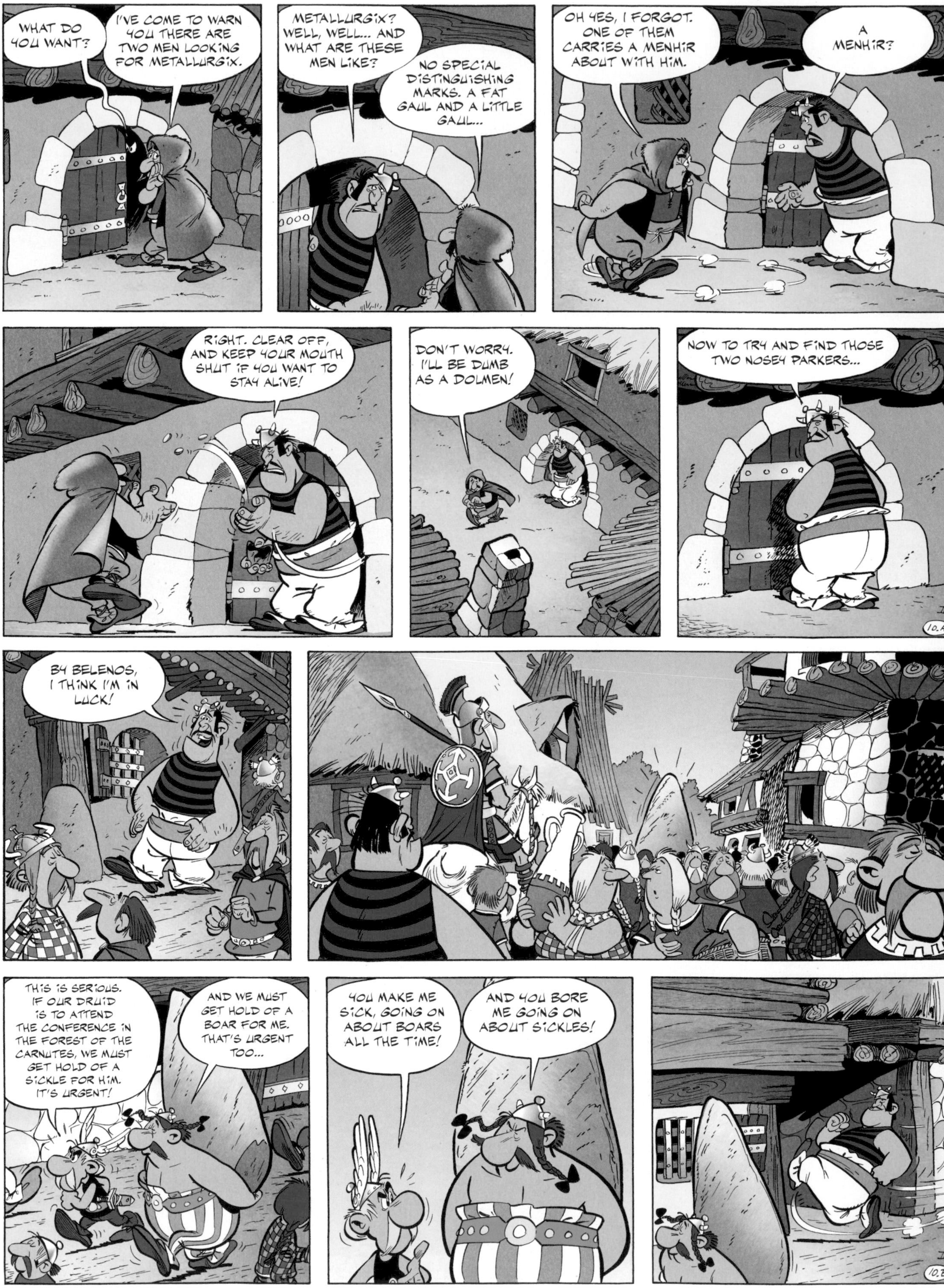
WHAT DO YOU WANT?
I'VE COME TO WARN YOU THERE ARE TWO MEN LOOKING FOR METALLURGIX.
METALLURGIX? WELL, WELL... AND WHAT ARE THESE MEN LIKE?
NO SPECIAL DISTINGUISHING MARKS. A FAT GAUL AND A LITTLE GAUL...
OH YES, I FORGOT. ONE OF THEM CARRIES A MENHIR ABOUT WITH HIM.
A MENHIR?
RIGHT. CLEAR OFF, AND KEEP YOUR MOUTH SHUT IF YOU WANT TO STAY ALIVE!
DON'T WORRY. I'LL BE DUMB AS A DOLMEN!
NOW TO TRY AND FIND THOSE TWO NOSEY PARKERS...
10.A
BY BELENOS, I THINK I'M IN LUCK!
THIS IS SERIOUS. IF OUR DRUID IS TO ATTEND THE CONFERENCE IN THE FOREST OF THE CARNUTES, WE MUST GET HOLD OF A SICKLE FOR HIM. IT'S URGENT!
AND WE MUST GET HOLD OF A BOAR FOR ME. THAT'S URGENT TOO...
YOU MAKE ME SICK, GOING ON ABOUT BOARS ALL THE TIME!
AND YOU BORE ME GOING ON ABOUT SICKLES!
10.B

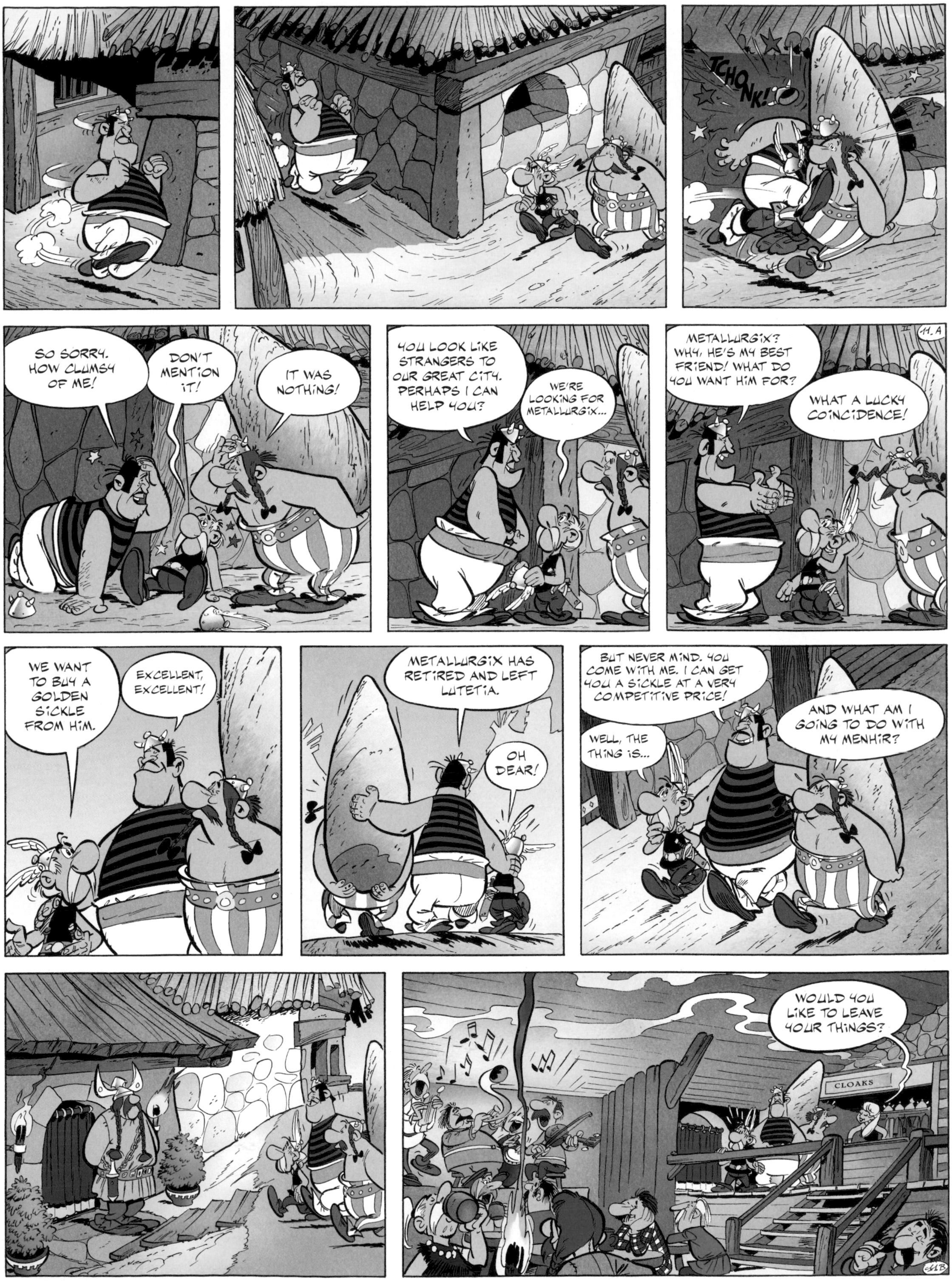
TCHONK!
SO SORRY. HOW CLUMSY OF ME!
DON'T MENTION IT!
IT WAS NOTHING!
YOU LOOK LIKE STRANGERS TO OUR GREAT CITY. PERHAPS I CAN HELP YOU?
WE'RE LOOKING FOR METALLURGIX...
METALLURGIX? WHY, HE'S MY BEST FRIEND! WHAT DO YOU WANT HIM FOR?
WHAT A LUCKY COINCIDENCE!
WE WANT TO BUY A GOLDEN SICKLE FROM HIM.
EXCELLENT, EXCELLENT!
METALLURGIX HAS RETIRED AND LEFT LUTETIA.
OH DEAR!
BUT NEVER MIND. YOU COME WITH ME. I CAN GET YOU A SICKLE AT A VERY COMPETITIVE PRICE!
WELL, THE THING IS...
AND WHAT AM I GOING TO DO WITH MY MENHIR?
CLOAKS
WOULD YOU LIKE TO LEAVE YOUR THINGS?

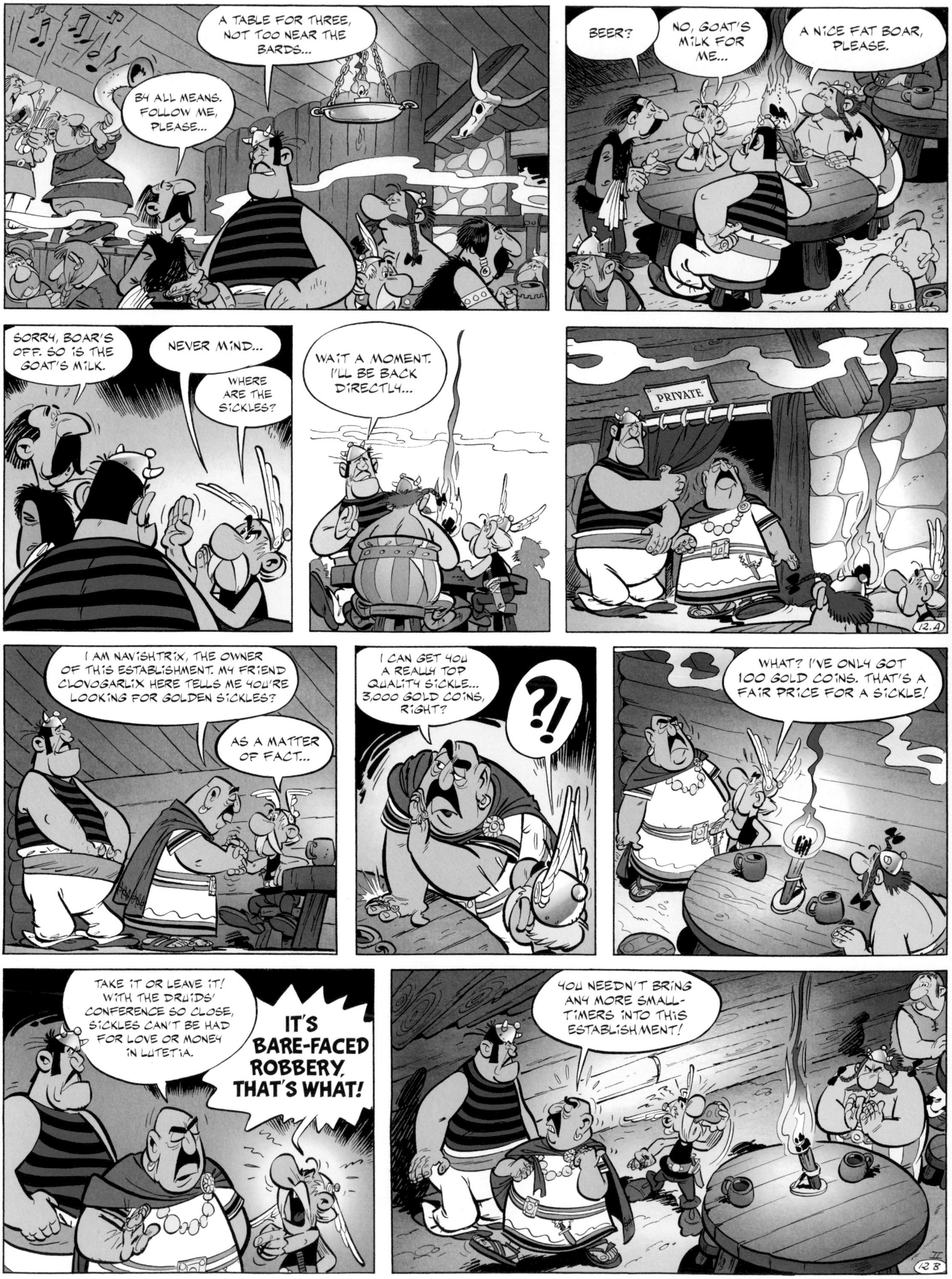
A TABLE FOR THREE, NOT TOO NEAR THE BARDS...
BY ALL MEANS. FOLLOW ME, PLEASE...
BEER?
NO, GOAT'S MILK FOR ME...
A NICE FAT BOAR, PLEASE.
SORRY, BOAR'S OFF. SO IS THE GOAT'S MILK.
NEVER MIND...
WHERE ARE THE SICKLES?
WAIT A MOMENT. I'LL BE BACK DIRECTLY...
PRIVATE
I AM NAVISHTRIX, THE OWNER OF THIS ESTABLISHMENT. MY FRIEND CLOVOGARLIX HERE TELLS ME YOU'RE LOOKING FOR GOLDEN SICKLES?
AS A MATTER OF FACT...
I CAN GET YOU A REALLY TOP QUALITY SICKLE... 3,000 GOLD COINS, RIGHT?
?!
WHAT? I'VE ONLY GOT 100 GOLD COINS. THAT'S A FAIR PRICE FOR A SICKLE!
TAKE IT OR LEAVE IT! WITH THE DRUIDS' CONFERENCE SO CLOSE, SICKLES CAN'T BE HAD FOR LOVE OR MONEY IN LUTETIA.
IT'S BARE-FACED ROBBERY, THAT'S WHAT!
YOU NEEDN'T BRING ANY MORE SMALL-TIMERS INTO THIS ESTABLISHMENT!

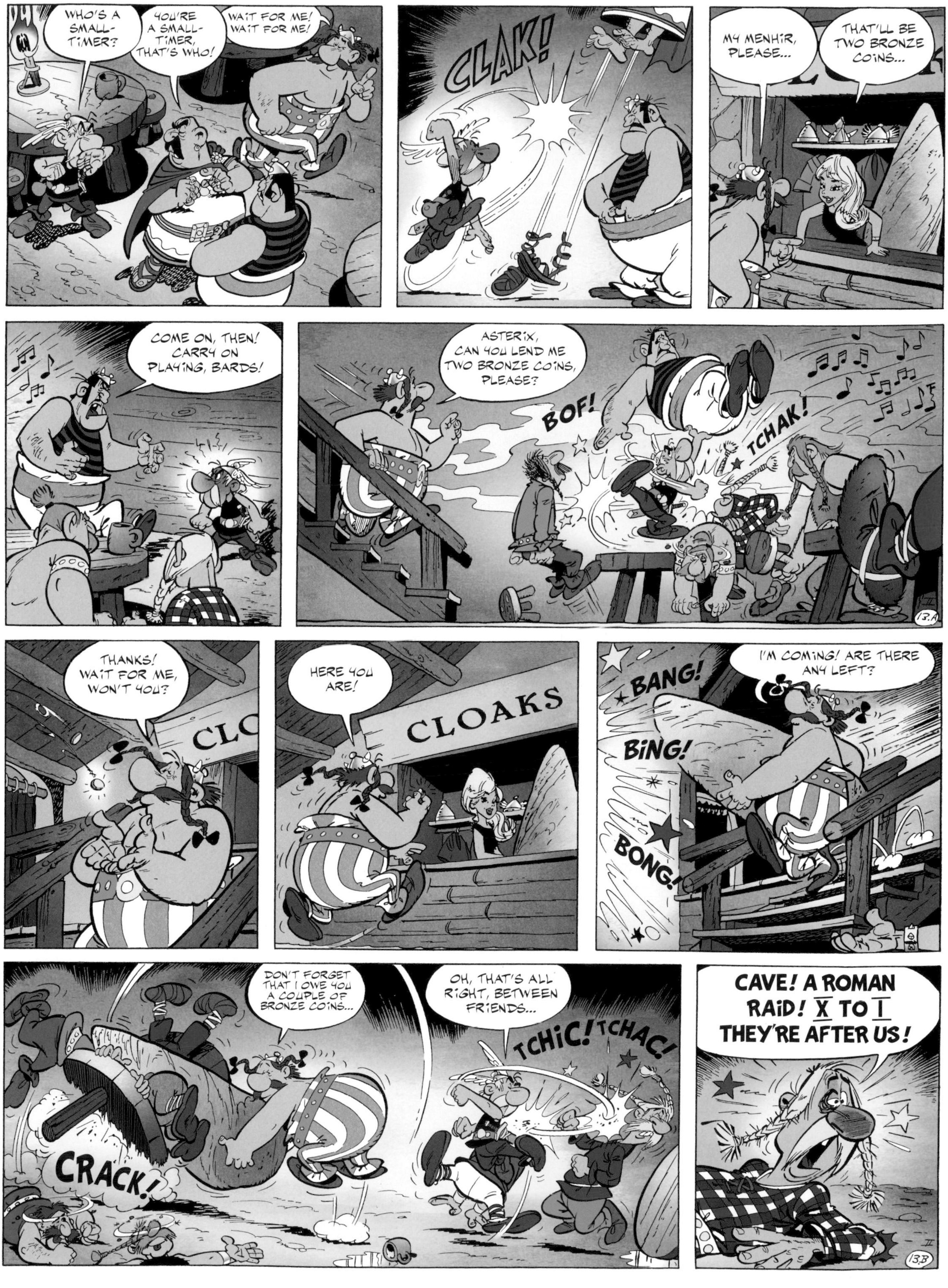
WHO'S A SMALL-TIMER?
YOU'RE A SMALL-TIMER, THAT'S WHO!
WAIT FOR ME! WAIT FOR ME!
CLAK!
MY MENHIR, PLEASE...
THAT'LL BE TWO BRONZE COINS...
COME ON, THEN! CARRY ON PLAYING, BARDS!
ASTERIX, CAN YOU LEND ME TWO BRONZE COINS, PLEASE?
BOF!
TCHAK!
THANKS! WAIT FOR ME, WON'T YOU?
CLO
HERE YOU ARE!
CLOAKS
I'M COMING! ARE THERE ANY LEFT?
BANG!
BING!
BONG!
DON'T FORGET THAT I OWE YOU A COUPLE OF BRONZE COINS...
OH, THAT'S ALL RIGHT, BETWEEN FRIENDS...
TCHIC! TCHAC!
CRACK!
CAVE! A ROMAN RAID! X TO I THEY'RE AFTER US!

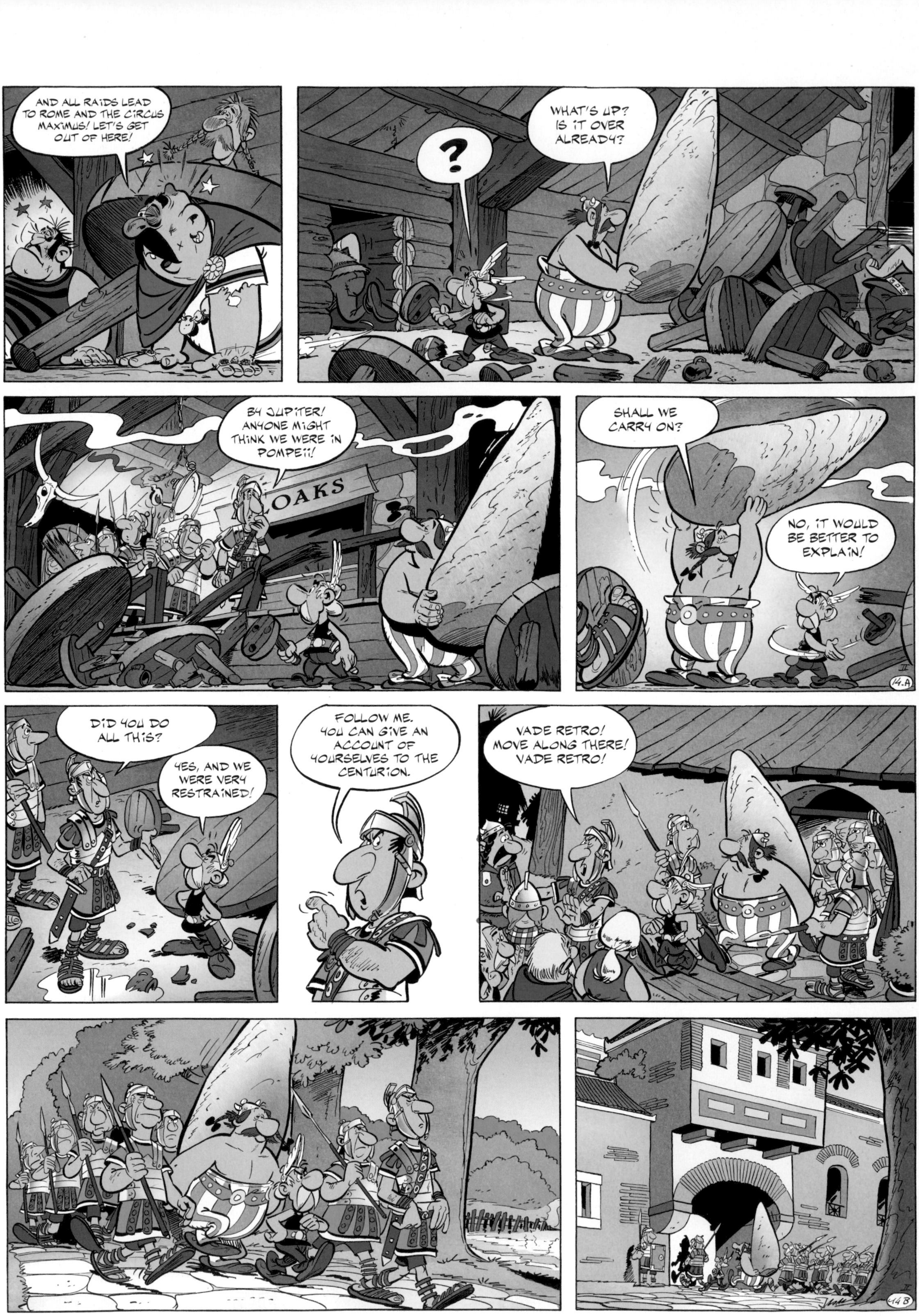
AND ALL RAIDS LEAD TO ROME AND THE CIRCUS MAXIMUS! LET'S GET OUT OF HERE!
?
WHAT'S UP? IS IT OVER ALREADY?
BY JUPITER! ANYONE MIGHT THINK WE WERE IN POMPEII!
OAKS
SHALL WE CARRY ON?
NO, IT WOULD BE BETTER TO EXPLAIN!
DID YOU DO ALL THIS?
YES, AND WE WERE VERY RESTRAINED!
FOLLOW ME. YOU CAN GIVE AN ACCOUNT OF YOURSELVES TO THE CENTURION.
VADE RETRO! MOVE ALONG THERE! VADE RETRO!

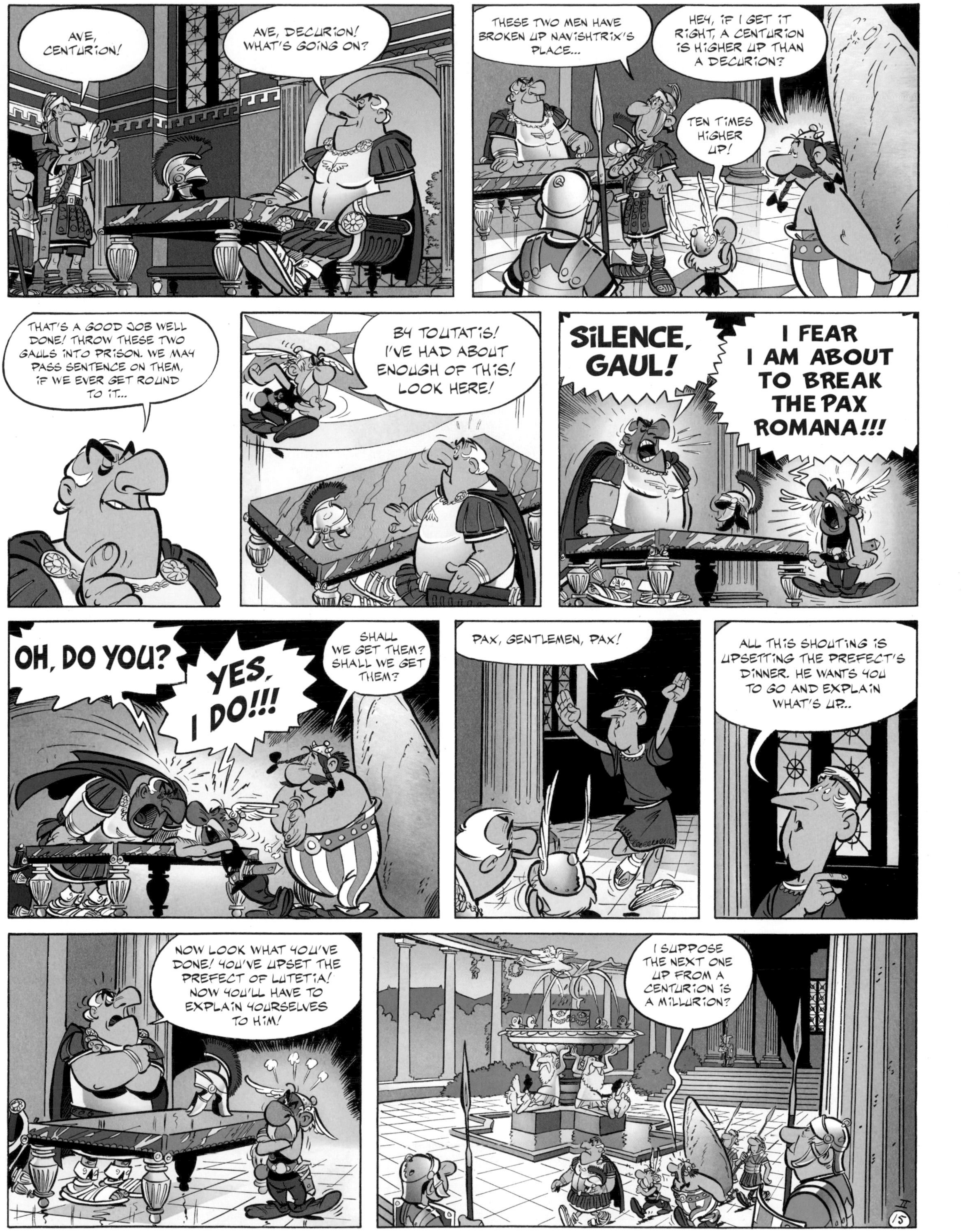

AVE, CENTURION!
AVE, DECURION! WHAT'S GOING ON?
THESE TWO MEN HAVE BROKEN UP NAVISHTRIX'S PLACE...
HEY, IF I GET IT RIGHT, A CENTURION IS HIGHER UP THAN A DECURION?
TEN TIMES HIGHER UP!
THAT'S A GOOD JOB WELL DONE! THROW THESE TWO GAULS INTO PRISON. WE MAY PASS SENTENCE ON THEM, IF WE EVER GET ROUND TO IT...
BY TOUTATIS! I'VE HAD ABOUT ENOUGH OF THIS! LOOK HERE!
SILENCE, GAUL!
I FEAR I AM ABOUT TO BREAK THE PAX ROMANA!!!
OH, DO YOU?
YES, I DO!!!
SHALL WE GET THEM? SHALL WE GET THEM?
PAX, GENTLEMEN, PAX!
ALL THIS SHOUTING IS UPSETTING THE PREFECT'S DINNER. HE WANTS YOU TO GO AND EXPLAIN WHAT'S UP..
NOW LOOK WHAT YOU'VE DONE! YOU'VE UPSET THE PREFECT OF LUTETIA! NOW YOU'LL HAVE TO EXPLAIN YOURSELVES TO HIM!
I SUPPOSE THE NEXT ONE UP FROM A CENTURION IS A MILLURION?
II 15

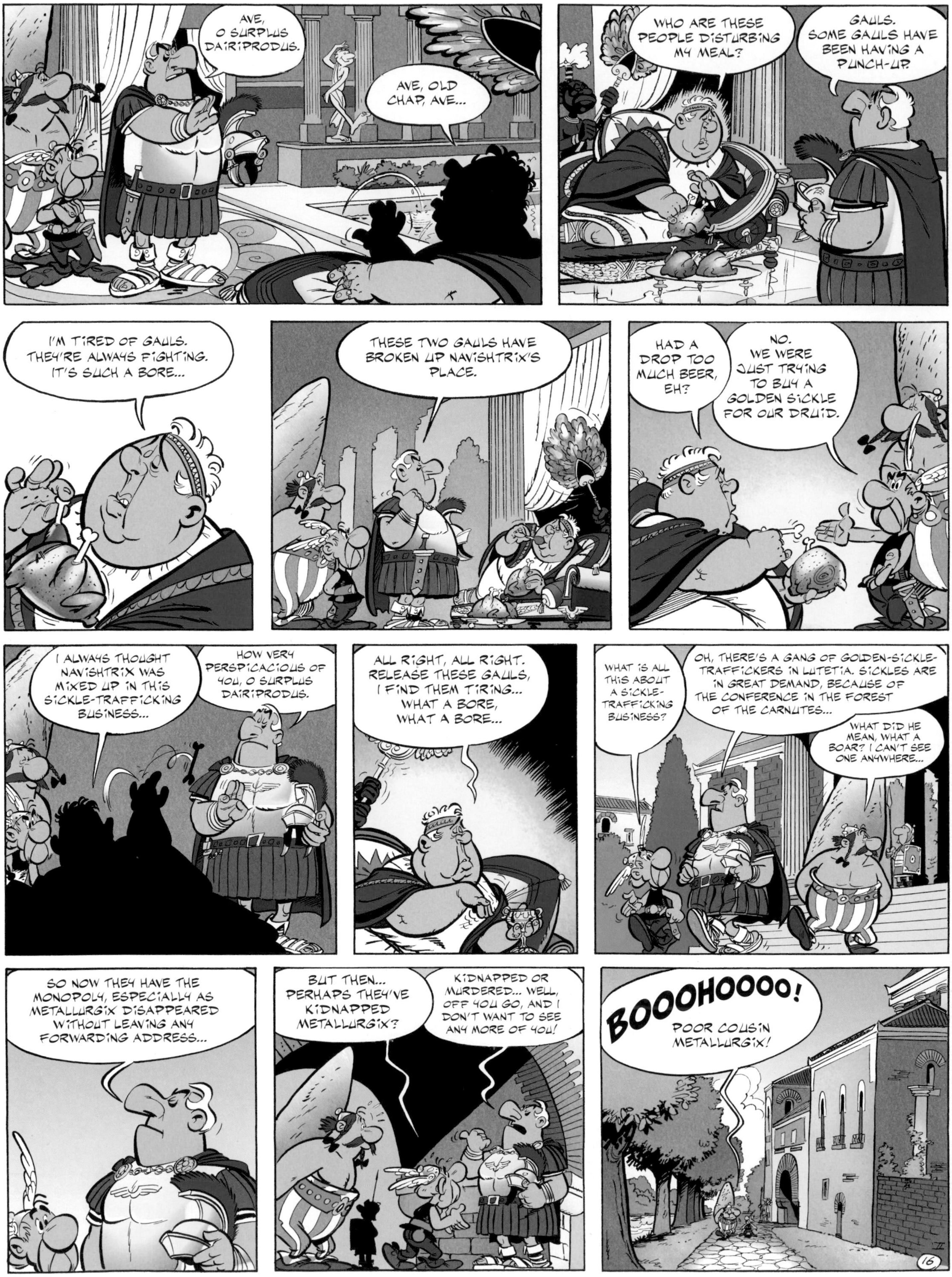
AVE, O SURPLUS DAIRIPRODUS.
AVE, OLD CHAP, AVE...
WHO ARE THESE PEOPLE DISTURBING MY MEAL?
GAULS. SOME GAULS HAVE BEEN HAVING A PUNCH-UP.
I'M TIRED OF GAULS. THEY'RE ALWAYS FIGHTING. IT'S SUCH A BORE...
THESE TWO GAULS HAVE BROKEN UP NAVISHTRIX'S PLACE.
HAD A DROP TOO MUCH BEER, EH?
NO. WE WERE JUST TRYING TO BUY A GOLDEN SICKLE FOR OUR DRUID.
I ALWAYS THOUGHT NAVISHTRIX WAS MIXED UP IN THIS SICKLE-TRAFFICKING BUSINESS...
HOW VERY PERSPICACIOUS OF YOU, O SURPLUS DAIRIPRODUS.
ALL RIGHT, ALL RIGHT. RELEASE THESE GAULS, I FIND THEM TIRING... WHAT A BORE, WHAT A BORE...
WHAT IS ALL THIS ABOUT A SICKLE-TRAFFICKING BUSINESS?
OH, THERE'S A GANG OF GOLDEN-SICKLE-TRAFFICKERS IN LUTETIA. SICKLES ARE IN GREAT DEMAND, BECAUSE OF THE CONFERENCE IN THE FOREST OF THE CARNUTES...
WHAT DID HE MEAN, WHAT A BOAR? I CAN'T SEE ONE ANYWHERE...
SO NOW THEY HAVE THE MONOPOLY, ESPECIALLY AS METALLURGIX DISAPPEARED WITHOUT LEAVING ANY FORWARDING ADDRESS...
BUT THEN... PERHAPS THEY'VE KIDNAPPED METALLURGIX?
KIDNAPPED OR MURDERED... WELL, OFF YOU GO, AND I DON'T WANT TO SEE ANY MORE OF YOU!
BOOOHOOOO!
POOR COUSIN METALLURGIX!
16

BOOOHOOOO! POOR COUSIN METALLURGIX!

WE'LL FIND HIM, OBELIX. FOR A START, WHAT DOES YOUR COUSIN LOOK LIKE?

WHAT DOES HE LOOK LIKE? I'VE NO IDEA. I'VE NEVER SET EYES ON HIM.

!

LET'S GO BACK TO HIS HOUSE. WE MIGHT FIND A CLUE THERE...

SO WE MIGHT. HOW CAN I BE EXPECTED TO KNOW WHAT HE LOOKS LIKE WHEN I'VE NEVER SEEN HIM....? SOMETIMES ASTERIX JUST DOESN'T STOP TO THINK!

THE DOOR'S LOCKED, OF COURSE...

LEAVE IT TO ME. I'LL OPEN IT...

CRAAASH!

THERE YOU ARE!

WHAT A MESS! THAT'S FUNNY; WE'RE RATHER TIDY IN MY FAMILY...

THERE'S BEEN A FIGHT HERE. LOOK, METALLURGIX HAS LEFT HIS PERSONAL BELONGINGS AND HIS KITCHEN UTENSILS BEHIND...

BUT HIS TOOLS, HIS SICKLES AND HIS MONEY ARE ALL MISSING. OBELIX, YOUR COUSIN'S BEEN KIDNAPPED BY THE SICKLE-TRAFFICKERS!

BOOHOOO! POOR METALLURGIX!

WELL, THIS PROVES METALLURGIX IS STILL ALIVE. WE'LL FIND HIM, BY TOUTATIS!

OH, GOODY!

LET'S MOVE IN HERE, AND FIRST, LET'S GO AND DO SOME SHOPPING.

GOOD IDEA!

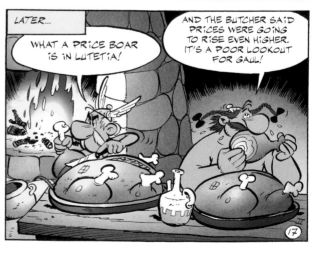
LATER...

WHAT A PRICE BOAR IS IN LUTETIA!

AND THE BUTCHER SAID PRICES WERE GOING TO RISE EVEN HIGHER. IT'S A POOR LOOKOUT FOR GAUL!

17

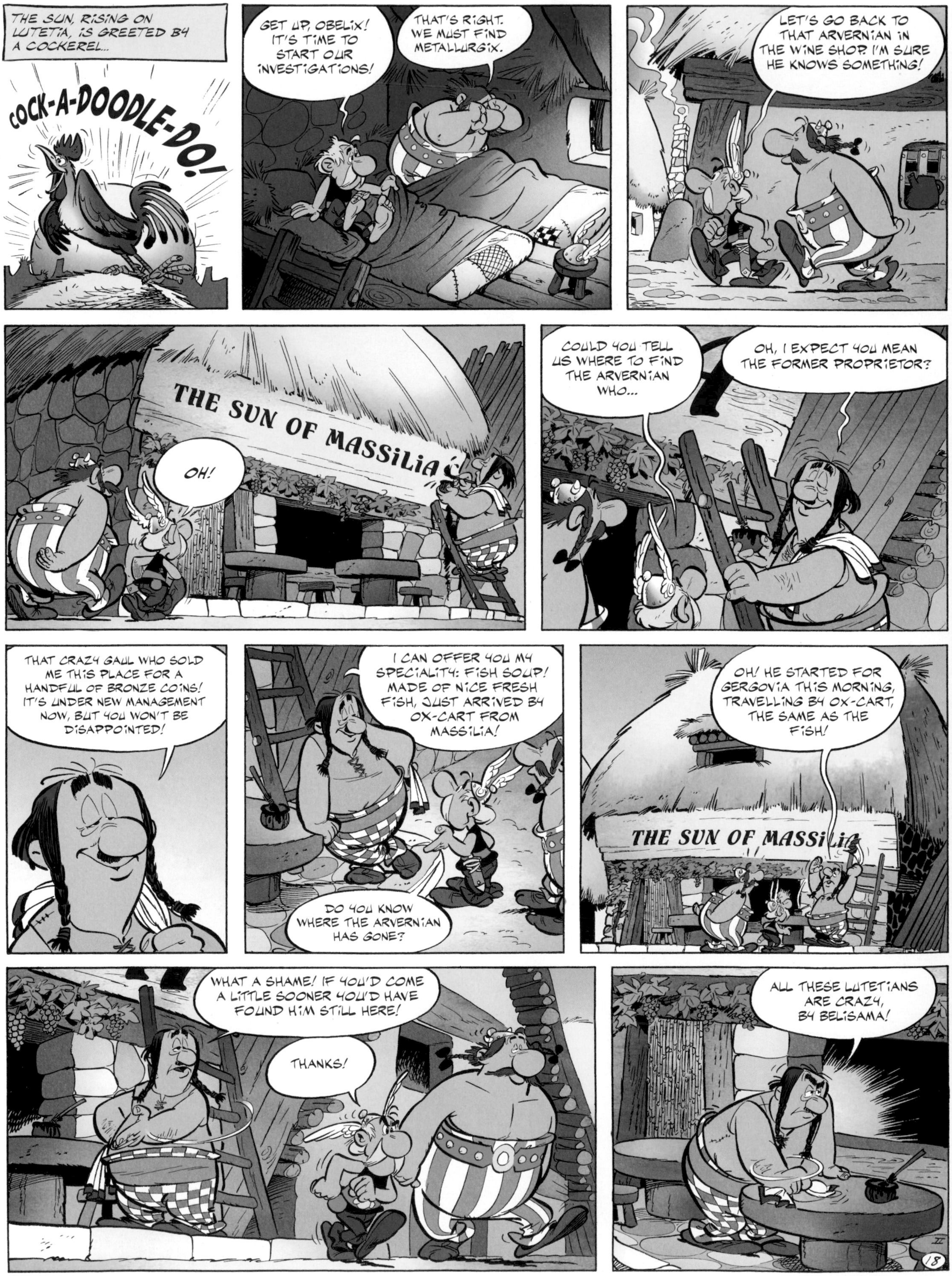
THE SUN, RISING ON LUTETIA, IS GREETED BY A COCKEREL...
COCK-A-DOODLE-DO!
GET UP, OBELIX! IT'S TIME TO START OUR INVESTIGATIONS!
THAT'S RIGHT. WE MUST FIND METALLURGIX.
LET'S GO BACK TO THAT ARVERNIAN IN THE WINE SHOP. I'M SURE HE KNOWS SOMETHING!
THE SUN OF MASSILIA
OH!
COULD YOU TELL US WHERE TO FIND THE ARVERNIAN WHO...
OH, I EXPECT YOU MEAN THE FORMER PROPRIETOR?
THAT CRAZY GAUL WHO SOLD ME THIS PLACE FOR A HANDFUL OF BRONZE COINS! IT'S UNDER NEW MANAGEMENT NOW, BUT YOU WON'T BE DISAPPOINTED!
I CAN OFFER YOU MY SPECIALITY: FISH SOUP! MADE OF NICE FRESH FISH, JUST ARRIVED BY OX-CART FROM MASSILIA!
DO YOU KNOW WHERE THE ARVERNIAN HAS GONE?
OH! HE STARTED FOR GERGOVIA THIS MORNING, TRAVELLING BY OX-CART, THE SAME AS THE FISH!
THE SUN OF MASSILIA
WHAT A SHAME! IF YOU'D COME A LITTLE SOONER YOU'D HAVE FOUND HIM STILL HERE!
THANKS!
ALL THESE LUTETIANS ARE CRAZY, BY BELISAMA!
18

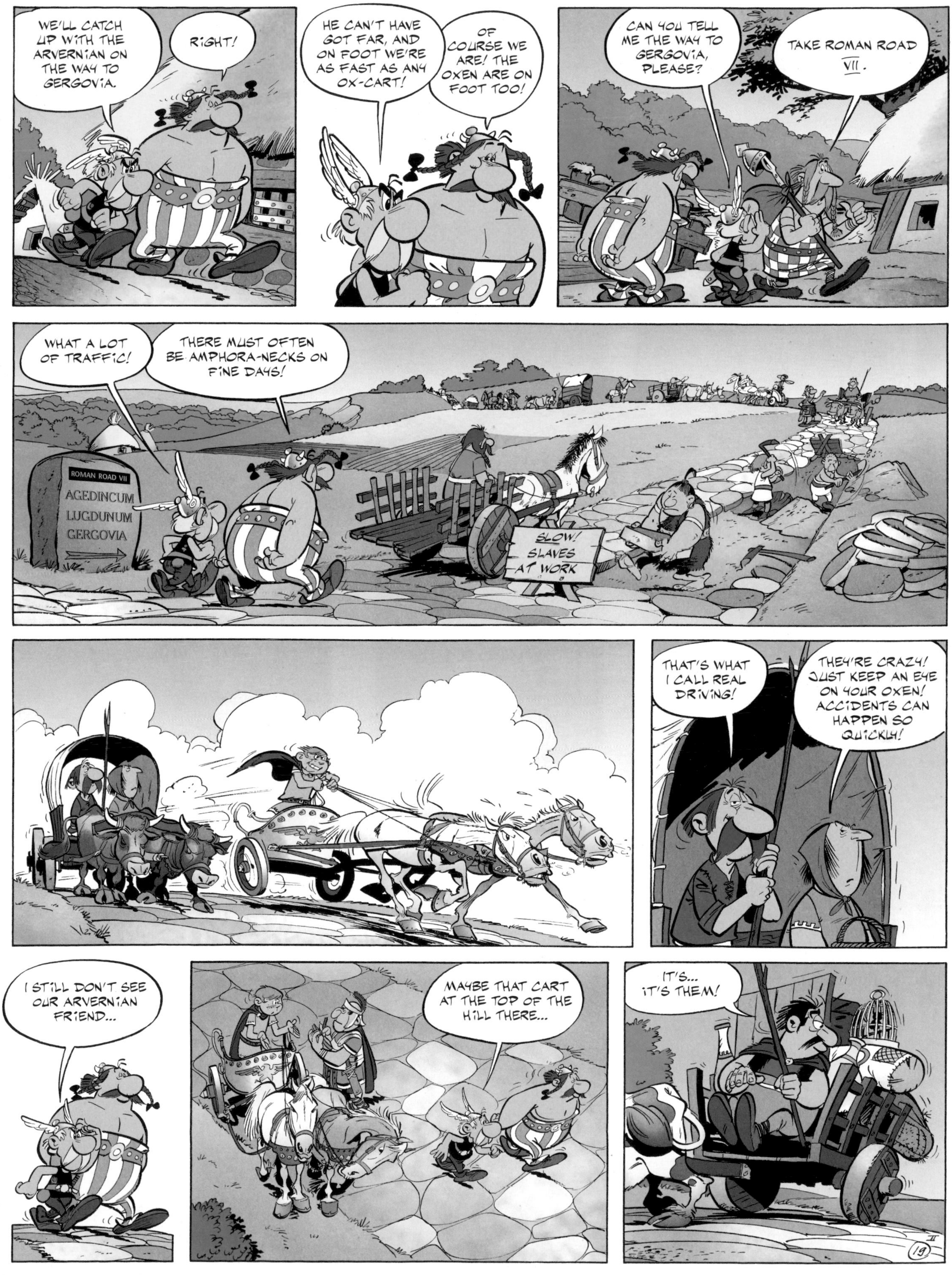
WE'LL CATCH UP WITH THE ARVERNIAN ON THE WAY TO GERGOVIA.
RIGHT!
HE CAN'T HAVE GOT FAR, AND ON FOOT WE'RE AS FAST AS ANY OX-CART!
OF COURSE WE ARE! THE OXEN ARE ON FOOT TOO!
CAN YOU TELL ME THE WAY TO GERGOVIA, PLEASE?
TAKE ROMAN ROAD VII.
WHAT A LOT OF TRAFFIC!
THERE MUST OFTEN BE AMPHORA-NECKS ON FINE DAYS!
ROMAN ROAD VII
AGEDINCUM
LUGDUNUM
GERGOVIA
SLOW! SLAVES AT WORK
THAT'S WHAT I CALL REAL DRIVING!
THEY'RE CRAZY! JUST KEEP AN EYE ON YOUR OXEN! ACCIDENTS CAN HAPPEN SO QUICKLY!
I STILL DON'T SEE OUR ARVERNIAN FRIEND...
MAYBE THAT CART AT THE TOP OF THE HILL THERE...
IT'S... IT'S THEM!
II
19

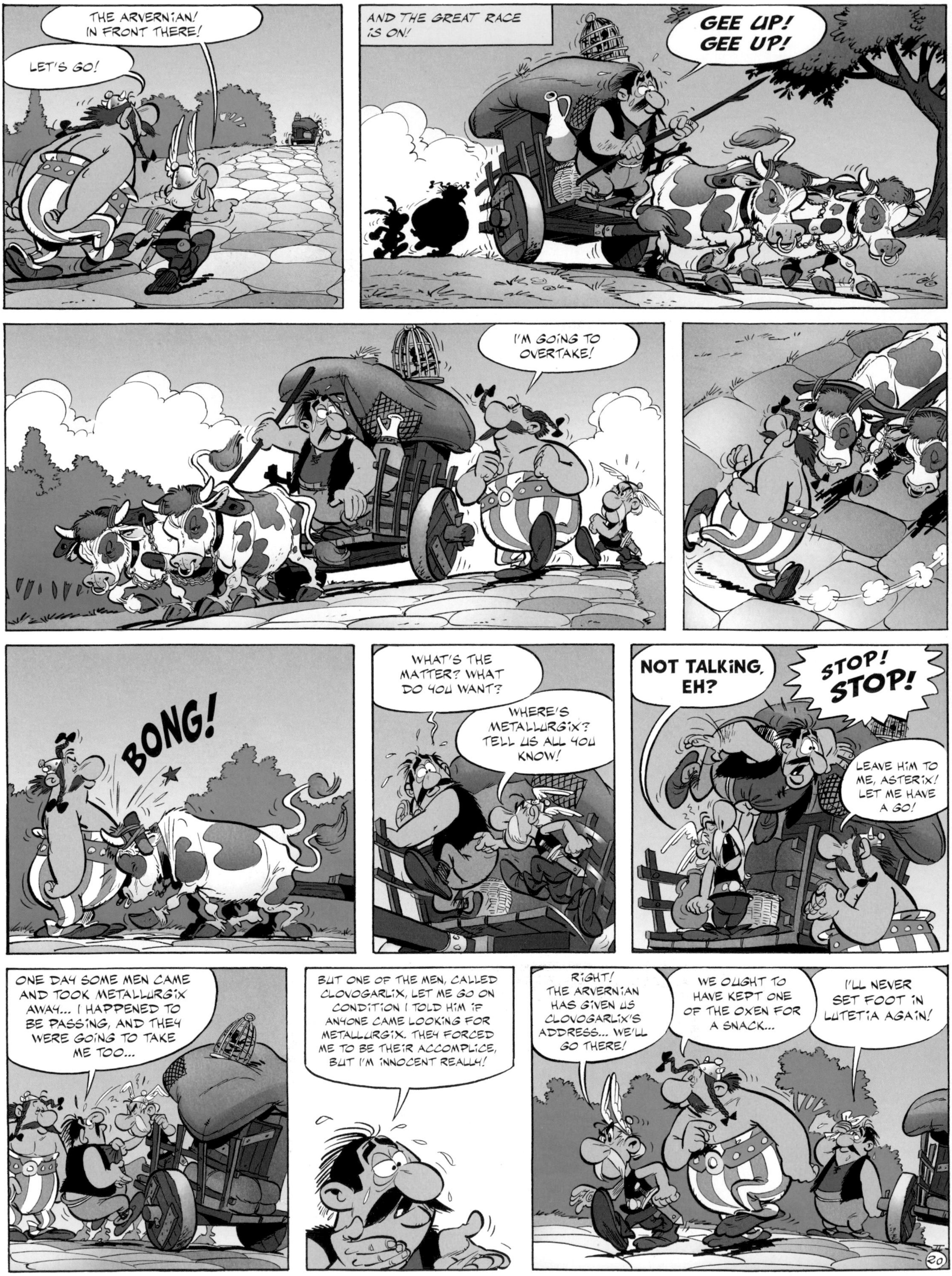
THE ARVERNIAN! IN FRONT THERE!
LET'S GO!
AND THE GREAT RACE IS ON!
GEE UP! GEE UP!
I'M GOING TO OVERTAKE!
BONG!
WHAT'S THE MATTER? WHAT DO YOU WANT?
WHERE'S METALLURGIX? TELL US ALL YOU KNOW!
NOT TALKING, EH?
STOP! STOP!
LEAVE HIM TO ME, ASTERIX! LET ME HAVE A GO!
ONE DAY SOME MEN CAME AND TOOK METALLURGIX AWAY... I HAPPENED TO BE PASSING, AND THEY WERE GOING TO TAKE ME TOO...
BUT ONE OF THE MEN, CALLED CLOVOGARLIX, LET ME GO ON CONDITION I TOLD HIM IF ANYONE CAME LOOKING FOR METALLURGIX. THEY FORCED ME TO BE THEIR ACCOMPLICE, BUT I'M INNOCENT REALLY!
RIGHT! THE ARVERNIAN HAS GIVEN US CLOVOGARLIX'S ADDRESS... WE'LL GO THERE!
WE OUGHT TO HAVE KEPT ONE OF THE OXEN FOR A SNACK...
I'LL NEVER SET FOOT IN LUTETIA AGAIN!
20

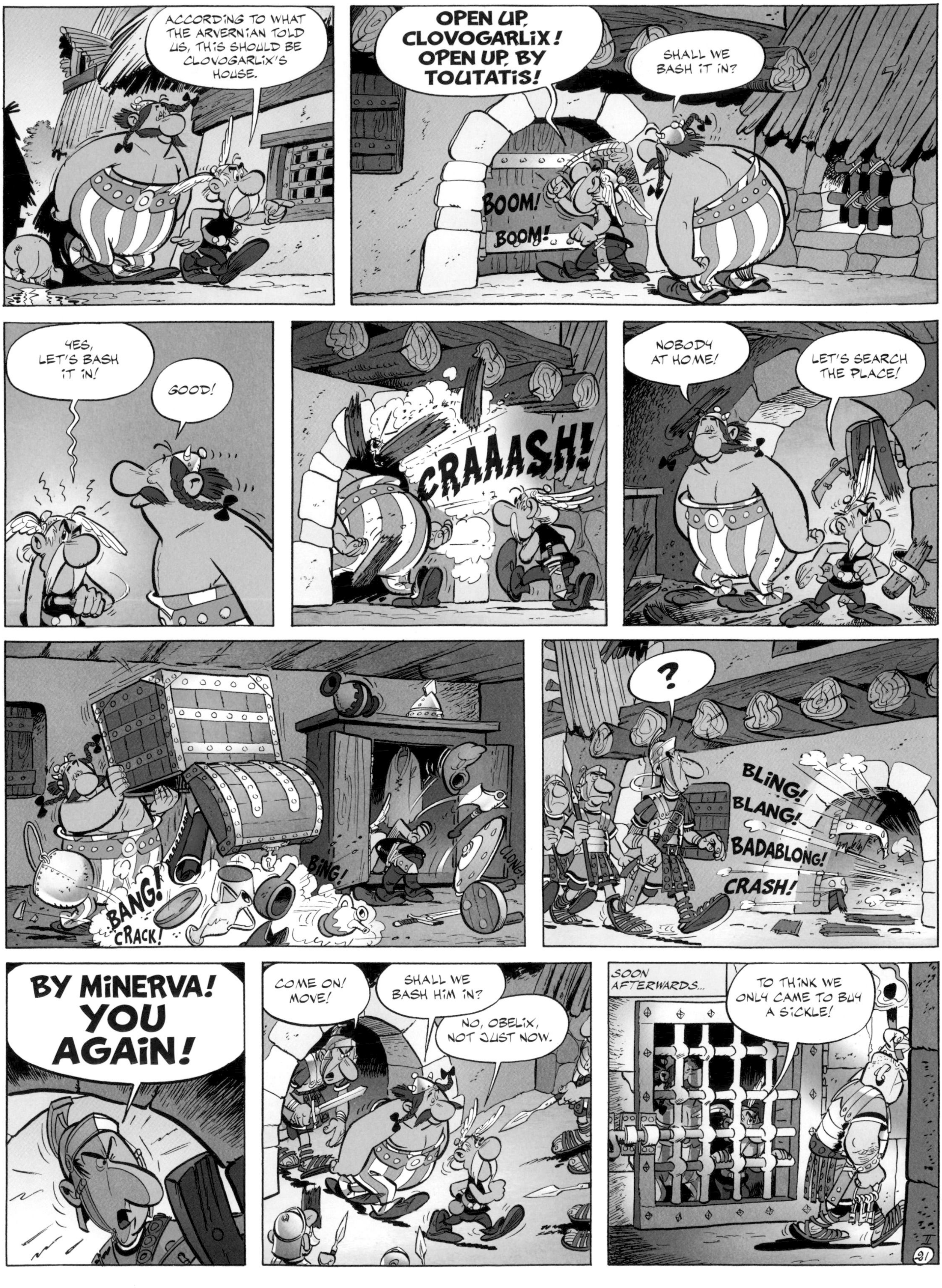
ACCORDING TO WHAT THE ARVERNIAN TOLD US, THIS SHOULD BE CLOVOGARLIX'S HOUSE.
OPEN UP, CLOVOGARLIX! OPEN UP, BY TOUTATIS!
BOOM!
BOOM!
SHALL WE BASH IT IN?
YES, LET'S BASH IT IN!
GOOD!
CRAAASH!
NOBODY AT HOME!
LET'S SEARCH THE PLACE!
BANG!
CRACK!
BING!
CLONG!
?
BLING!
BLANG!
BADABLONG!
CRASH!
BY MINERVA! YOU AGAIN!
COME ON! MOVE!
SHALL WE BASH HIM IN?
NO, OBELIX, NOT JUST NOW.
SOON AFTERWARDS...
TO THINK WE ONLY CAME TO BUY A SICKLE!
31

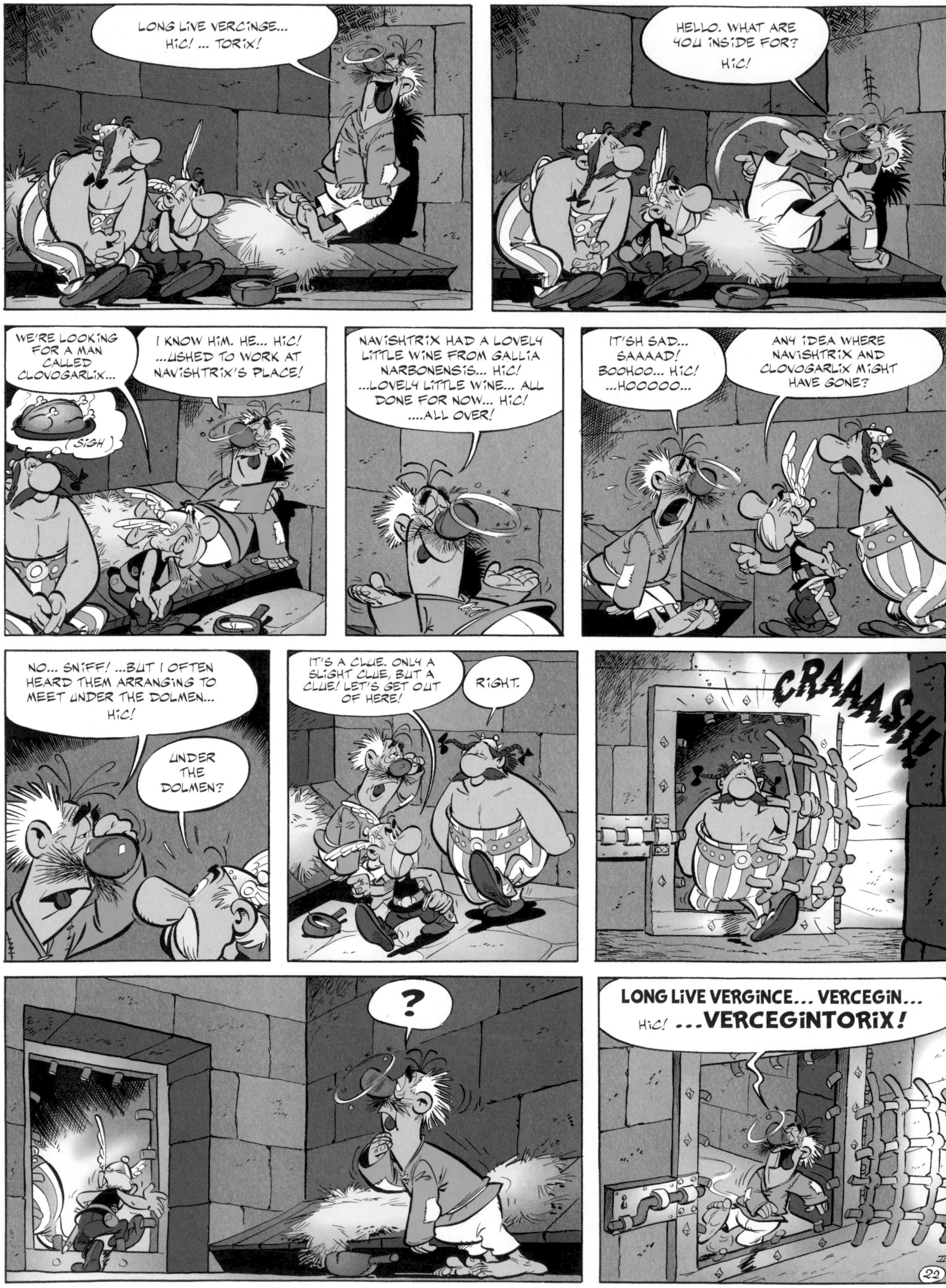
LONG LIVE VERCINGE... HIC! ... TORIX!
HELLO. WHAT ARE YOU INSIDE FOR? HIC!
WE'RE LOOKING FOR A MAN CALLED CLOVOGARLIX...
(SIGH)
I KNOW HIM. HE... HIC! ...USHED TO WORK AT NAVISHTRIX'S PLACE!
NAVISHTRIX HAD A LOVELY LITTLE WINE FROM GALLIA NARBONENSIS... HIC! ...LOVELY LITTLE WINE... ALL DONE FOR NOW... HIC! ....ALL OVER!
IT'SH SAD... SAAAAD! BOOHOO... HIC! ...HOOOOO...
ANY IDEA WHERE NAVISHTRIX AND CLOVOGARLIX MIGHT HAVE GONE?
NO... SNIFF! ...BUT I OFTEN HEARD THEM ARRANGING TO MEET UNDER THE DOLMEN... HIC!
UNDER THE DOLMEN?
IT'S A CLUE. ONLY A SLIGHT CLUE, BUT A CLUE! LET'S GET OUT OF HERE!
RIGHT.
CRAAASH!
?
LONG LIVE VERGINCE... VERCEGIN... HIC! ...VERCEGINTORIX!
22

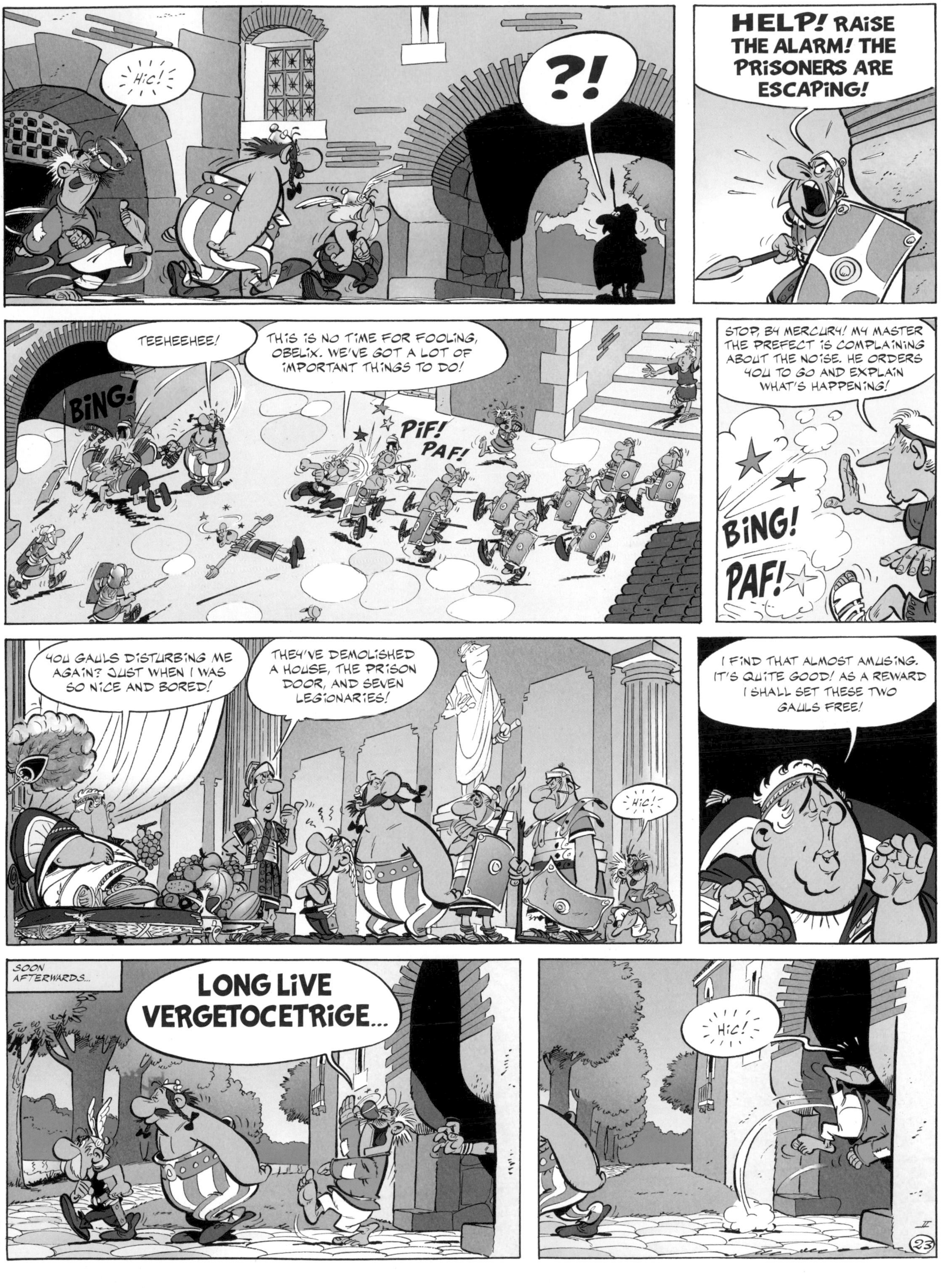

HIC!
?!
HELP! RAISE THE ALARM! THE PRISONERS ARE ESCAPING!
TEEHEEHEE!
THIS IS NO TIME FOR FOOLING, OBELIX. WE'VE GOT A LOT OF IMPORTANT THINGS TO DO!
BING!
PIF!
PAF!
STOP, BY MERCURY! MY MASTER THE PREFECT IS COMPLAINING ABOUT THE NOISE. HE ORDERS YOU TO GO AND EXPLAIN WHAT'S HAPPENING!
BING!
PAF!
YOU GAULS DISTURBING ME AGAIN? JUST WHEN I WAS SO NICE AND BORED!
THEY'VE DEMOLISHED A HOUSE, THE PRISON DOOR, AND SEVEN LEGIONARIES!
HIC!
I FIND THAT ALMOST AMUSING. IT'S QUITE GOOD! AS A REWARD I SHALL SET THESE TWO GAULS FREE!
SOON AFTERWARDS...
LONG LIVE VERGETOCETRIGE...
HIC!
23

WE MUST FIND THE DOLMEN WHERE CLOVOGARLIX AND NAVISHTRIX MEET!

IT WON'T BE EASY...

ALCOHOLIX AQUITANIAN WINES

YOU NEVER KNOW. THE LUTETIANS CAN'T HAVE MANY DOLMENS...

POOR THINGS!

WE SHOULD BE ABLE TO GET SOME INFORMATION OVER THERE...

Visit Lutetia
★ Claudius Omnibus, guide
★ ☆

LATIN SPOKEN
CELTIC SPOKEN
Gothic spoken

DO YOU WANT TO SEE OUR BEAUTIFUL CITY?

NO, WE WANT TO SEE SOME DOLMENS!

LUTETIA NIGHTS
Illuminations
Amusements
Gaiety
3 Sestertii

WE HAVEN'T ANY DOLMENS AROUND HERE!

(SIGH) POOR THINGS!

SURELY THERE MUST BE AT LEAST ONE!

LUTETIA NIGHTS
Illuminations
Amusements &
Gaiety
Sestertii

JUST A MINUTE... NOW I COME TO THINK OF IT, I HAVE HEARD OF A DOLMEN IN THE FOREST... THE FOREST OVER WHERE THE SUN SETS...

JUST THE JOB! TAKE US TO THAT FOREST!

**NO!** THERE ARE WOLVES AND BANDITS IN THAT FOREST!

WOULDN'T YOU RATHER SEE A SHOW AT THE FAMOUS MOLA RUBRA? 3 SESTERTII AND AS MUCH BEER AS YOU CAN DRINK!

Omnibus, guide

NO, THANK YOU!

LET'S GO AND FIND THAT FOREST OVER WHERE THE SUN SETS!

ONE SINGLE, SOLITARY DOLMEN... POOR THINGS!

Visit Lutetia

24

84

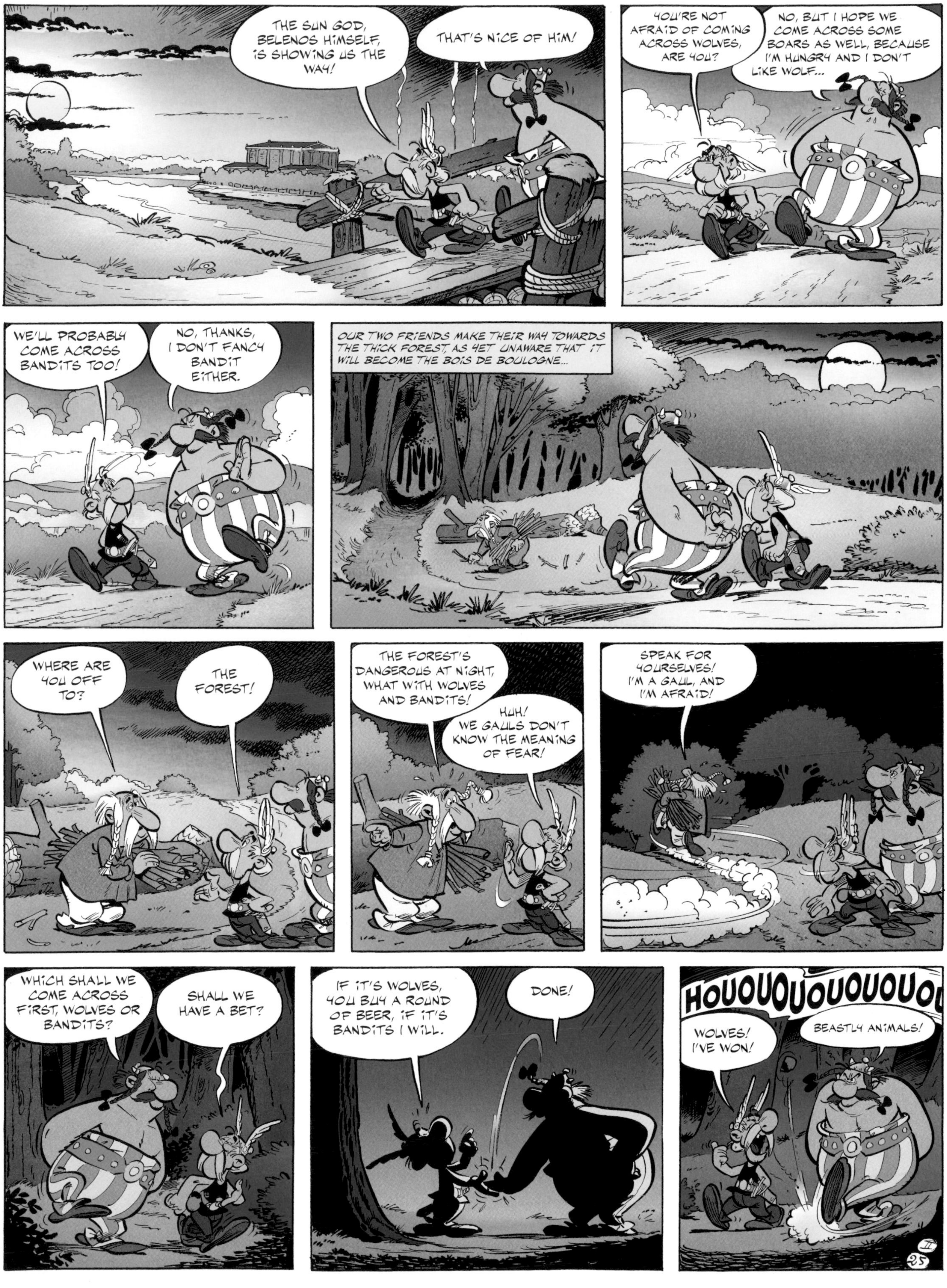
THE SUN GOD, BELENOS HIMSELF, IS SHOWING US THE WAY!
THAT'S NICE OF HIM!
YOU'RE NOT AFRAID OF COMING ACROSS WOLVES, ARE YOU?
NO, BUT I HOPE WE COME ACROSS SOME BOARS AS WELL, BECAUSE I'M HUNGRY AND I DON'T LIKE WOLF...
WE'LL PROBABLY COME ACROSS BANDITS TOO!
NO, THANKS, I DON'T FANCY BANDIT EITHER.
OUR TWO FRIENDS MAKE THEIR WAY TOWARDS THE THICK FOREST, AS YET UNAWARE THAT IT WILL BECOME THE BOIS DE BOULOGNE...
WHERE ARE YOU OFF TO?
THE FOREST!
THE FOREST'S DANGEROUS AT NIGHT, WHAT WITH WOLVES AND BANDITS!
HUH! WE GAULS DON'T KNOW THE MEANING OF FEAR!
SPEAK FOR YOURSELVES! I'M A GAUL, AND I'M AFRAID!
WHICH SHALL WE COME ACROSS FIRST, WOLVES OR BANDITS?
SHALL WE HAVE A BET?
IF IT'S WOLVES, YOU BUY A ROUND OF BEER, IF IT'S BANDITS I WILL.
DONE!
HOUOUOUOUOUOUOU
WOLVES! I'VE WON!
BEASTLY ANIMALS!

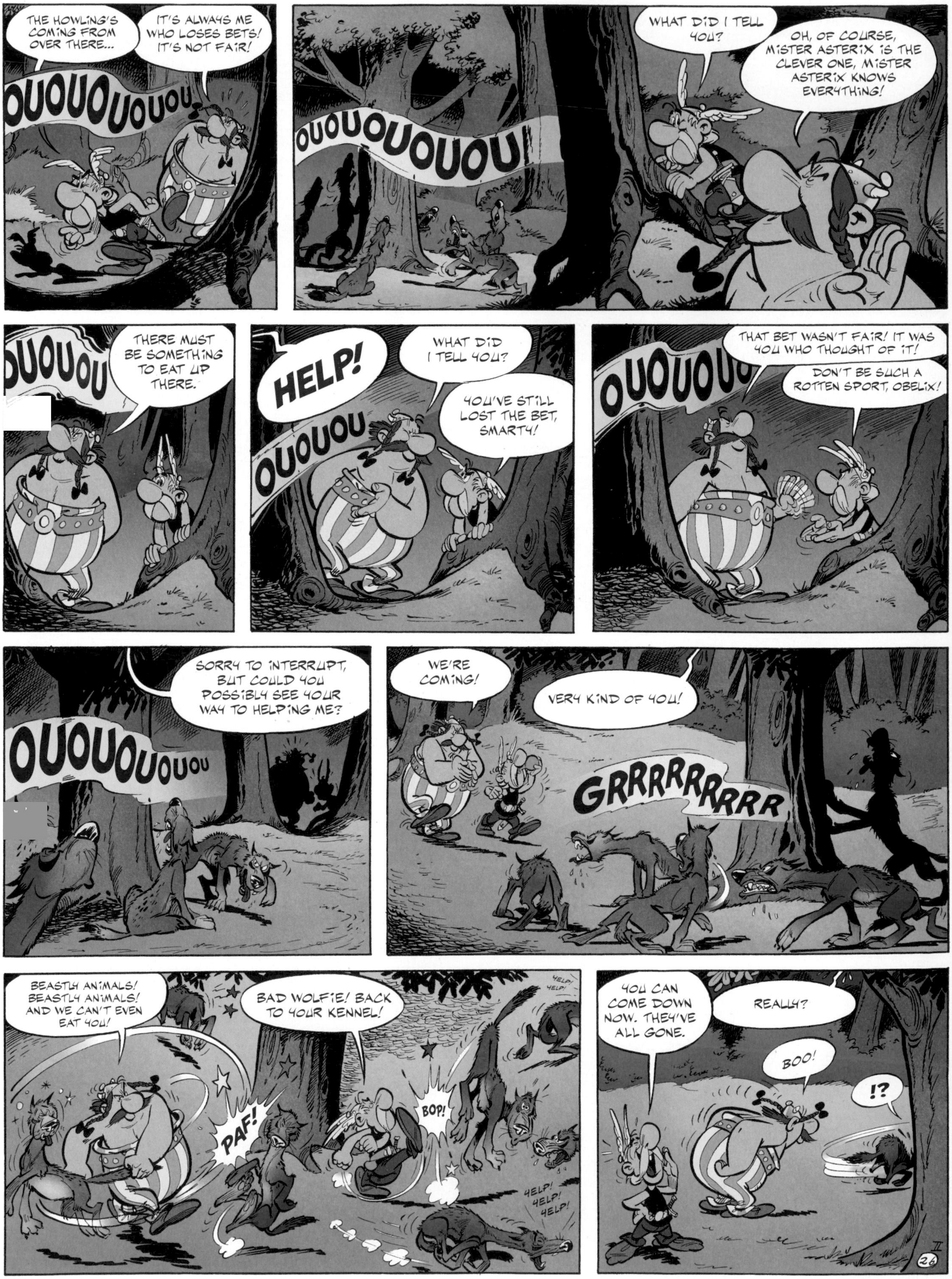
THE HOWLING'S COMING FROM OVER THERE...
IT'S ALWAYS ME WHO LOSES BETS! IT'S NOT FAIR!
OUOUOUOUOU
OUOUOUOUOUOU!
WHAT DID I TELL YOU?
OH, OF COURSE, MISTER ASTERIX IS THE CLEVER ONE, MISTER ASTERIX KNOWS EVERYTHING!
OUOUOU
THERE MUST BE SOMETHING TO EAT UP THERE.
HELP!
OUOUOU
WHAT DID I TELL YOU?
YOU'VE STILL LOST THE BET, SMARTY!
OUOUOU
THAT BET WASN'T FAIR! IT WAS YOU WHO THOUGHT OF IT!
DON'T BE SUCH A ROTTEN SPORT, OBELIX!
OUOUOUOUOU
SORRY TO INTERRUPT, BUT COULD YOU POSSIBLY SEE YOUR WAY TO HELPING ME?
WE'RE COMING!
VERY KIND OF YOU!
GRRRRRRRRR
BEASTLY ANIMALS! BEASTLY ANIMALS! AND WE CAN'T EVEN EAT YOU!
BAD WOLFIE! BACK TO YOUR KENNEL!
HELP! HELP!
PAF!
BOP!
HELP! HELP! HELP!
YOU CAN COME DOWN NOW. THEY'VE ALL GONE.
REALLY?
BOO!
!?

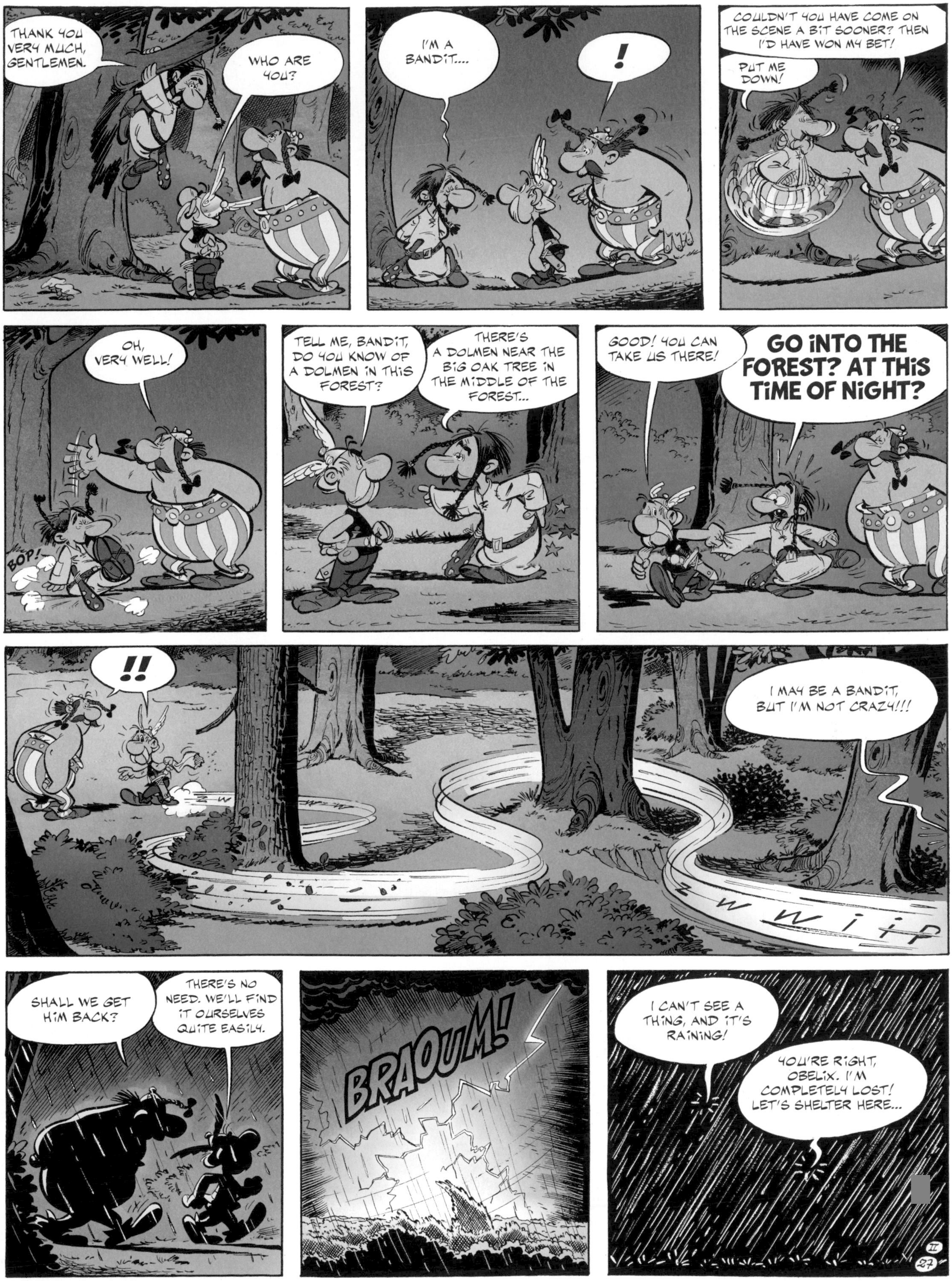
THANK YOU VERY MUCH, GENTLEMEN.
WHO ARE YOU?
I'M A BANDIT....
!
COULDN'T YOU HAVE COME ON THE SCENE A BIT SOONER? THEN I'D HAVE WON MY BET!
PUT ME DOWN!
OH, VERY WELL!
BOP!
TELL ME, BANDIT, DO YOU KNOW OF A DOLMEN IN THIS FOREST?
THERE'S A DOLMEN NEAR THE BIG OAK TREE IN THE MIDDLE OF THE FOREST...
GOOD! YOU CAN TAKE US THERE!
GO INTO THE FOREST? AT THIS TIME OF NIGHT?
!!
ZW
I MAY BE A BANDIT, BUT I'M NOT CRAZY!!!
ZWWIIP
SHALL WE GET HIM BACK?
THERE'S NO NEED. WE'LL FIND IT OURSELVES QUITE EASILY.
BRAOUM!
I CAN'T SEE A THING, AND IT'S RAINING!
YOU'RE RIGHT, OBELIX. I'M COMPLETELY LOST! LET'S SHELTER HERE...

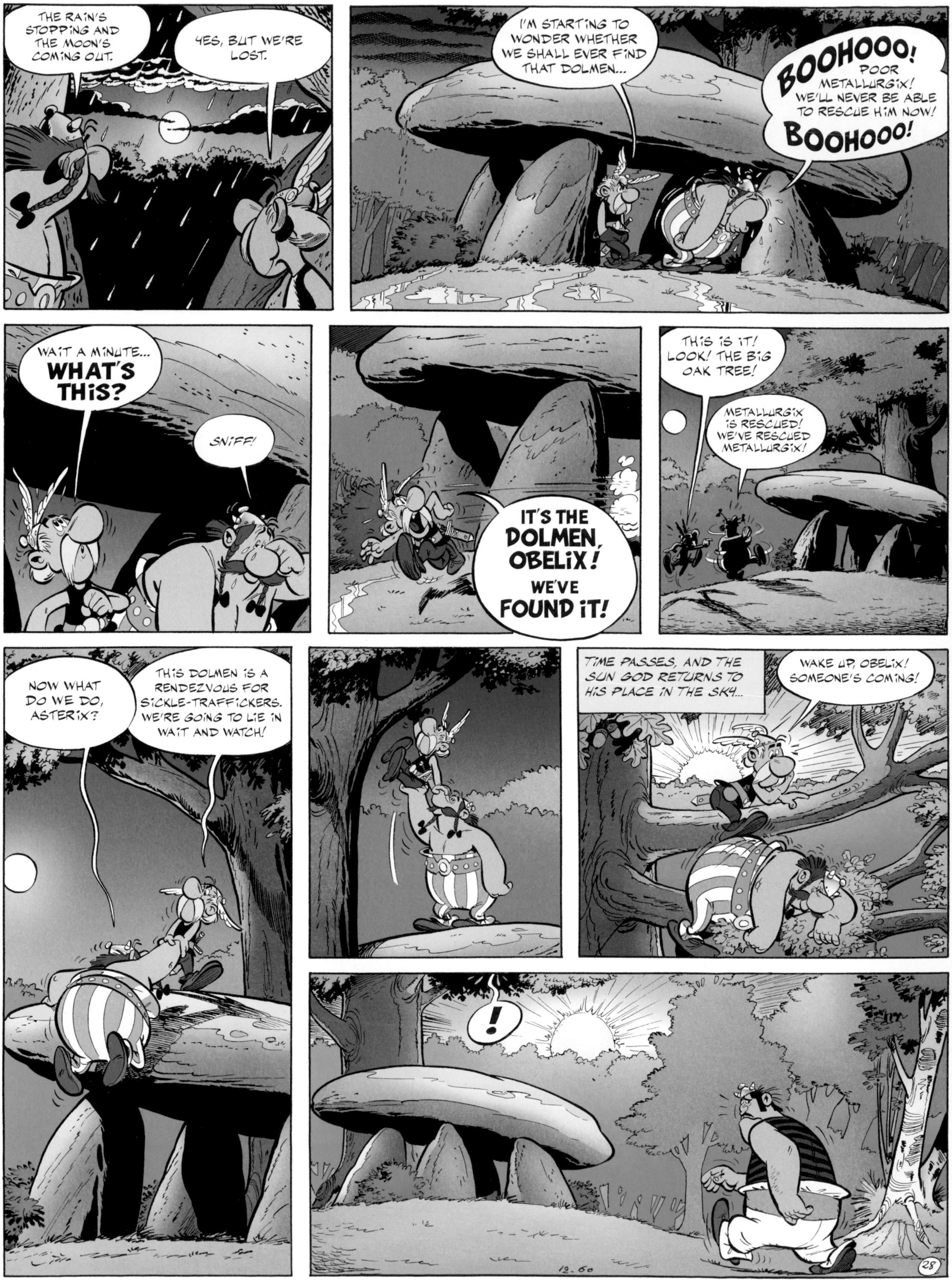

THE RAIN'S STOPPING AND THE MOON'S COMING OUT.
YES, BUT WE'RE LOST.
I'M STARTING TO WONDER WHETHER WE SHALL EVER FIND THAT DOLMEN...
BOOHOOO! POOR METALLURGIX! WE'LL NEVER BE ABLE TO RESCUE HIM NOW! BOOHOOO!
WAIT A MINUTE... WHAT'S THIS?
SNIFF!
IT'S THE DOLMEN, OBELIX! WE'VE FOUND IT!
THIS IS IT! LOOK! THE BIG OAK TREE!
METALLURGIX IS RESCUED! WE'VE RESCUED METALLURGIX!
NOW WHAT DO WE DO, ASTERIX?
THIS DOLMEN IS A RENDEZVOUS FOR SICKLE-TRAFFICKERS. WE'RE GOING TO LIE IN WAIT AND WATCH!
TIME PASSES, AND THE SUN GOD RETURNS TO HIS PLACE IN THE SKY...
WAKE UP, OBELIX! SOMEONE'S COMING!
!

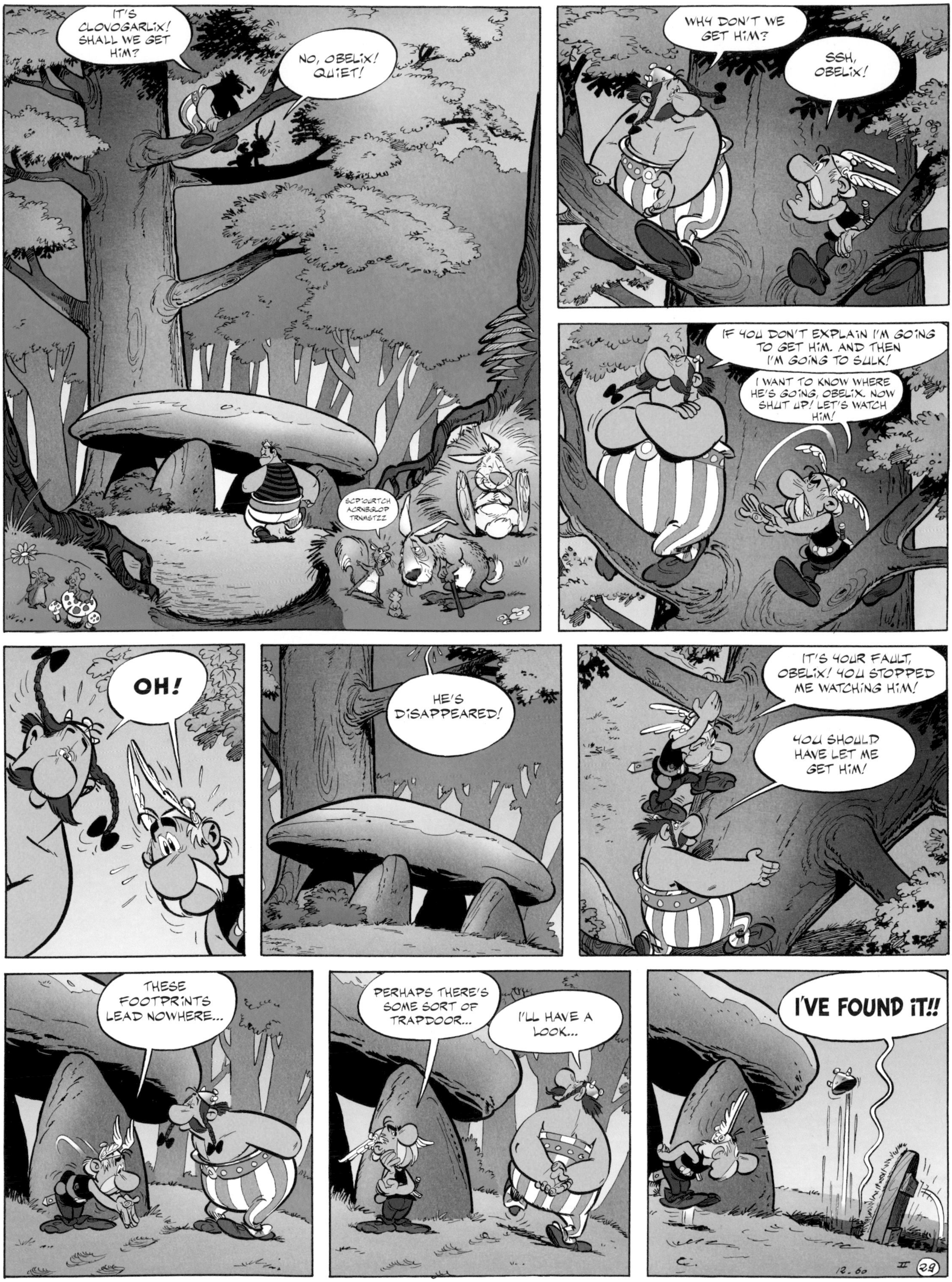
IT'S CLOVOGARLIX! SHALL WE GET HIM?
NO, OBELIX! QUIET!
SCP'IOURTCH ACRNBGLOP TRNMSTZZ
WHY DON'T WE GET HIM?
SSH, OBELIX!
IF YOU DON'T EXPLAIN I'M GOING TO GET HIM. AND THEN I'M GOING TO SULK!
I WANT TO KNOW WHERE HE'S GOING, OBELIX. NOW SHUT UP! LET'S WATCH HIM!
OH!
HE'S DISAPPEARED!
IT'S YOUR FAULT, OBELIX! YOU STOPPED ME WATCHING HIM!
YOU SHOULD HAVE LET ME GET HIM!
THESE FOOTPRINTS LEAD NOWHERE...
PERHAPS THERE'S SOME SORT OF TRAPDOOR...
I'LL HAVE A LOOK...
I'VE FOUND IT!!
12.60
II 29

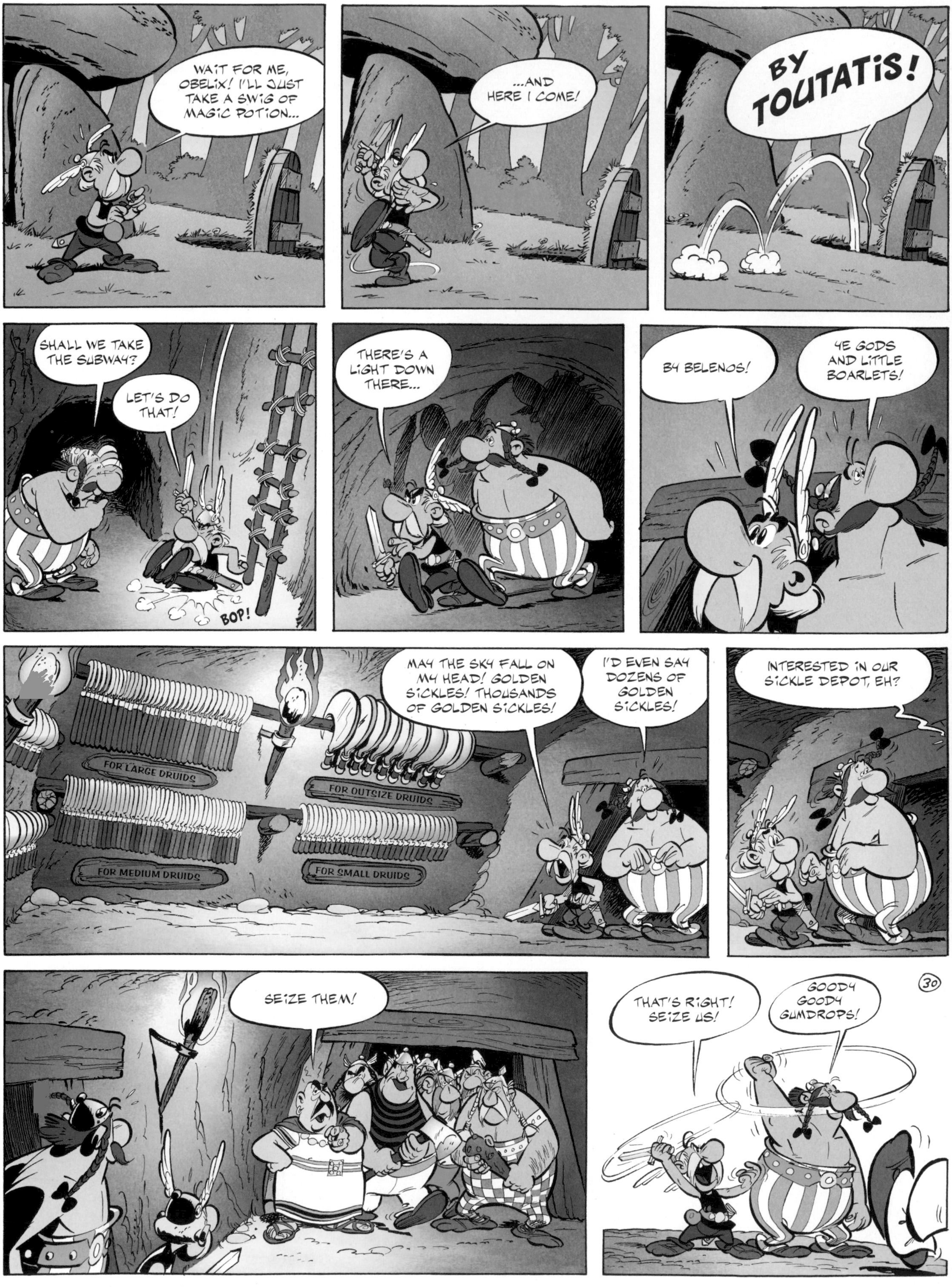
WAIT FOR ME, OBELIX! I'LL JUST TAKE A SWIG OF MAGIC POTION...
...AND HERE I COME!
BY TOUTATIS!
SHALL WE TAKE THE SUBWAY?
LET'S DO THAT!
BOP!
THERE'S A LIGHT DOWN THERE...
BY BELENOS!
YE GODS AND LITTLE BOARLETS!
FOR LARGE DRUIDS
FOR OUTSIZE DRUIDS
FOR MEDIUM DRUIDS
FOR SMALL DRUIDS
MAY THE SKY FALL ON MY HEAD! GOLDEN SICKLES! THOUSANDS OF GOLDEN SICKLES!
I'D EVEN SAY DOZENS OF GOLDEN SICKLES!
INTERESTED IN OUR SICKLE DEPOT, EH?
SEIZE THEM!
THAT'S RIGHT! SEIZE US!
GOODY GOODY GUMDROPS!
30

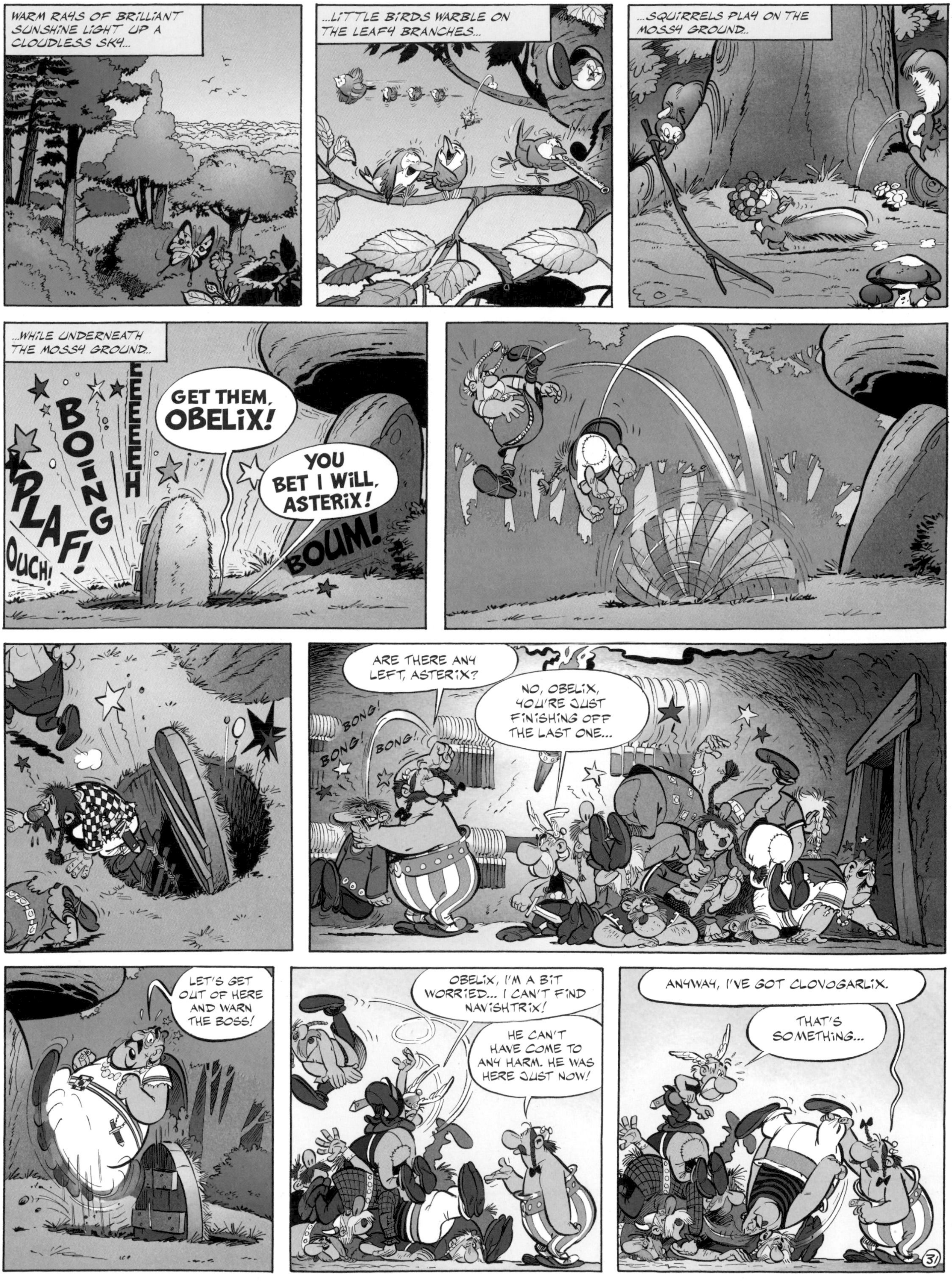
WARM RAYS OF BRILLIANT SUNSHINE LIGHT UP A CLOUDLESS SKY...
...LITTLE BIRDS WARBLE ON THE LEAFY BRANCHES...
...SQUIRRELS PLAY ON THE MOSSY GROUND...
...WHILE UNDERNEATH THE MOSSY GROUND...
EEEEEEH
BOiNG
PLAF!
OUCH!
GET THEM, OBELiX!
YOU BET I WiLL, ASTERiX!
BOUM!
ARE THERE ANY LEFT, ASTERIX?
BONG!
BONG!
BONG!
NO, OBELIX, YOU'RE JUST FINISHING OFF THE LAST ONE...
LET'S GET OUT OF HERE AND WARN THE BOSS!
OBELIX, I'M A BIT WORRIED... I CAN'T FIND NAVISHTRIX!
HE CAN'T HAVE COME TO ANY HARM. HE WAS HERE JUST NOW!
ANYWAY, I'VE GOT CLOVOGARLIX.
THAT'S SOMETHING...
31

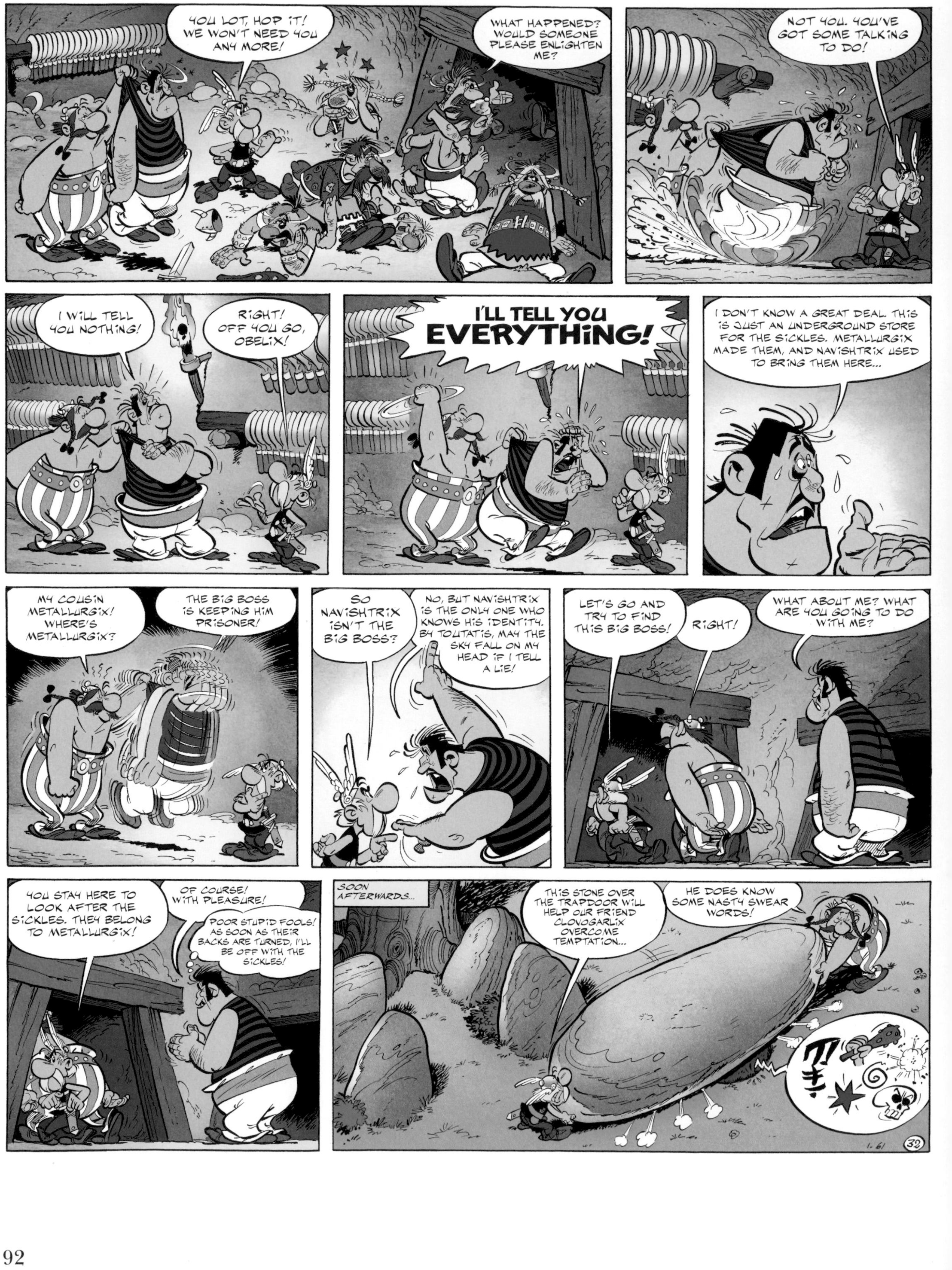
YOU LOT, HOP IT! WE WON'T NEED YOU ANY MORE!
WHAT HAPPENED? WOULD SOMEONE PLEASE ENLIGHTEN ME?
NOT YOU. YOU'VE GOT SOME TALKING TO DO!
I WILL TELL YOU NOTHING!
RIGHT! OFF YOU GO, OBELIX!
I'LL TELL YOU EVERYTHING!
I DON'T KNOW A GREAT DEAL. THIS IS JUST AN UNDERGROUND STORE FOR THE SICKLES. METALLURGIX MADE THEM, AND NAVISHTRIX USED TO BRING THEM HERE...
MY COUSIN METALLURGIX! WHERE'S METALLURGIX?
THE BIG BOSS IS KEEPING HIM PRISONER!
SO NAVISHTRIX ISN'T THE BIG BOSS?
NO, BUT NAVISHTRIX IS THE ONLY ONE WHO KNOWS HIS IDENTITY. BY TOUTATIS, MAY THE SKY FALL ON MY HEAD IF I TELL A LIE!
LET'S GO AND TRY TO FIND THIS BIG BOSS!
RIGHT!
WHAT ABOUT ME? WHAT ARE YOU GOING TO DO WITH ME?
YOU STAY HERE TO LOOK AFTER THE SICKLES. THEY BELONG TO METALLURGIX!
OF COURSE! WITH PLEASURE!
POOR STUPID FOOLS! AS SOON AS THEIR BACKS ARE TURNED, I'LL BE OFF WITH THE SICKLES!
SOON AFTERWARDS...
THIS STONE OVER THE TRAPDOOR WILL HELP OUR FRIEND CLOVOGARLIX OVERCOME TEMPTATION...
HE DOES KNOW SOME NASTY SWEAR WORDS!

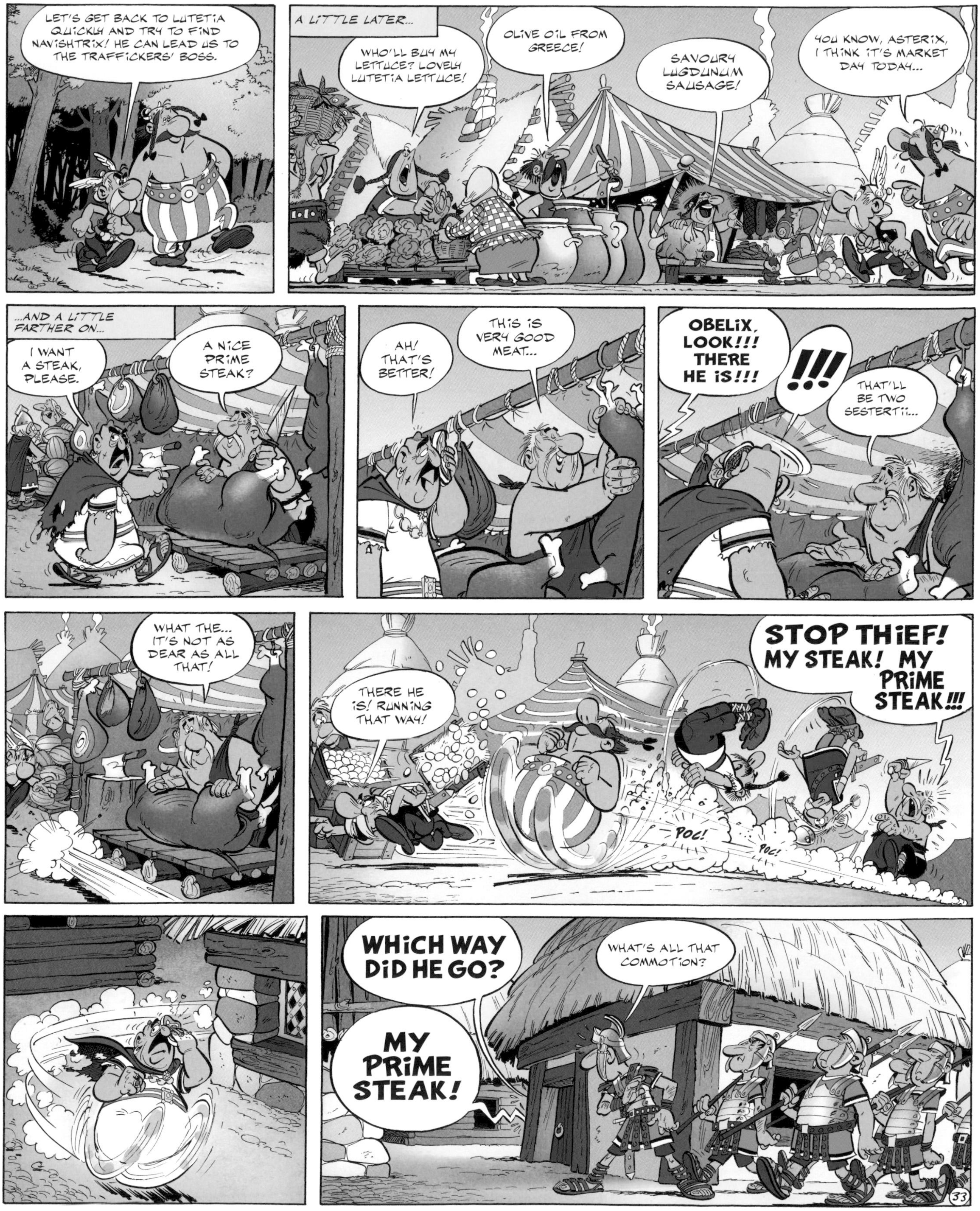

LET'S GET BACK TO LUTETIA QUICKLY AND TRY TO FIND NAVISHTRIX! HE CAN LEAD US TO THE TRAFFICKERS' BOSS.
A LITTLE LATER...
WHO'LL BUY MY LETTUCE? LOVELY LUTETIA LETTUCE!
OLIVE OIL FROM GREECE!
SAVOURY LUGDUNUM SAUSAGE!
YOU KNOW, ASTERIX, I THINK IT'S MARKET DAY TODAY...
...AND A LITTLE FARTHER ON...
I WANT A STEAK, PLEASE.
A NICE PRIME STEAK?
AH! THAT'S BETTER!
THIS IS VERY GOOD MEAT...
OBELIX, LOOK!!! THERE HE IS!!!
!!!
THAT'LL BE TWO SESTERTII...
WHAT THE... IT'S NOT AS DEAR AS ALL THAT!
THERE HE IS! RUNNING THAT WAY!
STOP THIEF! MY STEAK! MY PRIME STEAK!!!
POC!
POC!
WHICH WAY DID HE GO?
MY PRIME STEAK!
WHAT'S ALL THAT COMMOTION?
33

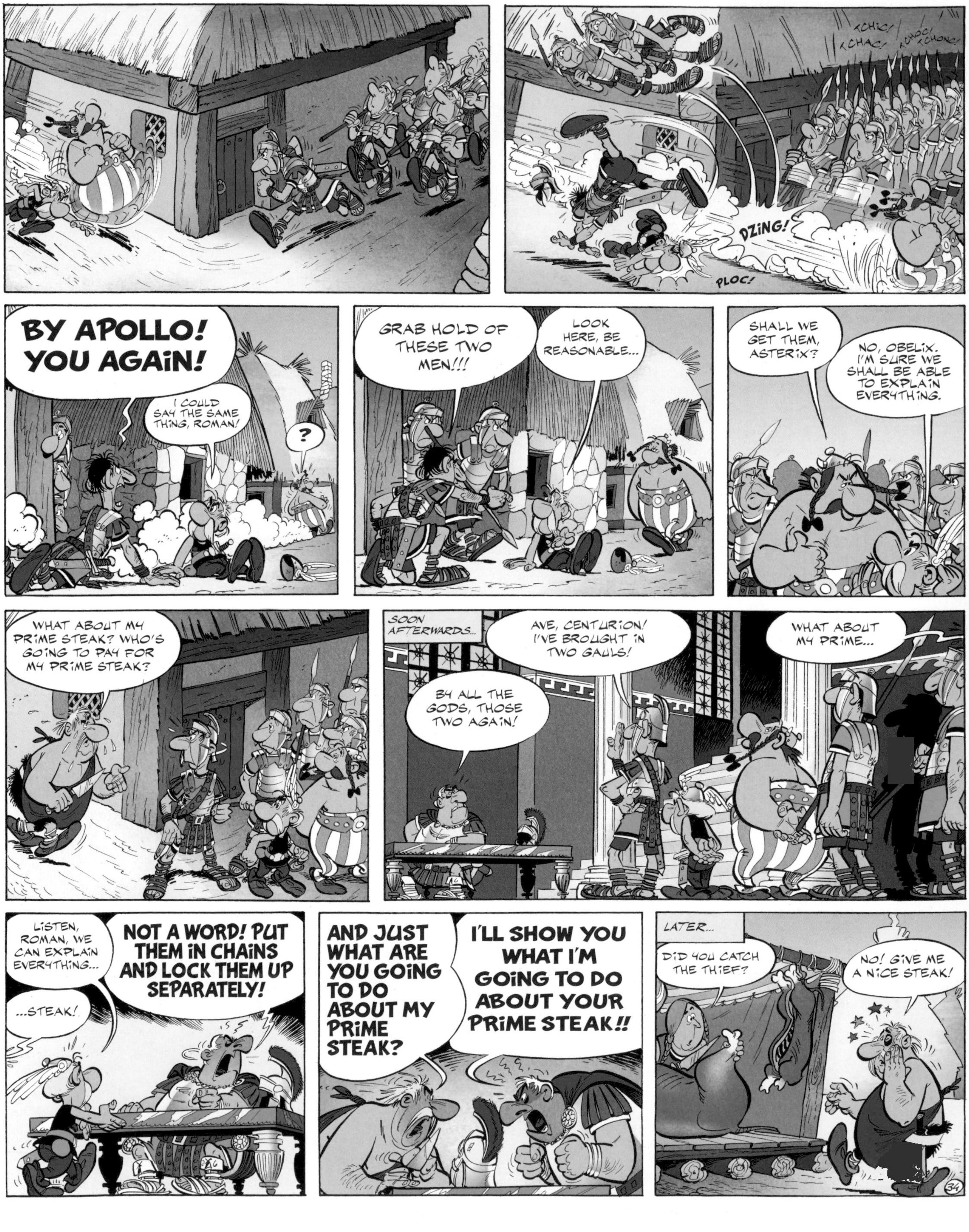

TCHIC!
TCHAC!
TCHOC!
TCHONC!
DZING!
PLOC!
BY APOLLO! YOU AGAIN!
I COULD SAY THE SAME THING, ROMAN!
?
GRAB HOLD OF THESE TWO MEN!!!
LOOK HERE, BE REASONABLE...
SHALL WE GET THEM, ASTERIX?
NO, OBELIX. I'M SURE WE SHALL BE ABLE TO EXPLAIN EVERYTHING.
WHAT ABOUT MY PRIME STEAK? WHO'S GOING TO PAY FOR MY PRIME STEAK?
SOON AFTERWARDS...
AVE, CENTURION! I'VE BROUGHT IN TWO GAULS!
BY ALL THE GODS, THOSE TWO AGAIN!
WHAT ABOUT MY PRIME...
LISTEN, ROMAN, WE CAN EXPLAIN EVERYTHING...
NOT A WORD! PUT THEM IN CHAINS AND LOCK THEM UP SEPARATELY!
...STEAK!
AND JUST WHAT ARE YOU GOING TO DO ABOUT MY PRIME STEAK?
I'LL SHOW YOU WHAT I'M GOING TO DO ABOUT YOUR PRIME STEAK!!
LATER...
DID YOU CATCH THE THIEF?
NO! GIVE ME A NICE STEAK!
34

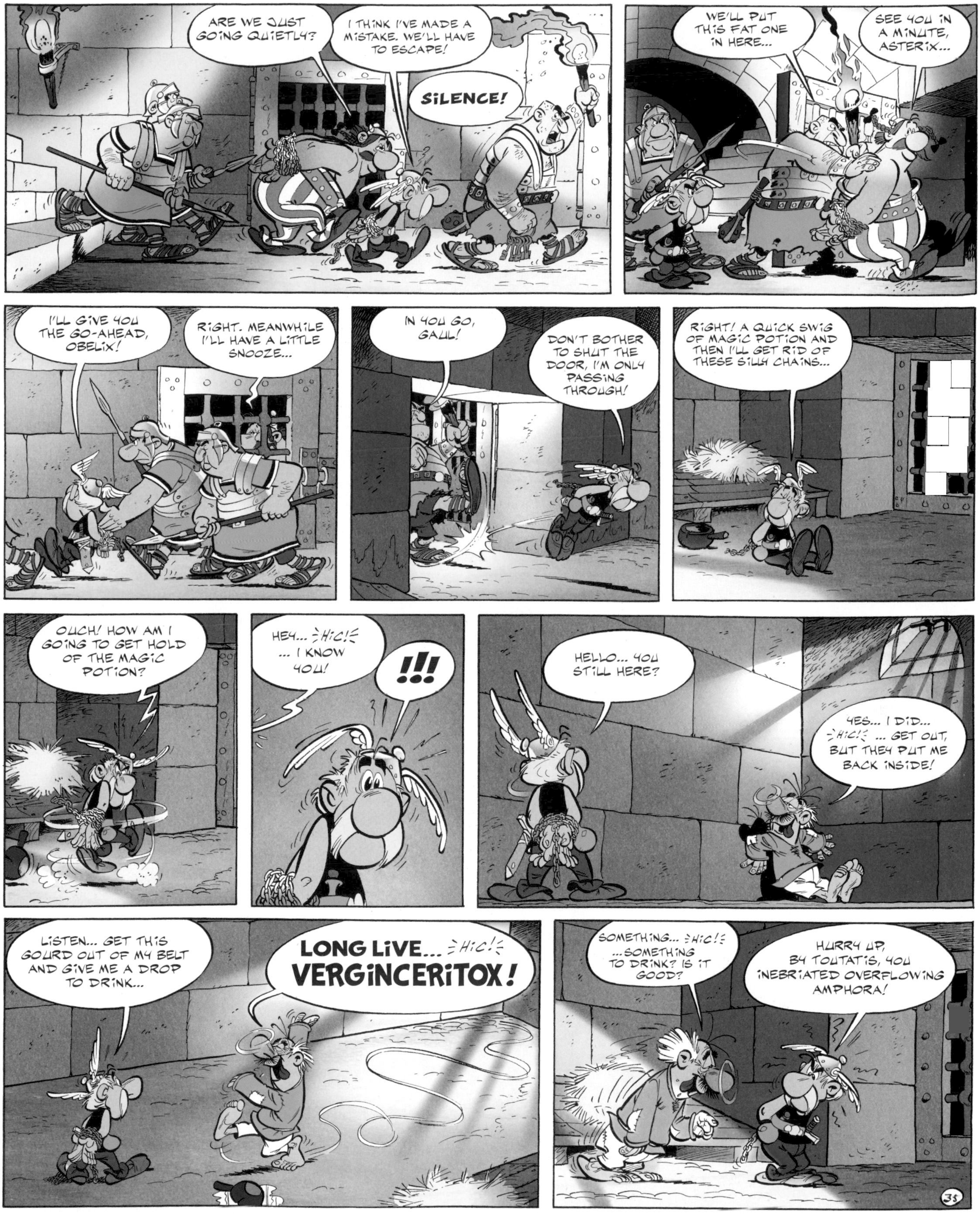
ARE WE JUST GOING QUIETLY?
I THINK I'VE MADE A MISTAKE. WE'LL HAVE TO ESCAPE!
SILENCE!
WE'LL PUT THIS FAT ONE IN HERE...
SEE YOU IN A MINUTE, ASTERIX...
I'LL GIVE YOU THE GO-AHEAD, OBELIX!
RIGHT. MEANWHILE I'LL HAVE A LITTLE SNOOZE...
IN YOU GO, GAUL!
DON'T BOTHER TO SHUT THE DOOR, I'M ONLY PASSING THROUGH!
RIGHT! A QUICK SWIG OF MAGIC POTION AND THEN I'LL GET RID OF THESE SILLY CHAINS...
OUCH! HOW AM I GOING TO GET HOLD OF THE MAGIC POTION?
HEY... HIC! ... I KNOW YOU!
!!!
HELLO... YOU STILL HERE?
YES... I DID... HIC! ... GET OUT, BUT THEY PUT ME BACK INSIDE!
LISTEN... GET THIS GOURD OUT OF MY BELT AND GIVE ME A DROP TO DRINK...
LONG LIVE... HIC! VERGINCERITOX!
SOMETHING... HIC! ...SOMETHING TO DRINK? IS IT GOOD?
HURRY UP, BY TOUTATIS, YOU INEBRIATED OVERFLOWING AMPHORA!
35

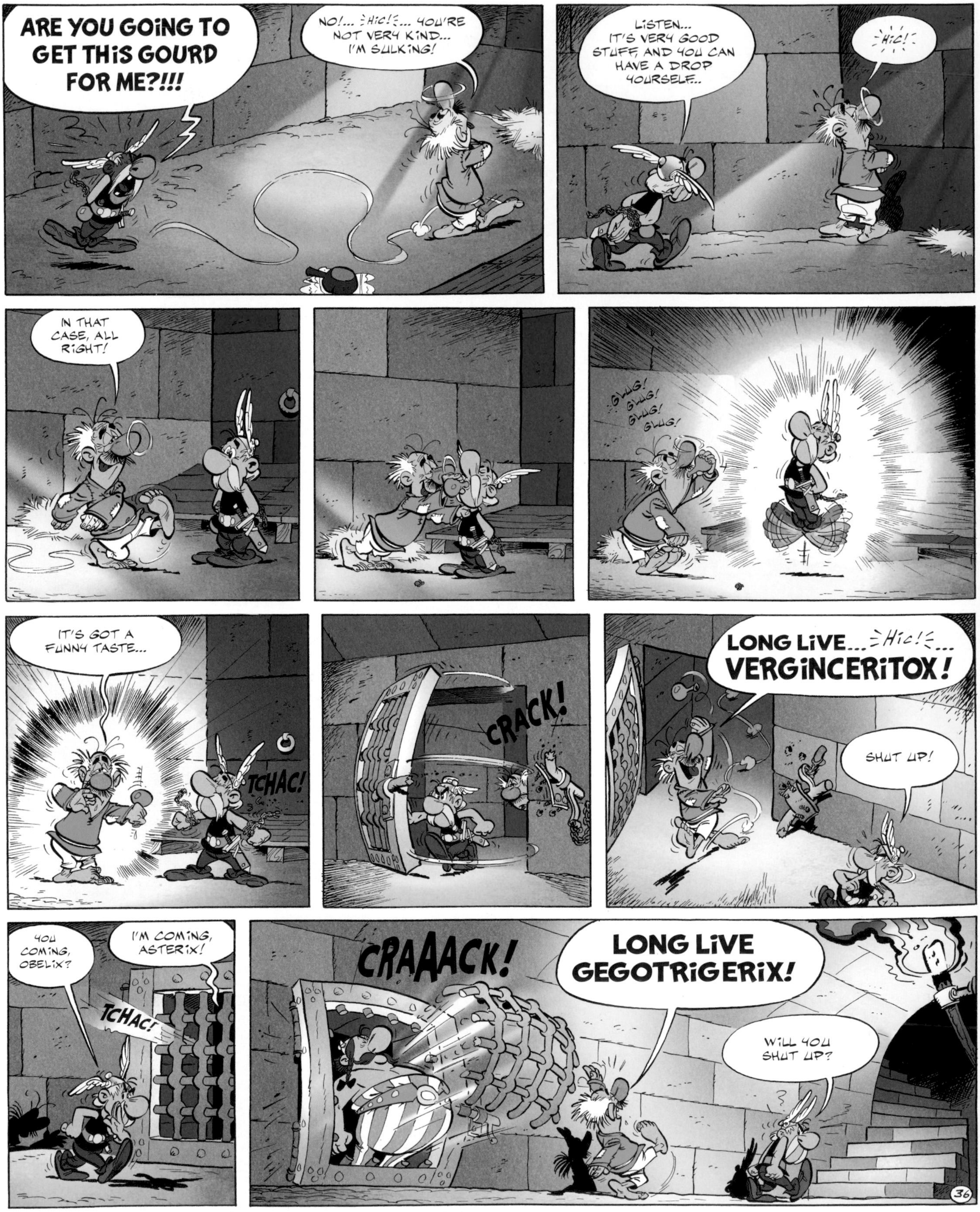
ARE YOU GOING TO GET THIS GOURD FOR ME?!!!
NO!... HIC!... YOU'RE NOT VERY KIND... I'M SULKING!
LISTEN... IT'S VERY GOOD STUFF, AND YOU CAN HAVE A DROP YOURSELF...
HIC!
IN THAT CASE, ALL RIGHT!
GLUG! GLUG! GLUG! GLUG!
IT'S GOT A FUNNY TASTE...
TCHAC!
CRACK!
LONG LIVE... HIC!... VERGINCERITOX!
SHUT UP!
YOU COMING, OBELIX?
I'M COMING, ASTERIX!
TCHAC!
CRAAACK!
LONG LIVE GEGOTRIGERIX!
WILL YOU SHUT UP?
36

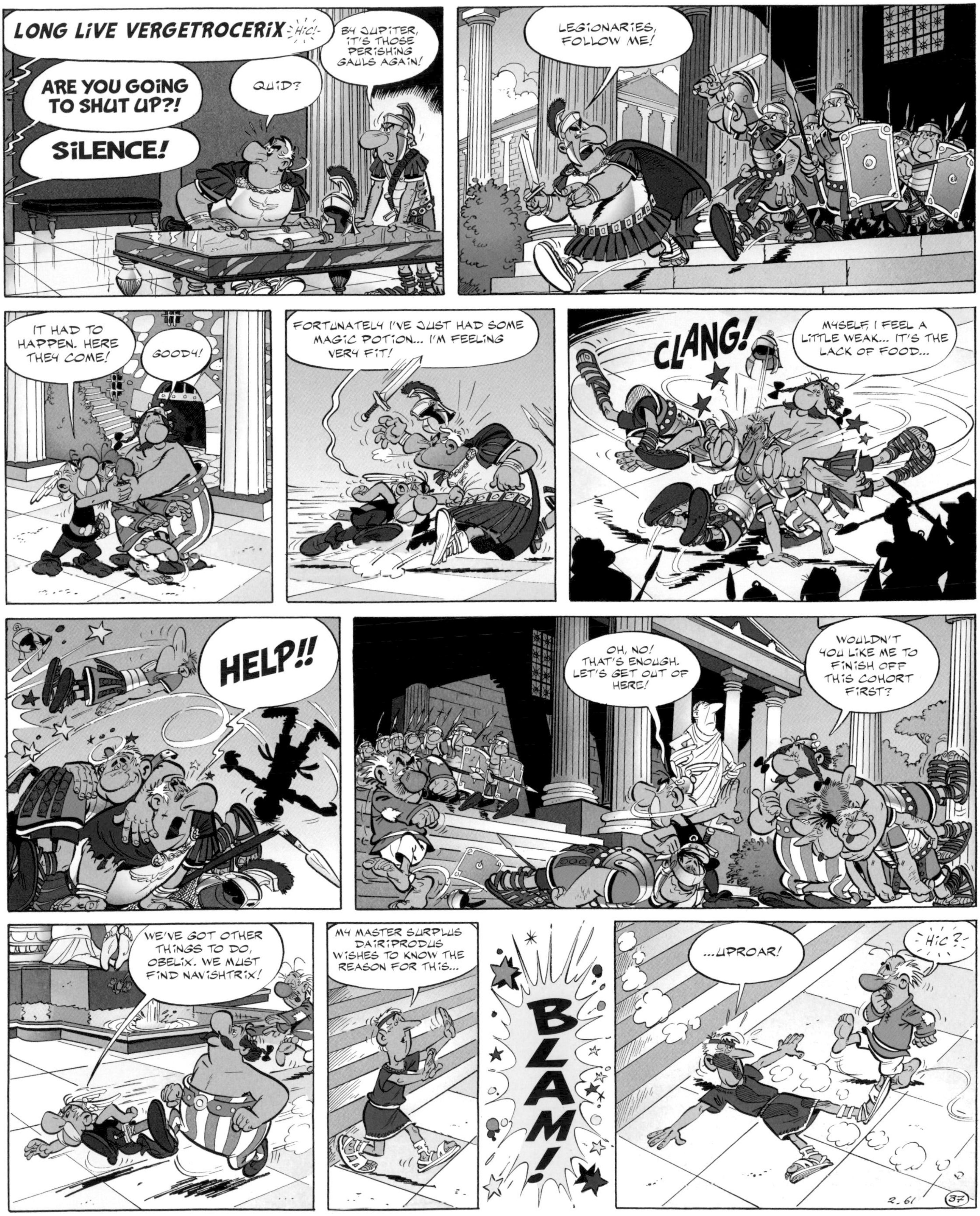
LONG LIVE VERGETROCERIX
HIC!
BY JUPITER, IT'S THOSE PERISHING GAULS AGAIN!
ARE YOU GOING TO SHUT UP?!
QUID?
SILENCE!
LEGIONARIES, FOLLOW ME!
IT HAD TO HAPPEN. HERE THEY COME!
GOODY!
FORTUNATELY I'VE JUST HAD SOME MAGIC POTION... I'M FEELING VERY FIT!
CLANG!
MYSELF, I FEEL A LITTLE WEAK... IT'S THE LACK OF FOOD...
HELP!!
OH, NO! THAT'S ENOUGH. LET'S GET OUT OF HERE!
WOULDN'T YOU LIKE ME TO FINISH OFF THIS COHORT FIRST?
WE'VE GOT OTHER THINGS TO DO, OBELIX. WE MUST FIND NAVISHTRIX!
MY MASTER SURPLUS DAIRIPRODUS WISHES TO KNOW THE REASON FOR THIS...
BLAM!
...UPROAR!
HIC?
2.61
37

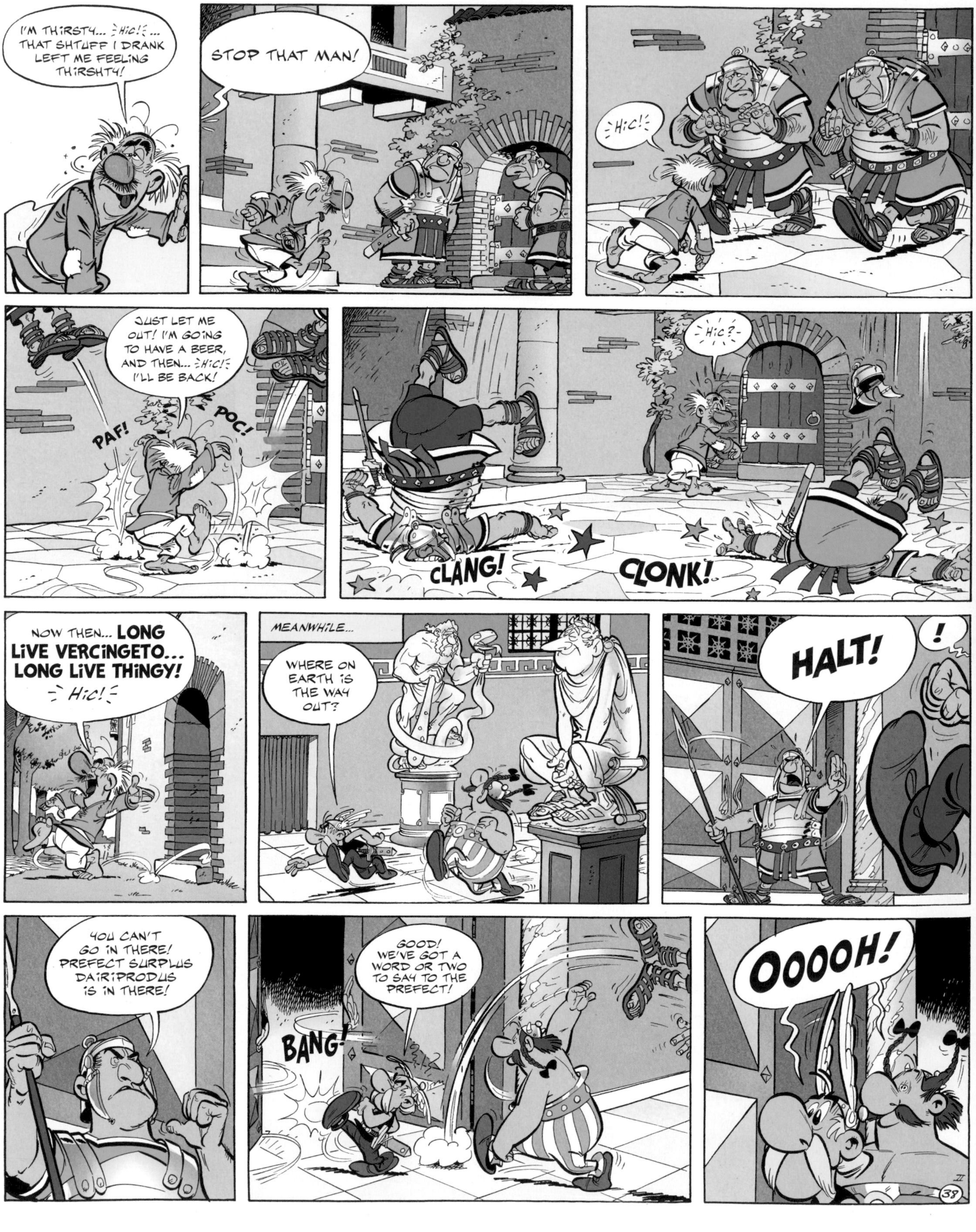
I'M THIRSTY... HIC! ... THAT SHTUFF I DRANK LEFT ME FEELING THIRSHTY!
STOP THAT MAN!
HIC!
JUST LET ME OUT! I'M GOING TO HAVE A BEER, AND THEN... HIC! I'LL BE BACK!
PAF!
POC!
HIC?
CLANG!
CLONK!
NOW THEN... LONG LIVE VERCINGETO... LONG LIVE THINGY!
HIC!
MEANWHILE...
WHERE ON EARTH IS THE WAY OUT?
HALT!
!
YOU CAN'T GO IN THERE! PREFECT SURPLUS DAIRIPRODUS IS IN THERE!
GOOD! WE'VE GOT A WORD OR TWO TO SAY TO THE PREFECT!
BANG!
OOOOH!
38

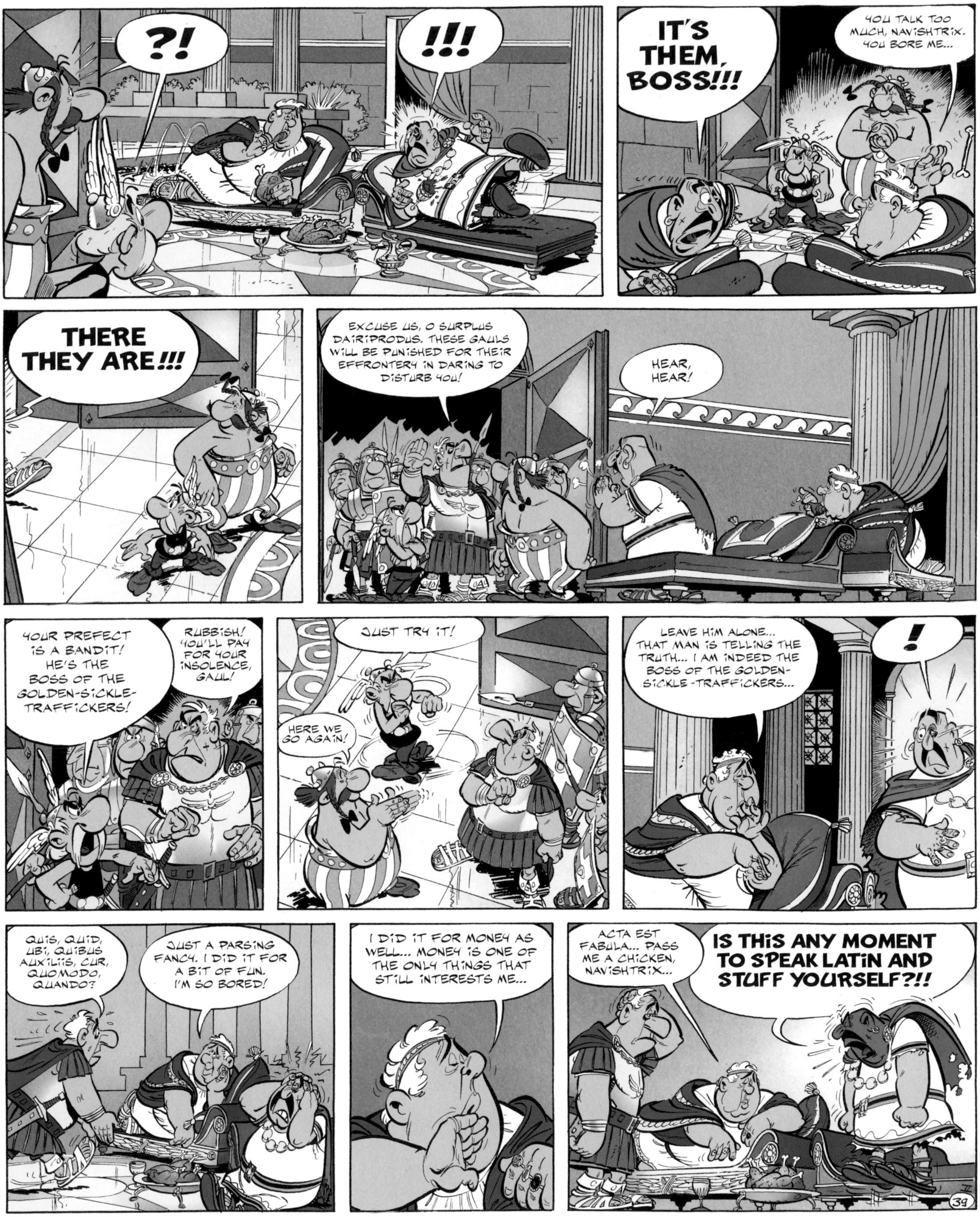
?!
!!!
IT'S THEM, BOSS!!!
YOU TALK TOO MUCH, NAVISHTRIX. YOU BORE ME...
THERE THEY ARE!!!
EXCUSE US, O SURPLUS DAIRIPRODUS. THESE GAULS WILL BE PUNISHED FOR THEIR EFFRONTERY IN DARING TO DISTURB YOU!
HEAR, HEAR!
YOUR PREFECT IS A BANDIT! HE'S THE BOSS OF THE GOLDEN-SICKLE-TRAFFICKERS!
RUBBISH! YOU'LL PAY FOR YOUR INSOLENCE, GAUL!
JUST TRY IT!
HERE WE GO AGAIN!
LEAVE HIM ALONE... THAT MAN IS TELLING THE TRUTH... I AM INDEED THE BOSS OF THE GOLDEN-SICKLE-TRAFFICKERS...
!
QUIS, QUID, UBI, QUIBUS AUXILIIS, CUR, QUOMODO, QUANDO?
JUST A PARSING FANCY. I DID IT FOR A BIT OF FUN. I'M SO BORED!
I DID IT FOR MONEY AS WELL... MONEY IS ONE OF THE ONLY THINGS THAT STILL INTERESTS ME...
ACTA EST FABULA... PASS ME A CHICKEN, NAVISHTRIX...
IS THIS ANY MOMENT TO SPEAK LATIN AND STUFF YOURSELF?!!
39

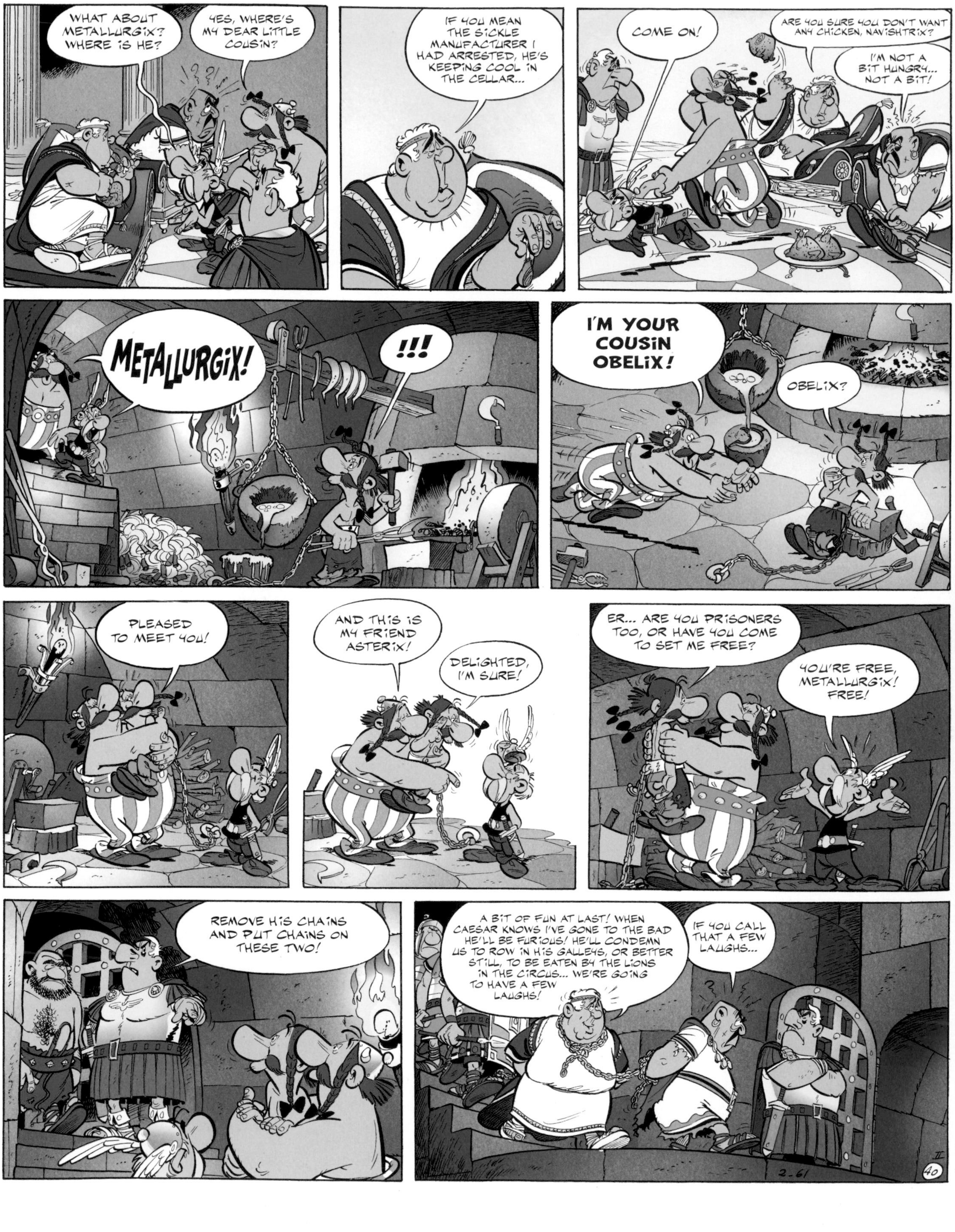
WHAT ABOUT METALLURGIX? WHERE IS HE?
YES, WHERE'S MY DEAR LITTLE COUSIN?
IF YOU MEAN THE SICKLE MANUFACTURER I HAD ARRESTED, HE'S KEEPING COOL IN THE CELLAR...
COME ON!
ARE YOU SURE YOU DON'T WANT ANY CHICKEN, NAVISHTRIX?
I'M NOT A BIT HUNGRY... NOT A BIT!
METALLURGIX!
!!!
I'M YOUR COUSIN OBELIX!
OBELIX?
PLEASED TO MEET YOU!
AND THIS IS MY FRIEND ASTERIX!
DELIGHTED, I'M SURE!
ER... ARE YOU PRISONERS TOO, OR HAVE YOU COME TO SET ME FREE?
YOU'RE FREE, METALLURGIX! FREE!
REMOVE HIS CHAINS AND PUT CHAINS ON THESE TWO!
A BIT OF FUN AT LAST! WHEN CAESAR KNOWS I'VE GONE TO THE BAD HE'LL BE FURIOUS! HE'LL CONDEMN US TO ROW IN HIS GALLEYS, OR BETTER STILL, TO BE EATEN BY THE LIONS IN THE CIRCUS... WE'RE GOING TO HAVE A FEW LAUGHS!
IF YOU CALL THAT A FEW LAUGHS...

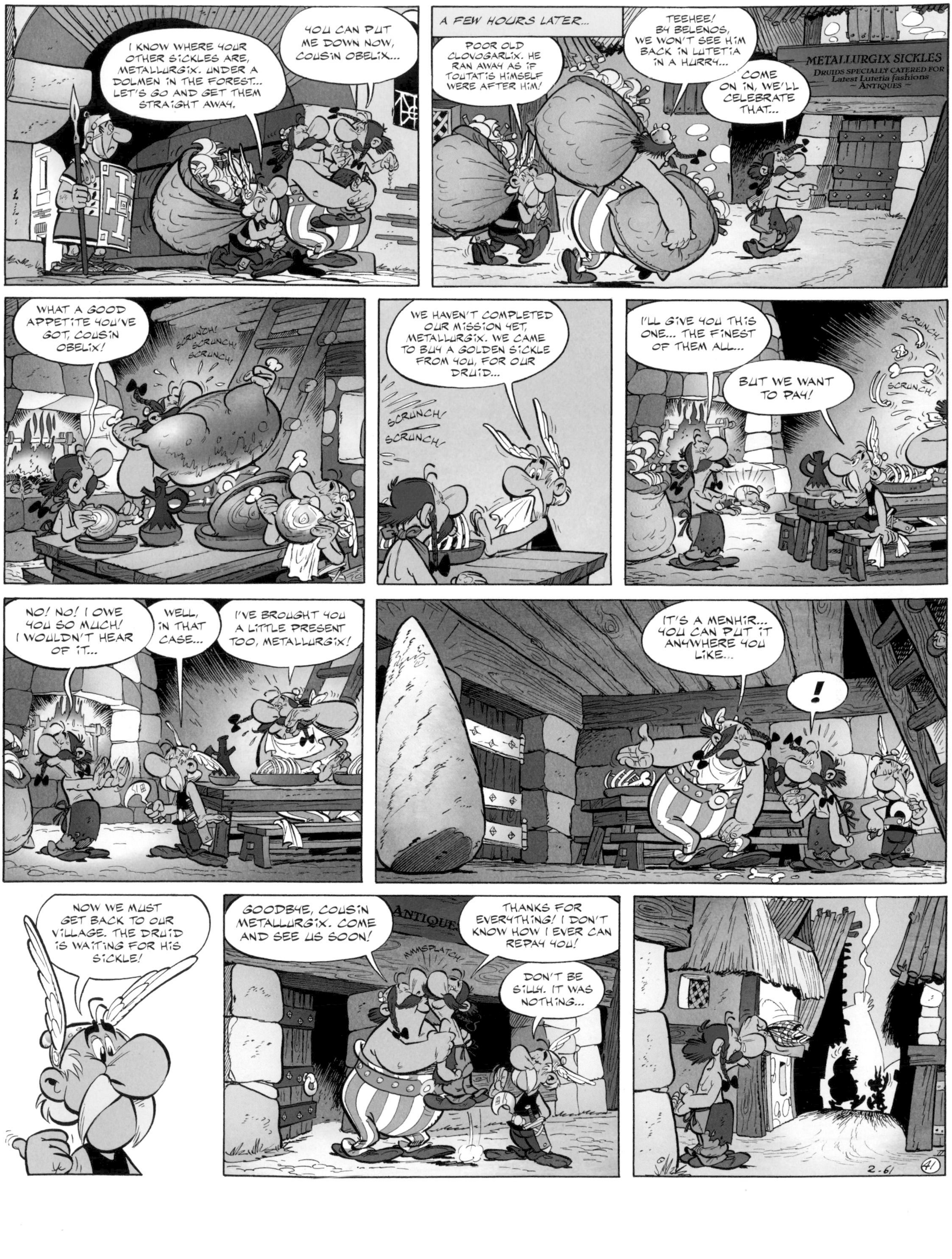
I KNOW WHERE YOUR OTHER SICKLES ARE, METALLURGIX. UNDER A DOLMEN IN THE FOREST... LET'S GO AND GET THEM STRAIGHT AWAY.
YOU CAN PUT ME DOWN NOW, COUSIN OBELIX...
A FEW HOURS LATER...
POOR OLD CLOVOGARLIX. HE RAN AWAY AS IF TOUTATIS HIMSELF WERE AFTER HIM!
TEEHEE! BY BELENOS, WE WON'T SEE HIM BACK IN LUTETIA IN A HURRY...
METALLURGIX SICKLES
DRUIDS SPECIALLY CATERED FOR
Latest Lutetia fashions
~ ANTIQUES ~
COME ON IN, WE'LL CELEBRATE THAT...
WHAT A GOOD APPETITE YOU'VE GOT, COUSIN OBELIX!
SCRUNCH! SCRUNCH! SCRUNCH!
WE HAVEN'T COMPLETED OUR MISSION YET, METALLURGIX. WE CAME TO BUY A GOLDEN SICKLE FROM YOU, FOR OUR DRUID...
SCRUNCH! SCRUNCH!
I'LL GIVE YOU THIS ONE... THE FINEST OF THEM ALL...
BUT WE WANT TO PAY!
SCRUNCH! SCRUNCH!
NO! NO! I OWE YOU SO MUCH! I WOULDN'T HEAR OF IT...
WELL, IN THAT CASE...
I'VE BROUGHT YOU A LITTLE PRESENT TOO, METALLURGIX!
IT'S A MENHIR... YOU CAN PUT IT ANYWHERE YOU LIKE...
!
NOW WE MUST GET BACK TO OUR VILLAGE. THE DRUID IS WAITING FOR HIS SICKLE!
GOODBYE, COUSIN METALLURGIX. COME AND SEE US SOON!
ANTIQUE
MMMSPLATCH!
THANKS FOR EVERYTHING! I DON'T KNOW HOW I EVER CAN REPAY YOU!
DON'T BE SILLY. IT WAS NOTHING...
2.61
41

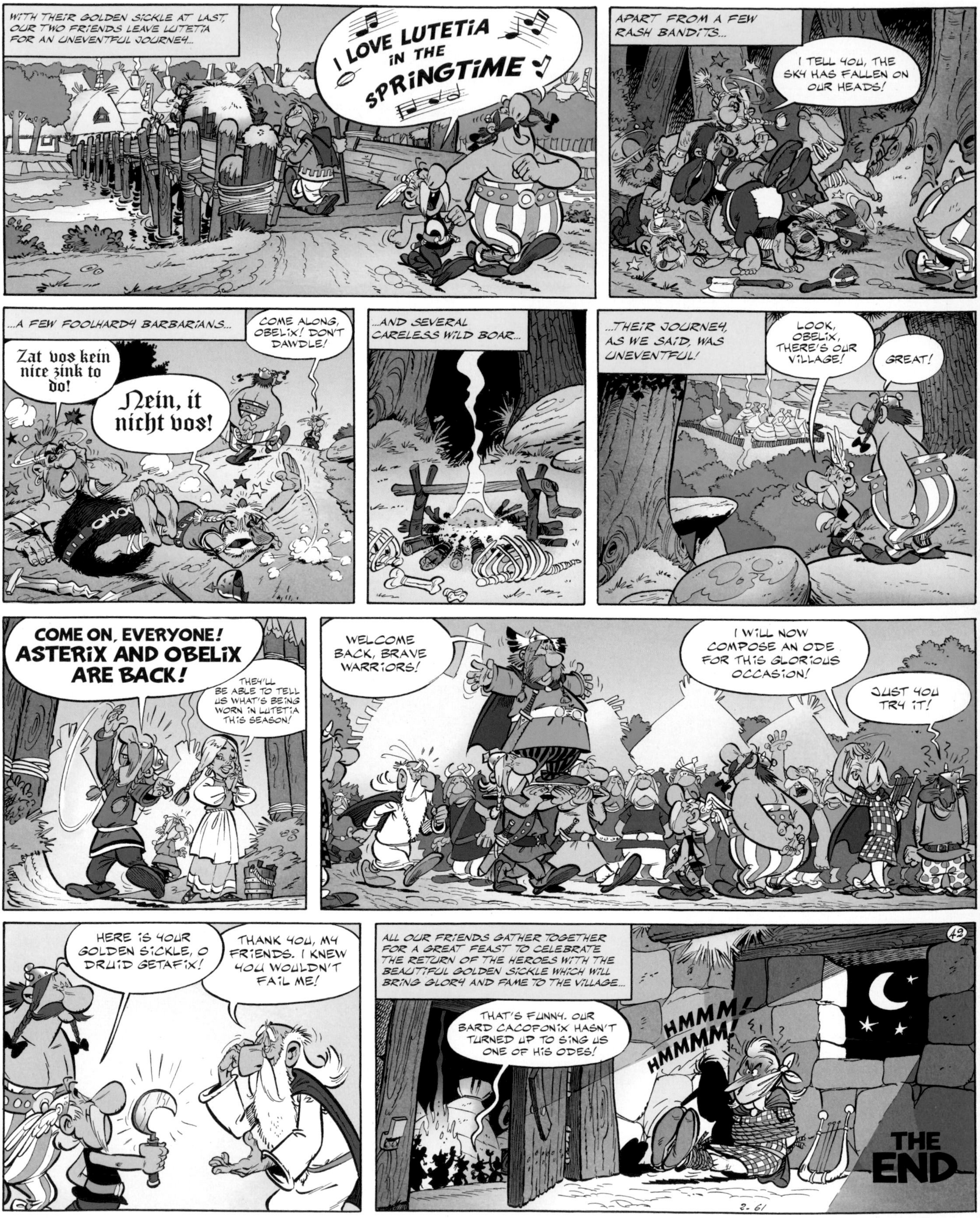

WITH THEIR GOLDEN SICKLE AT LAST, OUR TWO FRIENDS LEAVE LUTETIA FOR AN UNEVENTFUL JOURNEY...
I LOVE LUTETIA IN THE SPRINGTIME
APART FROM A FEW RASH BANDITS...
I TELL YOU, THE SKY HAS FALLEN ON OUR HEADS!
...A FEW FOOLHARDY BARBARIANS...
COME ALONG, OBELIX! DON'T DAWDLE!
Zat vos kein nice zink to do!
Nein, it nicht vos!
...AND SEVERAL CARELESS WILD BOAR...
...THEIR JOURNEY, AS WE SAID, WAS UNEVENTFUL!
LOOK, OBELIX, THERE'S OUR VILLAGE!
GREAT!
COME ON, EVERYONE! ASTERIX AND OBELIX ARE BACK!
THEY'LL BE ABLE TO TELL US WHAT'S BEING WORN IN LUTETIA THIS SEASON!
WELCOME BACK, BRAVE WARRIORS!
I WILL NOW COMPOSE AN ODE FOR THIS GLORIOUS OCCASION!
JUST YOU TRY IT!
HERE IS YOUR GOLDEN SICKLE, O DRUID GETAFIX!
THANK YOU, MY FRIENDS. I KNEW YOU WOULDN'T FAIL ME!
ALL OUR FRIENDS GATHER TOGETHER FOR A GREAT FEAST TO CELEBRATE THE RETURN OF THE HEROES WITH THE BEAUTIFUL GOLDEN SICKLE WHICH WILL BRING GLORY AND FAME TO THE VILLAGE...
THAT'S FUNNY. OUR BARD CACOFONIX HASN'T TURNED UP TO SING US ONE OF HIS ODES!
HMMM! HMMMM!
THE END

R. GOSCINNY **Asterix** A. UDERZO

# Asterix and the Goths

Written by René GOSCINNY

Illustrated by Albert UDERZO

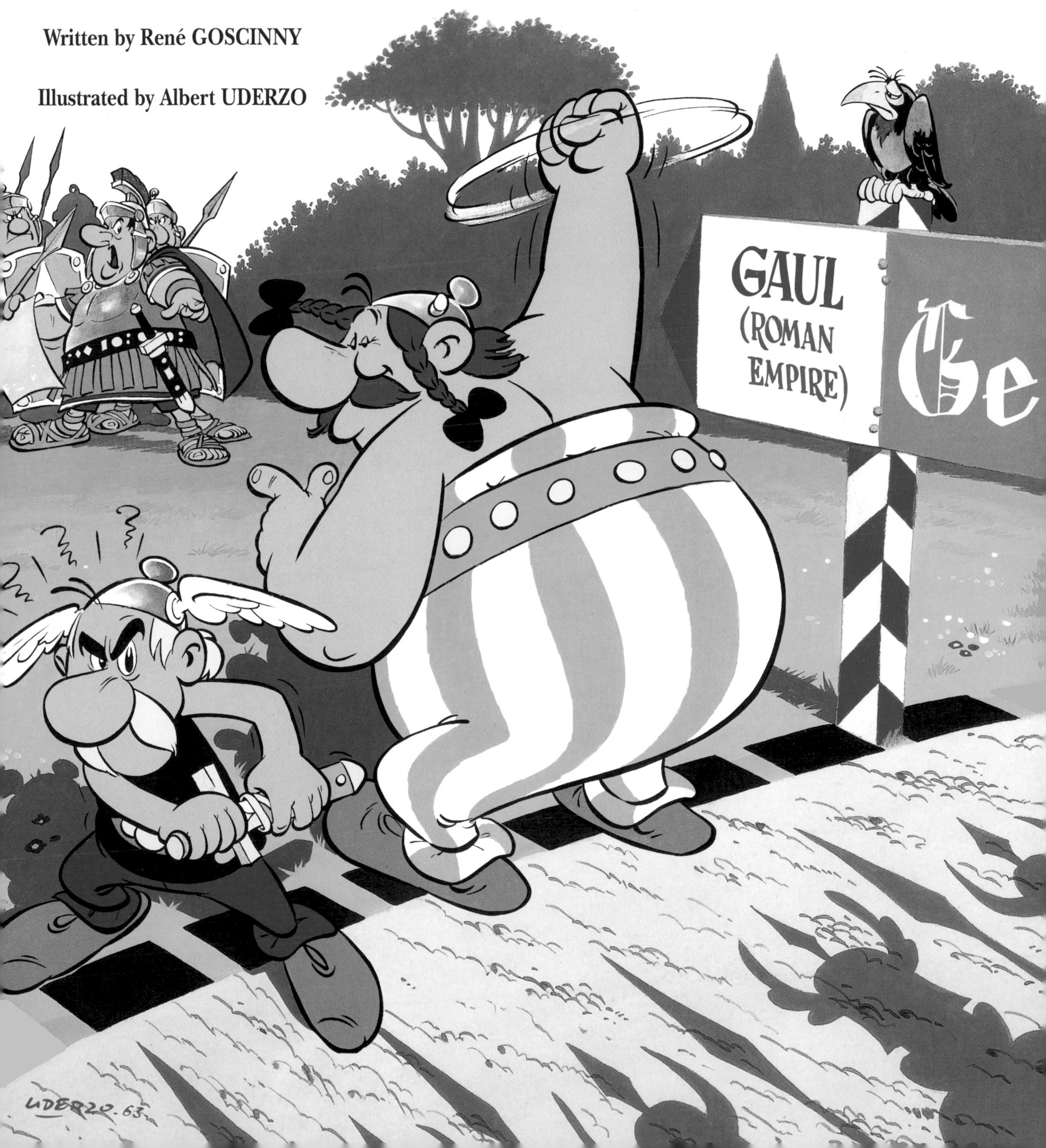
GAUL
(ROMAN
EMPIRE)
Ge
UDERZO. 63

GOSCINNY AND UDERZO

PRESENT

*An Asterix Adventure*

# ASTERIX
# AND THE
# GOTHS

*Written by* RENÉ GOSCINNY *and Illustrated by* ALBERT UDERZO

*Translated by* Anthea Bell *and* Derek Hockridge

Orion
Children's Books

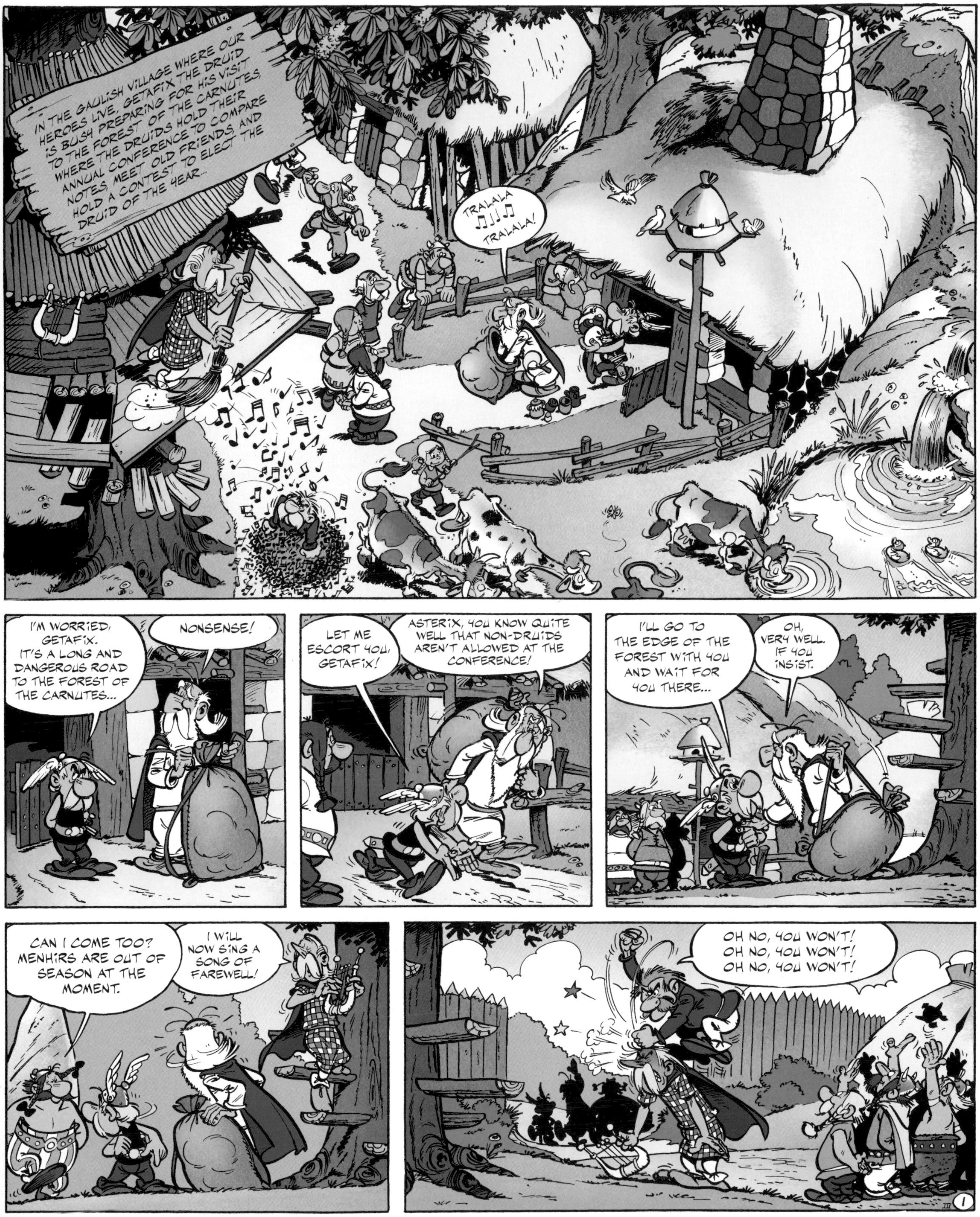

IN THE GAULISH VILLAGE WHERE OUR HEROES LIVE, GETAFIX THE DRUID IS BUSY PREPARING FOR HIS VISIT TO THE FOREST OF THE CARNUTES, WHERE THE DRUIDS HOLD THEIR ANNUAL CONFERENCE TO COMPARE NOTES, MEET OLD FRIENDS, AND HOLD A CONTEST TO ELECT THE DRUID OF THE YEAR...
TRALALA ♫♩♩♫ TRALALA!
I'M WORRIED, GETAFIX. IT'S A LONG AND DANGEROUS ROAD TO THE FOREST OF THE CARNUTES...
NONSENSE!
LET ME ESCORT YOU, GETAFIX!
ASTERIX, YOU KNOW QUITE WELL THAT NON-DRUIDS AREN'T ALLOWED AT THE CONFERENCE!
I'LL GO TO THE EDGE OF THE FOREST WITH YOU AND WAIT FOR YOU THERE...
OH, VERY WELL. IF YOU INSIST.
CAN I COME TOO? MENHIRS ARE OUT OF SEASON AT THE MOMENT.
I WILL NOW SING A SONG OF FAREWELL!
OH NO, YOU WON'T! OH NO, YOU WON'T! OH NO, YOU WON'T!
1

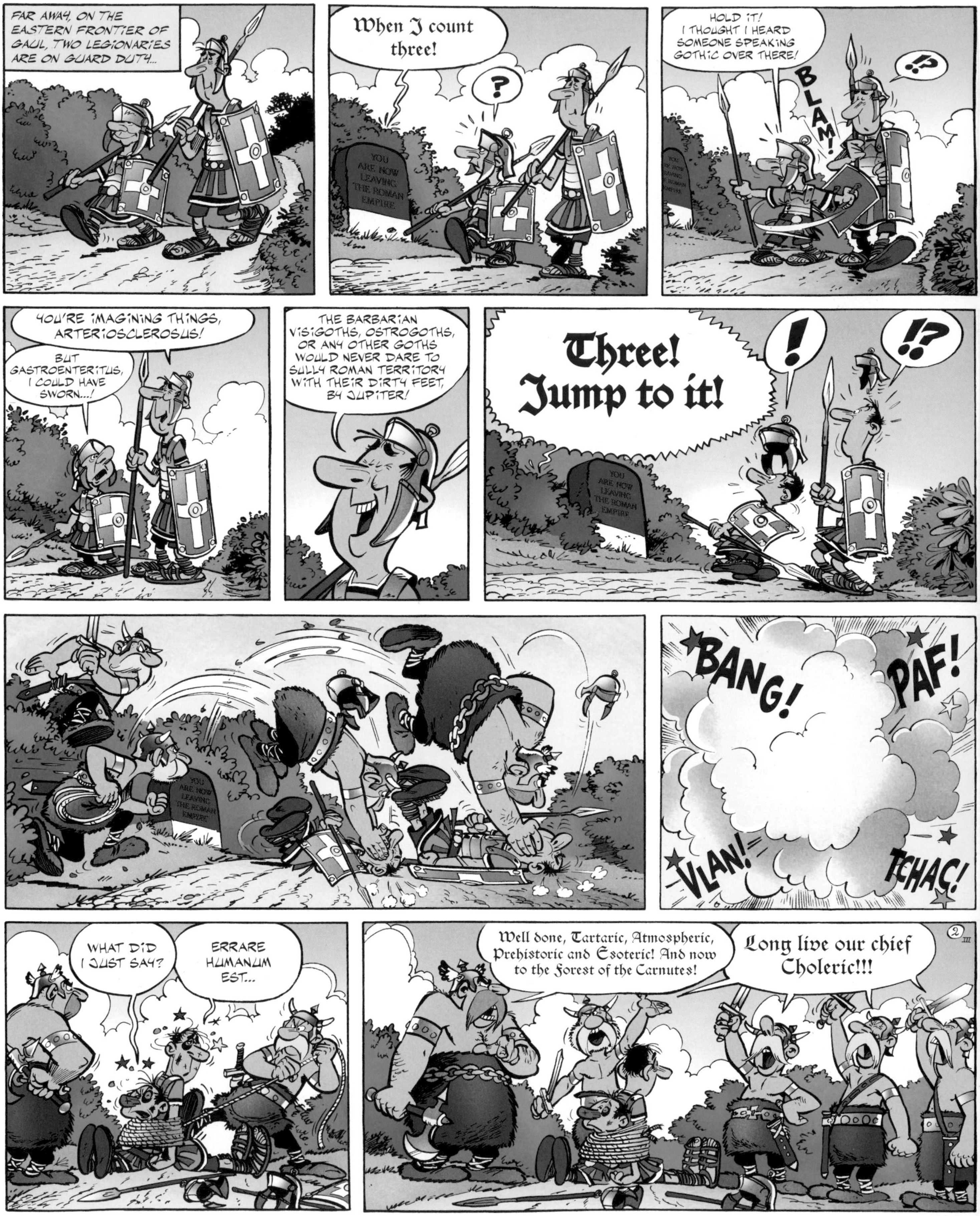
FAR AWAY, ON THE EASTERN FRONTIER OF GAUL, TWO LEGIONARIES ARE ON GUARD DUTY...
When I count three!
YOU ARE NOW LEAVING THE ROMAN EMPIRE
?
HOLD IT! I THOUGHT I HEARD SOMEONE SPEAKING GOTHIC OVER THERE!
BLAM!
!?
YOU'RE IMAGINING THINGS, ARTERIOSCLEROSUS!
BUT GASTROENTERITUS, I COULD HAVE SWORN...!
THE BARBARIAN VISIGOTHS, OSTROGOTHS, OR ANY OTHER GOTHS WOULD NEVER DARE TO SULLY ROMAN TERRITORY WITH THEIR DIRTY FEET, BY JUPITER!
Three! Jump to it!
!
!?
YOU ARE NOW LEAVING THE ROMAN EMPIRE
BANG!
PAF!
VLAN!
TCHAC!
WHAT DID I JUST SAY?
ERRARE HUMANUM EST...
Well done, Tartaric, Atmospheric, Prehistoric and Esoteric! And now to the Forest of the Carnutes!
Long live our chief Choleric!!!

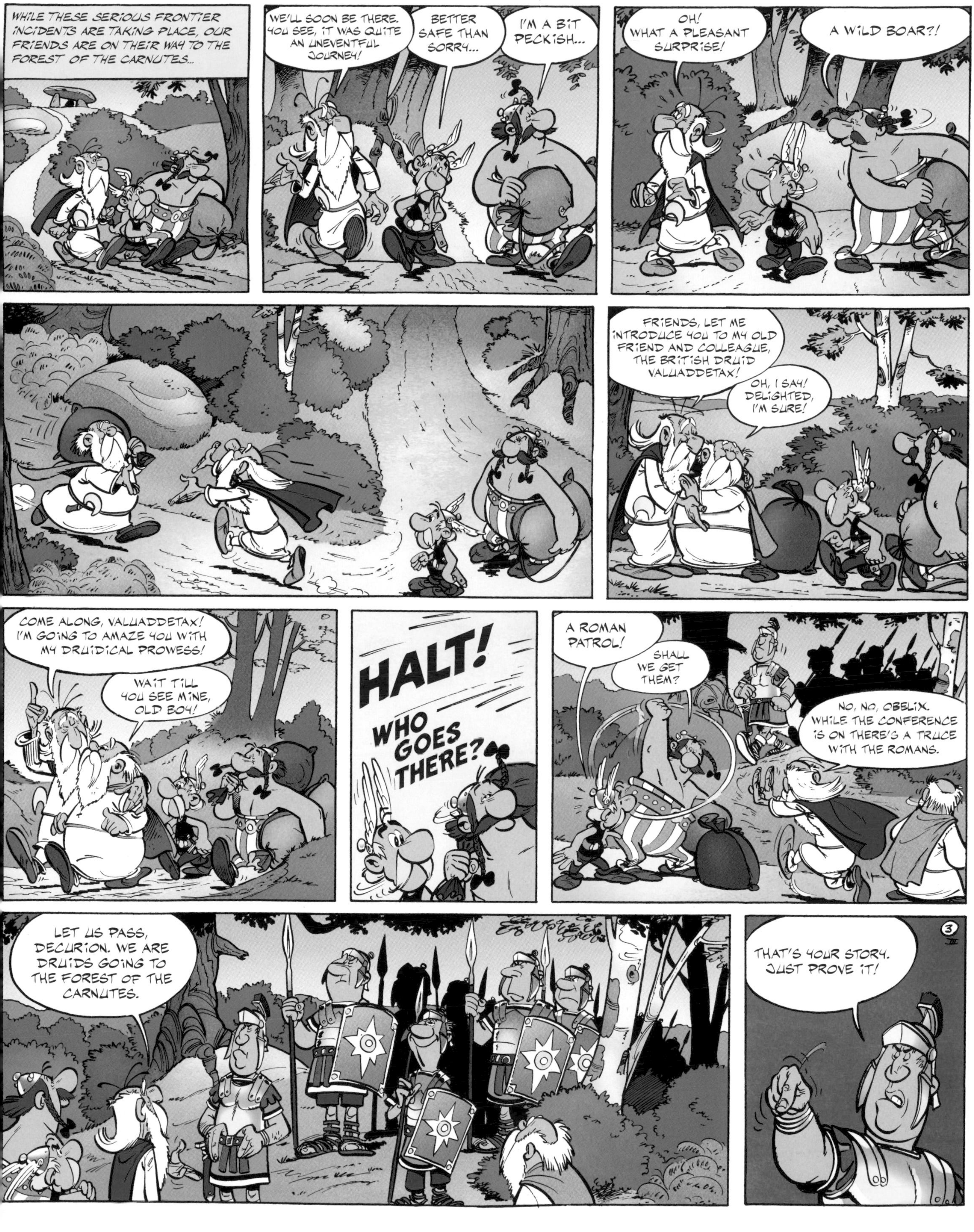
WHILE THESE SERIOUS FRONTIER INCIDENTS ARE TAKING PLACE, OUR FRIENDS ARE ON THEIR WAY TO THE FOREST OF THE CARNUTES...
WE'LL SOON BE THERE. YOU SEE, IT WAS QUITE AN UNEVENTFUL JOURNEY!
BETTER SAFE THAN SORRY...
I'M A BIT PECKISH...
OH! WHAT A PLEASANT SURPRISE!
A WILD BOAR?!
FRIENDS, LET ME INTRODUCE YOU TO MY OLD FRIEND AND COLLEAGUE, THE BRITISH DRUID VALUADDETAX!
OH, I SAY! DELIGHTED, I'M SURE!
COME ALONG, VALUADDETAX! I'M GOING TO AMAZE YOU WITH MY DRUIDICAL PROWESS!
WAIT TILL YOU SEE MINE, OLD BOY!
HALT!
WHO GOES THERE?
A ROMAN PATROL!
SHALL WE GET THEM?
NO, NO, OBELIX. WHILE THE CONFERENCE IS ON THERE'S A TRUCE WITH THE ROMANS.
LET US PASS, DECURION. WE ARE DRUIDS GOING TO THE FOREST OF THE CARNUTES.
3
THAT'S YOUR STORY. JUST PROVE IT!

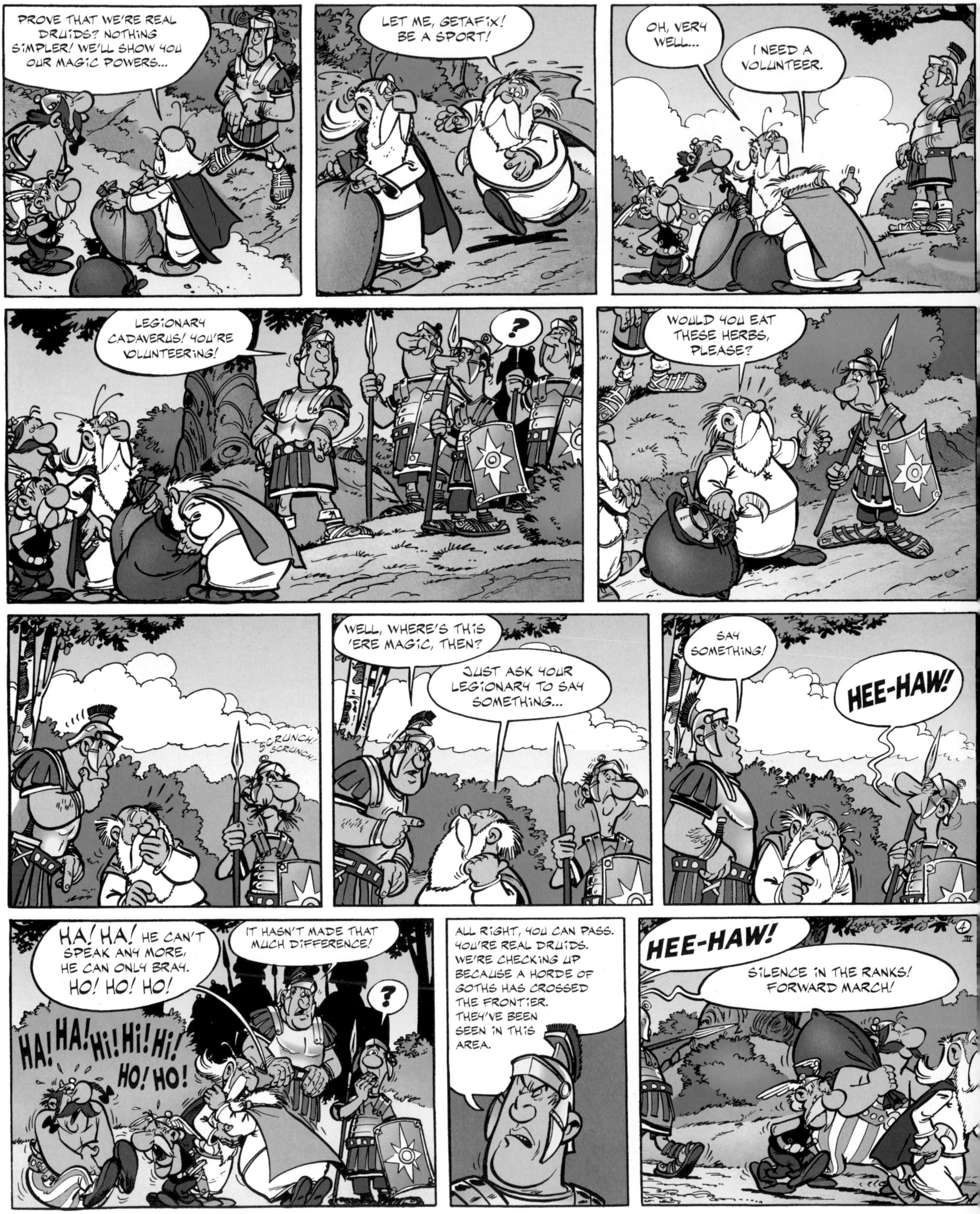
PROVE THAT WE'RE REAL DRUIDS? NOTHING SIMPLER! WE'LL SHOW YOU OUR MAGIC POWERS...
LET ME, GETAFIX! BE A SPORT!
OH, VERY WELL...
I NEED A VOLUNTEER.
LEGIONARY CADAVERUS! YOU'RE VOLUNTEERING!
?
WOULD YOU EAT THESE HERBS, PLEASE?
SCRUNCH! SCRUNCH!
WELL, WHERE'S THIS 'ERE MAGIC, THEN?
JUST ASK YOUR LEGIONARY TO SAY SOMETHING...
SAY SOMETHING!
HEE-HAW!
HA! HA! HE CAN'T SPEAK ANY MORE, HE CAN ONLY BRAY. HO! HO! HO!
IT HASN'T MADE THAT MUCH DIFFERENCE!
HA! HA! HI! HI! HI! HO! HO!
?
ALL RIGHT, YOU CAN PASS. YOU'RE REAL DRUIDS. WE'RE CHECKING UP BECAUSE A HORDE OF GOTHS HAS CROSSED THE FRONTIER. THEY'VE BEEN SEEN IN THIS AREA.
HEE-HAW!
SILENCE IN THE RANKS! FORWARD MARCH!

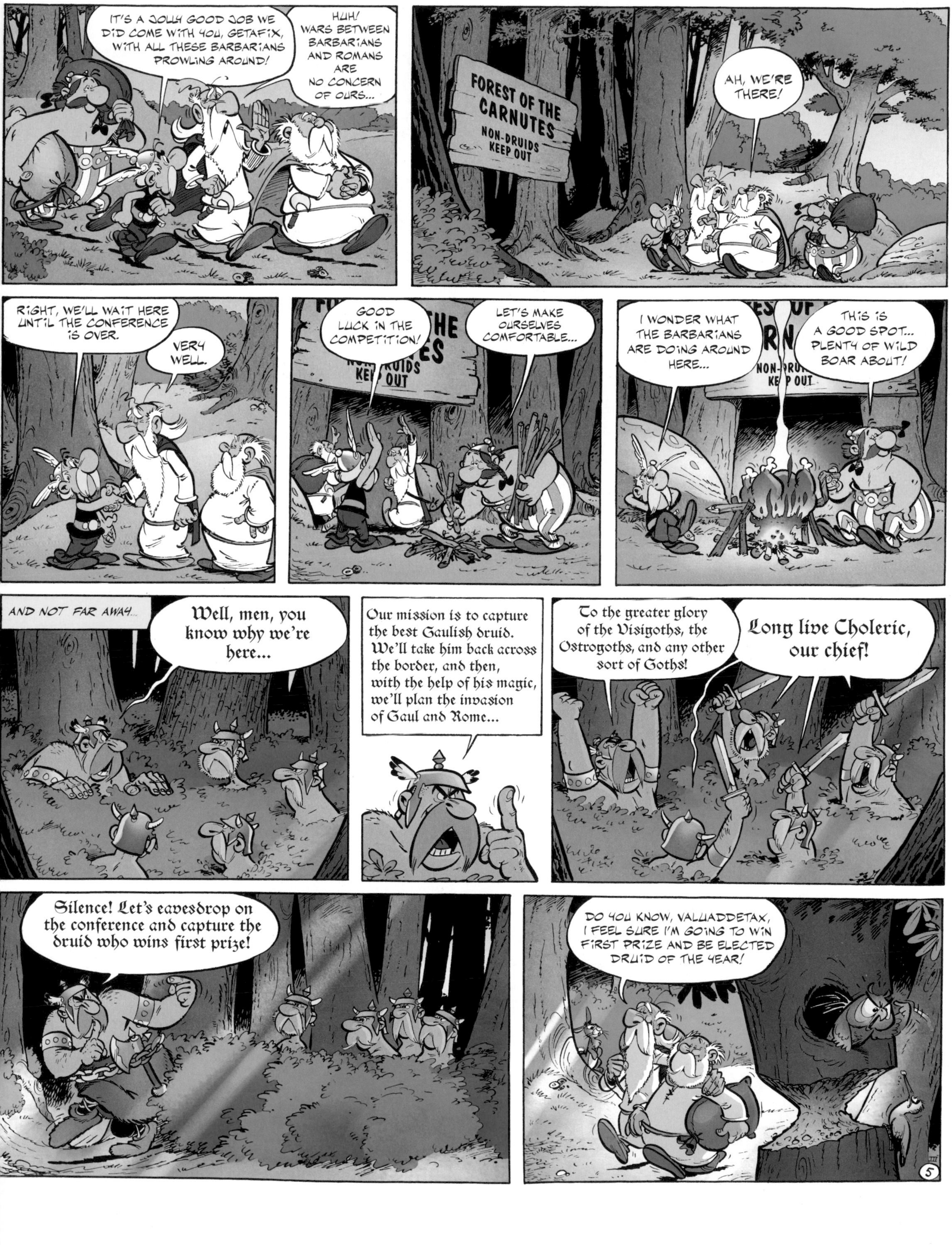
IT'S A JOLLY GOOD JOB WE DID COME WITH YOU, GETAFIX, WITH ALL THESE BARBARIANS PROWLING AROUND!
HUH! WARS BETWEEN BARBARIANS AND ROMANS ARE NO CONCERN OF OURS...
FOREST OF THE CARNUTES
NON-DRUIDS KEEP OUT
AH, WE'RE THERE!
RIGHT, WE'LL WAIT HERE UNTIL THE CONFERENCE IS OVER.
VERY WELL.
GOOD LUCK IN THE COMPETITION!
LET'S MAKE OURSELVES COMFORTABLE...
I WONDER WHAT THE BARBARIANS ARE DOING AROUND HERE...
THIS IS A GOOD SPOT... PLENTY OF WILD BOAR ABOUT!
AND NOT FAR AWAY...
Well, men, you know why we're here...
Our mission is to capture the best Gaulish druid. We'll take him back across the border, and then, with the help of his magic, we'll plan the invasion of Gaul and Rome...
To the greater glory of the Visigoths, the Ostrogoths, and any other sort of Goths!
Long live Choleric, our chief!
Silence! Let's eavesdrop on the conference and capture the druid who wins first prize!
DO YOU KNOW, VALUADDETAX, I FEEL SURE I'M GOING TO WIN FIRST PRIZE AND BE ELECTED DRUID OF THE YEAR!
5

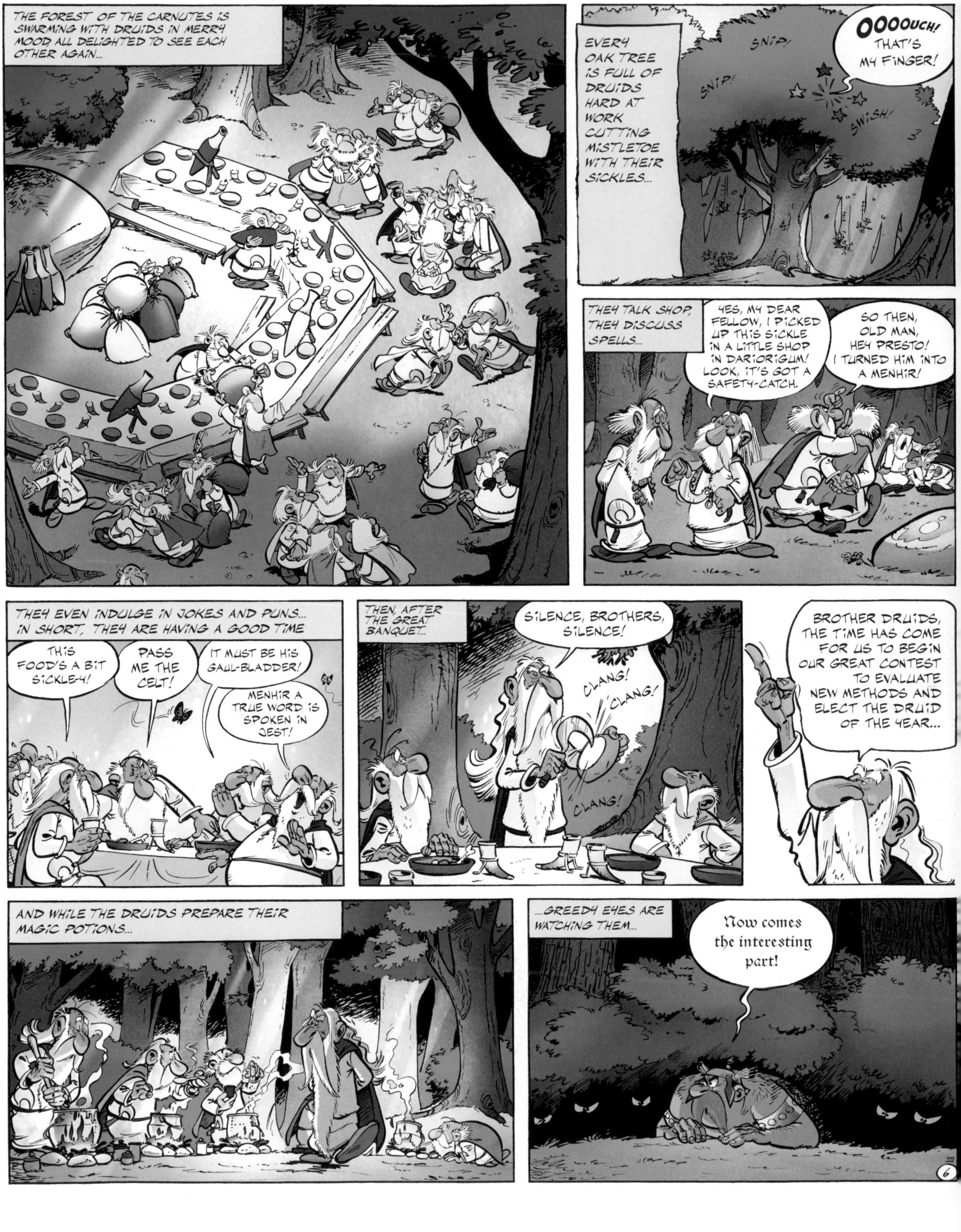
THE FOREST OF THE CARNUTES IS SWARMING WITH DRUIDS IN MERRY MOOD ALL DELIGHTED TO SEE EACH OTHER AGAIN...
EVERY OAK TREE IS FULL OF DRUIDS HARD AT WORK CUTTING MISTLETOE WITH THEIR SICKLES...
SNIP!
SNIP!
SWISH!
OOOOUCH! THAT'S MY FINGER!
THEY TALK SHOP, THEY DISCUSS SPELLS...
YES, MY DEAR FELLOW, I PICKED UP THIS SICKLE IN A LITTLE SHOP IN DARIORIGUM! LOOK, IT'S GOT A SAFETY-CATCH.
SO THEN, OLD MAN, HEY PRESTO! I TURNED HIM INTO A MENHIR!
THEY EVEN INDULGE IN JOKES AND PUNS... IN SHORT, THEY ARE HAVING A GOOD TIME
THIS FOOD'S A BIT SICKLE-Y!
PASS ME THE CELT!
IT MUST BE HIS GAUL-BLADDER!
MENHIR A TRUE WORD IS SPOKEN IN JEST!
THEN, AFTER THE GREAT BANQUET...
SILENCE, BROTHERS, SILENCE!
CLANG!
CLANG!
CLANG!
BROTHER DRUIDS, THE TIME HAS COME FOR US TO BEGIN OUR GREAT CONTEST TO EVALUATE NEW METHODS AND ELECT THE DRUID OF THE YEAR...
AND WHILE THE DRUIDS PREPARE THEIR MAGIC POTIONS...
...GREEDY EYES ARE WATCHING THEM...
Now comes the interesting part!

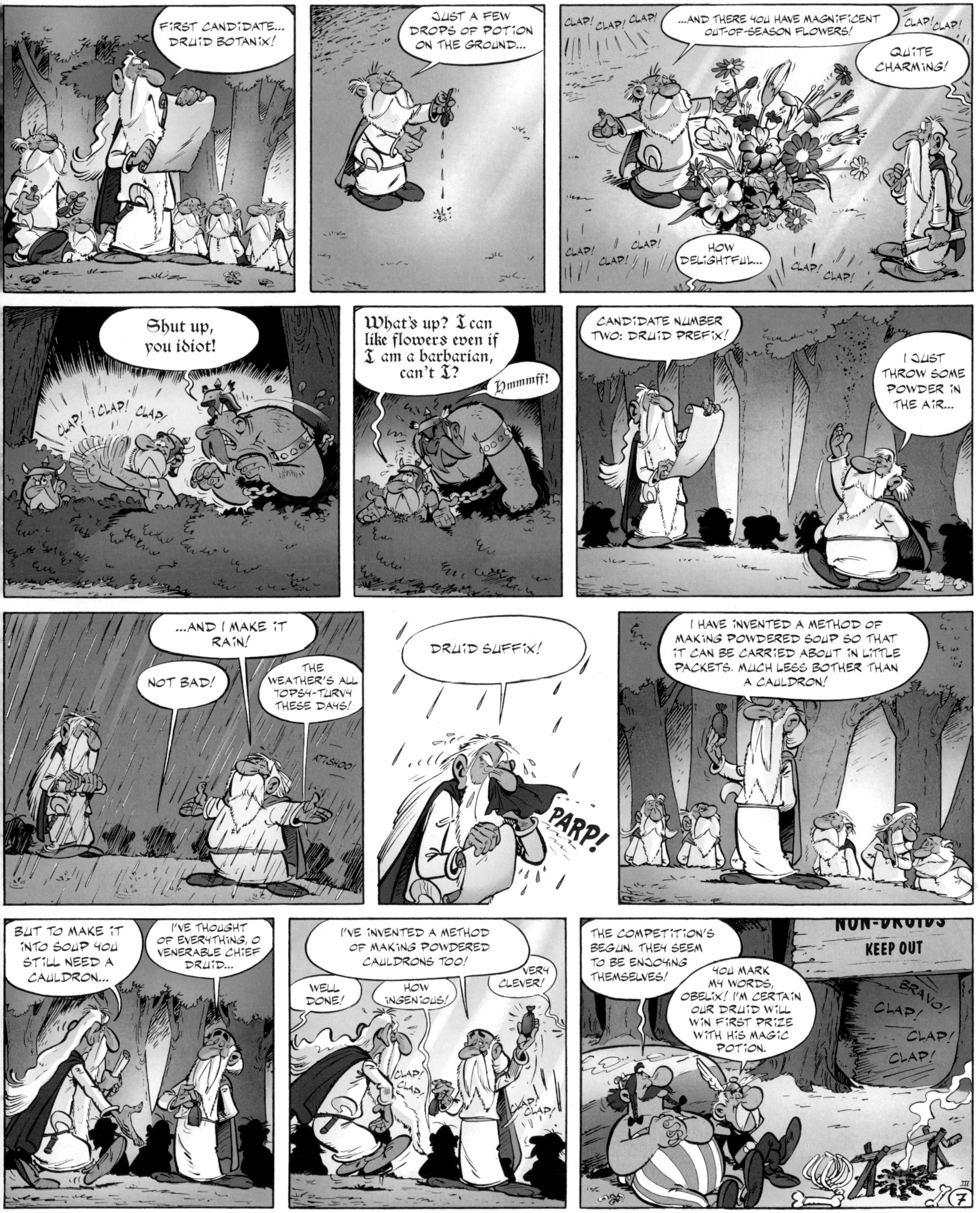

FIRST CANDIDATE... DRUID BOTANIX!
JUST A FEW DROPS OF POTION ON THE GROUND...
CLAP! CLAP! CLAP!
...AND THERE YOU HAVE MAGNIFICENT OUT-OF-SEASON FLOWERS!
CLAP! CLAP!
QUITE CHARMING!
CLAP! CLAP! CLAP!
HOW DELIGHTFUL...
CLAP! CLAP!
Shut up, you idiot!
CLAP! CLAP! CLAP!
What's up? I can like flowers even if I am a barbarian, can't I?
Hmmmff!
CANDIDATE NUMBER TWO: DRUID PREFIX!
I JUST THROW SOME POWDER IN THE AIR...
...AND I MAKE IT RAIN!
NOT BAD!
THE WEATHER'S ALL TOPSY-TURVY THESE DAYS!
ATISHOO!
DRUID SUFFIX!
PARP!
I HAVE INVENTED A METHOD OF MAKING POWDERED SOUP SO THAT IT CAN BE CARRIED ABOUT IN LITTLE PACKETS. MUCH LESS BOTHER THAN A CAULDRON!
BUT TO MAKE IT INTO SOUP YOU STILL NEED A CAULDRON...
I'VE THOUGHT OF EVERYTHING, O VENERABLE CHIEF DRUID...
I'VE INVENTED A METHOD OF MAKING POWDERED CAULDRONS TOO!
WELL DONE!
HOW INGENIOUS!
VERY CLEVER!
CLAP! CLAP!
CLAP! CLAP!
NON-DRUIDS KEEP OUT
THE COMPETITION'S BEGUN. THEY SEEM TO BE ENJOYING THEMSELVES!
YOU MARK MY WORDS, OBELIX! I'M CERTAIN OUR DRUID WILL WIN FIRST PRIZE WITH HIS MAGIC POTION.
BRAVO!
CLAP!
CLAP!
CLAP!
7

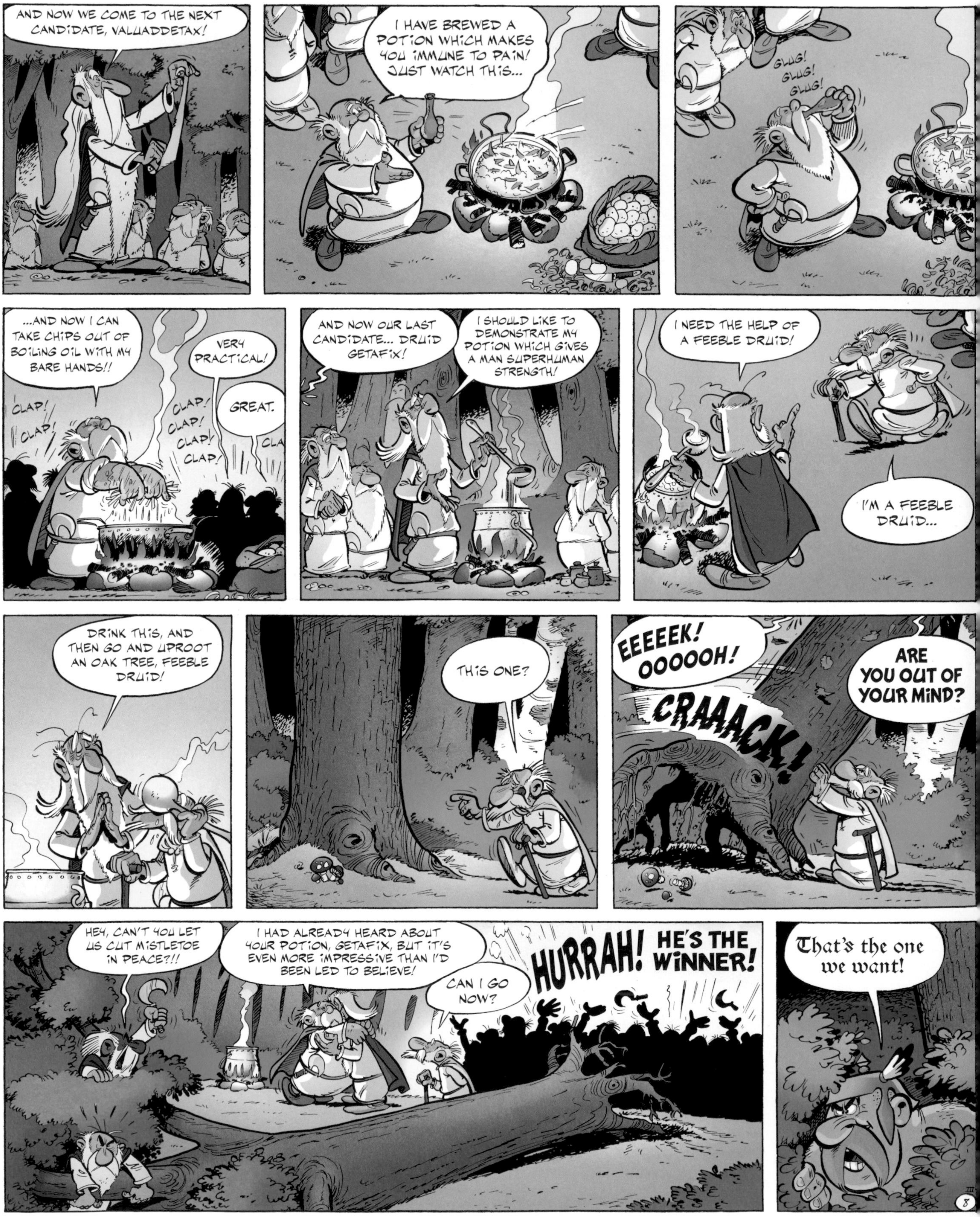
AND NOW WE COME TO THE NEXT CANDIDATE, VALUADDETAX!
I HAVE BREWED A POTION WHICH MAKES YOU IMMUNE TO PAIN! JUST WATCH THIS...
GLUG! GLUG! GLUG!
...AND NOW I CAN TAKE CHIPS OUT OF BOILING OIL WITH MY BARE HANDS!!
CLAP! CLAP!
VERY PRACTICAL!
CLAP! CLAP! CLAP! CLAP!
GREAT.
AND NOW OUR LAST CANDIDATE... DRUID GETAFIX!
I SHOULD LIKE TO DEMONSTRATE MY POTION WHICH GIVES A MAN SUPERHUMAN STRENGTH!
I NEED THE HELP OF A FEEBLE DRUID!
I'M A FEEBLE DRUID...
DRINK THIS, AND THEN GO AND UPROOT AN OAK TREE, FEEBLE DRUID!
THIS ONE?
EEEEEK! OOOOOH!
CRAAACK!
ARE YOU OUT OF YOUR MIND?
HEY, CAN'T YOU LET US CUT MISTLETOE IN PEACE?!!
I HAD ALREADY HEARD ABOUT YOUR POTION, GETAFIX, BUT IT'S EVEN MORE IMPRESSIVE THAN I'D BEEN LED TO BELIEVE!
CAN I GO NOW?
HURRAH! HE'S THE WINNER!
That's the one we want!
8

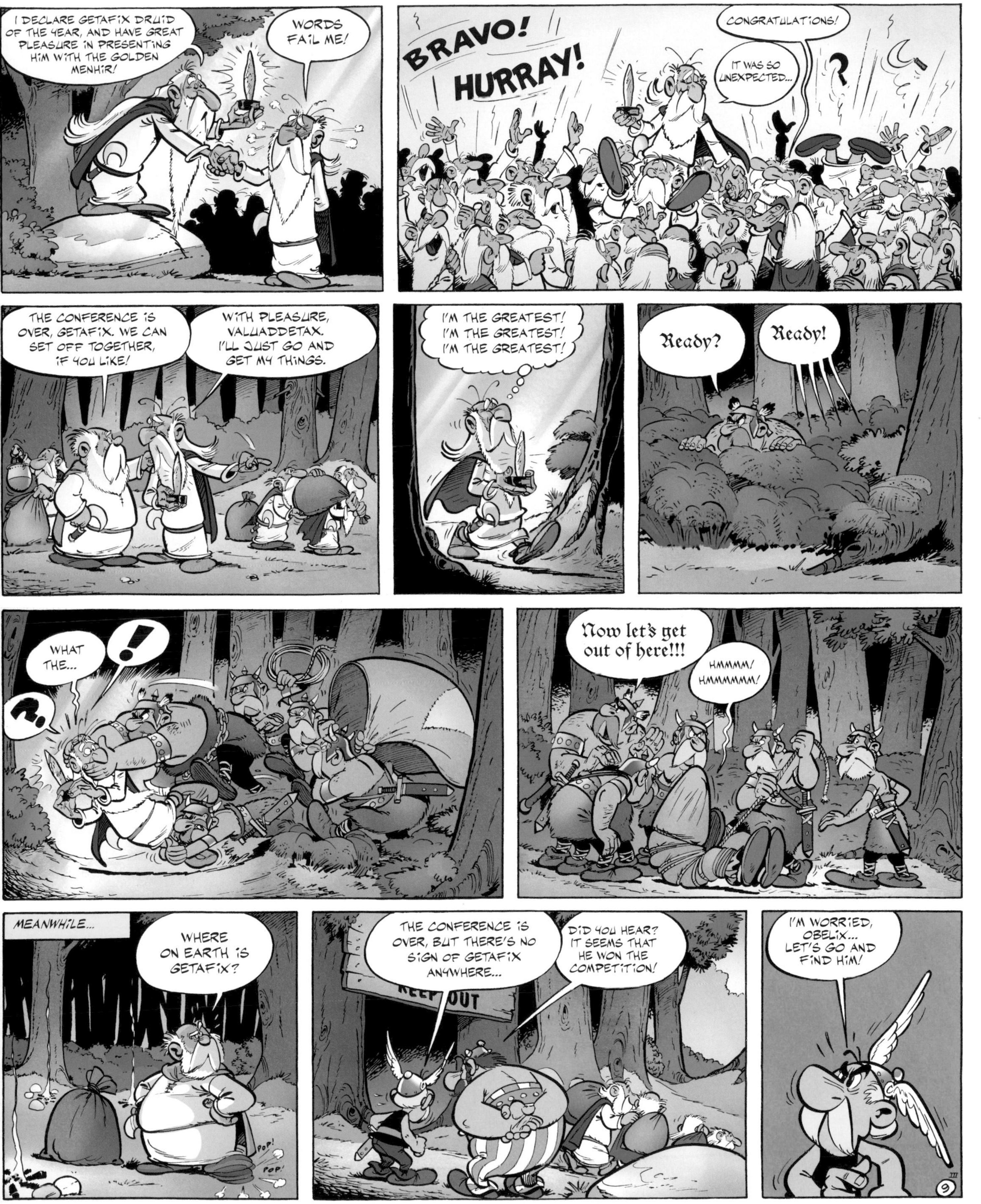
I DECLARE GETAFIX DRUID OF THE YEAR, AND HAVE GREAT PLEASURE IN PRESENTING HIM WITH THE GOLDEN MENHIR!
WORDS FAIL ME!
BRAVO!
HURRAY!
CONGRATULATIONS!
IT WAS SO UNEXPECTED...
?
THE CONFERENCE IS OVER, GETAFIX. WE CAN SET OFF TOGETHER, IF YOU LIKE!
WITH PLEASURE, VALUADDETAX. I'LL JUST GO AND GET MY THINGS.
I'M THE GREATEST! I'M THE GREATEST! I'M THE GREATEST!
Ready?
Ready!
WHAT THE...
!
?
Now let's get out of here!!!
HMMMM! HMMMMMM!
MEANWHILE...
WHERE ON EARTH IS GETAFIX?
POP!
POP!
THE CONFERENCE IS OVER, BUT THERE'S NO SIGN OF GETAFIX ANYWHERE...
DID YOU HEAR? IT SEEMS THAT HE WON THE COMPETITION!
I'M WORRIED, OBELIX... LET'S GO AND FIND HIM!
9

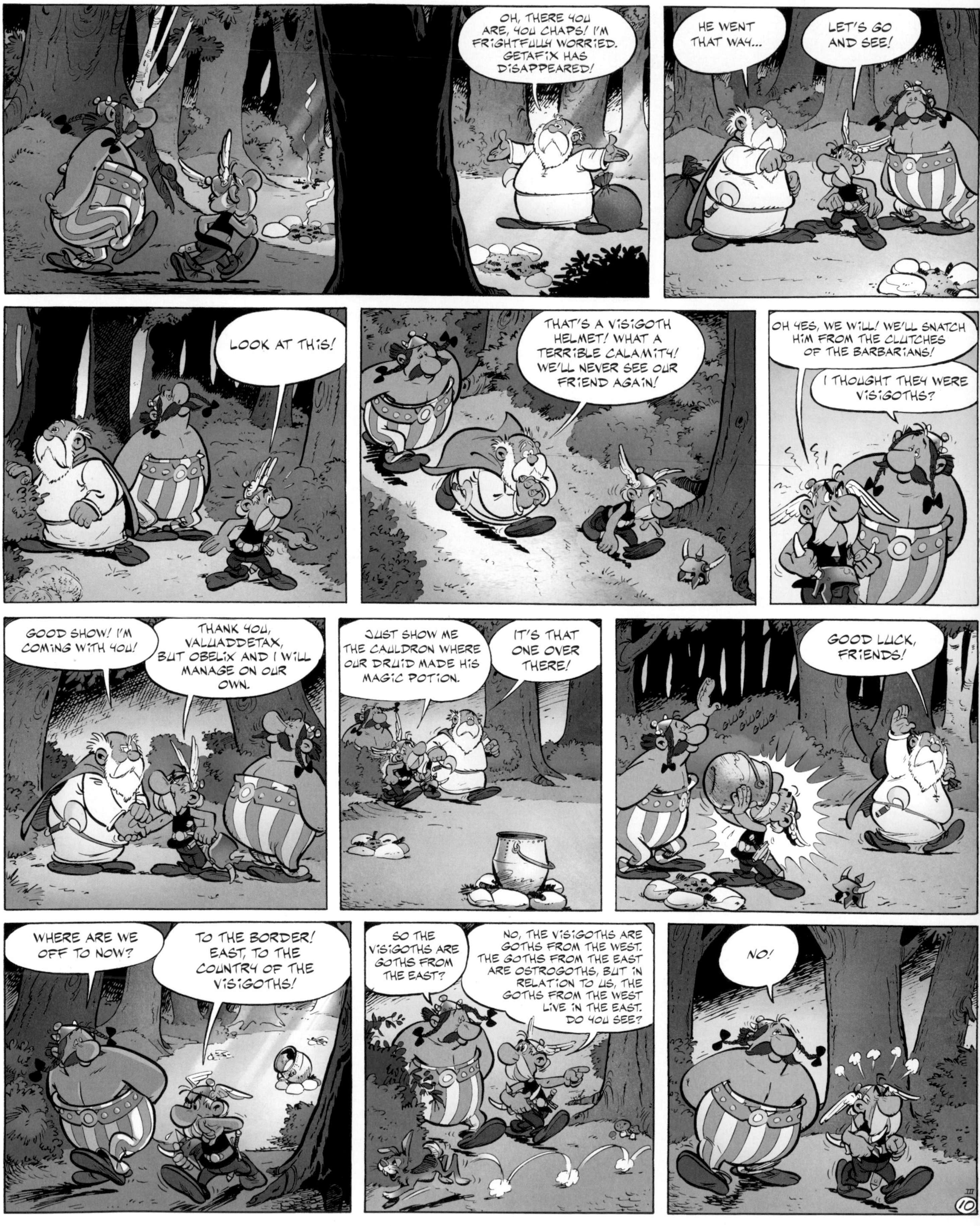
OH, THERE YOU ARE, YOU CHAPS! I'M FRIGHTFULLY WORRIED. GETAFIX HAS DISAPPEARED!
HE WENT THAT WAY...
LET'S GO AND SEE!
LOOK AT THIS!
THAT'S A VISIGOTH HELMET! WHAT A TERRIBLE CALAMITY! WE'LL NEVER SEE OUR FRIEND AGAIN!
OH YES, WE WILL! WE'LL SNATCH HIM FROM THE CLUTCHES OF THE BARBARIANS!
I THOUGHT THEY WERE VISIGOTHS?
GOOD SHOW! I'M COMING WITH YOU!
THANK YOU, VALUADDETAX, BUT OBELIX AND I WILL MANAGE ON OUR OWN.
JUST SHOW ME THE CAULDRON WHERE OUR DRUID MADE HIS MAGIC POTION.
IT'S THAT ONE OVER THERE!
GLUG! GLUG! GLUG!
GOOD LUCK, FRIENDS!
WHERE ARE WE OFF TO NOW?
TO THE BORDER! EAST, TO THE COUNTRY OF THE VISIGOTHS!
SO THE VISIGOTHS ARE GOTHS FROM THE EAST?
NO, THE VISIGOTHS ARE GOTHS FROM THE WEST. THE GOTHS FROM THE EAST ARE OSTROGOTHS, BUT IN RELATION TO US, THE GOTHS FROM THE WEST LIVE IN THE EAST. DO YOU SEE?
NO!
III
10

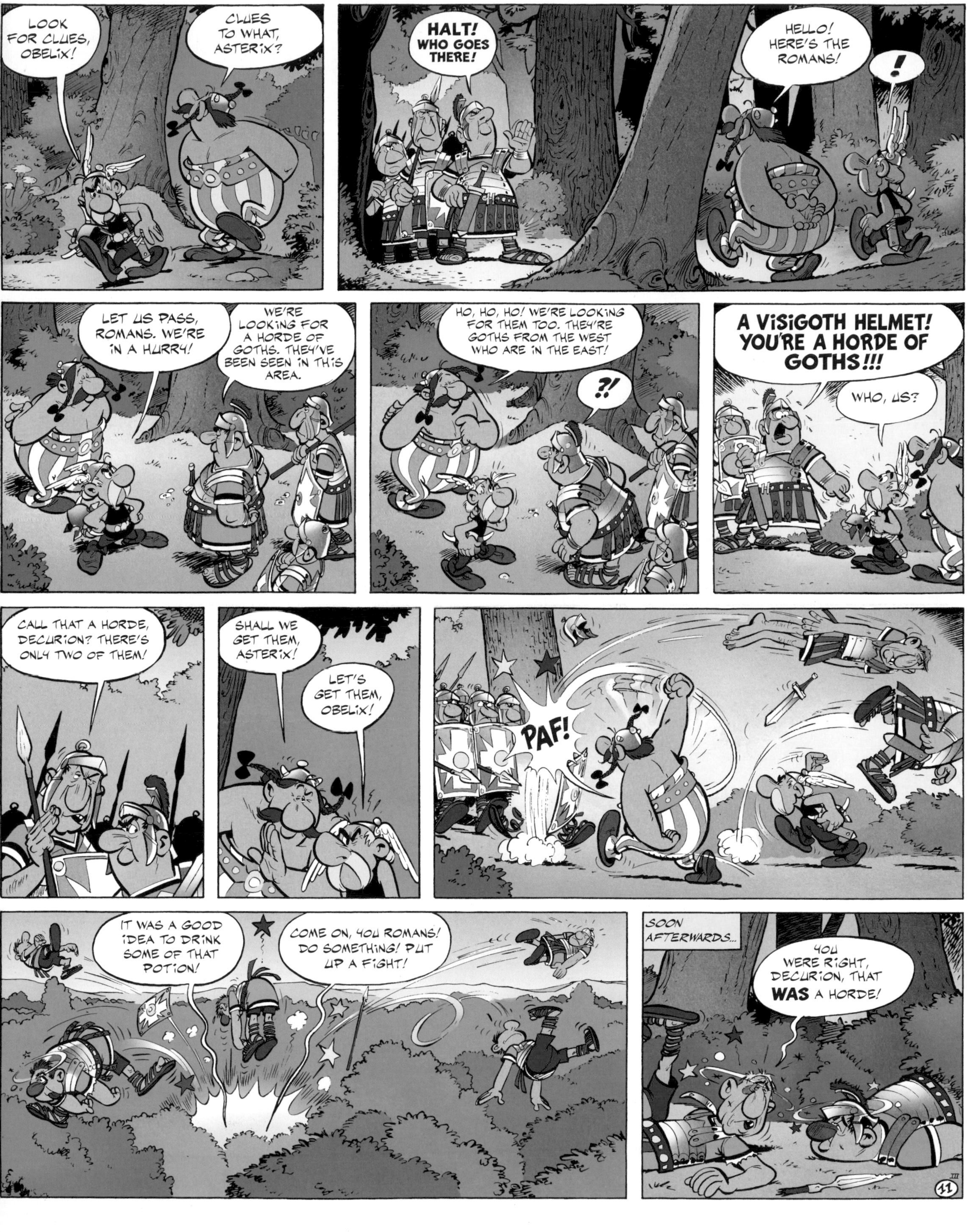

LOOK FOR CLUES, OBELIX!
CLUES TO WHAT, ASTERIX?
HALT! WHO GOES THERE!
HELLO! HERE'S THE ROMANS!
!
LET US PASS, ROMANS. WE'RE IN A HURRY!
WE'RE LOOKING FOR A HORDE OF GOTHS. THEY'VE BEEN SEEN IN THIS AREA.
HO, HO, HO! WE'RE LOOKING FOR THEM TOO. THEY'RE GOTHS FROM THE WEST WHO ARE IN THE EAST!
?!
A VISIGOTH HELMET! YOU'RE A HORDE OF GOTHS!!!
WHO, US?
CALL THAT A HORDE, DECURION? THERE'S ONLY TWO OF THEM!
SHALL WE GET THEM, ASTERIX?
LET'S GET THEM, OBELIX!
PAF!
IT WAS A GOOD IDEA TO DRINK SOME OF THAT POTION!
COME ON, YOU ROMANS! DO SOMETHING! PUT UP A FIGHT!
SOON AFTERWARDS...
YOU WERE RIGHT, DECURION, THAT WAS A HORDE!
11

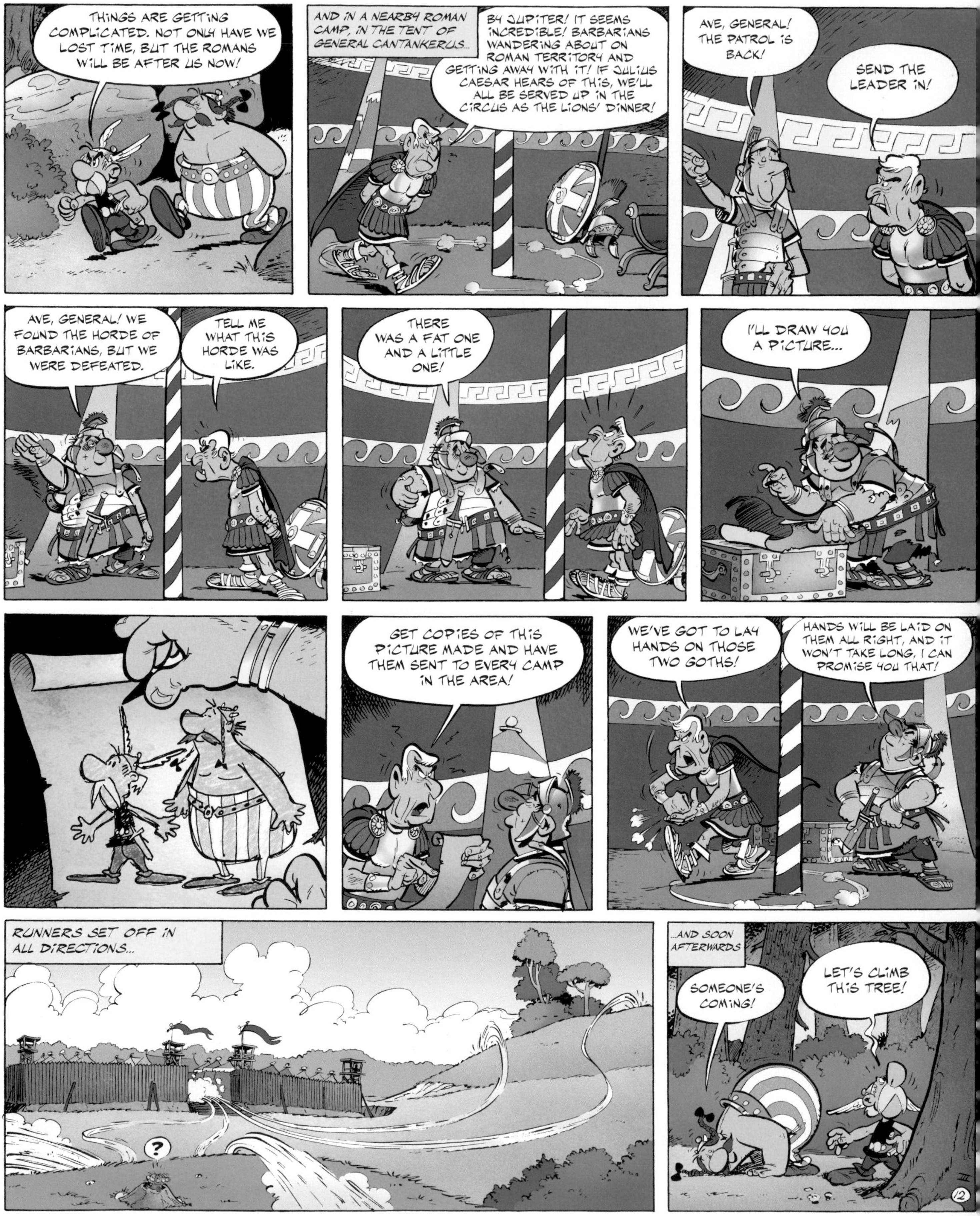
THINGS ARE GETTING COMPLICATED. NOT ONLY HAVE WE LOST TIME, BUT THE ROMANS WILL BE AFTER US NOW!
AND IN A NEARBY ROMAN CAMP, IN THE TENT OF GENERAL CANTANKERUS...
BY JUPITER! IT SEEMS INCREDIBLE! BARBARIANS WANDERING ABOUT ON ROMAN TERRITORY AND GETTING AWAY WITH IT! IF JULIUS CAESAR HEARS OF THIS, WE'LL ALL BE SERVED UP IN THE CIRCUS AS THE LIONS' DINNER!
AVE, GENERAL! THE PATROL IS BACK!
SEND THE LEADER IN!
AVE, GENERAL! WE FOUND THE HORDE OF BARBARIANS, BUT WE WERE DEFEATED.
TELL ME WHAT THIS HORDE WAS LIKE.
THERE WAS A FAT ONE AND A LITTLE ONE!
I'LL DRAW YOU A PICTURE...
GET COPIES OF THIS PICTURE MADE AND HAVE THEM SENT TO EVERY CAMP IN THE AREA!
WE'VE GOT TO LAY HANDS ON THOSE TWO GOTHS!
HANDS WILL BE LAID ON THEM ALL RIGHT, AND IT WON'T TAKE LONG, I CAN PROMISE YOU THAT!
RUNNERS SET OFF IN ALL DIRECTIONS...
?
...AND SOON AFTERWARDS
SOMEONE'S COMING!
LET'S CLIMB THIS TREE!
12

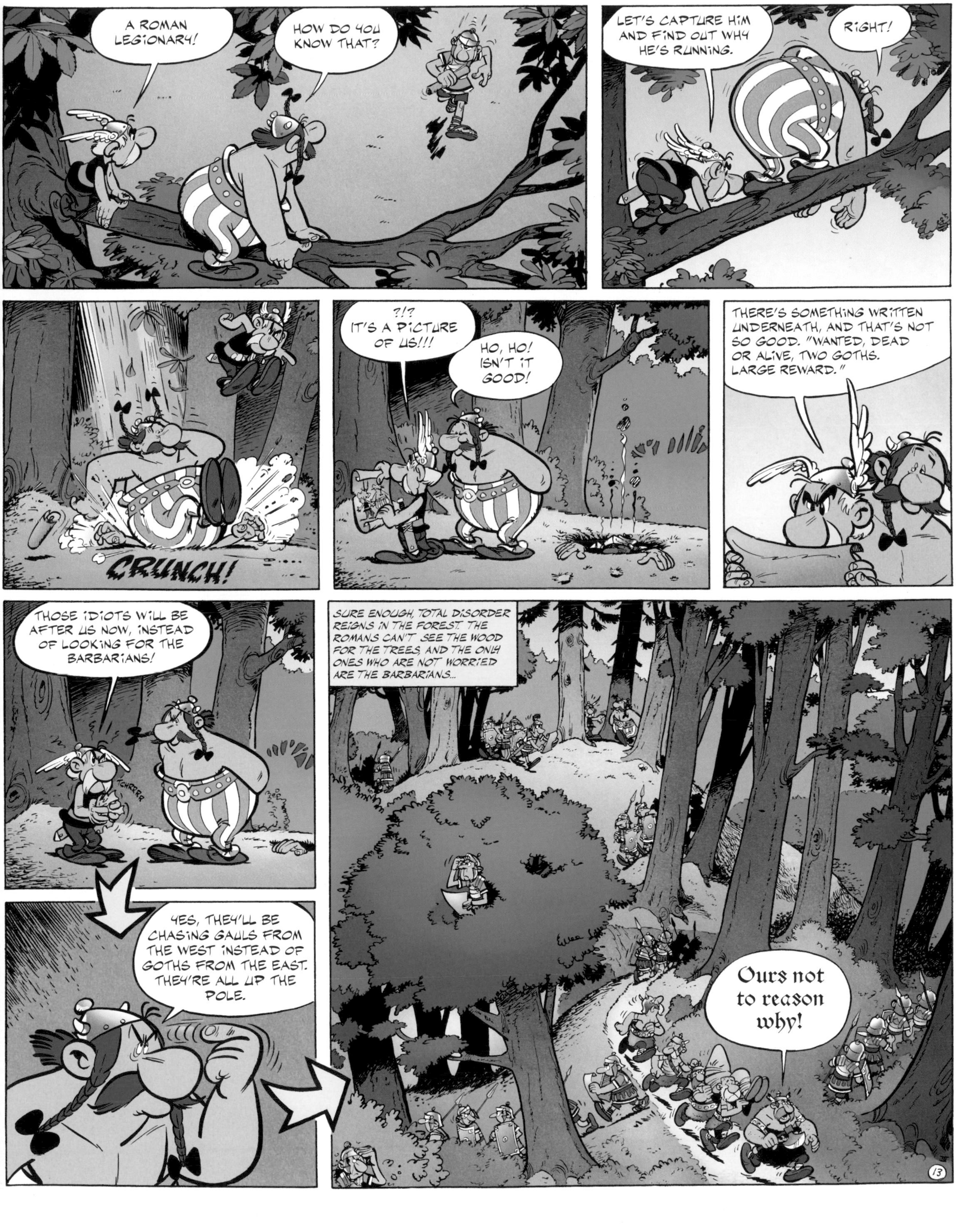
A ROMAN LEGIONARY!
HOW DO YOU KNOW THAT?
LET'S CAPTURE HIM AND FIND OUT WHY HE'S RUNNING.
RIGHT!
CRUNCH!
?!? IT'S A PICTURE OF US!!!
HO, HO! ISN'T IT GOOD!
THERE'S SOMETHING WRITTEN UNDERNEATH, AND THAT'S NOT SO GOOD. "WANTED, DEAD OR ALIVE, TWO GOTHS. LARGE REWARD."
THOSE IDIOTS WILL BE AFTER US NOW, INSTEAD OF LOOKING FOR THE BARBARIANS!
YES, THEY'LL BE CHASING GAULS FROM THE WEST INSTEAD OF GOTHS FROM THE EAST. THEY'RE ALL UP THE POLE.
SURE ENOUGH, TOTAL DISORDER REIGNS IN THE FOREST. THE ROMANS CAN'T SEE THE WOOD FOR THE TREES, AND THE ONLY ONES WHO ARE NOT WORRIED ARE THE BARBARIANS...
Ours not to reason why!
13

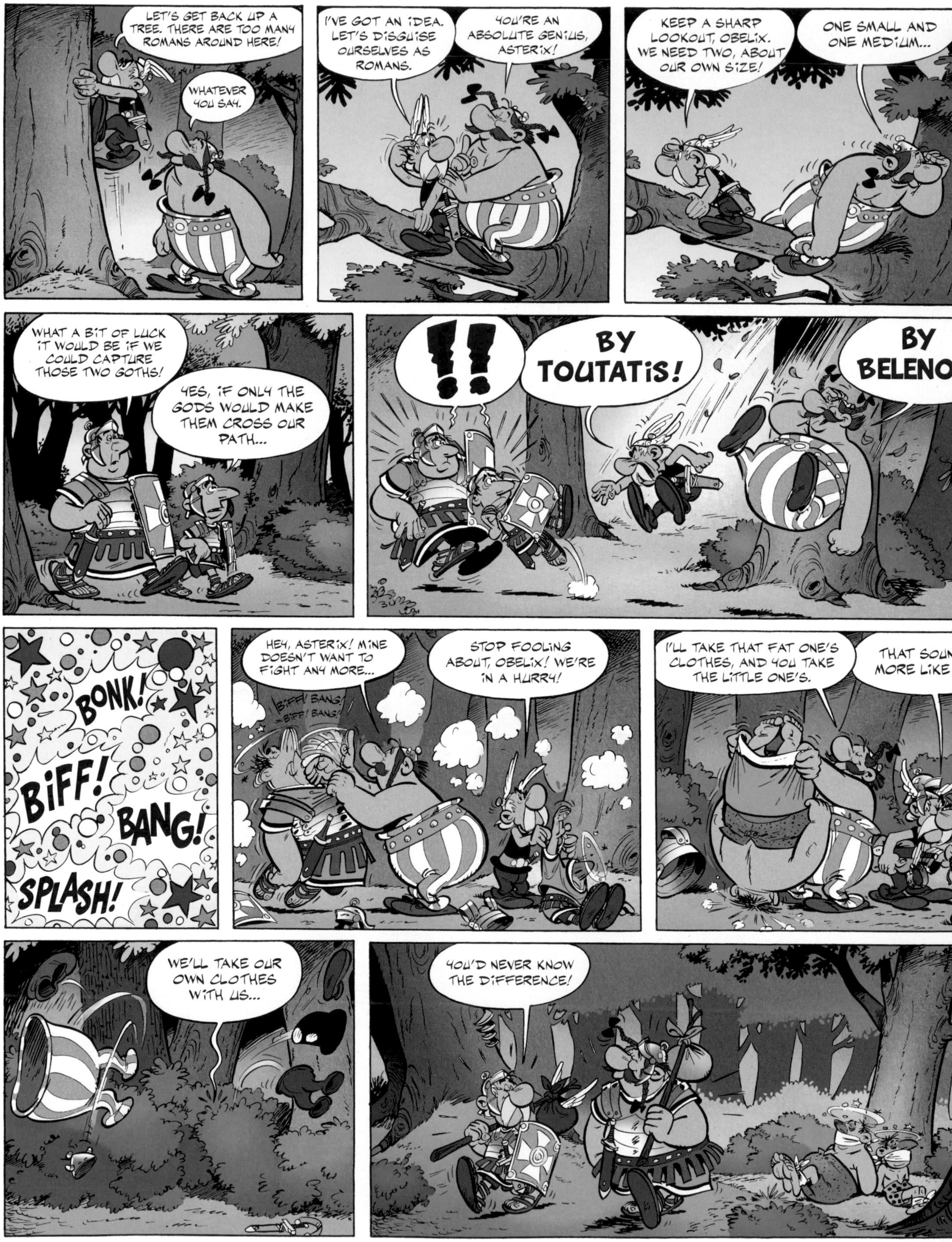

LET'S GET BACK UP A TREE. THERE ARE TOO MANY ROMANS AROUND HERE!
WHATEVER YOU SAY.
I'VE GOT AN IDEA. LET'S DISGUISE OURSELVES AS ROMANS.
YOU'RE AN ABSOLUTE GENIUS, ASTERIX!
KEEP A SHARP LOOKOUT, OBELIX. WE NEED TWO, ABOUT OUR OWN SIZE!
ONE SMALL AND ONE MEDIUM...
WHAT A BIT OF LUCK IT WOULD BE IF WE COULD CAPTURE THOSE TWO GOTHS!
YES, IF ONLY THE GODS WOULD MAKE THEM CROSS OUR PATH...
!!
BY TOUTATIS!
BY BELENOS!
BONK!
BIFF!
BANG!
SPLASH!
HEY, ASTERIX! MINE DOESN'T WANT TO FIGHT ANY MORE...
BIFF! BANG!
BIFF! BANG!
STOP FOOLING ABOUT, OBELIX! WE'RE IN A HURRY!
I'LL TAKE THAT FAT ONE'S CLOTHES, AND YOU TAKE THE LITTLE ONE'S.
THAT SOUNDS MORE LIKE IT...
WE'LL TAKE OUR OWN CLOTHES WITH US...
YOU'D NEVER KNOW THE DIFFERENCE!
14

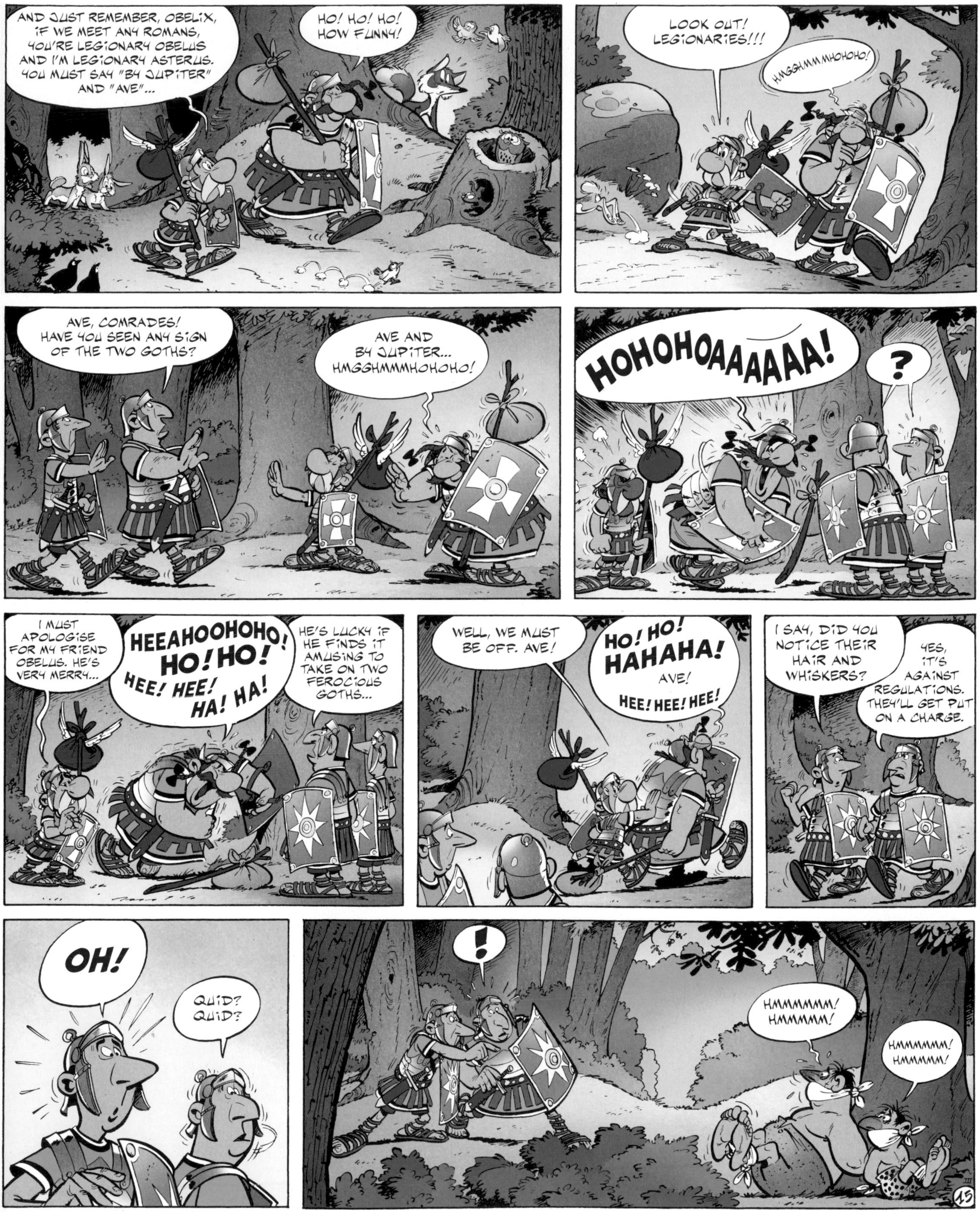
AND JUST REMEMBER, OBELIX, IF WE MEET ANY ROMANS, YOU'RE LEGIONARY OBELUS AND I'M LEGIONARY ASTERUS. YOU MUST SAY "BY JUPITER" AND "AVE"...
HO! HO! HO! HOW FUNNY!
LOOK OUT! LEGIONARIES!!!
HMGGHMMMHOHOHO!
AVE, COMRADES! HAVE YOU SEEN ANY SIGN OF THE TWO GOTHS?
AVE AND BY JUPITER... HMGGHMMMHOHOHO!
HOHOHOAAAAAA!
?
I MUST APOLOGISE FOR MY FRIEND OBELUS. HE'S VERY MERRY...
HEEAHOOHOHO! HO! HO! HEE! HEE! HA! HA!
HE'S LUCKY IF HE FINDS IT AMUSING TO TAKE ON TWO FEROCIOUS GOTHS...
WELL, WE MUST BE OFF. AVE!
HO! HO! HAHAHA! AVE! HEE! HEE! HEE!
I SAY, DID YOU NOTICE THEIR HAIR AND WHISKERS?
YES, IT'S AGAINST REGULATIONS. THEY'LL GET PUT ON A CHARGE.
OH!
QUID? QUID?
!
HMMMMMM! HMMMMM!
HMMMMMM! HMMMMM!
15

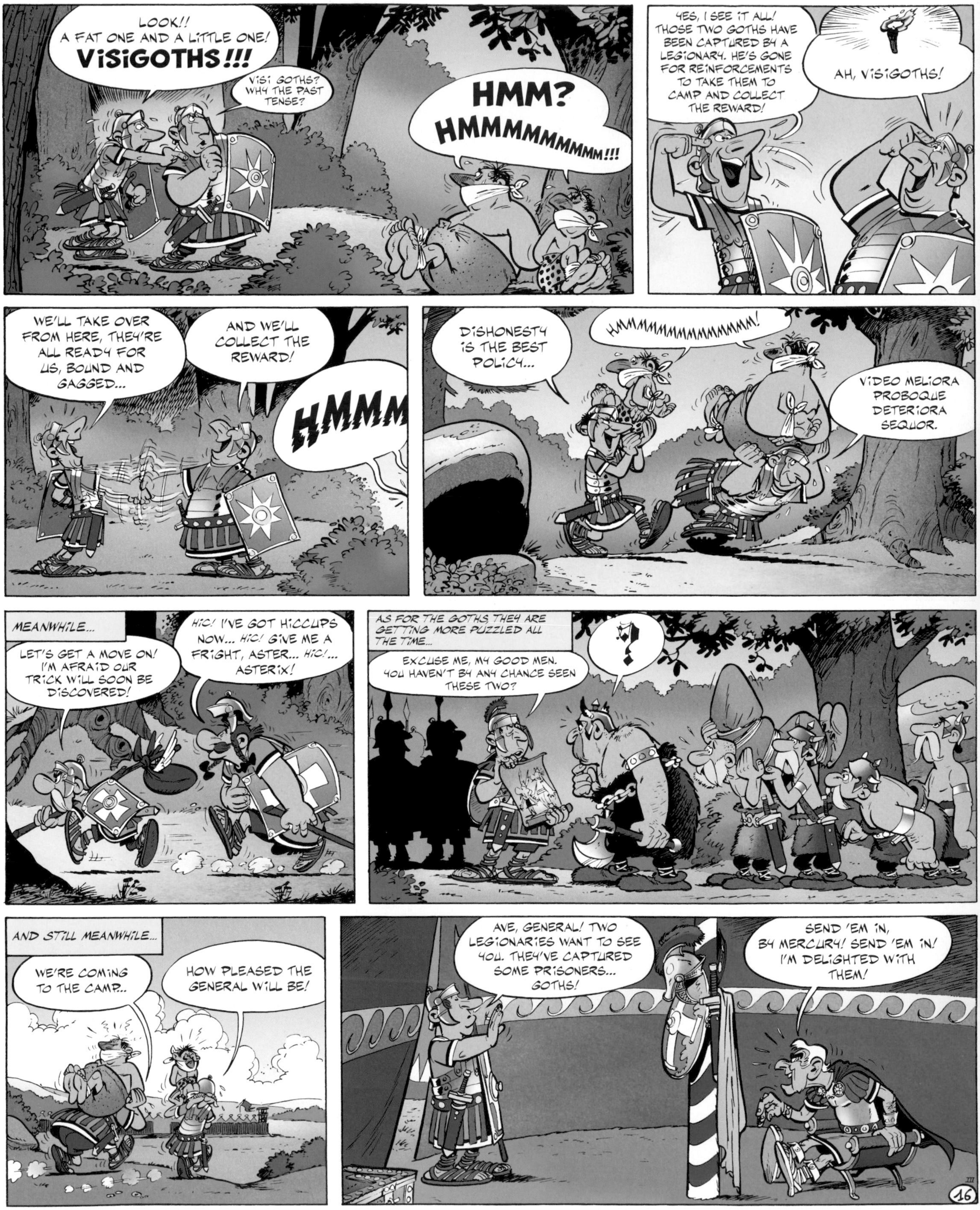
LOOK!! A FAT ONE AND A LITTLE ONE! VISIGOTHS!!!
VISI GOTHS? WHY THE PAST TENSE?
HMM? HMMMMMMMMM!!!
YES, I SEE IT ALL! THOSE TWO GOTHS HAVE BEEN CAPTURED BY A LEGIONARY. HE'S GONE FOR REINFORCEMENTS TO TAKE THEM TO CAMP AND COLLECT THE REWARD!
AH, VISIGOTHS!
WE'LL TAKE OVER FROM HERE, THEY'RE ALL READY FOR US, BOUND AND GAGGED...
AND WE'LL COLLECT THE REWARD!
HMMM
DISHONESTY IS THE BEST POLICY...
HMMMMMMMMMMMMMM!
VIDEO MELIORA PROBOQUE DETERIORA SEQUOR.
MEANWHILE...
LET'S GET A MOVE ON! I'M AFRAID OUR TRICK WILL SOON BE DISCOVERED!
HIC! I'VE GOT HICCUPS NOW... HIC! GIVE ME A FRIGHT, ASTER... HIC!... ASTERIX!
AS FOR THE GOTHS THEY ARE GETTING MORE PUZZLED ALL THE TIME...
EXCUSE ME, MY GOOD MEN. YOU HAVEN'T BY ANY CHANCE SEEN THESE TWO?
AND STILL MEANWHILE...
WE'RE COMING TO THE CAMP...
HOW PLEASED THE GENERAL WILL BE!
AVE, GENERAL! TWO LEGIONARIES WANT TO SEE YOU. THEY'VE CAPTURED SOME PRISONERS... GOTHS!
SEND 'EM IN, BY MERCURY! SEND 'EM IN! I'M DELIGHTED WITH THEM!
16

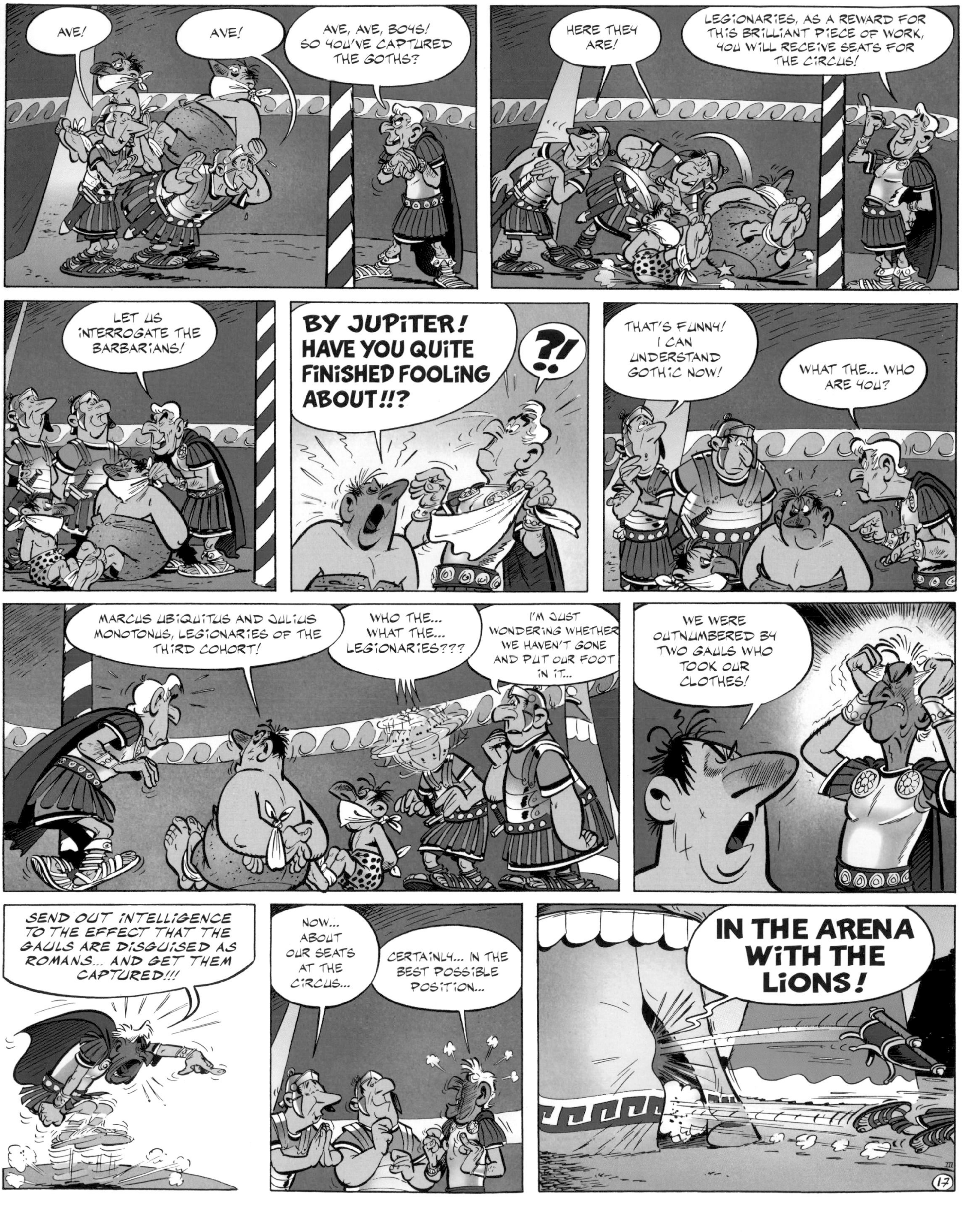
AVE!
AVE!
AVE, AVE, BOYS! SO YOU'VE CAPTURED THE GOTHS?
HERE THEY ARE!
LEGIONARIES, AS A REWARD FOR THIS BRILLIANT PIECE OF WORK, YOU WILL RECEIVE SEATS FOR THE CIRCUS!
LET US INTERROGATE THE BARBARIANS!
BY JUPITER! HAVE YOU QUITE FINISHED FOOLING ABOUT!!?
?!
THAT'S FUNNY! I CAN UNDERSTAND GOTHIC NOW!
WHAT THE... WHO ARE YOU?
MARCUS UBIQUITUS AND JULIUS MONOTONUS, LEGIONARIES OF THE THIRD COHORT!
WHO THE... WHAT THE... LEGIONARIES???
I'M JUST WONDERING WHETHER WE HAVEN'T GONE AND PUT OUR FOOT IN IT...
WE WERE OUTNUMBERED BY TWO GAULS WHO TOOK OUR CLOTHES!
SEND OUT INTELLIGENCE TO THE EFFECT THAT THE GAULS ARE DISGUISED AS ROMANS... AND GET THEM CAPTURED!!!
NOW... ABOUT OUR SEATS AT THE CIRCUS...
CERTAINLY... IN THE BEST POSSIBLE POSITION...
IN THE ARENA WITH THE LIONS!
17

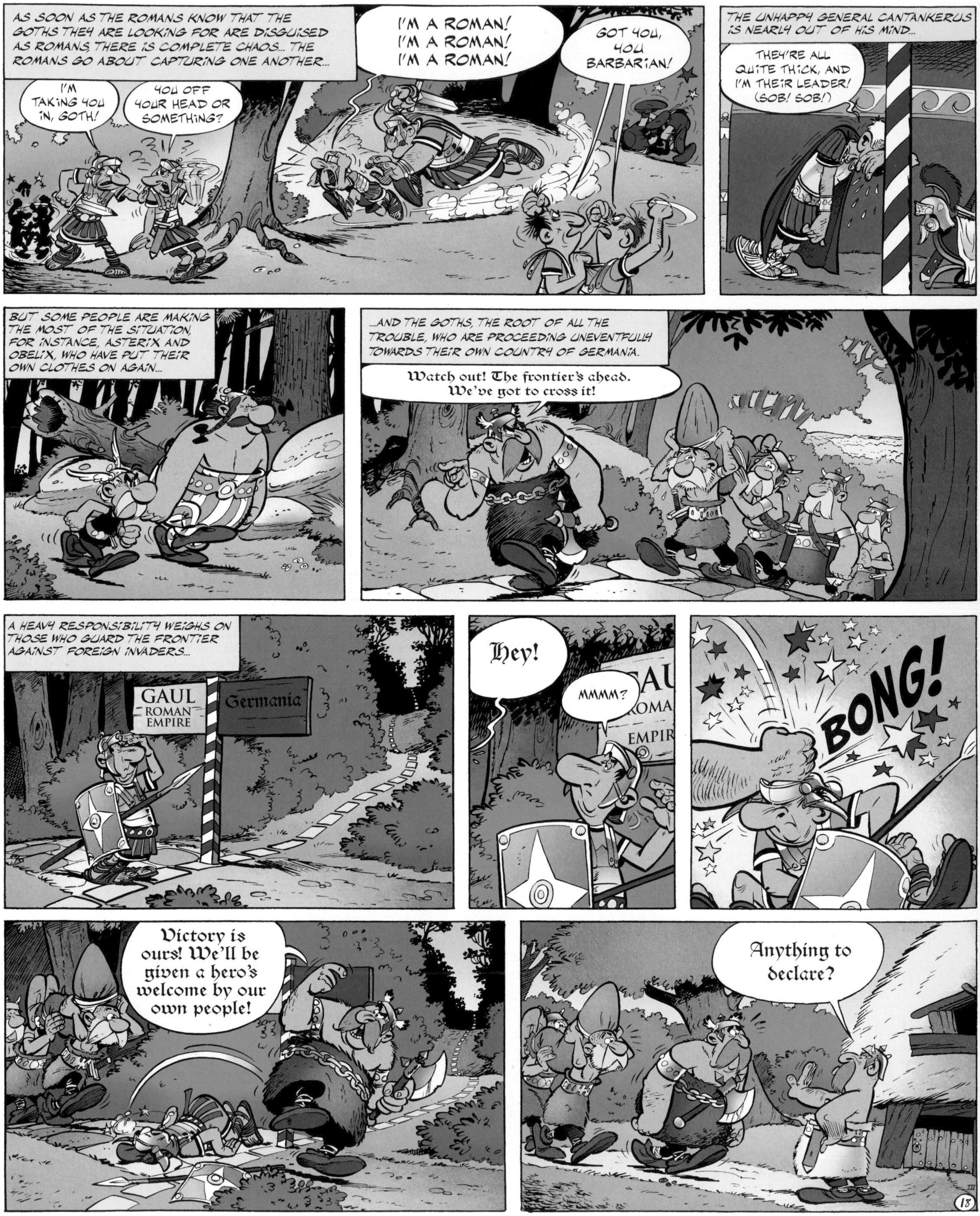
AS SOON AS THE ROMANS KNOW THAT THE GOTHS THEY ARE LOOKING FOR ARE DISGUISED AS ROMANS, THERE IS COMPLETE CHAOS... THE ROMANS GO ABOUT CAPTURING ONE ANOTHER...
I'M TAKING YOU IN, GOTH!
YOU OFF YOUR HEAD OR SOMETHING?
I'M A ROMAN! I'M A ROMAN! I'M A ROMAN!
GOT YOU, YOU BARBARIAN!
THE UNHAPPY GENERAL CANTANKERUS IS NEARLY OUT OF HIS MIND...
THEY'RE ALL QUITE THICK, AND I'M THEIR LEADER! (SOB! SOB!)
BUT SOME PEOPLE ARE MAKING THE MOST OF THE SITUATION, FOR INSTANCE, ASTERIX AND OBELIX, WHO HAVE PUT THEIR OWN CLOTHES ON AGAIN...
...AND THE GOTHS, THE ROOT OF ALL THE TROUBLE, WHO ARE PROCEEDING UNEVENTFULLY TOWARDS THEIR OWN COUNTRY OF GERMANIA.
Watch out! The frontier's ahead. We've got to cross it!
A HEAVY RESPONSIBILITY WEIGHS ON THOSE WHO GUARD THE FRONTIER AGAINST FOREIGN INVADERS...
GAUL ROMAN EMPIRE
Germania
Hey!
MMMM?
BONG!
Victory is ours! We'll be given a hero's welcome by our own people!
Anything to declare?
18

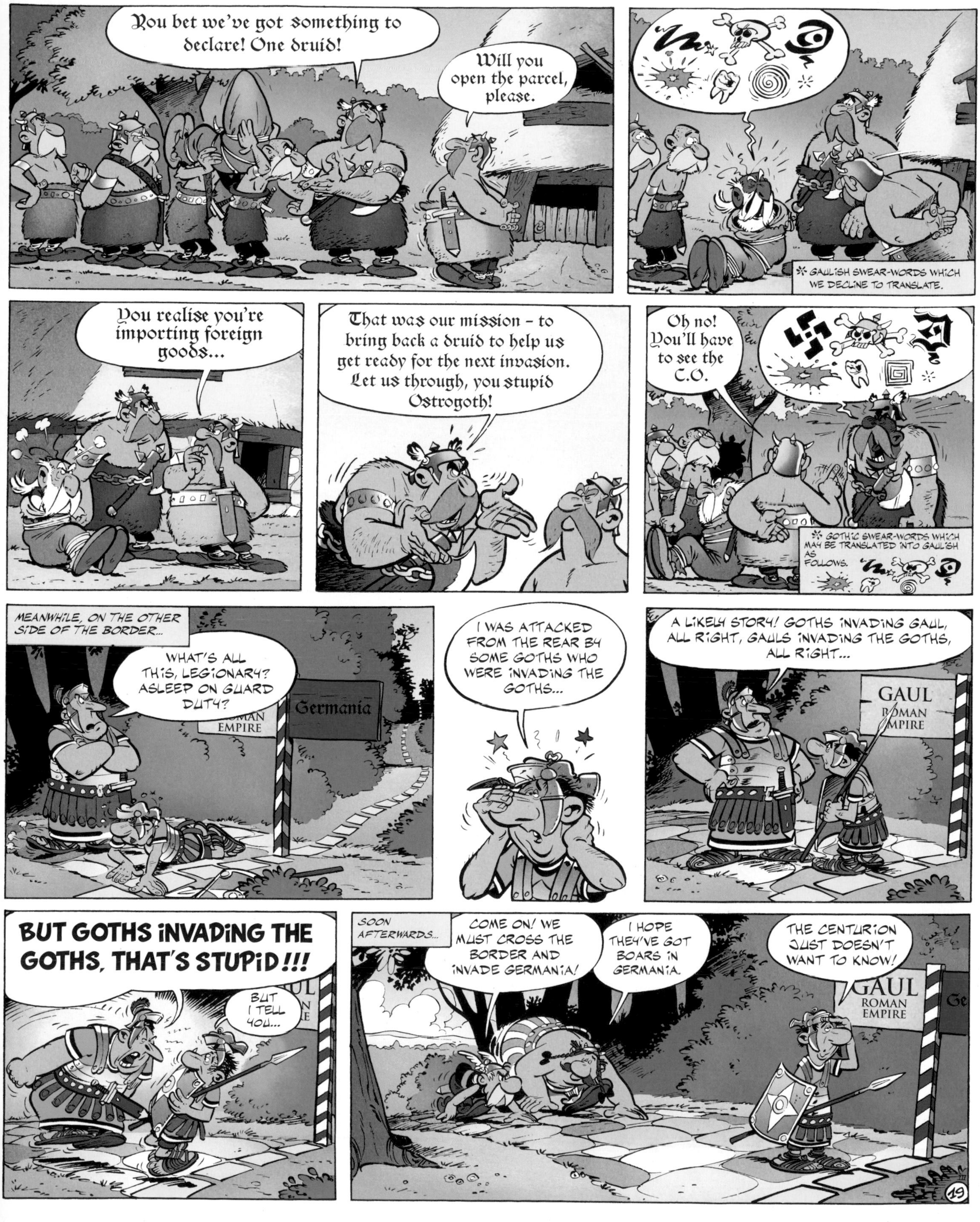

You bet we've got something to declare! One druid!
Will you open the parcel, please.
✲ GAULISH SWEAR-WORDS WHICH WE DECLINE TO TRANSLATE.
You realise you're importing foreign goods...
That was our mission – to bring back a druid to help us get ready for the next invasion. Let us through, you stupid Ostrogoth!
Oh no! You'll have to see the C.O.
✲ GOTHIC SWEAR-WORDS WHICH MAY BE TRANSLATED INTO GAULISH AS FOLLOWS.
MEANWHILE, ON THE OTHER SIDE OF THE BORDER...
WHAT'S ALL THIS, LEGIONARY? ASLEEP ON GUARD DUTY?
Germania
ROMAN EMPIRE
I WAS ATTACKED FROM THE REAR BY SOME GOTHS WHO WERE INVADING THE GOTHS...
A LIKELY STORY! GOTHS INVADING GAUL, ALL RIGHT, GAULS INVADING THE GOTHS, ALL RIGHT...
GAUL
ROMAN EMPIRE
BUT GOTHS INVADING THE GOTHS, THAT'S STUPID!!!
BUT I TELL YOU...
SOON AFTERWARDS...
COME ON! WE MUST CROSS THE BORDER AND INVADE GERMANIA!
I HOPE THEY'VE GOT BOARS IN GERMANIA.
THE CENTURION JUST DOESN'T WANT TO KNOW!
GAUL
ROMAN EMPIRE
19

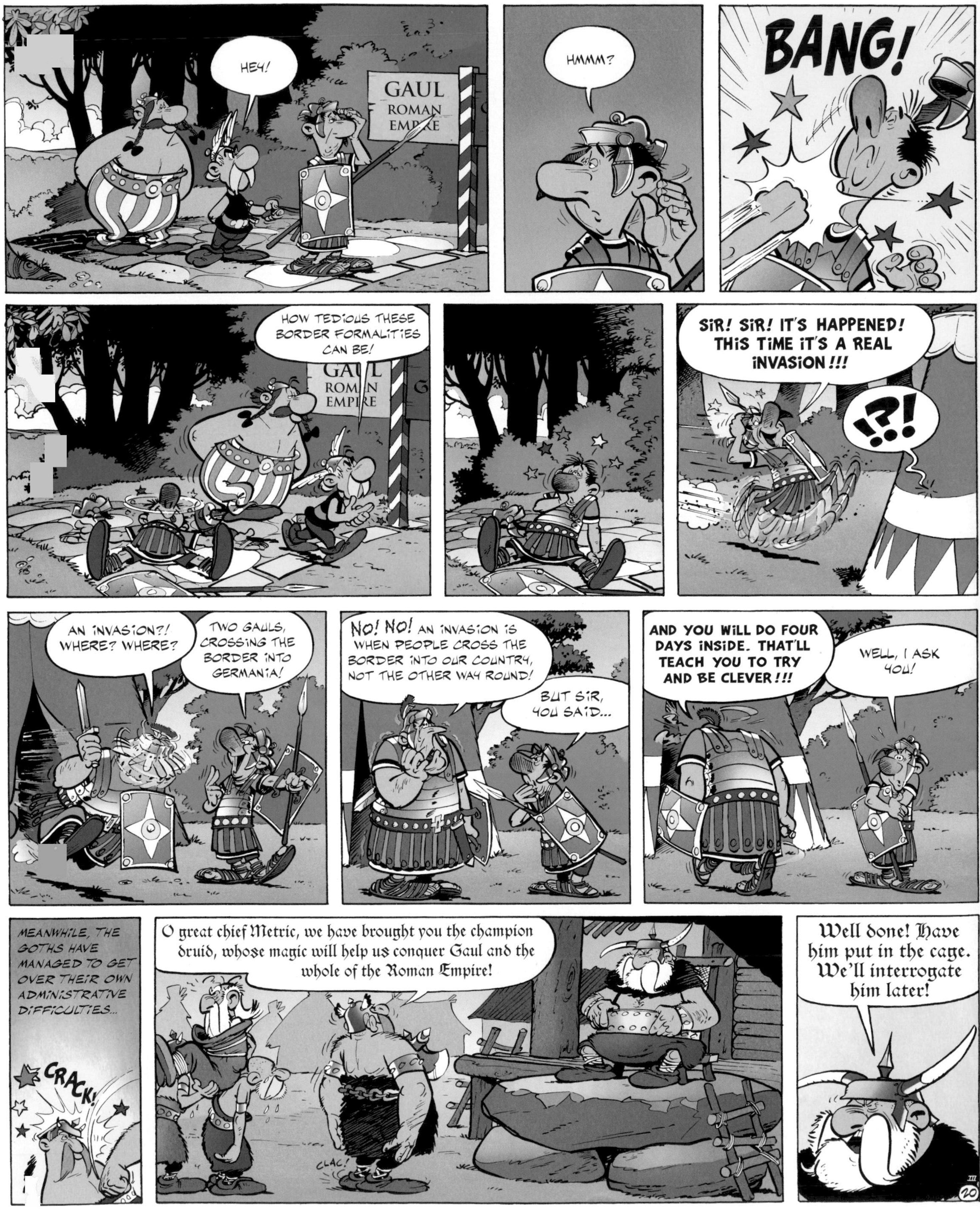
HEY!
GAUL
ROMAN EMPIRE
HMMM?
BANG!
HOW TEDIOUS THESE BORDER FORMALITIES CAN BE!
SIR! SIR! IT'S HAPPENED! THIS TIME IT'S A REAL INVASION!!!
!?!
AN INVASION?! WHERE? WHERE?
TWO GAULS, CROSSING THE BORDER INTO GERMANIA!
NO! NO! AN INVASION IS WHEN PEOPLE CROSS THE BORDER INTO OUR COUNTRY, NOT THE OTHER WAY ROUND!
BUT SIR, YOU SAID...
AND YOU WILL DO FOUR DAYS INSIDE. THAT'LL TEACH YOU TO TRY AND BE CLEVER!!!
WELL, I ASK YOU!
MEANWHILE, THE GOTHS HAVE MANAGED TO GET OVER THEIR OWN ADMINISTRATIVE DIFFICULTIES...
CRACK!
O great chief Metric, we have brought you the champion druid, whose magic will help us conquer Gaul and the whole of the Roman Empire!
CLAC!
Well done! Have him put in the cage. We'll interrogate him later!

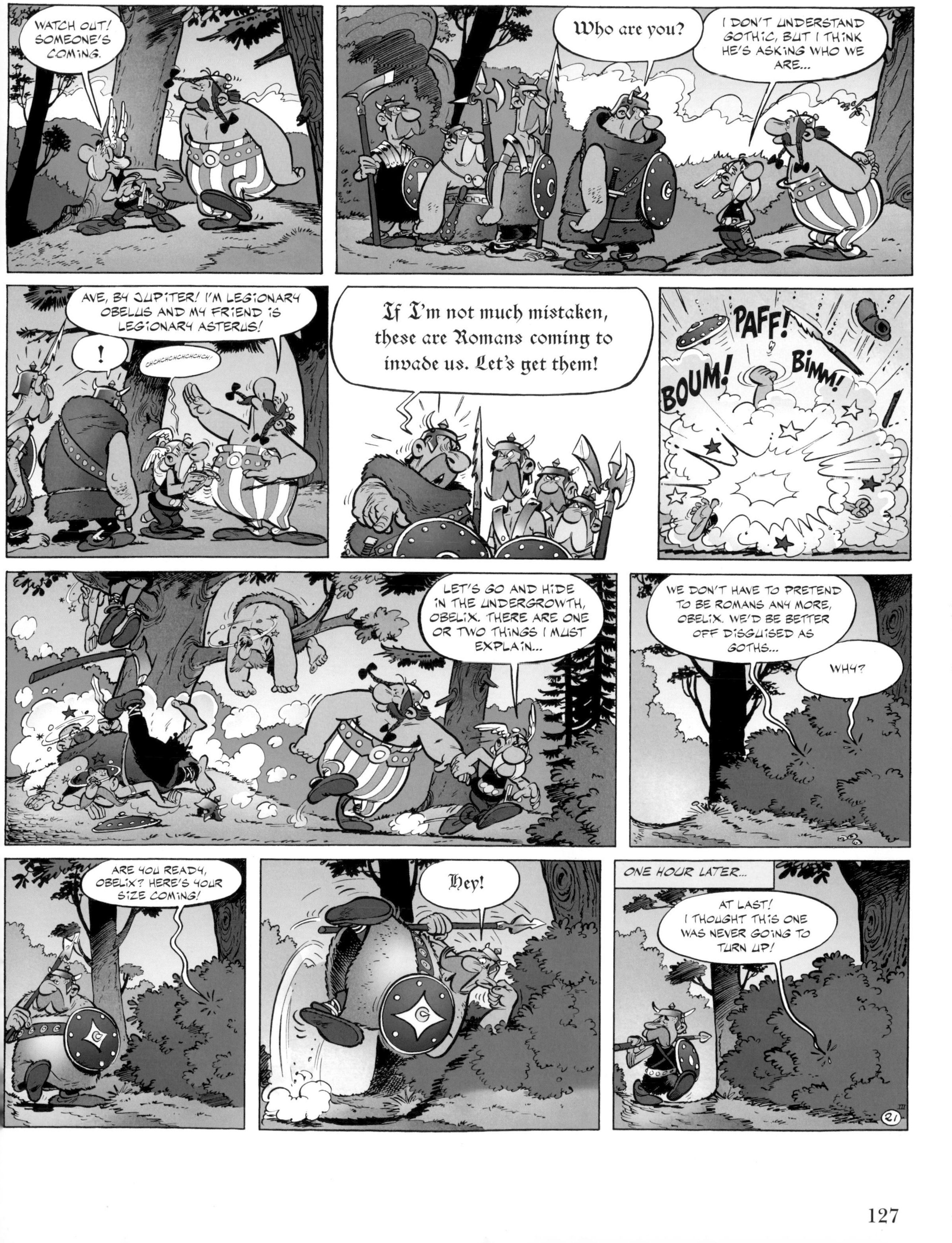
WATCH OUT! SOMEONE'S COMING.
Who are you?
I DON'T UNDERSTAND GOTHIC, BUT I THINK HE'S ASKING WHO WE ARE...
AVE, BY JUPITER! I'M LEGIONARY OBELUS AND MY FRIEND IS LEGIONARY ASTERUS!
!
If I'm not much mistaken, these are Romans coming to invade us. Let's get them!
PAFF!
BOUM!
BIMM!
LET'S GO AND HIDE IN THE UNDERGROWTH, OBELIX. THERE ARE ONE OR TWO THINGS I MUST EXPLAIN...
WE DON'T HAVE TO PRETEND TO BE ROMANS ANY MORE, OBELIX. WE'D BE BETTER OFF DISGUISED AS GOTHS...
WHY?
ARE YOU READY, OBELIX? HERE'S YOUR SIZE COMING!
Hey!
ONE HOUR LATER...
AT LAST! I THOUGHT THIS ONE WAS NEVER GOING TO TURN UP!
21

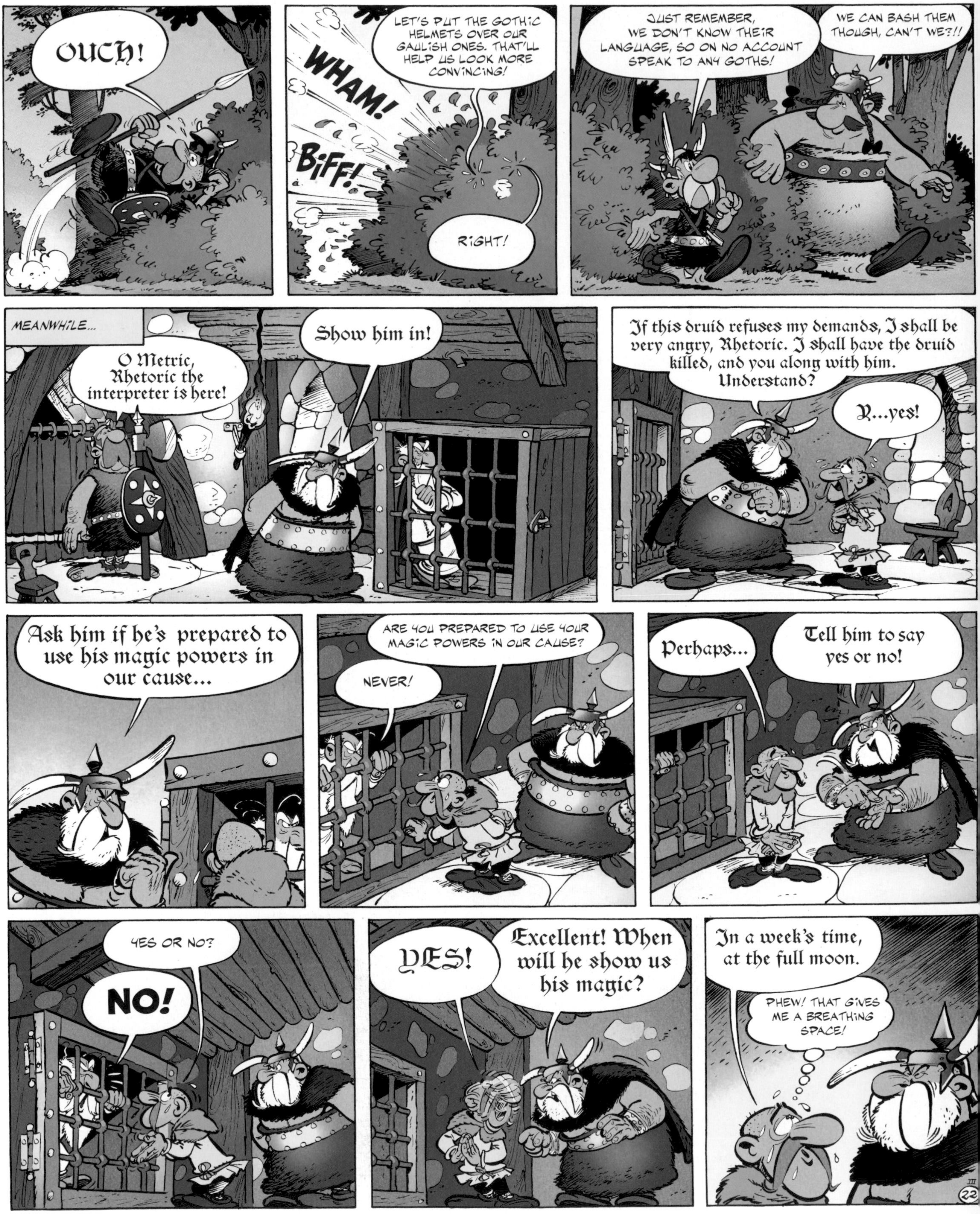
OUCH!
LET'S PUT THE GOTHIC HELMETS OVER OUR GAULISH ONES. THAT'LL HELP US LOOK MORE CONVINCING!
WHAM!
BIFF!
RIGHT!
JUST REMEMBER, WE DON'T KNOW THEIR LANGUAGE, SO ON NO ACCOUNT SPEAK TO ANY GOTHS!
WE CAN BASH THEM THOUGH, CAN'T WE?!!
MEANWHILE...
O Metric, Rhetoric the interpreter is here!
Show him in!
If this druid refuses my demands, I shall be very angry, Rhetoric. I shall have the druid killed, and you along with him. Understand?
Y...yes!
Ask him if he's prepared to use his magic powers in our cause...
ARE YOU PREPARED TO USE YOUR MAGIC POWERS IN OUR CAUSE?
NEVER!
Perhaps...
Tell him to say yes or no!
YES OR NO?
NO!
YES!
Excellent! When will he show us his magic?
In a week's time, at the full moon.
PHEW! THAT GIVES ME A BREATHING SPACE!
III 22

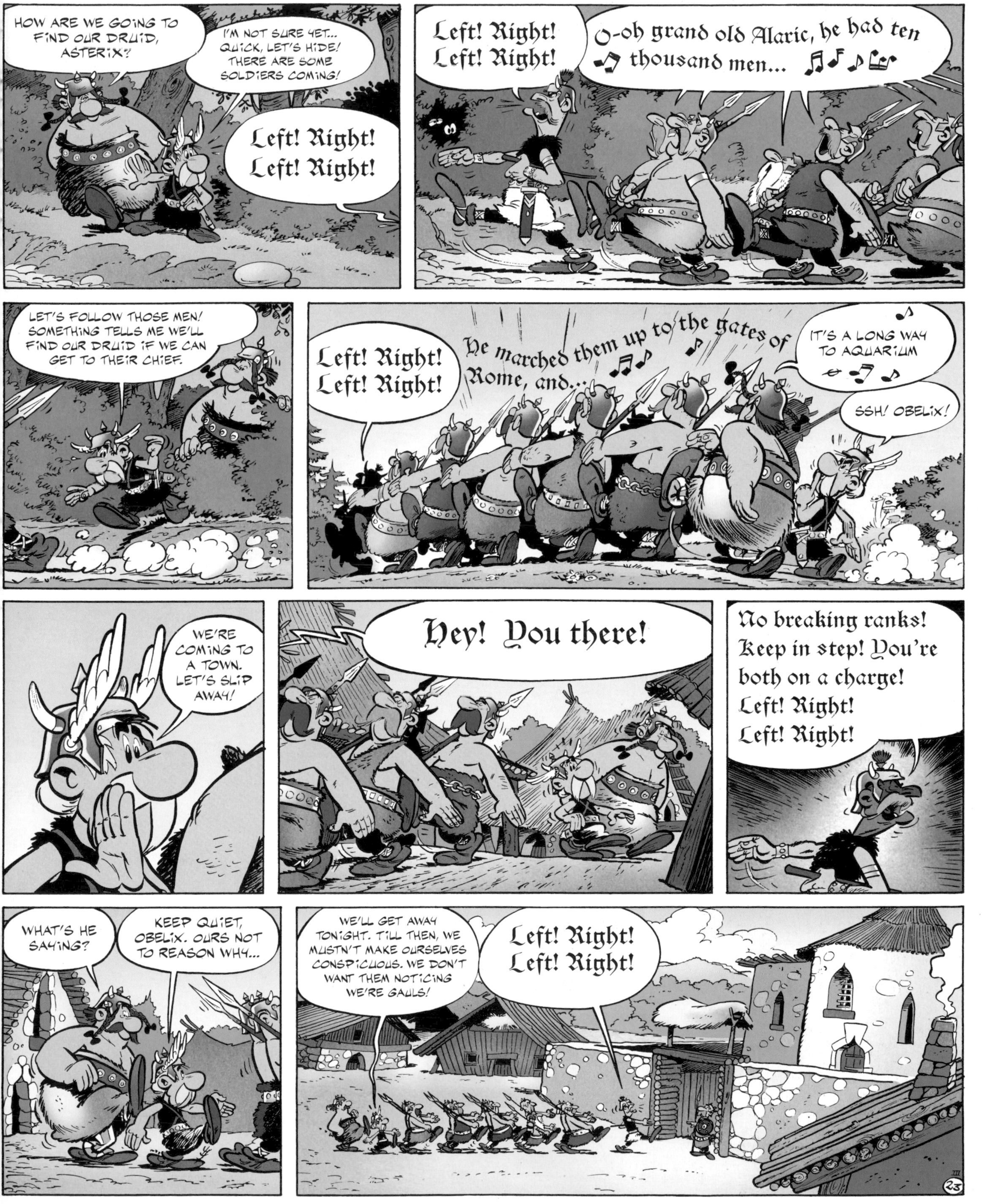

HOW ARE WE GOING TO FIND OUR DRUID, ASTERIX?
I'M NOT SURE YET... QUICK, LET'S HIDE! THERE ARE SOME SOLDIERS COMING!
Left! Right! Left! Right!
Left! Right! Left! Right!
O-oh grand old Alaric, he had ten thousand men...
LET'S FOLLOW THOSE MEN! SOMETHING TELLS ME WE'LL FIND OUR DRUID IF WE CAN GET TO THEIR CHIEF.
Left! Right! Left! Right!
He marched them up to the gates of Rome, and...
IT'S A LONG WAY TO AQUARIUM
SSH! OBELIX!
WE'RE COMING TO A TOWN. LET'S SLIP AWAY!
Hey! You there!
No breaking ranks! Keep in step! You're both on a charge! Left! Right! Left! Right!
WHAT'S HE SAYING?
KEEP QUIET, OBELIX. OURS NOT TO REASON WHY...
WE'LL GET AWAY TONIGHT. TILL THEN, WE MUSTN'T MAKE OURSELVES CONSPICUOUS. WE DON'T WANT THEM NOTICING WE'RE GAULS!
Left! Right! Left! Right!
23

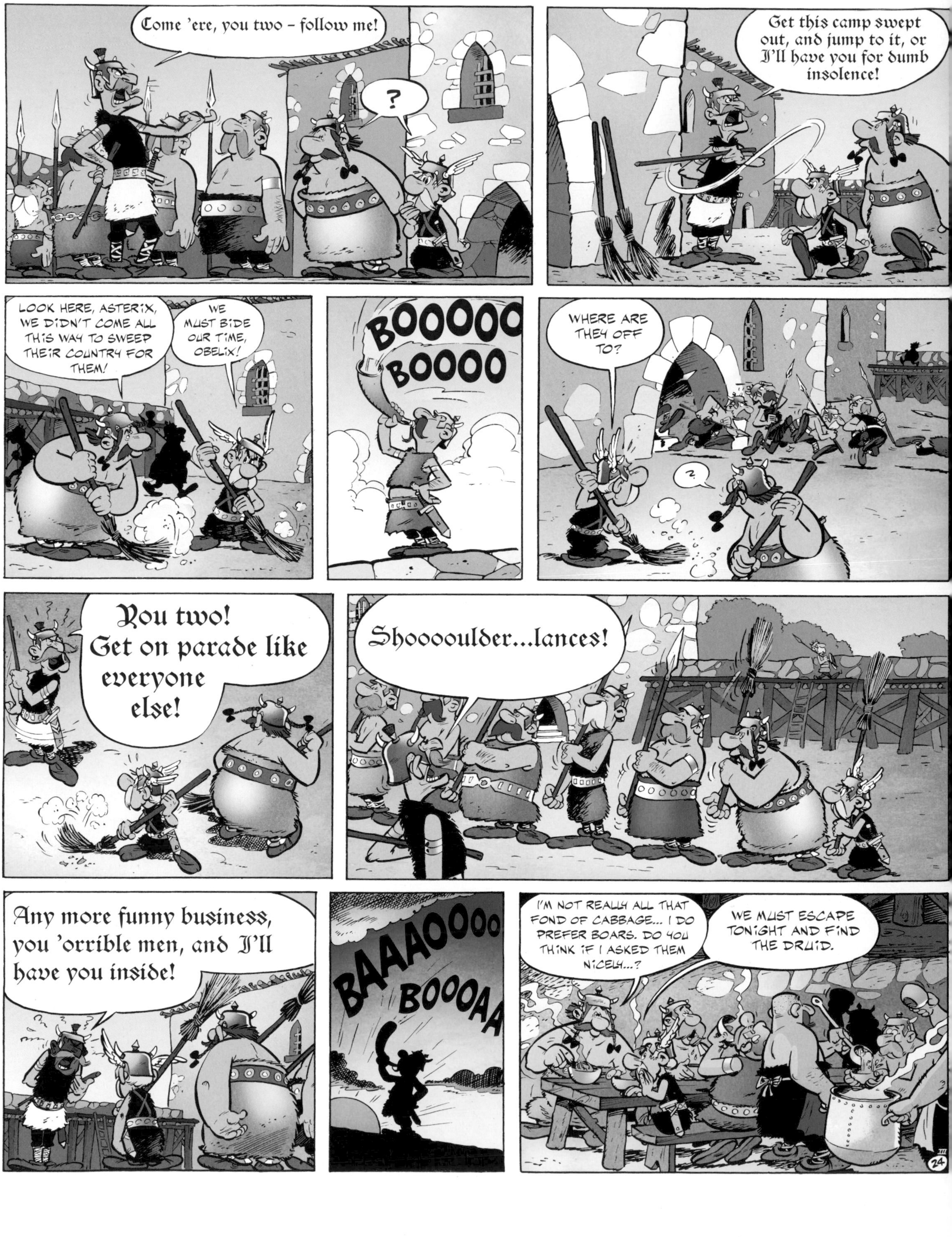

Come 'ere, you two – follow me!
?
Get this camp swept out, and jump to it, or I'll have you for dumb insolence!
LOOK HERE, ASTERIX, WE DIDN'T COME ALL THIS WAY TO SWEEP THEIR COUNTRY FOR THEM!
WE MUST BIDE OUR TIME, OBELIX!
BOOOOO BOOOO
WHERE ARE THEY OFF TO?
?
You two! Get on parade like everyone else!
Shoooooulder...lances!
Any more funny business, you 'orrible men, and I'll have you inside!
BAAAOOOO BOOOAA
I'M NOT REALLY ALL THAT FOND OF CABBAGE... I DO PREFER BOARS. DO YOU THINK IF I ASKED THEM NICELY...?
WE MUST ESCAPE TONIGHT AND FIND THE DRUID.

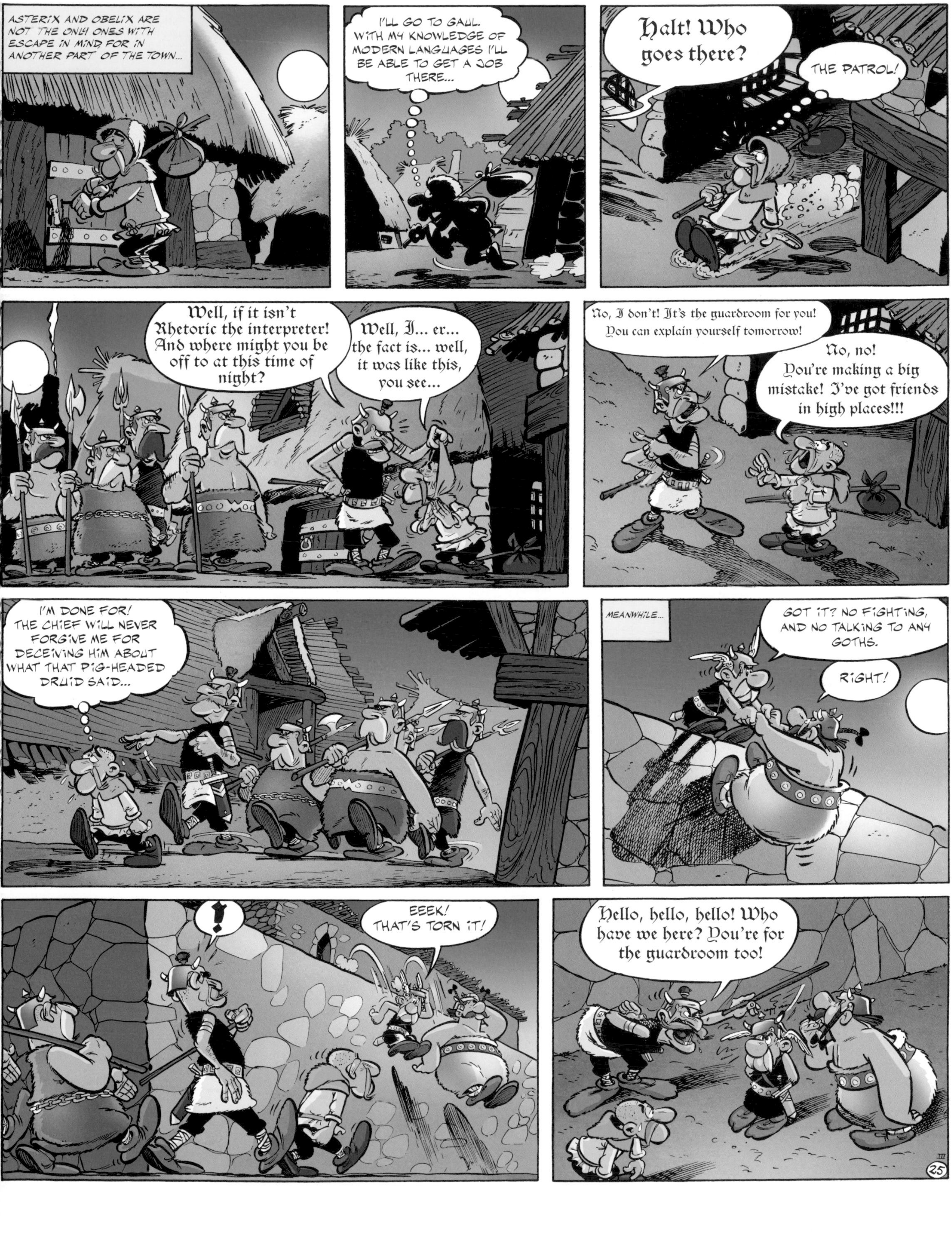
ASTERIX AND OBELIX ARE NOT THE ONLY ONES WITH ESCAPE IN MIND FOR IN ANOTHER PART OF THE TOWN...
I'LL GO TO GAUL. WITH MY KNOWLEDGE OF MODERN LANGUAGES I'LL BE ABLE TO GET A JOB THERE...
Halt! Who goes there?
THE PATROL!
Well, if it isn't Rhetoric the interpreter! And where might you be off to at this time of night?
Well, I... er... the fact is... well, it was like this, you see...
No, I don't! It's the guardroom for you! You can explain yourself tomorrow!
No, no! You're making a big mistake! I've got friends in high places!!!
I'M DONE FOR! THE CHIEF WILL NEVER FORGIVE ME FOR DECEIVING HIM ABOUT WHAT THAT PIG-HEADED DRUID SAID...
MEANWHILE...
GOT IT? NO FIGHTING, AND NO TALKING TO ANY GOTHS.
RIGHT!
!
EEEK! THAT'S TORN IT!
Hello, hello, hello! Who have we here? You're for the guardroom too!
25

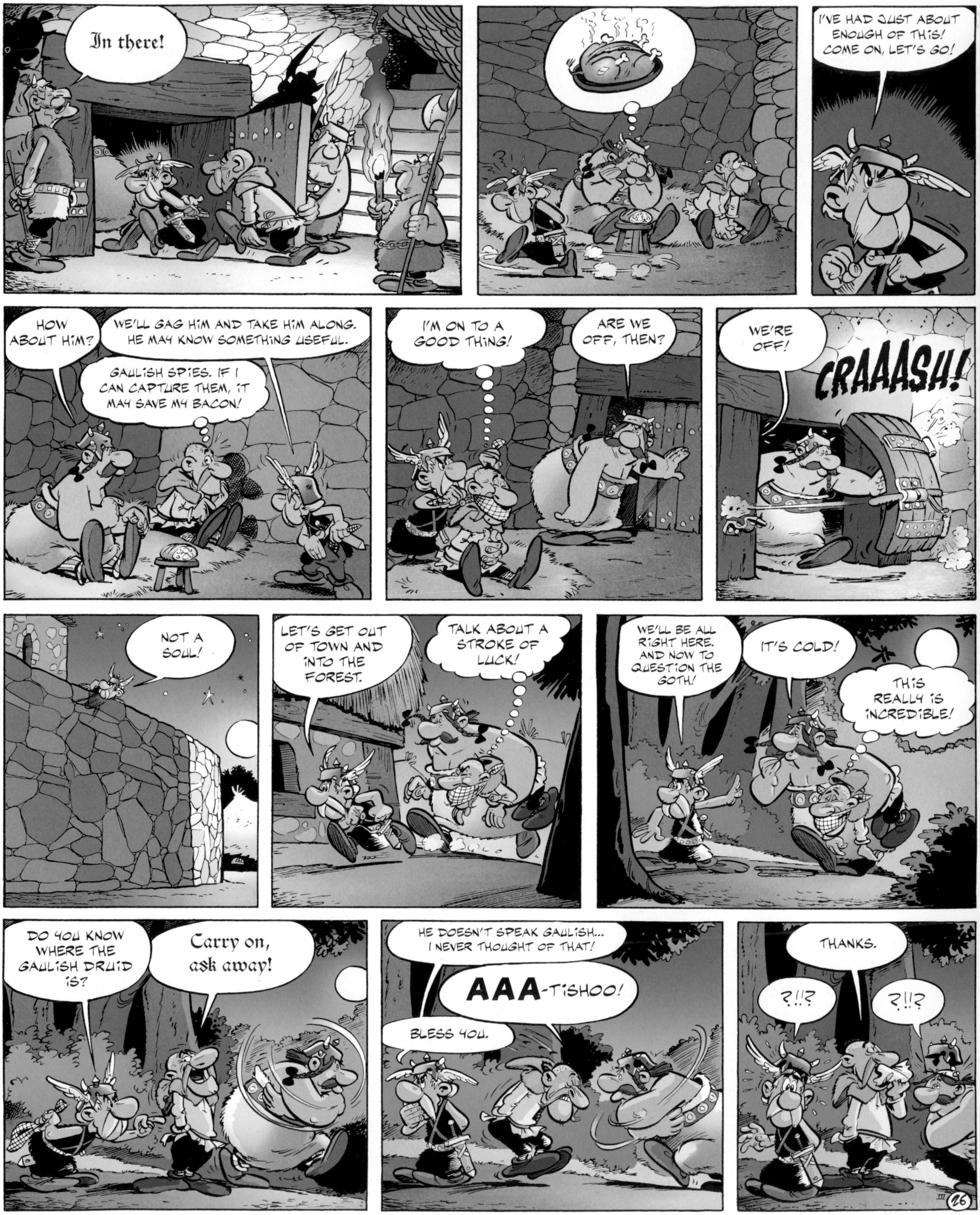
In there!
I'VE HAD JUST ABOUT ENOUGH OF THIS! COME ON, LET'S GO!
HOW ABOUT HIM?
WE'LL GAG HIM AND TAKE HIM ALONG. HE MAY KNOW SOMETHING USEFUL.
GAULISH SPIES. IF I CAN CAPTURE THEM, IT MAY SAVE MY BACON!
I'M ON TO A GOOD THING!
ARE WE OFF, THEN?
WE'RE OFF!
CRAAASH!
NOT A SOUL!
LET'S GET OUT OF TOWN AND INTO THE FOREST.
TALK ABOUT A STROKE OF LUCK!
WE'LL BE ALL RIGHT HERE. AND NOW TO QUESTION THE GOTH!
IT'S COLD!
THIS REALLY IS INCREDIBLE!
DO YOU KNOW WHERE THE GAULISH DRUID IS?
Carry on, ask away!
HE DOESN'T SPEAK GAULISH... I NEVER THOUGHT OF THAT!
AAA-TISHOO!
BLESS YOU.
THANKS.
?!!?
?!!?

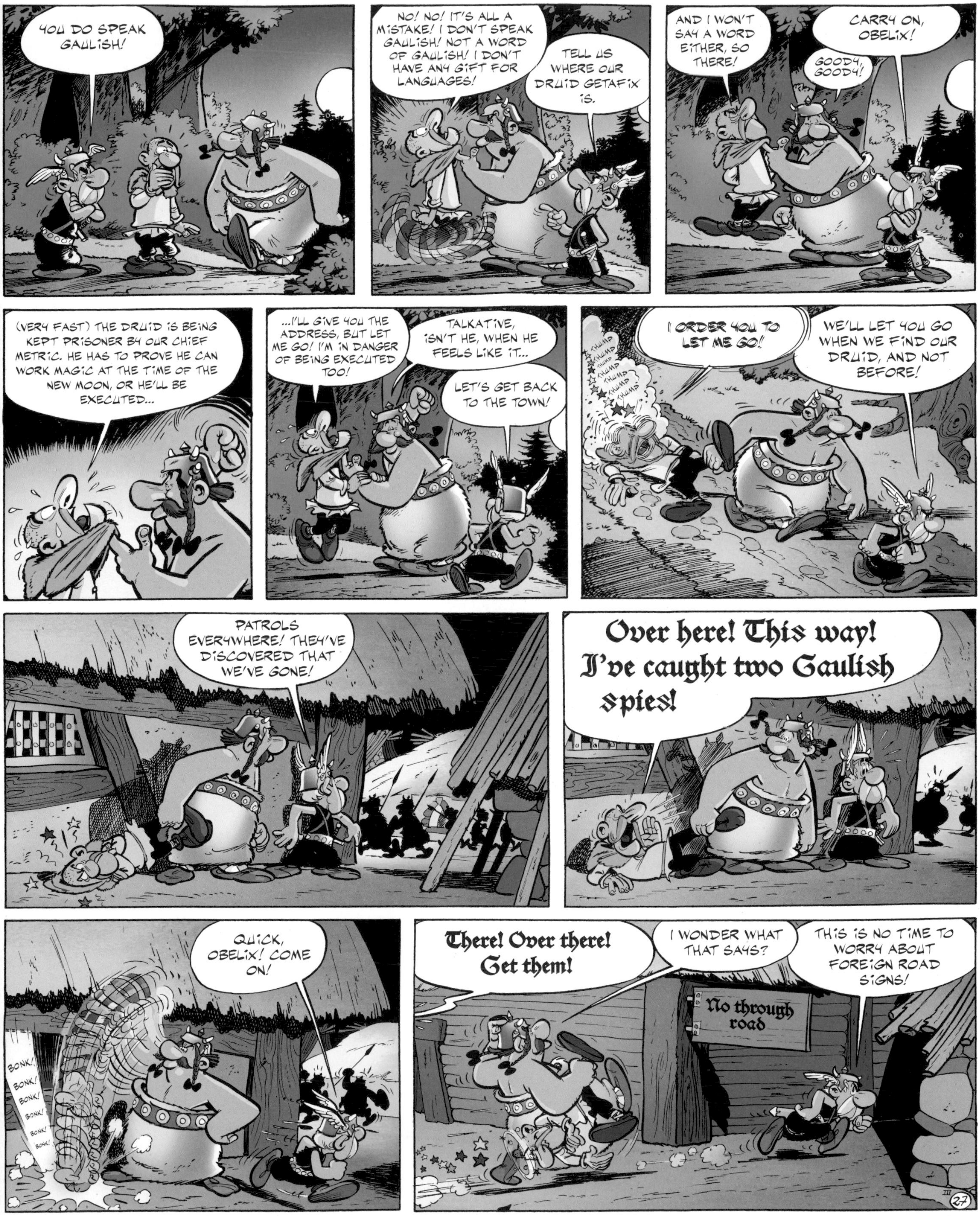

YOU DO SPEAK GAULISH!
NO! NO! IT'S ALL A MISTAKE! I DON'T SPEAK GAULISH! NOT A WORD OF GAULISH! I DON'T HAVE ANY GIFT FOR LANGUAGES!
TELL US WHERE OUR DRUID GETAFIX IS.
AND I WON'T SAY A WORD EITHER, SO THERE!
CARRY ON, OBELIX!
GOODY, GOODY!
(VERY FAST) THE DRUID IS BEING KEPT PRISONER BY OUR CHIEF METRIC. HE HAS TO PROVE HE CAN WORK MAGIC AT THE TIME OF THE NEW MOON, OR HE'LL BE EXECUTED...
...I'LL GIVE YOU THE ADDRESS, BUT LET ME GO! I'M IN DANGER OF BEING EXECUTED TOO!
TALKATIVE, ISN'T HE, WHEN HE FEELS LIKE IT...
LET'S GET BACK TO THE TOWN!
I ORDER YOU TO LET ME GO!
WE'LL LET YOU GO WHEN WE FIND OUR DRUID, AND NOT BEFORE!
PATROLS EVERYWHERE! THEY'VE DISCOVERED THAT WE'VE GONE!
Over here! This way! I've caught two Gaulish spies!
QUICK, OBELIX! COME ON!
BONK! BONK! BONK! BONK! BONK! BONK!
There! Over there! Get them!
I WONDER WHAT THAT SAYS?
THIS IS NO TIME TO WORRY ABOUT FOREIGN ROAD SIGNS!
No through road
III 27

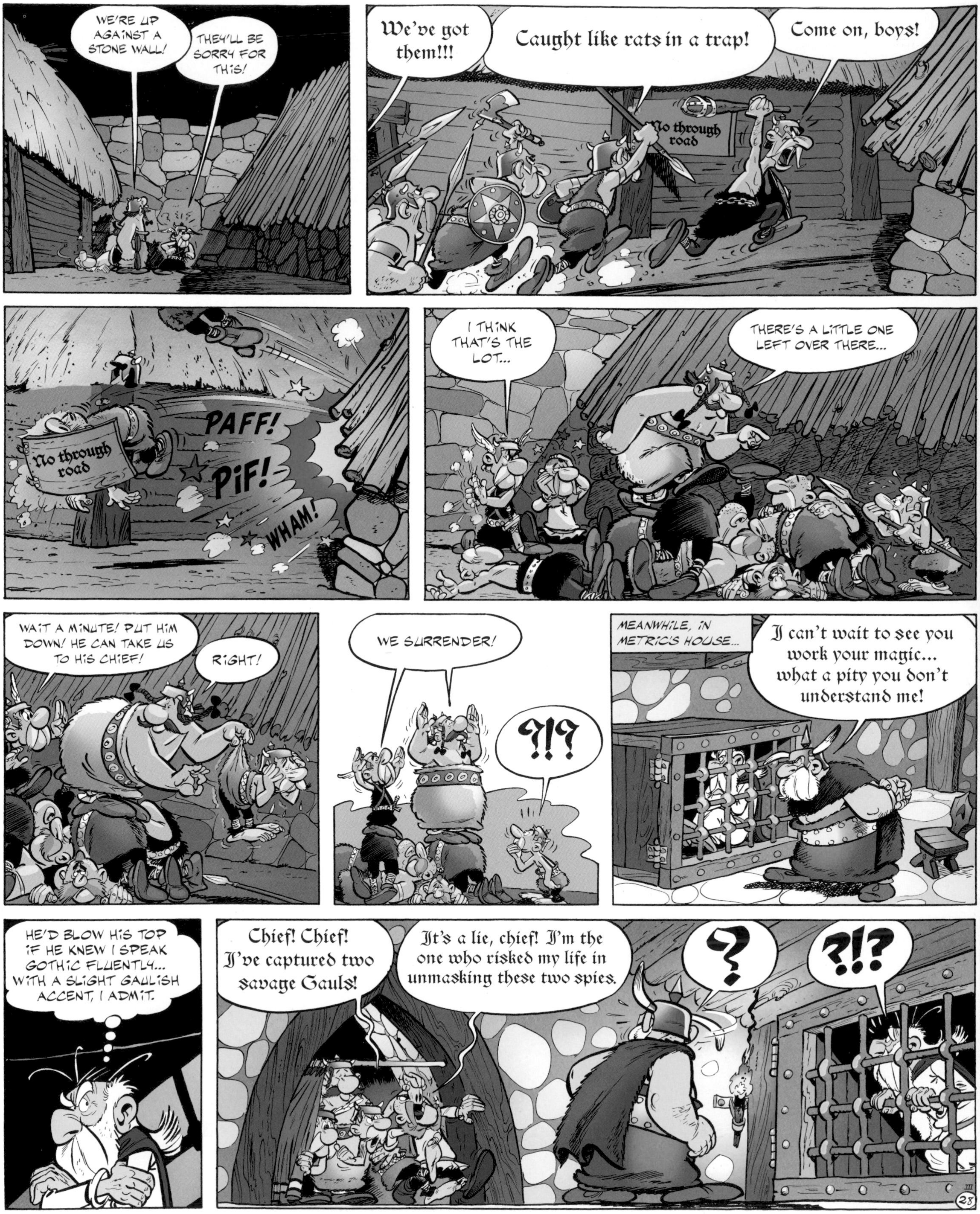
WE'RE UP AGAINST A STONE WALL!
THEY'LL BE SORRY FOR THIS!
We've got them!!!
Caught like rats in a trap!
Come on, boys!
No through road
No through road
PAFF!
PIF!
WHAM!
I THINK THAT'S THE LOT...
THERE'S A LITTLE ONE LEFT OVER THERE...
WAIT A MINUTE! PUT HIM DOWN! HE CAN TAKE US TO HIS CHIEF!
RIGHT!
WE SURRENDER!
?!?
MEANWHILE, IN METRICS HOUSE...
I can't wait to see you work your magic... what a pity you don't understand me!
HE'D BLOW HIS TOP IF HE KNEW I SPEAK GOTHIC FLUENTLY... WITH A SLIGHT GAULISH ACCENT, I ADMIT.
Chief! Chief! I've captured two savage Gauls!
It's a lie, chief! I'm the one who risked my life in unmasking these two spies.
?
?!?

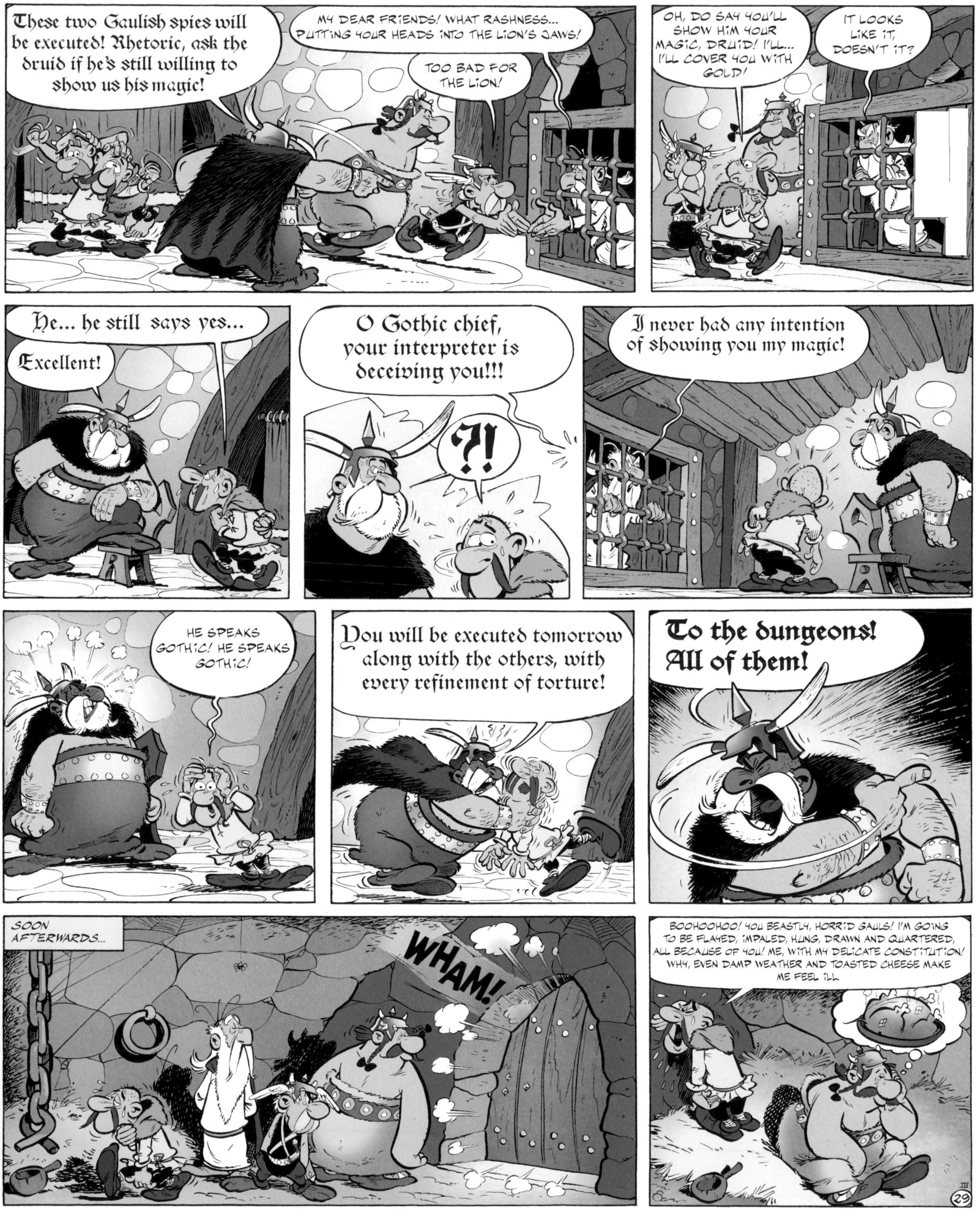
These two Gaulish spies will be executed! Rhetoric, ask the druid if he's still willing to show us his magic!
MY DEAR FRIENDS! WHAT RASHNESS... PUTTING YOUR HEADS INTO THE LION'S JAWS!
TOO BAD FOR THE LION!
OH, DO SAY YOU'LL SHOW HIM YOUR MAGIC, DRUID! I'LL... I'LL COVER YOU WITH GOLD!
IT LOOKS LIKE IT, DOESN'T IT?
He... he still says yes...
Excellent!
O Gothic chief, your interpreter is deceiving you!!!
?!
I never had any intention of showing you my magic!
HE SPEAKS GOTHIC! HE SPEAKS GOTHIC!
You will be executed tomorrow along with the others, with every refinement of torture!
To the dungeons! All of them!
SOON AFTERWARDS...
WHAM!
BOOHOOHOO! YOU BEASTLY, HORRID GAULS! I'M GOING TO BE FLAYED, IMPALED, HUNG, DRAWN AND QUARTERED, ALL BECAUSE OF YOU! ME, WITH MY DELICATE CONSTITUTION! WHY, EVEN DAMP WEATHER AND TOASTED CHEESE MAKE ME FEEL ILL.
III 29

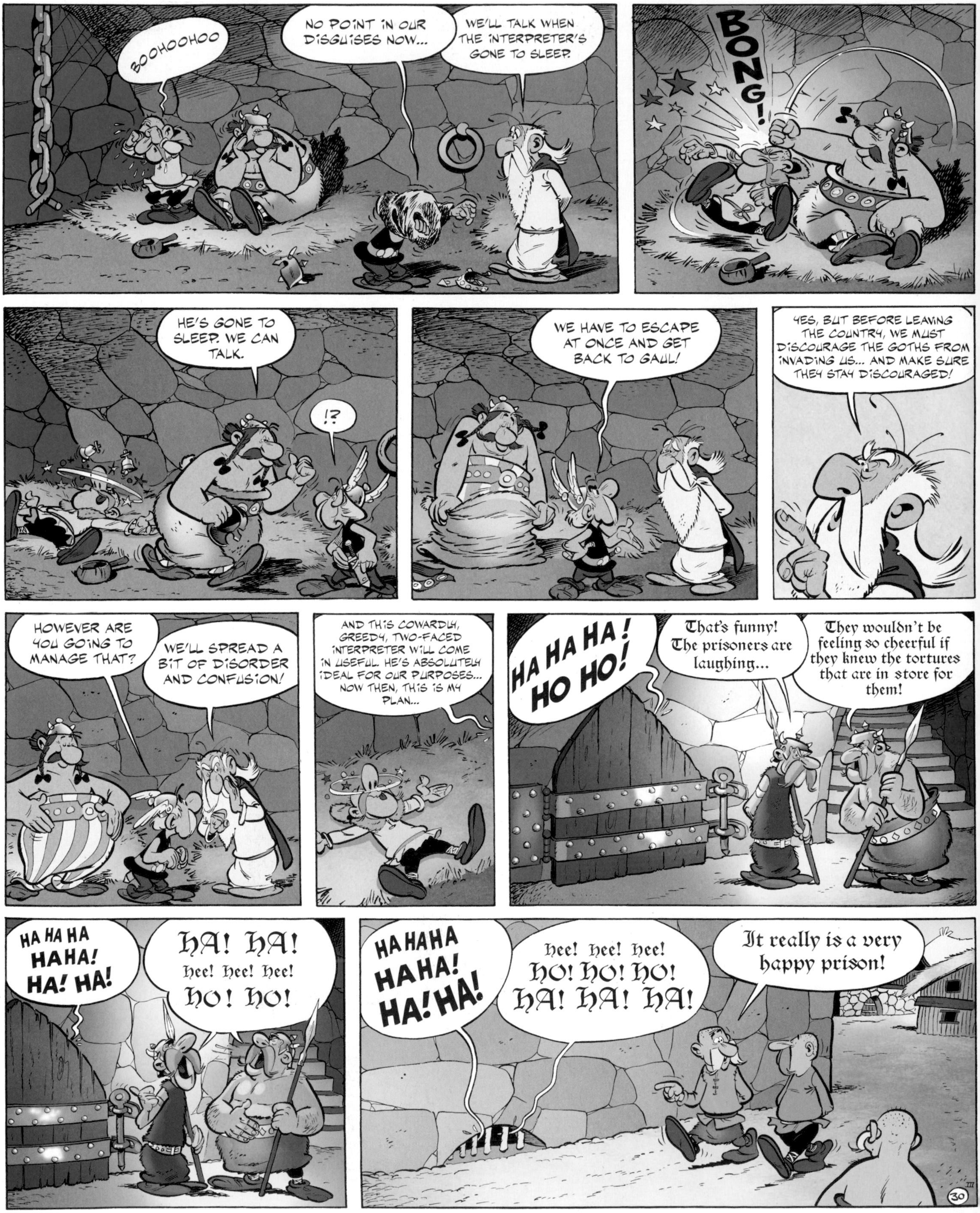
BOOHOOHOO
NO POINT IN OUR DISGUISES NOW...
WE'LL TALK WHEN THE INTERPRETER'S GONE TO SLEEP.
BONG!
HE'S GONE TO SLEEP. WE CAN TALK.
!?
WE HAVE TO ESCAPE AT ONCE AND GET BACK TO GAUL!
YES, BUT BEFORE LEAVING THE COUNTRY, WE MUST DISCOURAGE THE GOTHS FROM INVADING US... AND MAKE SURE THEY STAY DISCOURAGED!
HOWEVER ARE YOU GOING TO MANAGE THAT?
WE'LL SPREAD A BIT OF DISORDER AND CONFUSION!
AND THIS COWARDLY, GREEDY, TWO-FACED INTERPRETER WILL COME IN USEFUL. HE'S ABSOLUTELY IDEAL FOR OUR PURPOSES... NOW THEN, THIS IS MY PLAN...
HA HA HA! HO HO!
That's funny! The prisoners are laughing...
They wouldn't be feeling so cheerful if they knew the tortures that are in store for them!
HA HA HA HAHA! HA! HA!
HA! HA! Hee! Hee! Hee! HO! HO!
HA HAHA HAHA! HA!HA!
Hee! Hee! Hee! HO! HO! HO! HA! HA! HA!
It really is a very happy prison!
30

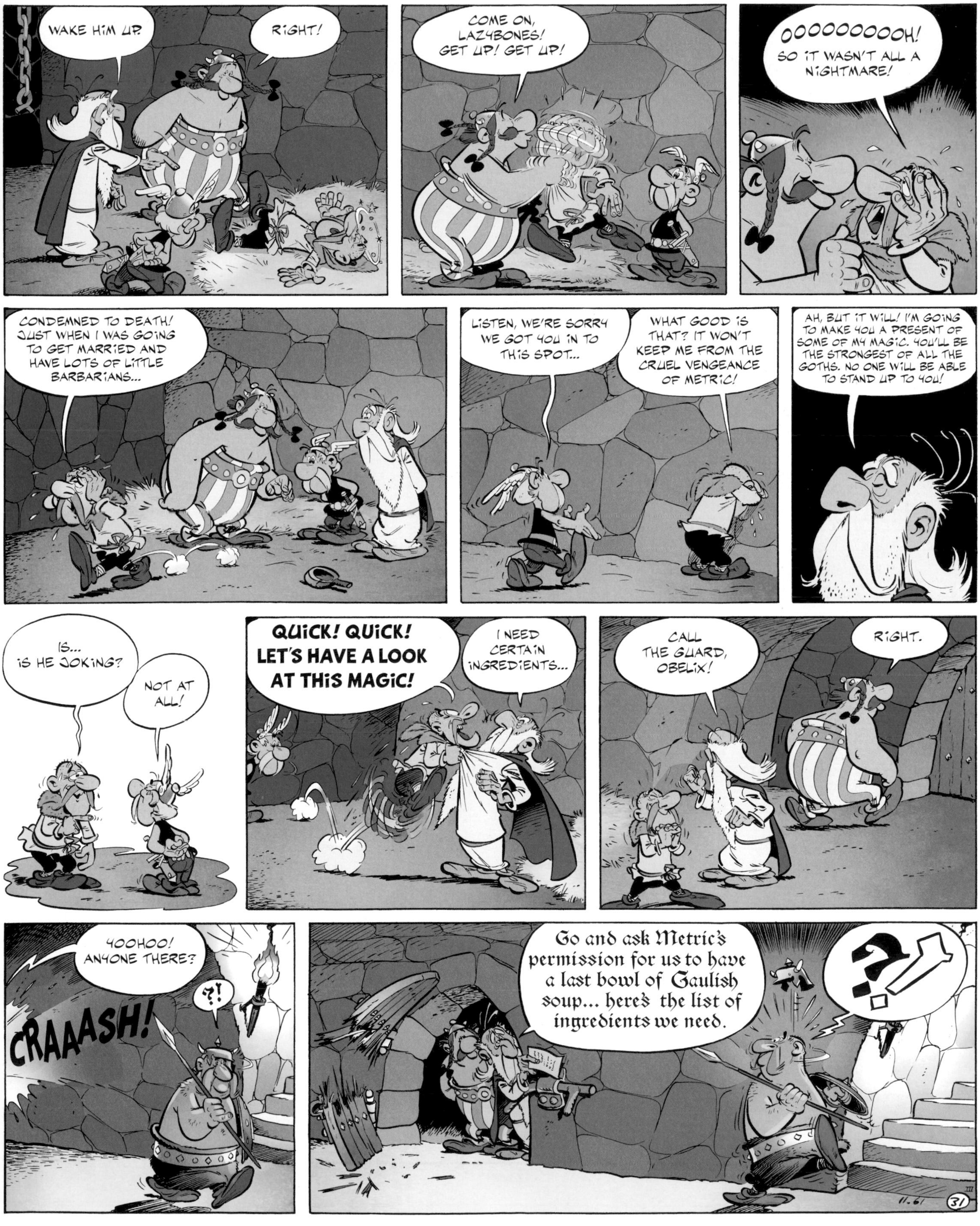
WAKE HIM UP.
RIGHT!
COME ON, LAZYBONES! GET UP! GET UP!
OOOOOOOOOH! SO IT WASN'T ALL A NIGHTMARE!
CONDEMNED TO DEATH! JUST WHEN I WAS GOING TO GET MARRIED AND HAVE LOTS OF LITTLE BARBARIANS...
LISTEN, WE'RE SORRY WE GOT YOU IN TO THIS SPOT...
WHAT GOOD IS THAT? IT WON'T KEEP ME FROM THE CRUEL VENGEANCE OF METRIC!
AH, BUT IT WILL! I'M GOING TO MAKE YOU A PRESENT OF SOME OF MY MAGIC. YOU'LL BE THE STRONGEST OF ALL THE GOTHS. NO ONE WILL BE ABLE TO STAND UP TO YOU!
IS... IS HE JOKING?
NOT AT ALL!
QUICK! QUICK! LET'S HAVE A LOOK AT THIS MAGIC!
I NEED CERTAIN INGREDIENTS...
CALL THE GUARD, OBELIX!
RIGHT.
YOOHOO! ANYONE THERE?
CRAAASH!
?!
Go and ask Metric's permission for us to have a last bowl of Gaulish soup... here's the list of ingredients we need.
?!
11.61
31

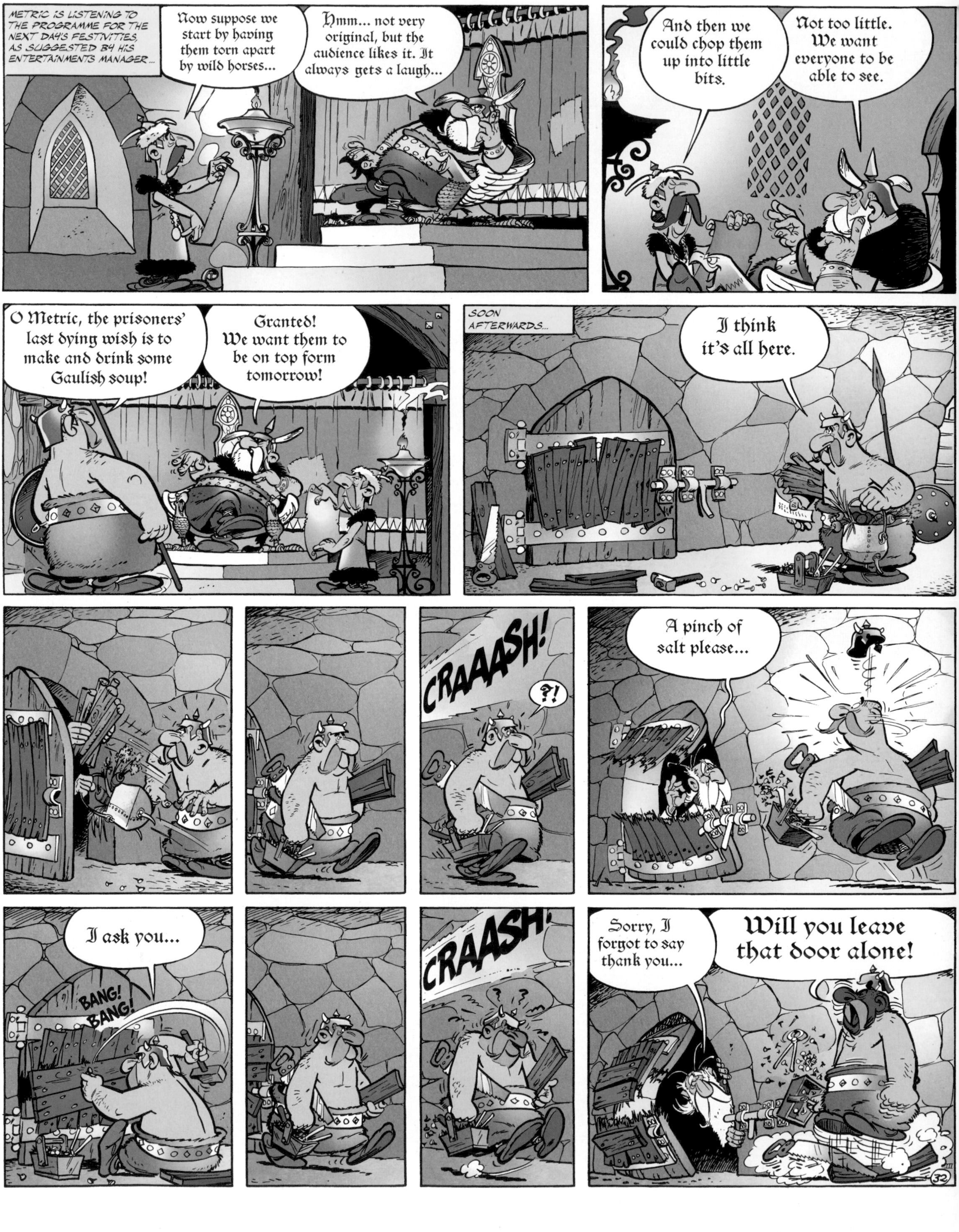
METRIC IS LISTENING TO THE PROGRAMME FOR THE NEXT DAY'S FESTIVITIES, AS SUGGESTED BY HIS ENTERTAINMENTS MANAGER ...
Now suppose we start by having them torn apart by wild horses...
Hmm... not very original, but the audience likes it. It always gets a laugh...
And then we could chop them up into little bits.
Not too little. We want everyone to be able to see.
O Metric, the prisoners' last dying wish is to make and drink some Gaulish soup!
Granted! We want them to be on top form tomorrow!
SOON AFTERWARDS...
I think it's all here.
CRAAASH!
?!
A pinch of salt please...
I ask you...
BANG! BANG!
CRAASH!
Sorry, I forgot to say thank you...
Will you leave that door alone!
32

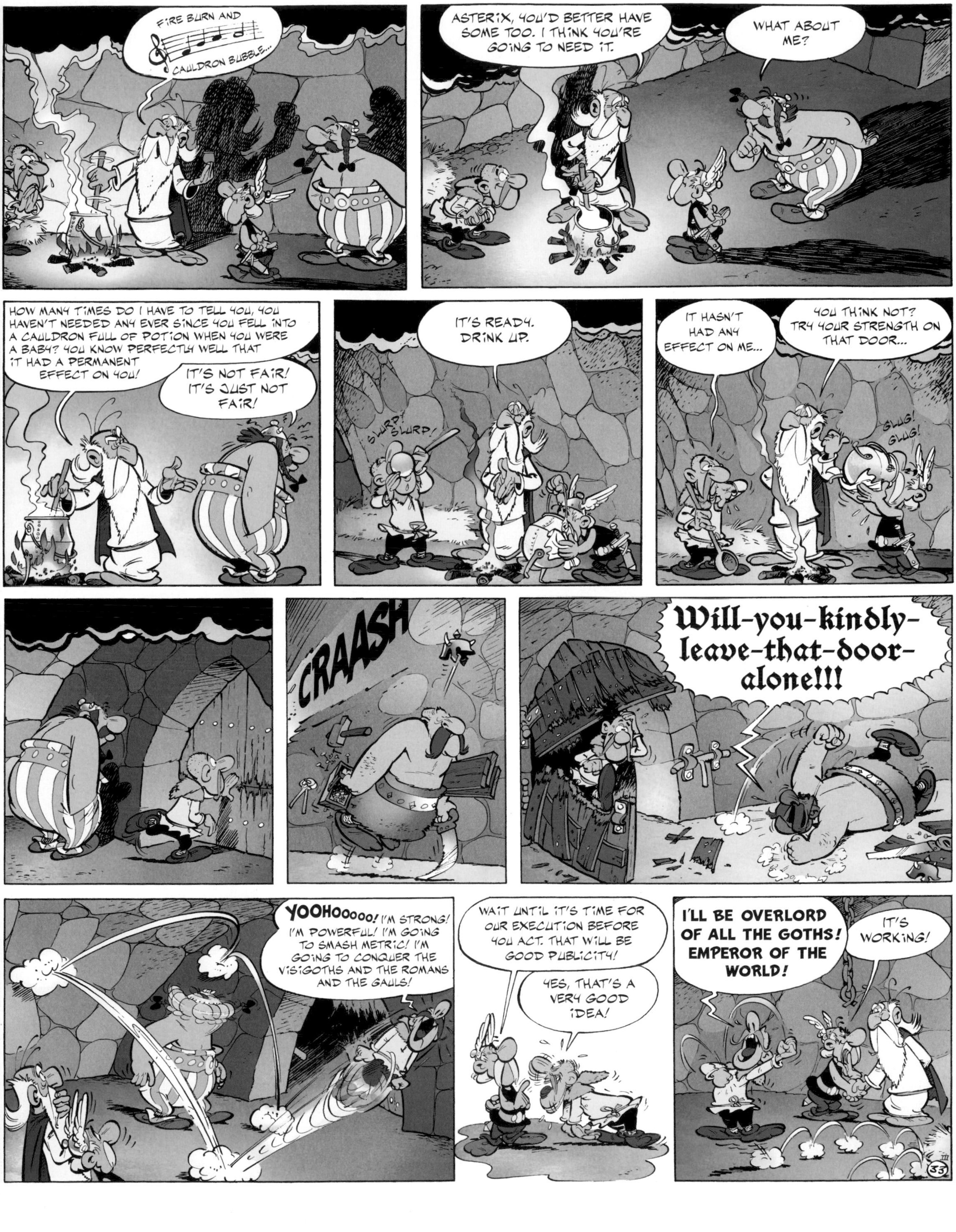

FIRE BURN AND CAULDRON BUBBLE...
ASTERIX, YOU'D BETTER HAVE SOME TOO. I THINK YOU'RE GOING TO NEED IT.
WHAT ABOUT ME?
HOW MANY TIMES DO I HAVE TO TELL YOU, YOU HAVEN'T NEEDED ANY EVER SINCE YOU FELL INTO A CAULDRON FULL OF POTION WHEN YOU WERE A BABY? YOU KNOW PERFECTLY WELL THAT IT HAD A PERMANENT EFFECT ON YOU!
IT'S NOT FAIR! IT'S JUST NOT FAIR!
IT'S READY. DRINK UP.
SLURP! SLURP!
IT HASN'T HAD ANY EFFECT ON ME...
YOU THINK NOT? TRY YOUR STRENGTH ON THAT DOOR...
GLUG! GLUG!
CRAASH
Will-you-kindly-leave-that-door-alone!!!
YOOHOooooo! I'M STRONG! I'M POWERFUL! I'M GOING TO SMASH METRIC! I'M GOING TO CONQUER THE VISIGOTHS AND THE ROMANS AND THE GAULS!
WAIT UNTIL IT'S TIME FOR OUR EXECUTION BEFORE YOU ACT. THAT WILL BE GOOD PUBLICITY!
YES, THAT'S A VERY GOOD IDEA!
I'LL BE OVERLORD OF ALL THE GOTHS! EMPEROR OF THE WORLD!
IT'S WORKING!

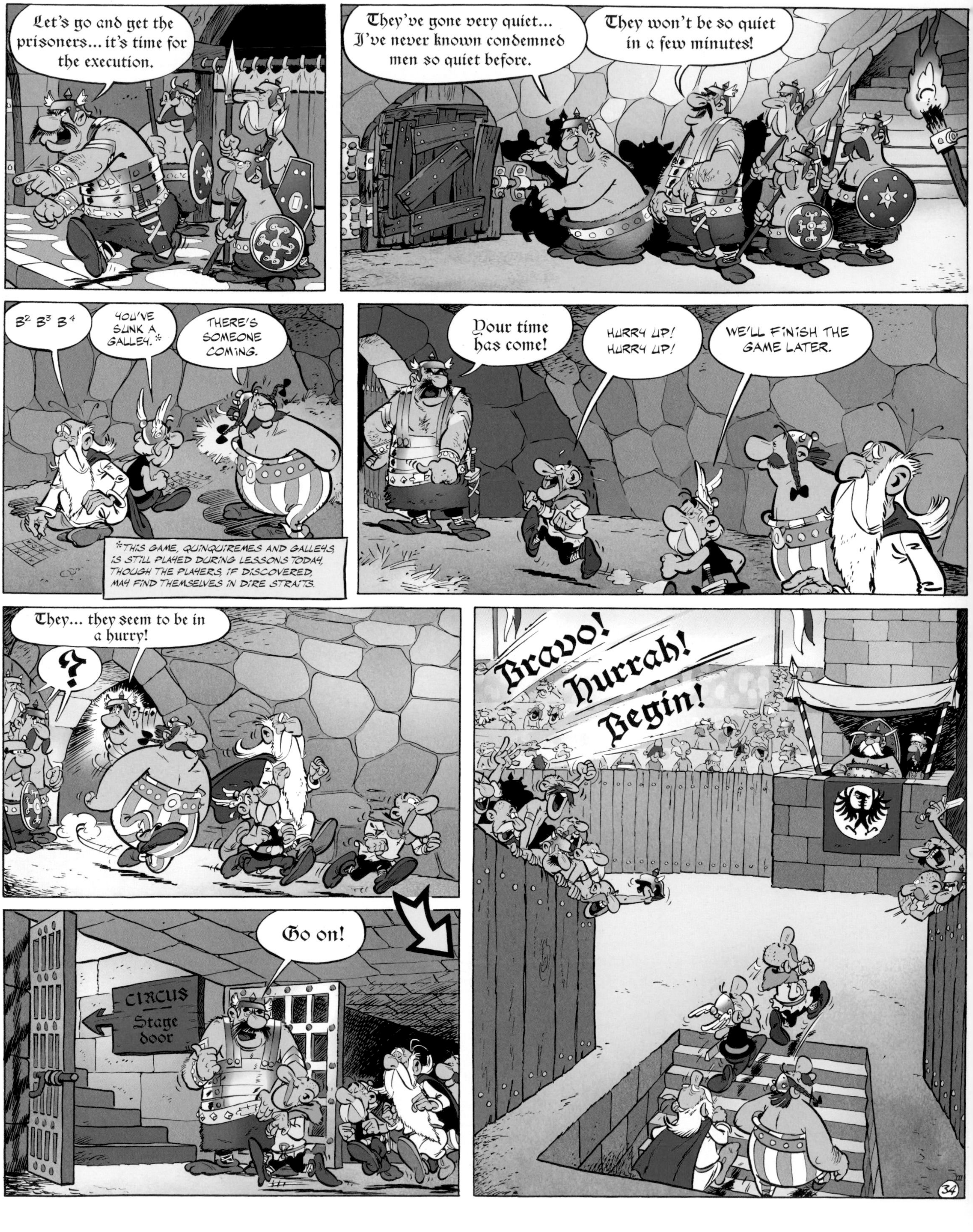
Let's go and get the prisoners... it's time for the execution.
They've gone very quiet... I've never known condemned men so quiet before.
They won't be so quiet in a few minutes!
B² B³ B⁴
YOU'VE SUNK A GALLEY.*
THERE'S SOMEONE COMING.
*THIS GAME, QUINQUIREMES AND GALLEYS, IS STILL PLAYED DURING LESSONS TODAY, THOUGH THE PLAYERS, IF DISCOVERED, MAY FIND THEMSELVES IN DIRE STRAITS.
Your time has come!
HURRY UP! HURRY UP!
WE'LL FINISH THE GAME LATER.
They... they seem to be in a hurry!
?
Go on!
CIRCUS
Stage door
Bravo!
Hurrah!
Begin!
34

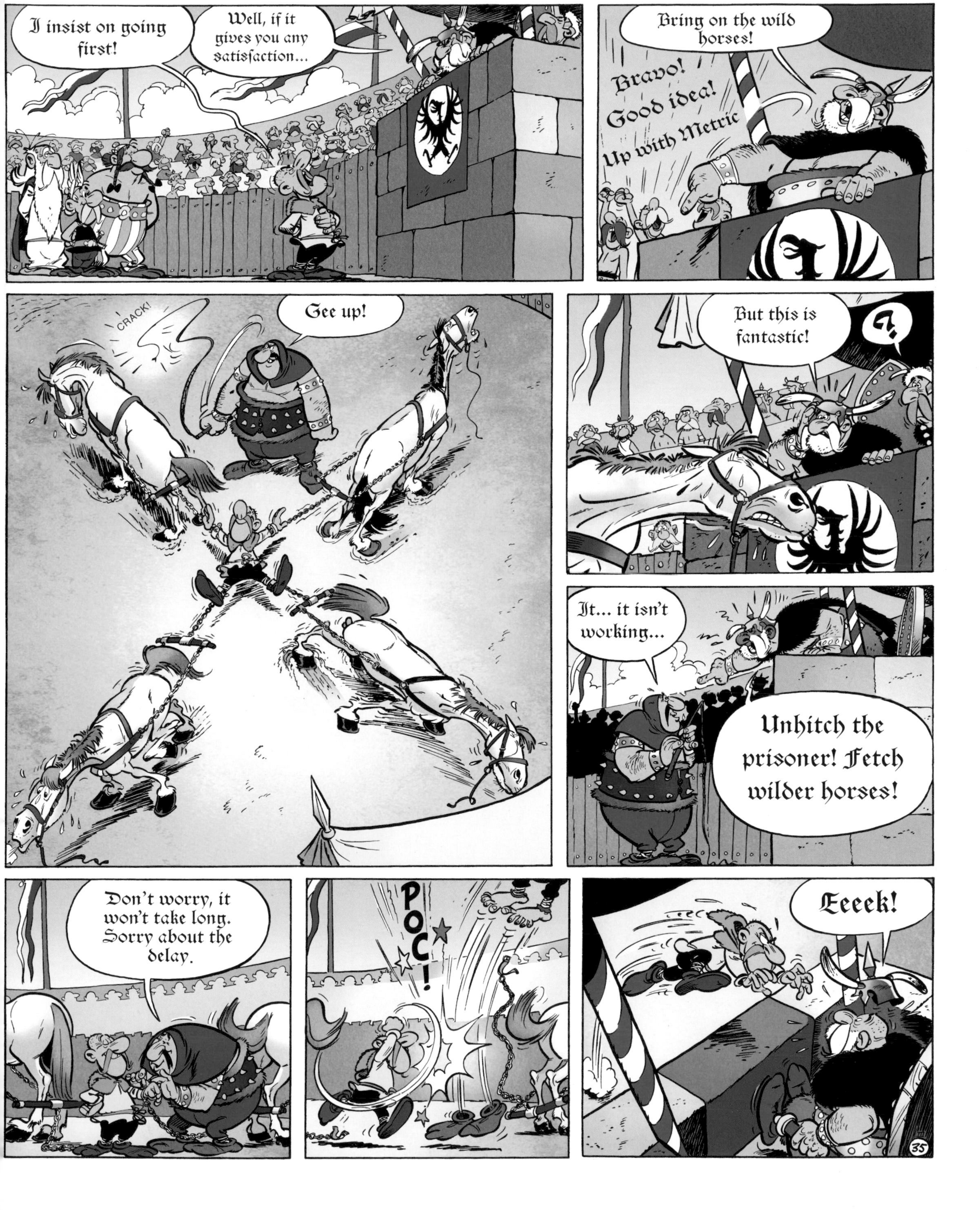
I insist on going first!
Well, if it gives you any satisfaction...
Bring on the wild horses!
Bravo!
Good idea!
Up with Metric
Gee up!
CRACK!
But this is fantastic!
?
It... it isn't working...
Unhitch the prisoner! Fetch wilder horses!
Don't worry, it won't take long. Sorry about the delay.
POC!
Eeeek!
35

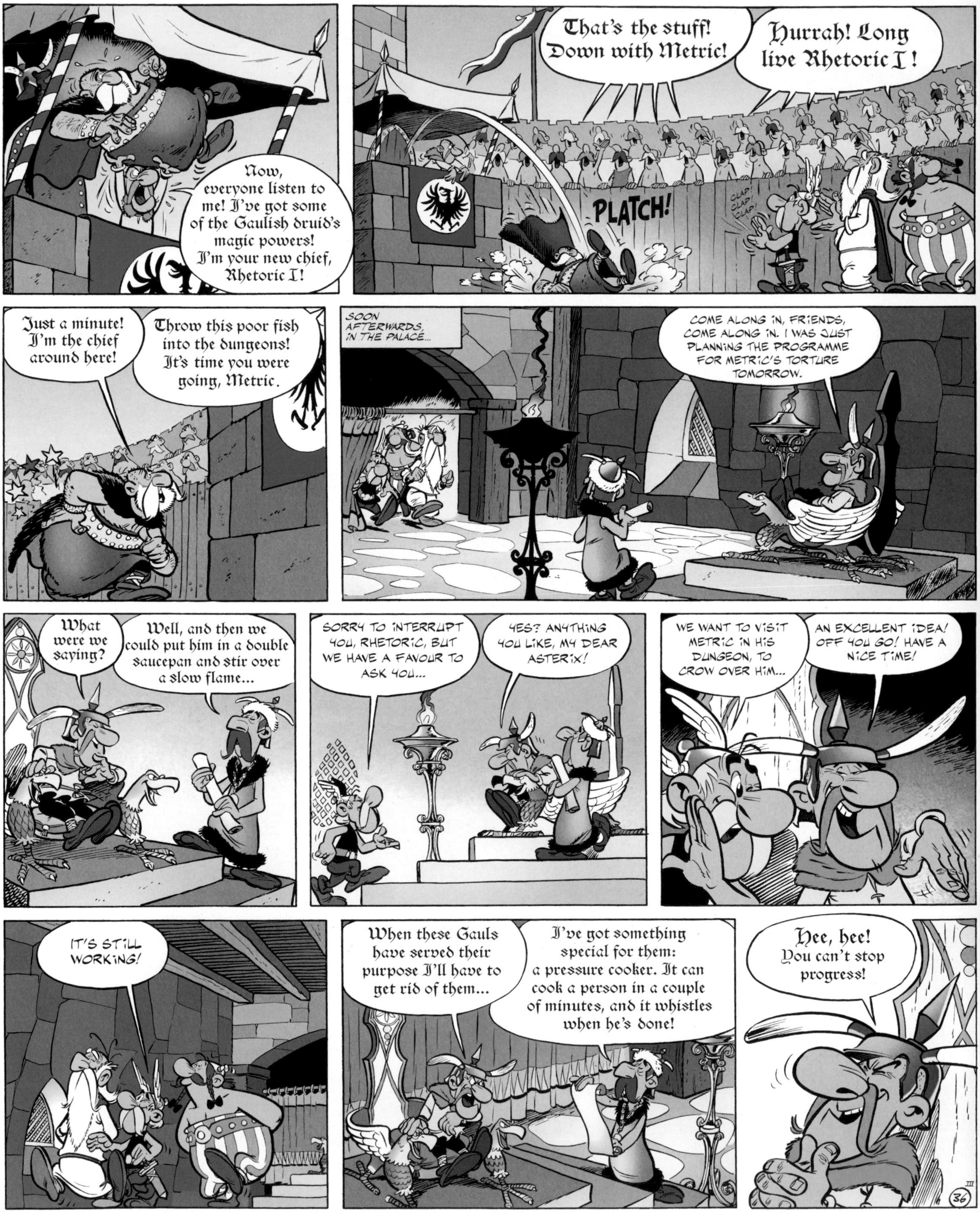
Now, everyone listen to me! I've got some of the Gaulish druid's magic powers! I'm your new chief, Rhetoric I!
That's the stuff! Down with Metric!
Hurrah! Long live Rhetoric I!
PLATCH!
CLAP! CLAP! CLAP!
Just a minute! I'm the chief around here!
Throw this poor fish into the dungeons! It's time you were going, Metric.
SOON AFTERWARDS, IN THE PALACE...
COME ALONG IN, FRIENDS, COME ALONG IN. I WAS JUST PLANNING THE PROGRAMME FOR METRIC'S TORTURE TOMORROW.
What were we saying?
Well, and then we could put him in a double saucepan and stir over a slow flame...
SORRY TO INTERRUPT YOU, RHETORIC, BUT WE HAVE A FAVOUR TO ASK YOU...
YES? ANYTHING YOU LIKE, MY DEAR ASTERIX!
WE WANT TO VISIT METRIC IN HIS DUNGEON, TO CROW OVER HIM...
AN EXCELLENT IDEA! OFF YOU GO! HAVE A NICE TIME!
IT'S STILL WORKING!
When these Gauls have served their purpose I'll have to get rid of them...
I've got something special for them: a pressure cooker. It can cook a person in a couple of minutes, and it whistles when he's done!
Hee, hee! You can't stop progress!
36

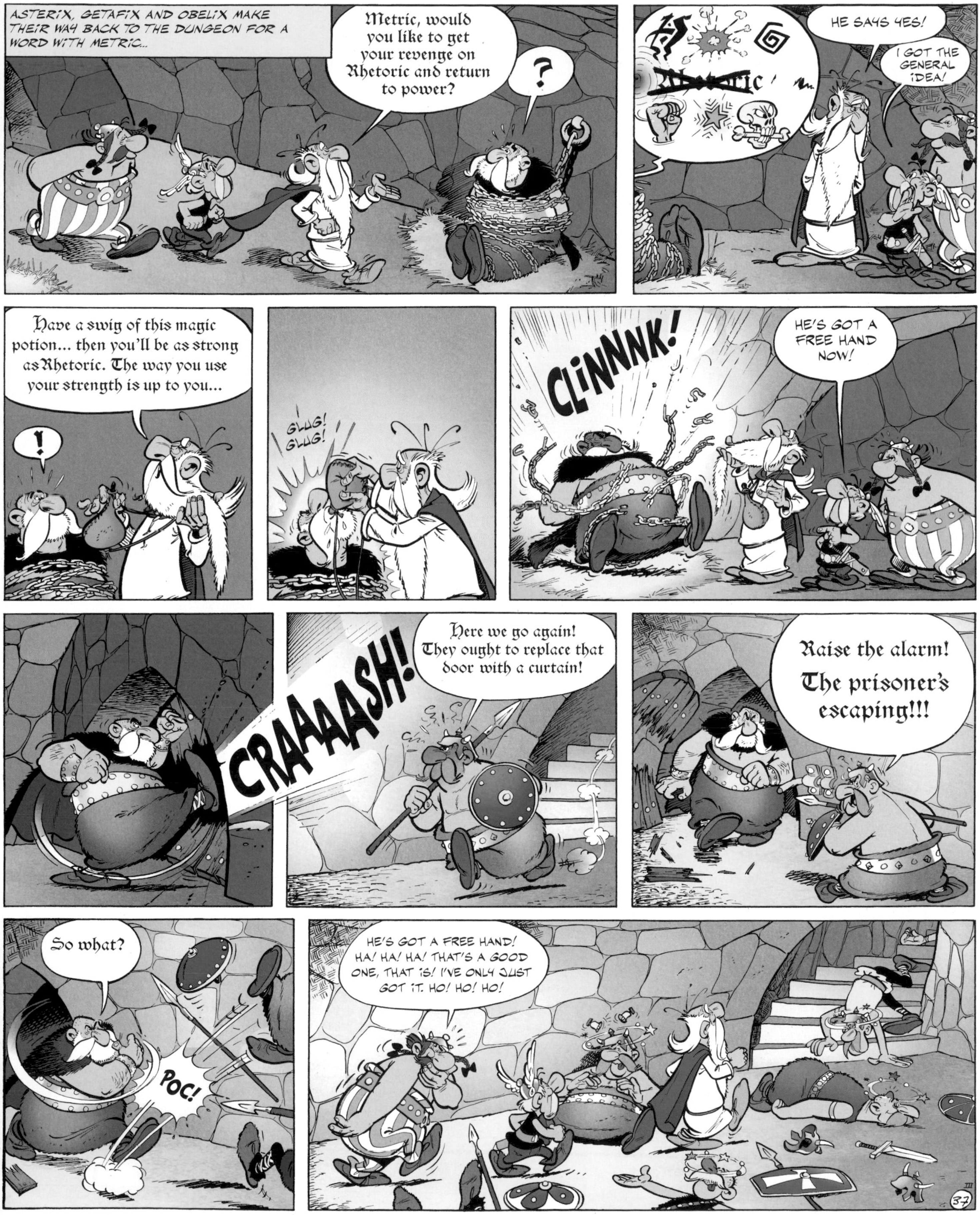
ASTERIX, GETAFIX AND OBELIX MAKE THEIR WAY BACK TO THE DUNGEON FOR A WORD WITH METRIC...
Metric, would you like to get your revenge on Rhetoric and return to power?
?
HE SAYS YES!
I GOT THE GENERAL IDEA!
Have a swig of this magic potion... then you'll be as strong as Rhetoric. The way you use your strength is up to you...
!
GLUG! GLUG!
CLINNNK!
HE'S GOT A FREE HAND NOW!
CRAAAASH!
Here we go again! They ought to replace that door with a curtain!
Raise the alarm! The prisoner's escaping!!!
So what?
POC!
HE'S GOT A FREE HAND! HA! HA! HA! THAT'S A GOOD ONE, THAT IS! I'VE ONLY JUST GOT IT. HO! HO! HO!

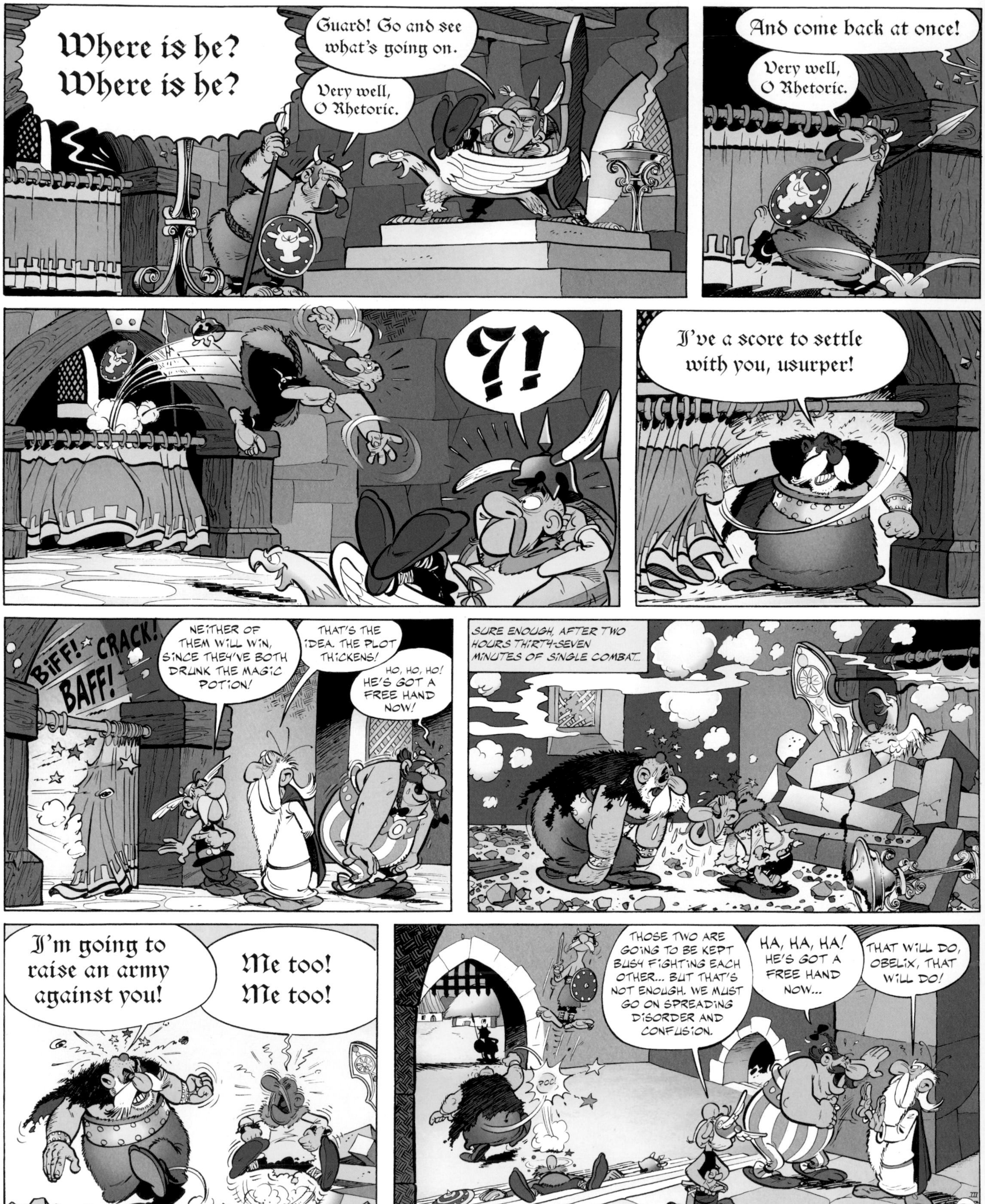
Where is he? Where is he?
Guard! Go and see what's going on.
Very well, O Rhetoric.
And come back at once!
Very well, O Rhetoric.
?!
I've a score to settle with you, usurper!
BIFF! CRACK! BAFF!
NEITHER OF THEM WILL WIN, SINCE THEY'VE BOTH DRUNK THE MAGIC POTION!
THAT'S THE IDEA. THE PLOT THICKENS!
HO, HO, HO! HE'S GOT A FREE HAND NOW!
SURE ENOUGH, AFTER TWO HOURS THIRTY-SEVEN MINUTES OF SINGLE COMBAT...
I'm going to raise an army against you!
Me too! Me too!
THOSE TWO ARE GOING TO BE KEPT BUSY FIGHTING EACH OTHER... BUT THAT'S NOT ENOUGH. WE MUST GO ON SPREADING DISORDER AND CONFUSION.
HA, HA, HA! HE'S GOT A FREE HAND NOW...
THAT WILL DO, OBELIX, THAT WILL DO!

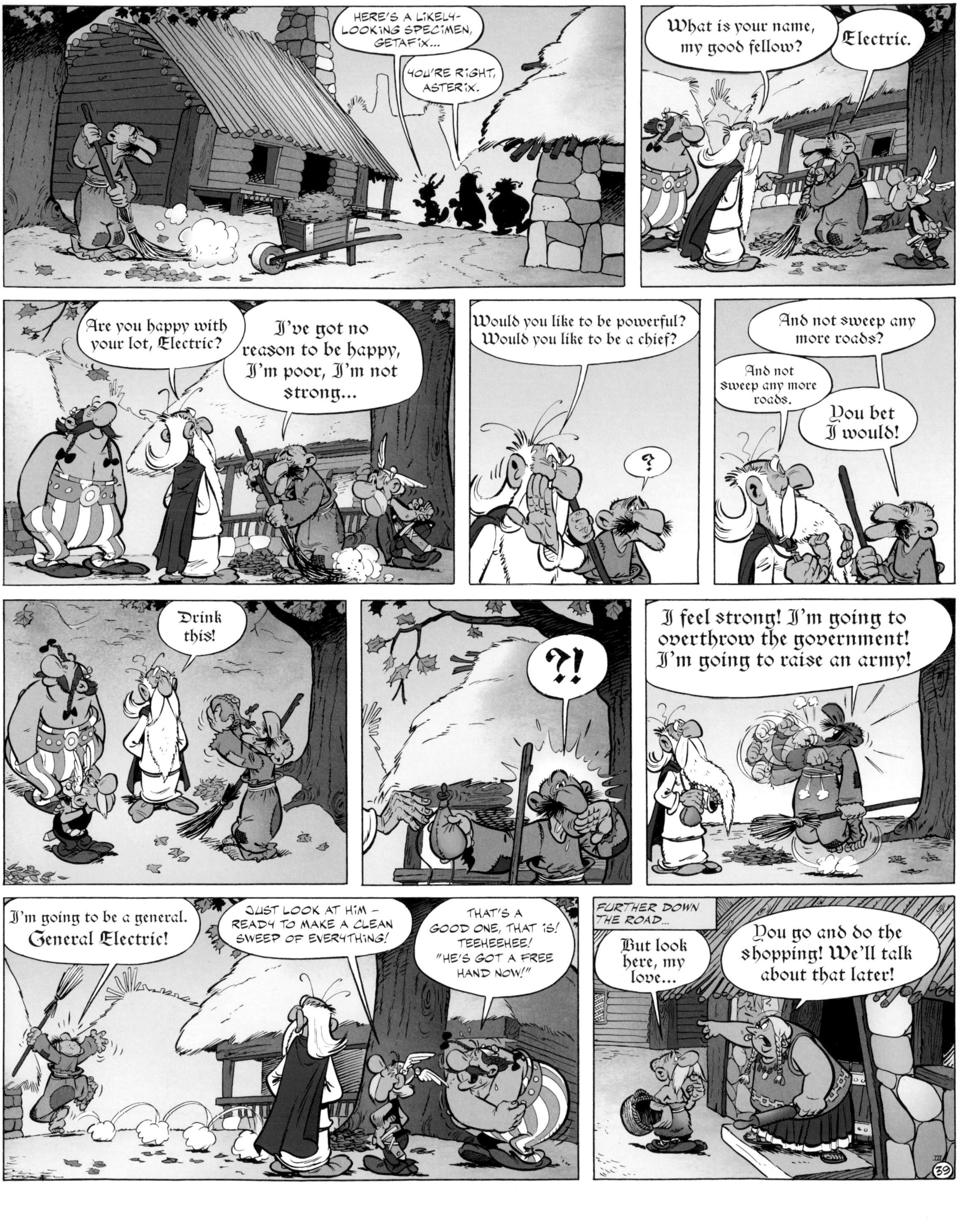
HERE'S A LIKELY-LOOKING SPECIMEN, GETAFIX...
YOU'RE RIGHT, ASTERIX.
What is your name, my good fellow?
Electric.
Are you happy with your lot, Electric?
I've got no reason to be happy, I'm poor, I'm not strong...
Would you like to be powerful? Would you like to be a chief?
?
And not sweep any more roads?
And not sweep any more roads.
You bet I would!
Drink this!
?!
I feel strong! I'm going to overthrow the government! I'm going to raise an army!
I'm going to be a general. General Electric!
JUST LOOK AT HIM – READY TO MAKE A CLEAN SWEEP OF EVERYTHING!
THAT'S A GOOD ONE, THAT IS! TEEHEEHEE! "HE'S GOT A FREE HAND NOW!"
FURTHER DOWN THE ROAD...
But look here, my love...
You go and do the shopping! We'll talk about that later!
III 39

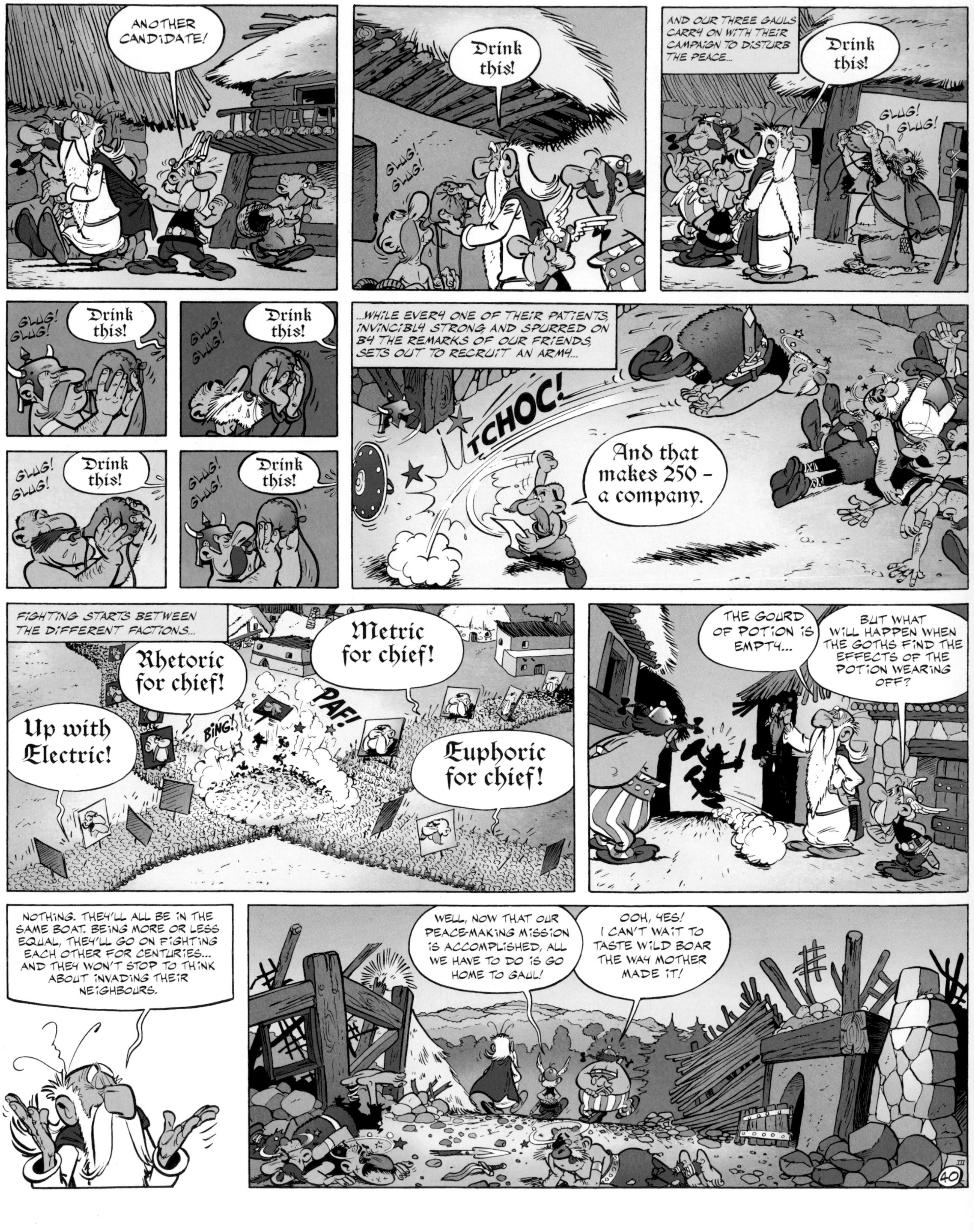

ANOTHER CANDIDATE!
Drink this!
GLUG! GLUG!
AND OUR THREE GAULS CARRY ON WITH THEIR CAMPAIGN TO DISTURB THE PEACE...
Drink this!
GLUG! GLUG!
GLUG! GLUG!
Drink this!
GLUG! GLUG!
Drink this!
GLUG! GLUG!
Drink this!
GLUG! GLUG!
Drink this!
...WHILE EVERY ONE OF THEIR PATIENTS, INVINCIBLY STRONG AND SPURRED ON BY THE REMARKS OF OUR FRIENDS, SETS OUT TO RECRUIT AN ARMY...
TCHOC!
And that makes 250 – a company.
FIGHTING STARTS BETWEEN THE DIFFERENT FACTIONS...
Up with Electric!
Rhetoric for chief!
BING!
PAF!
Metric for chief!
Euphoric for chief!
THE GOURD OF POTION IS EMPTY...
BUT WHAT WILL HAPPEN WHEN THE GOTHS FIND THE EFFECTS OF THE POTION WEARING OFF?
NOTHING. THEY'LL ALL BE IN THE SAME BOAT. BEING MORE OR LESS EQUAL, THEY'LL GO ON FIGHTING EACH OTHER FOR CENTURIES... AND THEY WON'T STOP TO THINK ABOUT INVADING THEIR NEIGHBOURS.
WELL, NOW THAT OUR PEACE-MAKING MISSION IS ACCOMPLISHED, ALL WE HAVE TO DO IS GO HOME TO GAUL!
OOH, YES! I CAN'T WAIT TO TASTE WILD BOAR THE WAY MOTHER MADE IT!
40

SOME OF THE CHIEFS

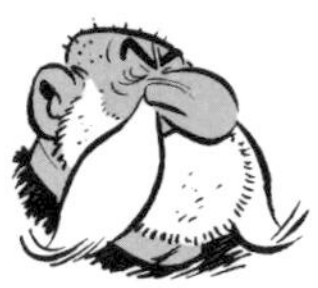

Metric

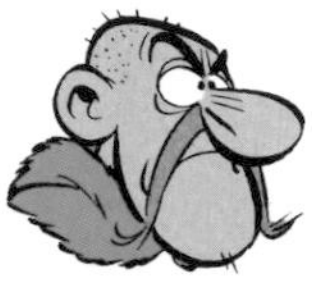

Rhetoric

# THE ASTERIXIAN WARS

## A Tangled Web...

The ruse employed by Asterix, Getafix and Obelix succeeded beyond their wildest dreams. After drinking the druid's magic potion, the Goths fought each other tooth and nail. Here is a brief summary to help you follow the history of these famous wars.

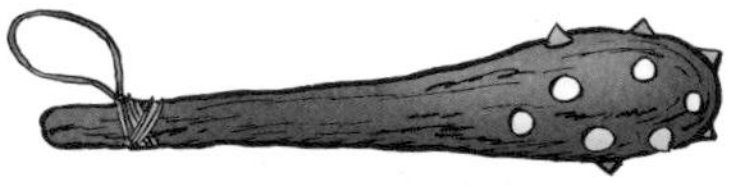

*The favourite and devastating weapon of the combatants.*

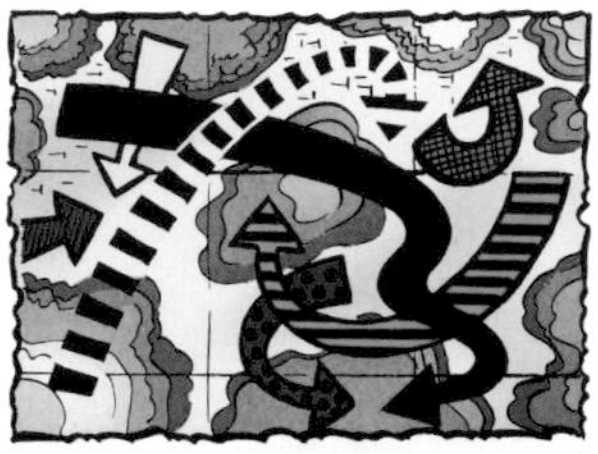

*Diagram indicating the course of events.*

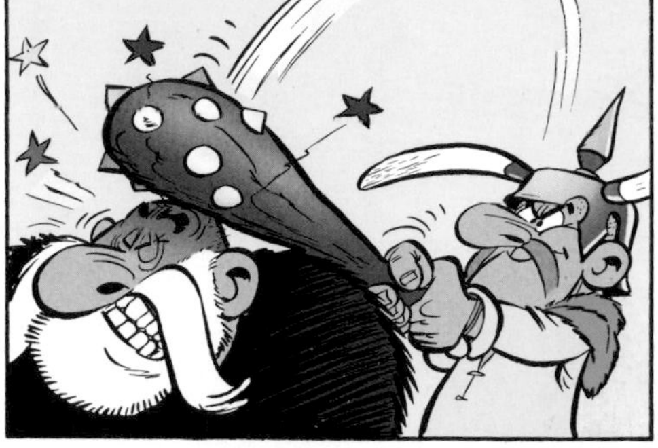

The first victory is won outright by Rhetoric, who, having surprised Metric by an outflanking movement, lets him have it – bonk! – and inflicts a crushing defeat on him. This defeat, however, is only temporary...

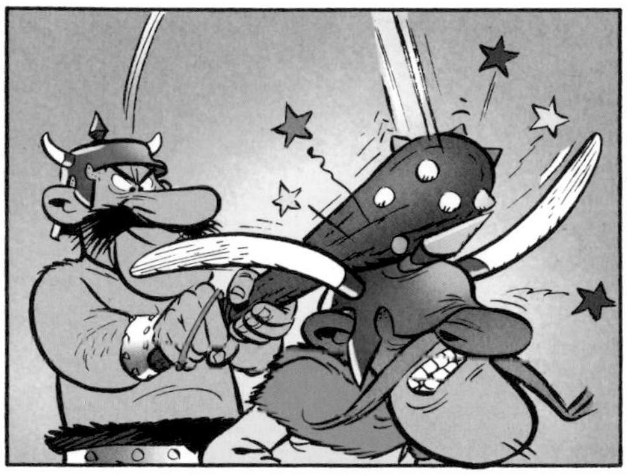

Rhetoric has no time to celebrate his victory, for, having completed his outflanking movement, he is taken in the rear by his own ally, Lyric. Lyric instantly proclaims himself supreme chief of all the Goths, much to the amusement of the other chiefs...

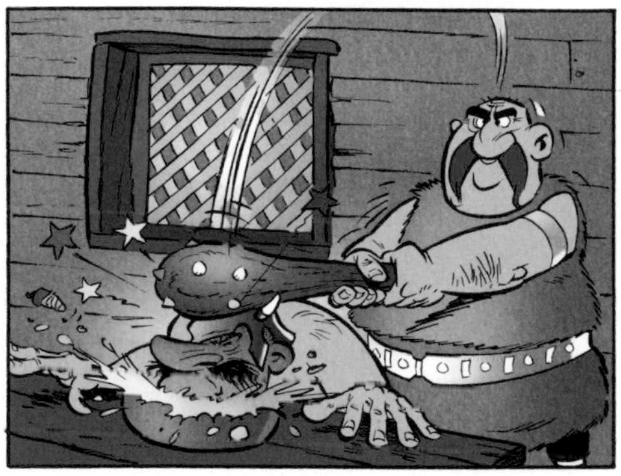

Who turn out to be right, for Lyric's brother-in-law Satiric lays an ambush for him, pretending to invite him to a family reunion, and Lyric falls into the trap. It was upon this occasion that the proposition that blood is thicker than water was first put to the test...

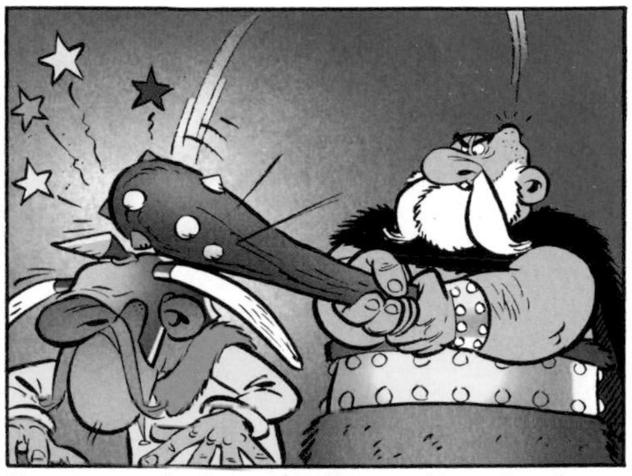

Rhetoric goes after Lyric, with the avowed intention of "bashing him up" (archaic), but his rearguard is surprised by Metric's vanguard. Bonk! This manoeuvre is known as the Metric System.

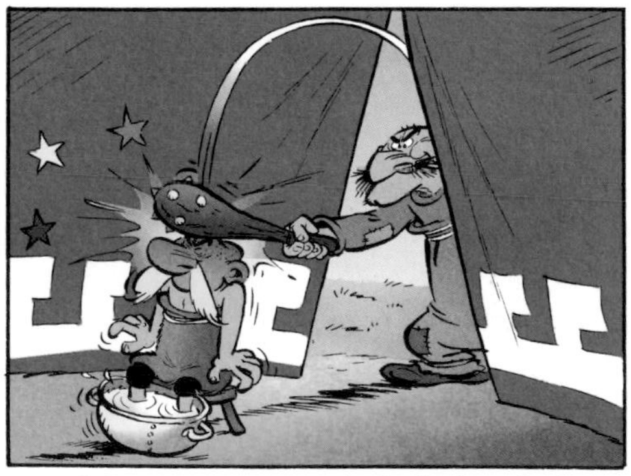

General Electric manages to surprise Euphoric meditating on the conduct of his next few campaigns. Euphoric's morale is distinctly lowered, but he has the last word, with his famous remark, "I'll short-circuit him yet".

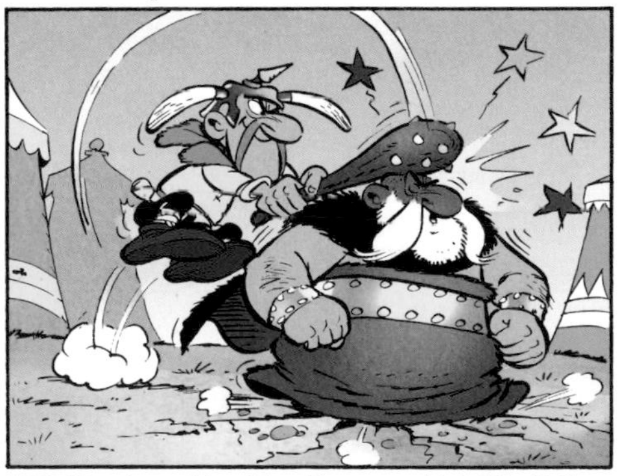

While Electric proclaims himself supreme chief of the Goths, to the amusement of all and sundry, it is the turn of Metric's rearguard to be surprised by Rhetoric's vanguard. Bonk! "This is bad for my system," is the comment of the exasperated Metric.

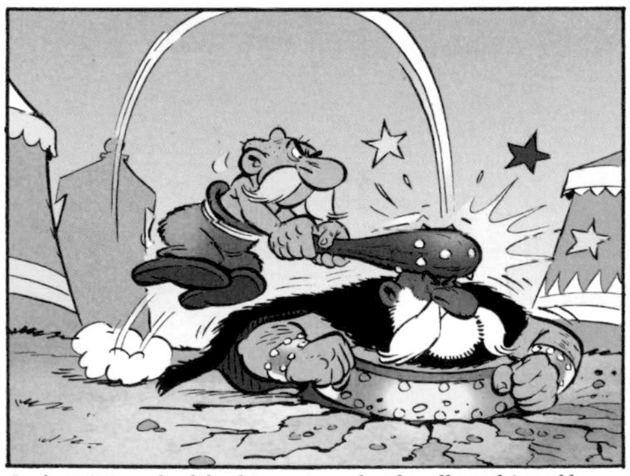

In fact, it is so bad for his system that he allows himself to be surprised by Euphoric. The battle is short and sharp. Euphoric, a wily politician, instantly proclaims himself supreme chief of the Goths. The other supreme chiefs are in fits...

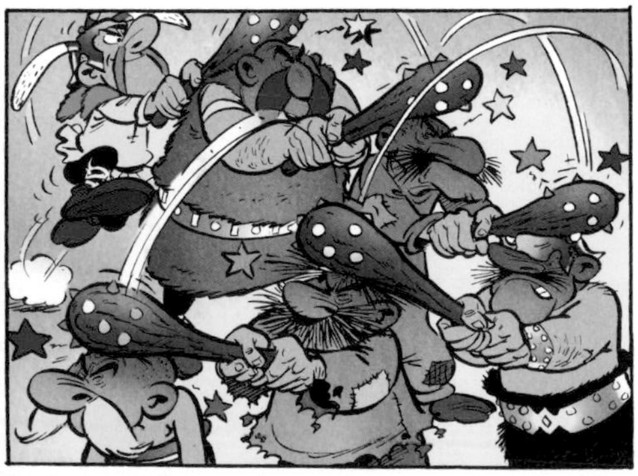

Euphoric, much annoyed, sets up camp and decides to sulk. He is surprised by Eccentric, who in his turn is attacked by Lyric, subsequently to be defeated by Electric. Electric is destined to be betrayed by Satiric, who will be beaten by Rhetoric.

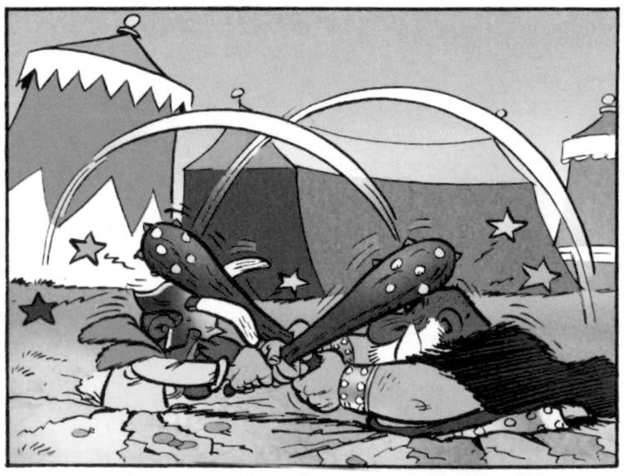

Going round a corner, Rhetoric's vanguard bumps into Metric's vanguard. Bonk! Bonk! This battle is famous in the Asterixian wars as the "Battle of the Two Losers". And so the war goes on...

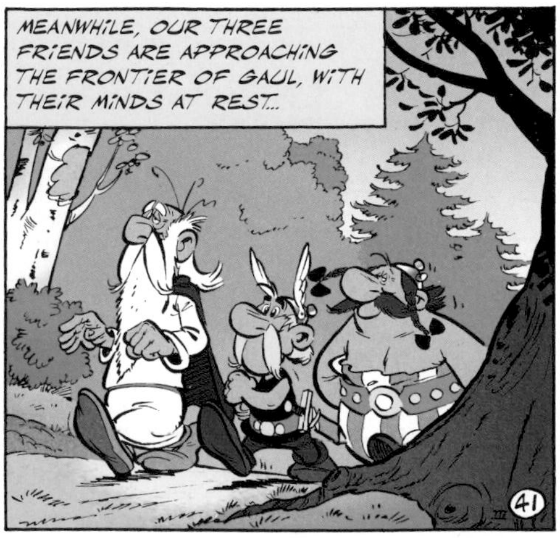
MEANWHILE, OUR THREE FRIENDS ARE APPROACHING THE FRONTIER OF GAUL, WITH THEIR MINDS AT REST...
41

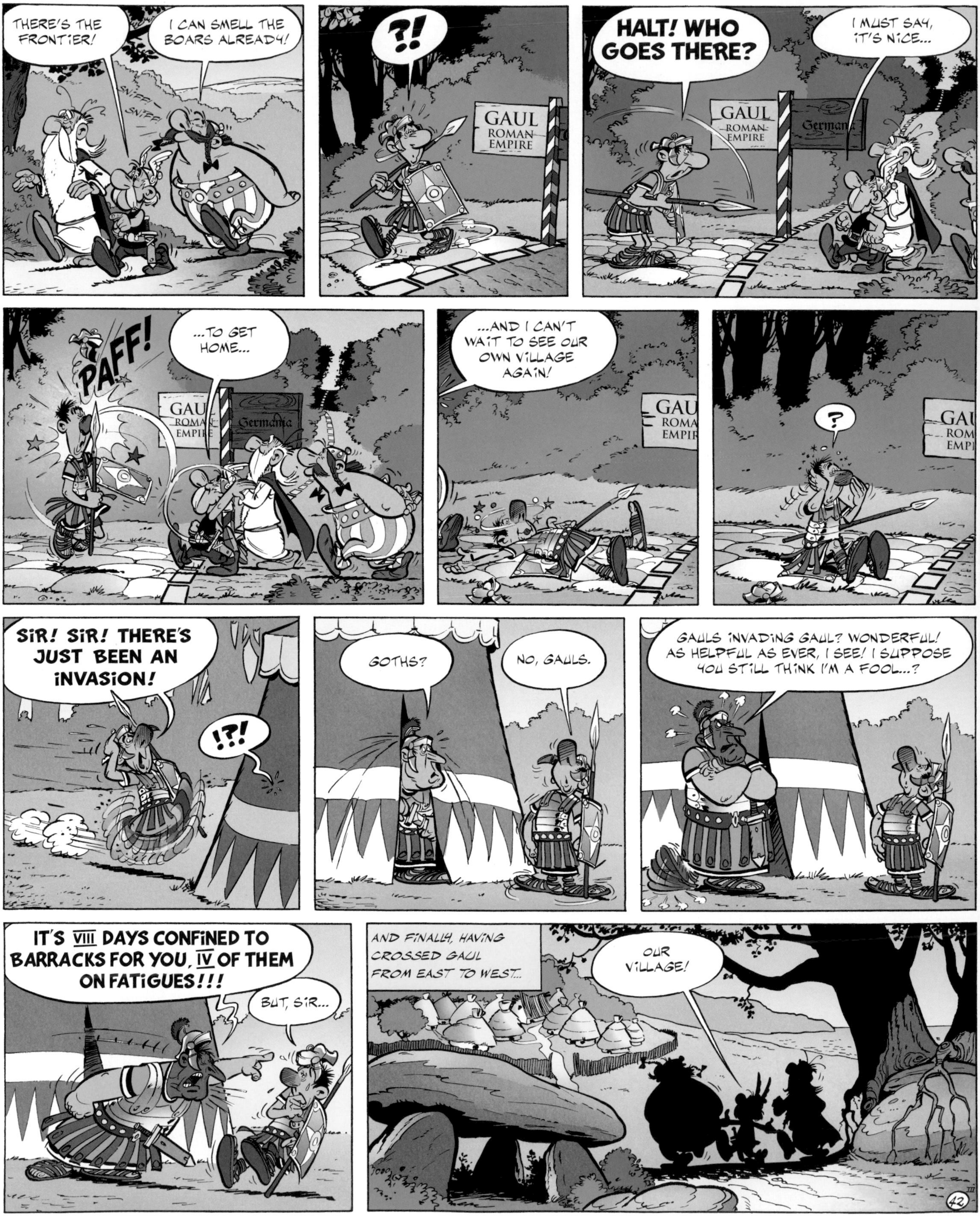
THERE'S THE FRONTIER!
I CAN SMELL THE BOARS ALREADY!
SNIFF SNIFF
?!
GAUL ROMAN EMPIRE
HALT! WHO GOES THERE?
I MUST SAY, IT'S NICE...
Germania
PAFF!
...TO GET HOME...
...AND I CAN'T WAIT TO SEE OUR OWN VILLAGE AGAIN!
?
SIR! SIR! THERE'S JUST BEEN AN INVASION!
!?!
GOTHS?
NO, GAULS.
GAULS INVADING GAUL? WONDERFUL! AS HELPFUL AS EVER, I SEE! I SUPPOSE YOU STILL THINK I'M A FOOL...?
IT'S VIII DAYS CONFINED TO BARRACKS FOR YOU, IV OF THEM ON FATIGUES!!!
BUT, SIR...
AND FINALLY, HAVING CROSSED GAUL FROM EAST TO WEST...
OUR VILLAGE!
42

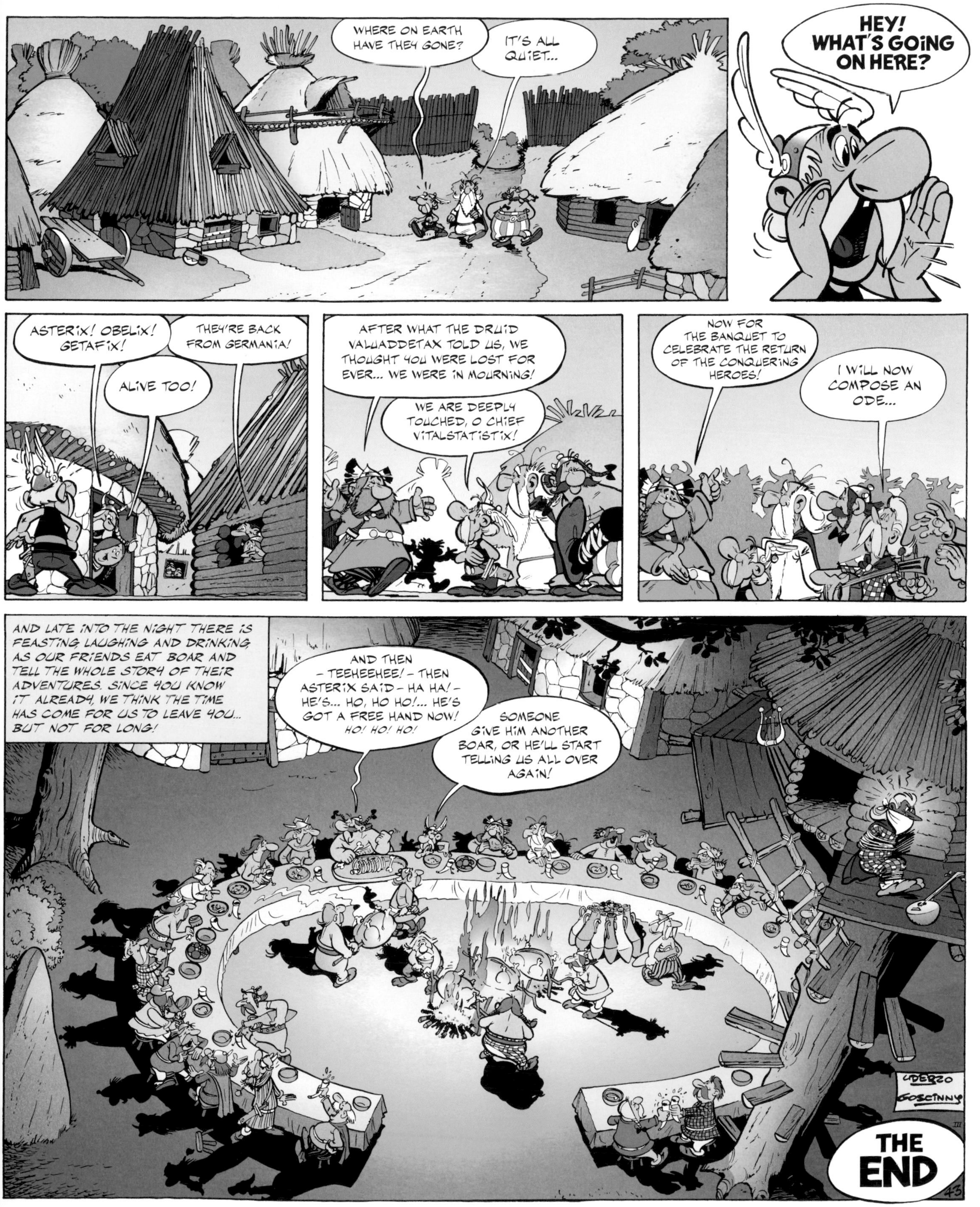
WHERE ON EARTH HAVE THEY GONE?
IT'S ALL QUIET...
HEY! WHAT'S GOING ON HERE?
ASTERIX! OBELIX! GETAFIX!
THEY'RE BACK FROM GERMANIA!
ALIVE TOO!
AFTER WHAT THE DRUID VALUADDETAX TOLD US, WE THOUGHT YOU WERE LOST FOR EVER... WE WERE IN MOURNING!
WE ARE DEEPLY TOUCHED, O CHIEF VITALSTATISTIX!
NOW FOR THE BANQUET TO CELEBRATE THE RETURN OF THE CONQUERING HEROES!
I WILL NOW COMPOSE AN ODE...
AND LATE INTO THE NIGHT THERE IS FEASTING LAUGHING AND DRINKING AS OUR FRIENDS EAT BOAR AND TELL THE WHOLE STORY OF THEIR ADVENTURES. SINCE YOU KNOW IT ALREADY, WE THINK THE TIME HAS COME FOR US TO LEAVE YOU... BUT NOT FOR LONG!
AND THEN – TEEHEEHEE! – THEN ASTERIX SAID – HA HA! – HE'S... HO, HO HO!... HE'S GOT A FREE HAND NOW! HO! HO! HO!
SOMEONE GIVE HIM ANOTHER BOAR, OR HE'LL START TELLING US ALL OVER AGAIN!
UDERZO
GOSCINNY
THE END
43

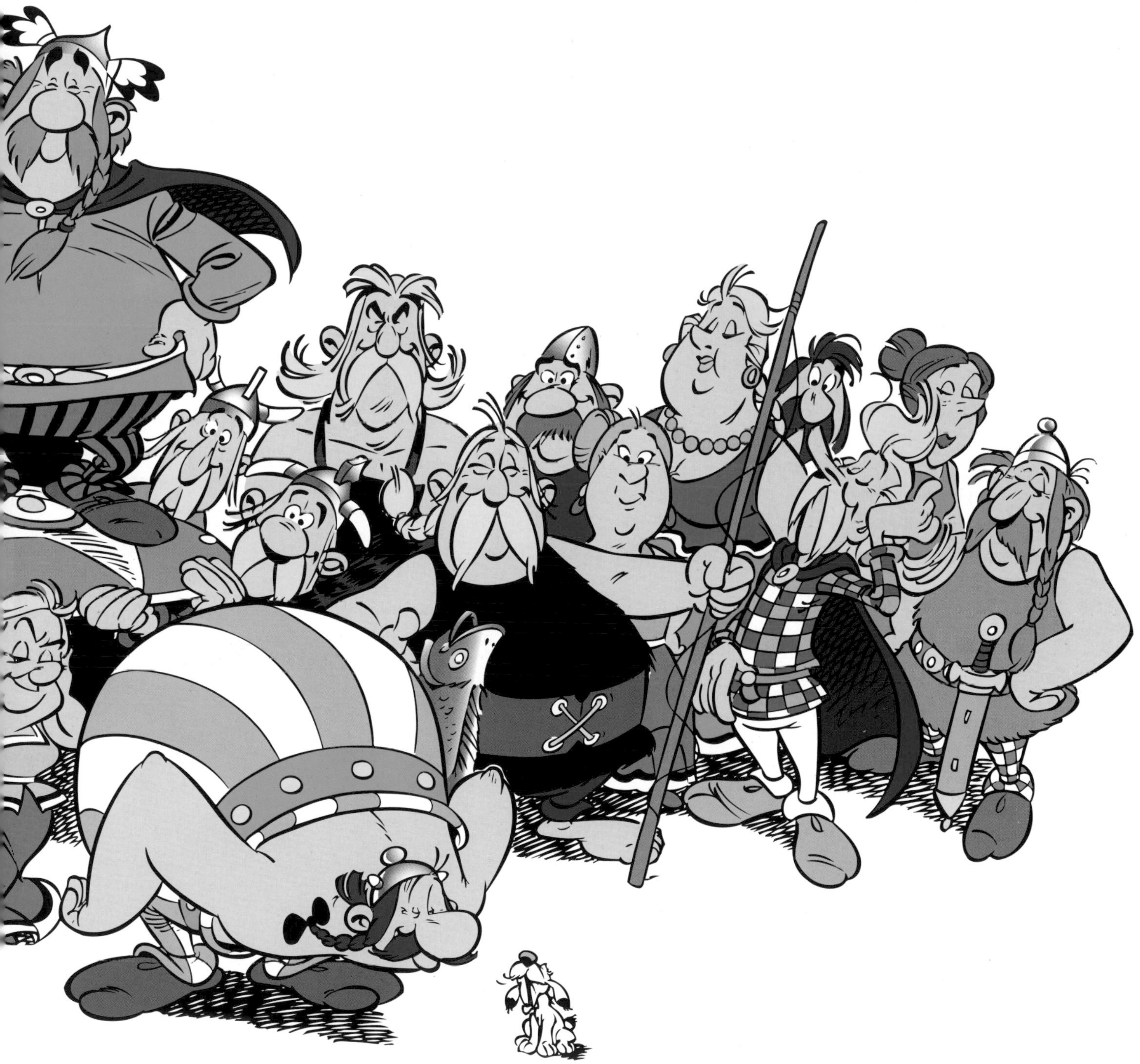